A Clash of Tomorrows

Book One: Gaia

What people are saying about *A Clash of Tomorrows*.

"This dazzling novel is a hero's journey, full of twists, turns, and unexpected surprises. "
---Simona Moroni, *Hollywood Daze*

"This is a great story. I was captured by every character. I really enjoyed how the story took you on an adventure along the way. Can't wait for Book 2."
---Debbie Fogle, *A Bohemian Christmas*

"I found *A Clash of Tomorrows* an exhilarating story filled with adventure on every page."
---D. Straight, Colorado Springs

"The story itself is intriguing. It is difficult to put the book down when necessary... I would not hesitate to recommend this book to middle school libraries and students."
--- P. Blevins, Retired M.S. Reading Specialist

"It was hard to put down and kept my interest all the way through... The description of things and people made it come to life for me."

--- P. Ellis, Holly Lake Ranch, TX

A Clash of Tomorrows

Book One: Gaia

Bruce M. Baker

Soonershoot Press

Oklahoma City, Oklahoma

Copyright©2024
Bruce M. Baker

All Rights Reserved.

This manuscript and associated documentation are the sole property of Soonershoot Press.

No part of this book may be reproduced by any mechanical, photographic, or electronic process or in the form of a phonographic recording; nor may it be stored in a retrieval system, transmitted, or otherwise copied for public or private use—other than for "fair use" as brief quotations embodied in articles and reviews—without prior written permission of the author/publisher.

ISBN: 978-1-7361995-6-5
Library of Congress Control Number: 2024900284

Cover Art: Darksouls1 (Pixabay)
https://pixabay.com/users/darksouls1-2189876/

This is a work of fiction. Any resemblance to people, living or dead, is coincidental. The geography and place names are real, although liberally represented. As to events…anything is possible.

Other works by Bruce M. Baker

The Chance - The true story of one girl's journey to freedom

Faith through Trial - A true story of hope and survival

Dedication

For my wonderful wife, Deborah, who has stood beside me for the past fifty years and is my constant muse.

"To see a World in a Grain of Sand
And a Heaven in a Wild Flower
Hold Infinity in the palm of your hand
And Eternity in an hour."

Excerpt from *Auguries of Innocence*
William Blake, 1803

Chapter 1 – The Beginning

There was war.

There had always been war.

The planet Aeden trembled as it endured the constant assault. Wanton destruction and loss of life radiated from all the combatants and seemed to be an integral part of their shared evolution. Humans had battled the other races since before history became history. Brief respites of peace popped up over the centuries of conflict as if to remind them that there was another way. Aeden never went that way. She swam in the blood of countless dead, blood whose only purpose was to fuel the flames of vengeance for battles yet to come.

Amid these untold ages of conflict, pure chance and a wayward wind tossed a small boat and its crew of elves off course and onto a new continent. Here in the West, Origen, the sole survivor of his race, revealed himself to the elven men. He spoke to them of possibilities they had never considered.

To call Origen a race is insufficient, as is to call him a specific gender, yet the races have always called him a "he." Origen was not organic. He was a sentient crystal who had arrived upon the Western

Continent eons earlier, long before the other races had elevated themselves above their ancestral non-sentient beginnings. Origen had since grown to where his crystalline essence permeated all living things in the West. Although he did not physically appear to those gathered on the shore that day, his presence resonated in their minds. The elves were in awe of what they had found. Many erroneously thought they had found their god.

The crystal intelligence offered the newcomers the entirety of the Western Continent to be their domain. In the West, the three races could share the bounty that Origen had built and leave their human adversaries an ocean away. Origen's only requirement was that the races would allow Origen's crystal nanites to infuse their bodies. He would live through them, and in return, the symbiotic joining would significantly extend their lives and enhance their strength. Most importantly, with humans far behind them, they could have peace at last.

The High Council considered the news. Not all agreed, and the arguments over the decision continued for months. In the end, a massive attack by the humans on an elven outpost solidified their resolve. The elves, pixies, and fairies decided they had nothing to lose and accepted Origen's offer, migrating their tribes to the West and abandoning the humans in sole control of the East.

Over time, as they acclimated to their new home, the immigrants found that diseases became a distant memory. Their bodies' crystal nanites crushed any invaders that would cause them harm. Science and the arts blossomed in the glow of lasting health and peace. It was a golden age.

The pixies, alone among the three races, never forgot the human threat they had left behind. They built the port city of Galadel on the Aerealan Peninsula as an outpost against a future human invasion. This small strip of land was where the first elven ship had landed in the West and was the closest point to the Eastern Continent. Logic indicated that any invasion would start there.

Unfortunately, the people of Galadel forgot their purpose over the years. The settlement prospered and even established relationships with human traders across the sea. The animosity between them ceased to exist. This new relationship gave rise to the hope that humans and the races might coexist peacefully.

A handful of centuries passed, and the memories of war faded with them. Galadel's once formidable defenses decayed from neglect even as its merchants prospered. Everyone rejoiced as they anticipated the beginning of a new age.

This newly forged alliance made the human attack on Galadel even more unexpected, and its ferocity was without precedent. There was no warning, no indication that anything was amiss. The invaders launched such fury upon the village that few in the community survived the onslaught. The humans showed no mercy as they reduced the city's fabled crystalline structures into glittering dust clouds floating on the wind. Only a lucky few of Galadel's thousands escaped when the battle subsided, fleeing into the surrounding hills and woodlands. Of those, even fewer survived to tell their tale.

"Remember Galadel" became the slogan that rekindled the new Human Wars. The elves, pixies, and fairies rebuilt their defenses rapidly and began to assault the human scourge with a vengeance. The ferocity of their battles ravaged both continents for over a hundred years. The conflict didn't discriminate; both sides suffered greatly, with no regard for combatants or civilians. Age or sex had no say in who died. Ultimately, half of Aeden's population perished in the wanton destruction. The war finally ended on the field of Ragnarök on the Eastern Continent when the elven and pixie armies vanquished the humans.

After the carnage, many elders of the non-human races wanted to find a permanent solution to the human problem. Since hundreds of years of separation hadn't settled the animosity between them, the elders felt only extermination could ensure the end of the conflicts once and for all. The fairies, being natural healers, refused to be part of the plan and left the assembly. The elves and pixies proceeded with their plan to eliminate their nemesis.

Though Origen had not spoken to the races in a millennium, the crystal nanites still connected them. Through them, Origen became aware of their decision and was appalled that they would consider such a dire outcome. As of old, he spoke directly to their minds. At first, they had no idea who this voice represented. To them, Origen was a being of legend, something contrived to scare children, not an actual entity. Besides, why would he talk to them now, and why would he side with the humans? Where was he when millions were slaughtered? The people were angry...and frightened.

Origen stated that he would not stand by while the races destroyed humankind. He argued that no crime was so severe that it warranted extinguishing an entire race of sentient beings. Origen proposed an alternative – exile. He instructed the elves and pixies to prepare one of the exoplanets, Gaia, for human habitation—a place where humans could live completely isolated, find their destiny, and never come to Aeden again.

Excerpt from <u>*The History of the Races, Fourth Edition*</u>

Chapter 2 - Kandi

The wayward breeze tickled her ears as she alternated between running and flying over the landscape. The rains had ended at moonrise, and the heady scent of wet soil permeated the air. This was Kandi's time when the passage of seconds slowed to a trickle, and her senses came completely alive. She lived for this time alone, in tune with her body as her wings beat the air and her legs pumped against the ground below.

Kandi Mehra paused to consider her life. Time is a fickle companion. Everything changes, yet everything stays the same. She remembered her first day home from her six-year tour as a Watcher on Gaia. Even though she knew the time dilation effect would happen, she was still shocked to find only a day had passed here at home. The disconnect made her head hurt. One of the many conundrums of travel between worlds was that the passage of local time did not correspond to time spent elsewhere. When a Watcher left Aeden, the Institute attached a tachyon stream to that person. That connection remained fixed on the home planet. No matter how long they were on the alien world, they always returned to the place and time they left. It was disconcerting, to say the least.

Even understanding the science, Kandi still found it disquieting that her Aedenian friends remembered details of conversations with her in their yesterday when she had difficulty remembering the day in question or, in some cases, the person themselves from her years gone. For her, the past six years of patrolling Gaian streets, subduing errant humans, attending Gaian temples, eating disgusting Gaian food, and breathing the toxic Gaian air had blurred her vision of Aeden - of home. It seemed somewhat unfair that only a day had transpired here on her home world. She remembered every day of her exile on Gaia. She had changed - tougher and more agile than she ever had been before.

Kandi chuckled as she remembered her friends' reactions that first day back. Even though they knew where she had been and the vagaries of time travel, the changes to her were startling to them. Her hair had been jet black and cropped short, just like the males in her squadron when she left. Six years of the bright, yellow Gaian sun had bleached it, so it was now a rich brown and shoulder length. Years under Gaia's much higher solar radiation had also significantly darkened her ordinarily fair skin. She hated the look and how it made her stand out from all the others and hoped it would fade to her original alabaster hue given time.

Kandi shook the memory from her mind as she continued her pre-dawn run around the city, finally stopping again to enjoy the view at the top of Mandril Plateau. She believed this was the perfect time of day between twilight and day. There was no natural darkness on Aeden, only the eternal between guaranteed by her two moons as they danced across the Aedenian sky in perfect sync with the rising sun. Darkness never stood a chance in their light.

Kandi shuddered as she remembered the first time she had experienced authentic blackness during her first month as a Watcher on Gaia. That world's single moon occasionally went out of phase and cast no light. On one such night, when heavy clouds blotted out the stars, darkness was complete, and the experience had been terrifying.

She had served Aeden with distinction for the rest of her tour. She had been shuttled to various posts around the planet: Gomorrah, Dorado, Nazca, and finally ending up – or rewarded with a cushy assignment in Babel. The local archangel, Ibless, had demanded a personal security detail and had selected her for the job. For personal reasons, the posting didn't work out. When she demanded either a transfer or a dismissal from the Corps, she received a message from the Director of the Institute on Aeden. He asked her to join them at headquarters as an instructor, accompanied by the promotion in rank to Master Watcher. The offer was better than she could have dreamed. Now, she was home, and the problems of Babel were a thousand light-years behind her.

Kandi was on the downhill portion of her run now. The other instructors couldn't understand why she ran. She had wings. Why not fly? She laughed at them. They had been isolated here for too long. Running was a benefit for the whole body. Her integration guide on Gaia had introduced the exercise to her, and after six years, it had become a part of her daily routine. She still flew, of course. How could she not? She would never abandon such a valuable tool. In battle, anything that gave you an advantage over your adversary was worth keeping in shape.

Kandi rounded a bend in the trail. From here, she could see the Institute's crystalline walls peeking out of the hillside before her. The engineers had fashioned the Institute mostly underground, primarily for defensive reasons. This also cut it off from the rest of Atlantia, Aeden's capital, which suited the population. The Institute was home to the Watcher Corps, now the only military organization on the planet. It reminded people of the war - and of humans. Therefore, they wanted it far removed from their everyday life. Beneath her, the sparkling spires of Atlantia shimmered in the valley below. The city glowed with iridescent colors as the lights from the setting moon Santar and the moon Tirith, now at the apex of its orbit, set it ablaze.

Kandi began to sprint toward the Institute's gym, interrupted only by the occasional night creature and the delightful aroma of the taroon blossoms, which only opened during the lunar exchange and whose fragrance was the only thing that seemed to overcome the Gaian poison in her lungs. It was as if they exuded their fabulous fragrances into the air for her and her alone. She loved being home.

As Kandi slowed to enter the facility, the gym's arched doorway seemed to welcome her into its embrace, the latticed crystal ceiling concentrating the reflected outside light to illuminate the interior. As the building registered her body heat, it would supplement the existing light with energy gathered during the Aedenian daylight hours.

Kandi was anxious to begin. Her morning run was just a warmup for her real daily workout. She fervently believed that sparring was the only way to keep her battle skills in top form and, in turn, make her a better instructor. Hand-to-hand combat had proven to be invaluable to the Corps. Even though Gaian armories had advanced weaponry, the head of each garrison would only authorize their use in a dire emergency, so great was the fear that the instruments would fall into human hands.

Consequently, at the Institute, hand-to-hand combat training was intense. With training and their augmented strength, an adequately trained warrior could disable several attackers single-handedly. Of course, if any Gaian weapons were lying around, they were fair game. More than once, Kandi had used the sword and shield of a disarmed warrior against the human foe with satisfying results.

Kandi smiled as she remembered the pleasure killing humans gave her. She hated them – all of them. The only good one was a dead one. More than once, she had wished for a force blaster or plasma disruptor so that she could lay waste to an entire city of the vermin infesting it. She had been one of the strongest voices favoring the extermination of the species before Origen had butted in. Even now, if it were up to her, Aeden would sterilize Gaia and be done with the human problem forever.

Kandi forced herself to refocus. Emotions could blind a fighter to other avenues of attack. Although not usually a prideful person, she had the satisfaction of being the youngest Master in a Watcher Corps that traditionally didn't value the young or the female. She intended to be the best. As a distinguished veteran of the Human Wars, she knew better than most of the challenges and dangers humans presented. She vowed to maintain fighting readiness to keep herself as an example for her cadets. She knew that a wasted second in battle could also be your last.

The AI control module had registered her entry into the building and initiated the framework for her battle simulation in area three. She shucked off her tunic, revealing only her skintight Durcon battle armor. Then, she prepared for her robotic opponent to arrive. Others had their favorites, AIs they fought all the time. She preferred allowing the simulator to choose her opponent. Since she couldn't select her adversary in a real battle, why should she do so in practice?

Kandi was surprised and pleased when she saw Sheda approach the battle ring — surprised because they had enjoyed sparring together only last week and pleased because Sheda was exceptionally good. Some of the cadets and even instructors thought all AIs were the same. They were incorrect. They each had an individuality that belied that belief. Examining the markings on the AI's body proved that. Sheda had dozens of markings highlighting her victories in the ring. At least one pointed to Kandi as the victim of Sheda's assault. Sheda was the quickest and most adaptable sparring opponent that Kandi had faced. All the AIs were good. Sheda was exceptional.

Only last week, Kandi had struggled to force a draw against Sheda, so Kandi knew she had to be at the top of her game this morning. "Good morning, Sheda." Although it was not standard practice, Kandi greeted her AI opponent as she would a human sparring partner, warmly and friendly before the fight commenced. Most of the cadets treated the AIs with contempt, which appalled Kandi. She considered AIs as people without the flesh and blood problems she and others had to overcome. In some ways, she envied them.

"Good morning, Master Watcher Mehra." Sheda's response was formal, with a hint of annoyance as she stepped into the ring.

"Sheda, it's me, Kandi. There is no need for titles here." Kandi was a little insulted by the AI's formal tone.

Sheda explained, "Master Watcher Mehra. The Council has registered several complaints with the controller, indicating AIs are getting far too familiar with our sparring partners. Control has ordered that we only use formal greetings from this point forward."

Kandi wasn't sure what was funnier, the idea that anyone would complain about the AI's speech or that a Council member would care. Kandi guessed that the problems lay more with how the AIs wiped up the mats with the cadets, not their familiarity. When dealing with snotty trainees, AIs could be a little vindictive. "Well," Kandi casually looked around the empty chamber, "I don't see any Council members around now, do you?" She smiled.

Sheda picked up on her meaning immediately. "No, Master Watch...Kandi. My sensors indicate that they are not present."

"Let us begin then."

After an hour of fierce combat, neither Kandi nor Sheda showed any indication of ending their session. They appeared perfectly matched, their bodies a blur, spinning around the ring in a macabre ballet. In that hour, neither challenger scored a hit on the other. Finally, a small opening appeared in Sheda's defense that Kandi's highly trained eye took advantage of. Executing a move that should have been physically impossible, Kandi feinted and got in a punch that surprised the AI-enhanced humanoid robot.

"Well thrown, Kandi!" Sheda practically shouted her compliment as the two broke apart for a quick rest.

"Thanks. I'll file it away for future reference when I fight one of the others. I'll never be able to use it on you again, right?" Kandi knew Sheda had already cataloged the move and calculated at least five countermoves for future attempts. "You won't tell, will you?" Kandi was slightly out of breath from the exertion.

"Kandi! We don't share battle techniques. Each of us has unique storage to keep battle information separate. For the training to be valid, each opponent must be fresh and unique."

While Sheda was speaking, Kandi noticed an almost imperceptible change in the robot's stance. She was ready if Kandi was foolish enough to try it again. Kandi chuckled as she imagined the poor cadet that drew Sheda next. Sheda wouldn't be averse to using Kandi's move for herself. That was how the training program continued to improve. Kandi knew that you rarely learned from your victories. Failures were what drove people forward.

Their battle proceeded, and the two opponents became so focused on each other that Kandi committed what would have been a fatal error in the field. She allowed someone to enter the gym and approach her without noticing. Four elven males moved silently to the edge of the ring where she and Sheda fought. After recovering from the initial shock of their approach, Kandi ignored them, hoping they would disappear as quietly as they had come. That, however, was not to be. One of the elves dared to speak, "What time do you get here, Master Watcher?" he asked with false innocence and a slight sneer to his tone.

The intrusion was enough to make Kandi miss a step, which, in turn, allowed Sheda to score a point of her own. Her lapse in concentration aggravated her more than the elf's interruption had. Not wanting to give Sheda a second opening, her only response to his words was a death glare. That look was enough for Kandi to recognize him. He was one of the cadets in her cadre – Dari? Alongside him, she noted three companions, all of them elves. She thought, *If four inexperienced cadets can get by you, you must be slipping, Kandi.*

Kandi had allowed a fraction of her mind a second to analyze the quartet. In her view, that was all the four were worth. Now, that moment was over. A hardened mask again took hold of her face as she resumed her duel with Sheda. She showed no outward sign that she had even heard the elf, which seemed to vex him terribly, so he decided to try again, this time a little louder, assuming she hadn't heard him the first time. "You know? No matter when I arrive, I always walk in on you in the heat of battle - wearing your body armor, no less! As if your AI would cause you any real injury."

Kandi was here every morning, and neither Dari nor his friends had ever darkened the doors – until today. As to the armor comment, she had composed her program to allow damage to the point of death. The body armor was more than necessary to keep the simulation accurate. Without it, the simulations would result in extensive medical help after every bout. No. His seedy stare indicated the elf was far more interested in what was under the semi-transparent shield than the armor itself. Thinking back, she could recall his ogling eyes and side comments during her group training simulations on more than one occasion. She had considered him a child then, and from what she could see, nothing had changed to alter that opinion.

Aeden had a long-standing equality between male and female citizens, but that did not mean this unwanted attention was unusual. Being a young master, Kandi often had to put up with a great deal of "attention" from the male students at the Institute. Her war record and Watcher career made her a bit of a celebrity among the cadets, and the fact that she was physically attractive only seemed to fascinate them more. The males in Kandi's squadron on Gaia had outgrown their fantasies even as their respect for her abilities increased. They hardly saw her as female anymore; that was how she liked it. To her comrades, she had been a valued ally, a trusted partner.

Undeterred by her inattention to his needling, Dari continued with his comments, ever louder in his shouts, "You can't beat the AI, of course. That would be impossible, but if you were grappling with a real opponent - like me, I'm sure we could make that very interesting. Want to give me a try?" The other three elves laughed at the comment, jostling each other like immature adolescents.

There was no mistaking the sexual innuendo in his words, but Kandi considered them unworthy of response. She knew the elf would take any reply as an encouragement to continue, and she refused to fall into that trap. She shook her head to clear the cobwebs and returned to her opponent with a vengeance, scoring two unanswered points. Sheda was not happy, resetting her stance and preparing to resume.

Dari was now angry. No one ever ignored him. Thanks to his family, the community respected him and even feared him, and he loved the attention. This pixie witch would pay for her indifference. He practically shouted in his rage, "You know, with a body like yours, I can see how you moved up the ranks so quickly. I imagine every senior officer in the corps was "satisfied" with your performance and has some great stories about you. I'd guess you were pretty good to move up this far this fast. How about you show us some of those techniques, Master Watcher?" His voice was tinged with disdain as he flung her title at her.

His cohorts laughed, cheered, and whistled in response to his comments. However, Kandi never acknowledged his presence during his tirade, preferring to continue her duel while mentally adding up the punishments she would inflict on those bastards during their next training session. A flicker of a smile crossed her lips as she considered her options. Paybacks could be hell, as well as a valuable training tool.

"Damn!" Kandi was shocked back into the fight by a series of blows Sheda aimed at her torso. Kandi was knocked back a few steps by the severity of the attack.

"Mind wandering?" Sheda said. Kandi could practically hear the laugh in the AI's voice even though the battle bot had no face to reflect it.

That did it. Even though Kandi's training screamed at her to ignore this latest insult, she felt she had no choice but to respond. Believing she would be able to return to her exercise soon, she paused the battle simulation and turned her undivided attention toward the foursome. Her steeled voice reverberated in the gymnasium, perfectly reflecting the disdain that consumed her, "How about you, little boys, leave now." *While you still can*, she mentally added. Her voice was strong and intense, as much a part of her skillset as her fighting abilities. With that voice, she had stopped full-blown riots on Gaia, and human leaders had often withered under the sound, especially when coupled with the stare from her ice-blue eyes. The four elves inched backward, looking to each other for support under the intensity of the onslaught. Dari shook the spell off first and goaded the others into a unified front. "Stay where you are. There is still only one of her and four of us. Don't let her mind games fool you."

The elf's comments only aggravated Kandi more, as their conversation indicated their plans. Still, she never allowed her annoyance to show, even as her anger increased. Outwardly, she appeared almost too calm as she continued. "Gentlemen, I'd recommend you rethink your decision. As you know, training requires concentration and discipline, something you four are obviously lacking. I, on the other hand, train daily. I have the speed and strength to overcome a small tribe of humans. Do you really want to try your luck?" She recognized the other three now. They were all low performers in their cadet classes, and several instructors had reported them for insufficient work. She doubted they would make the final cut – especially after she registered this stunt with the Director.

Unrepentant and encouraged by finally getting her attention, Dari laughed as he continued, "Don't get your wings in a bunch, Kandi. I get it. Physical exercise is the best way to improve a lot of things. It's just that the guys and I believe you should teach us how to exercise all our muscles. Besides beating up on a machine, there are far more enjoyable things to do as a workout." Out of the corner of her eye, she saw one of the other elves making crude motions with his body as the others laughed.

Kandi was not amused, "That is Master Watcher to you, cadet!" Funny, she could put up with the taunting and the juvenile sexual comments and actions, but breaking protocol was inexcusable.

Cadets had to respect rank, even if they didn't respect common decency.

"Oh, excuse me, Master Watcher. Is that what the Director calls you in your evening meetings? What DID you have to do to gain your promotion?" Dari was treading on dangerous ground here. Kandi and the director were comrades-in-arms. They had served together in several campaigns during the final years of the Human Wars. Additionally, he was a trusted friend, and his reputation was beyond reproach. She would not allow this punk to put a great man down.

Looking up at their tall bodies from her comparatively diminutive height, she placed her hands firmly on her hips before taunting them, "You mentioned some exercises. What exactly would those be?" Her voice changed temperament before continuing, "Before responding, you should remember that I am your commanding officer."

Dari chuckled as Mert, one of the other elves, spoke with a slight slur, "Pretty sure you know exactly what we mean, ma'am. We don't want anything special, just a little taste of your fairy dust." The others jeered and laughed in response. "Yeah, "they chuckled, "just a bit of that sweet fairy dust."

Her eyebrows arched slightly at this latest insult. Her eye movement, almost imperceptible, would be the only indication the boys would get of the rage growing within her. They were oblivious and paid no heed. She continued in the same commanding voice as earlier, "Cadets. Trust me – this isn't the direction you want to go. Leave this facility immediately, or I'll notify the Director and see you brought up on charges. I will have no lack of evidence."

Dari grinned. "Is that it? Are you shy? Afraid of people watching? Don't you worry your pretty head about that. I took the liberty of rerouting the memory cache to a different storage area, which will auto-delete a few seconds later. Whatever happens here stays here. No one will ever know." Kandi reached for her wrist communicator as Dari continued. "Oh, don't bother with the mechanical comms either. For some mysterious reason, they won't work here. Someone must have configured a signal jammer." His smile grew into a leer as he winked at his compatriots.

His revelation visibly shook her. There was no way this was possible, especially on the Institute grounds. When she got control again, she said, "I can see where you might get a scrambler for the comms, but rerouting and deleting the memory cache is far above even my grade level, let alone yours. I don't believe you."

Dari continued condescendingly, "You should, Kandi," intentionally using her first name again, "You really should. After all, what good is having a father on the Council if you can't get the access codes for the things you need?"

What a jerk, she thought, *and he has relatives on the Council, a father no less*. Kandi tried to remain nonplused by the news as she began putting together multiple scenarios for how this morning might end. She just needed a little more time, "So, Daddy just gave you the codes, huh? It's a pretty risky move if you ask me. What happens if someone finds out? Daddy won't be happy if this rolls back on him."

"No one will ever know; even if they did, they wouldn't believe it. My father would see it swept away just like he's done before. The public's memory is very short." He continued, "Sweetheart, You should understand. I pretty much get anything I want. Anything – or anyone, if you see what I mean."

Kandi definitely "saw" what he meant. She also saw that the odds this encounter would end peacefully were getting slimmer by the minute. Several of her projected scenarios had already faded into obsolescence. The remaining ones were almost all violent. Part of her smiled. These boys were starting to tick her off, and quite honestly, she wasn't sure she wanted a peaceful conclusion anymore. Still, her position as their commanding officer dictated that she should at least try to resolve this situation non-violently, so she continued, "So…if I understand you correctly, all the audio and video feeds from this morning are being destroyed?"

"Right, first time."

"And the personal comms are disabled as well?"

"Correct again."

"You four seemed to have analyzed this encounter pretty thoroughly."

Dari answered with a laugh and a knowing smile echoed by his friends.

Kandi confronted the four with an abrupt statement, "Let me get this straight. Are you four prepared to rape me?"

The other boys were startled by her forwardness, but Dari didn't bat an eye, leering as he responded, "We hope it doesn't come to that. Ideally, you will cooperate and...enjoy our company like we know we'll enjoy yours. That way, it isn't rape at all, is it?" The men responded to Dari's bravado. They recovered their composure and joined him in a throaty, conspiratorial laugh.

The last non-violent scenario trashed; Kandi resolved herself to a more interactive resolution to the conflict. Dari's comment had ignited something primal inside her. Something that, once kindled, grew until the underlying emotion overcame her senses of propriety and duty. As the internal transformation progressed, an impish grin snaked across her face. The elves were clueless. They were, unfortunately, totally unaware of the nuances of pixie behavior. The earlier lifted eyebrow was a warning; the impish grin promised terrible things on the horizon. Her grin would have caused Gaian marauders to surrender and her fellow Watchers to shake in their boots, anticipating what would happen if the humans failed to give up. That grin should've set off alarms – run for the hills kind of alarms. This grin was not a friendly, welcoming smile. This smile was feral, fueled by warrior instincts that her ancestors had honed since her race began.

The four elves were too emboldened by their actions to notice or, for that matter, care about Kandi's change in mood. In their sexually stimulated minds, four-to-one odds seemed pretty good, and they looked forward to some sport at Kandi's expense. Quickly, before they lost their nerve, they encircled her so she couldn't escape.

Silly boys, Why would I want to escape?

Even in her heightened state, her training won out, and she gave a peaceful solution one last try. "With or without the sensor readings, you must realize I will take this to the Director. You will pay dearly for today's actions."

Dari smiled broadly in amusement. "Seriously? Your word against the four of us. You wouldn't stand a chance. My father already has me on a short track to the Council. The others here are all sons of leading Atlantean citizens. Don't make me laugh. We'll tell them that you arranged it. You wanted to have your way with us. You destroyed the sensor feeds. You longed for us. No one, especially my father, will believe otherwise."

Kandi shrugged her shoulders. Well, she had tried.

Despite the disparity of numbers, the four elves never stood a chance. Even with their crystal-enhanced muscle strength, they lacked the discipline and training to maximize their potential. The four surrounded her, jeering, daring her to break free. While Dari bragged, Kandi analyzed vectors and strategies until one of the other elves, Batar, got a little too daring, snaking out his arm while attempting to grab her left breast.

Batar's attempt was enough to generate an instinctive response from Kandi, whose senses and nerves were at battle readiness. She intercepted and yanked his hand away, breaking his wrist in a single fluid motion. Using his forward momentum, she threw him into the elf directly behind her, following the move with a solid kick to Batar's midsection to speed him along. The sound of his ribs breaking elicited an impromptu giggle from the pixie's mouth. The two male bodies merged under the force of impact and fell to the ground, with Batar moaning pitifully. Kandi didn't take time to notice. She was in full battle mode now.

Even before the elves hit the ground, Kandi used the force of her kick to propel herself through the air, targeting Mert's solar plexus with her fist and using his body mass to swing herself over his head so that she faced her opponent. His mouth gaped in disbelief as his body spasmed in response to the vicious assault. An attempt to scream resulted in a quick jab to the jaw, effectively silencing him. As a bonus, the force of the hit neatly sliced off the tip of his tongue before rendering him unconscious. Mert dropped like a stone, blood trickling from his mouth as a wayward tooth bounced across the floor.

Now, only Dari remained untouched. Kandi spotted the would-be rapist turned coward as he ran frantically toward the exit, trying his best to escape. Kandi's malevolent grin grew more prominent. There was no way she would allow him to leave on his own power. A brief sprint and a kick to his knee were all she required to disable the elf. Dari's screams echoed throughout the facility as he slid across the floor, writhing in pain, begging her to spare him.

Kandi was not in a merciful mood. Before finishing with Dari, there was a loose end she needed to tie up. She looked over her shoulder and saw Zenah attempting to disentangle himself from Batar.

She walked over toward them. Calling his name made him look up – just in time to receive the knockout punch. The backward motion from that strike caused Zenah to fall back on his friend, renewing Batar's cries of pain. Apparently, broken ribs don't like people falling on them.

The entire battle had lasted less than thirty seconds. Bodies and bodily fluids littered the floor of the gym. Kandi had barely broken a sweat.

Still screaming in pain, Dari drew her attention back toward him. Kandi was confident that she had broken either his knee or his leg, possibly both – she didn't care. Her objective had been to immobilize him; the terrible pain was a bonus. She slowly walked across the gym floor toward the sniveling elf. She bent over his writhing body as he held his hands outward in a pathetic attempt at defense. Her viselike hands reached around and grabbed the back of his head, pulling him forward and forcing his complete attention on her, his face mere inches away from hers.

He got quiet. His body shivered in a combination of pain and fear. His fun morning "entertainment" was in ruins. He had planned for a sexual conquest and the subsequent bragging rights, not this. Dari's biggest concern was no longer carnal conquest but survival. As he stared into the pixie's eyes, he conjured up a dozen terrible things she could do to him, the least of which was death.

Kandi slapped the boy hard with her free hand, the echo reverberating in the now quiet gym. She wanted to be positive she had Dari's complete and undivided attention. She then spoke to him in a calm, steady voice that belied the vicious beast he now knew was inside the petite form. "Listen very carefully, little boy. I'm only going to say this once. Remember every word." Dari nodded his assent. "You will never try anything like this again, not with me or anyone else. If you do, or if I hear of you ambushing another woman, I'll find you, and we'll finish our sparring session, only next time I won't be as gentle."

Dari gulped. He did not doubt for one second that she meant what she said. She continued, "Understand this. I am one 'someone' you will never 'get' no matter who your daddy is. This is my body, and the list of people I share it with is short and doesn't nor will it ever include little boys like you."

Kandi dropped his head, relishing its hollow sound as it struck the gym floor. She then took her time to place her tunic over her armor. Her adrenaline levels were returning to normal. Every movement reminded her how tired she was. She triggered the call button on her wrist comm and feigned shock when there was no response. "Oh, I forgot. The comm links aren't working here. Too bad. I'll have to call medical when I'm outside the range of your scrambler."

She laughed at her 'joke' before speaking again, this time in a normal tone just loud enough to be heard over the crying and moaning, "Boys, for future reference, please note that I am a pixie, not a fairy. Perhaps, during your recovery, you can study the differences, but I'll give you one for free. Pixies don't do 'dust.' We generally avoid fairies altogether – they are too soft for our liking. Medics will be here soon. Don't go anywhere – little boys."

Origen and the nature of time travel from the Aedenian Archives

Time is a soup – a stew made from infinite bits of random materials - some savory, some not. Our perception of time is an organization of a few bites of that stew presented in a four-dimensional reality – a time stream. Bits of time can be arranged in any order; no logic is required. When considered in their entirety, the possibilities become endless.

Origen's travels spanned hundreds of worlds before arriving on Aeden millennia ago via his transport portal, the Wellspring. The other planets proved unsuitable for crystal life forms. They either contained too many heavy metals or sustained excessive solar radiation levels, which would damage and possibly kill him.

Once on Aeden, he realized he had found a perfect location. The radiation from the red sun was low, and heavy metals were almost non-existent, at least on the Western Continent. That was where he stayed and grew, living solitary until the races crossed his path eons later.

As part of his pact with the elves, pixies, and fairies, Origen shaped the future of life on this planet – joining organic and inorganic into a symbiotic relationship where all parties thrived. The races gained a long life without disease and a bountiful food supply. They also received the gift of space travel - the ability to go to the other worlds he had found. For his part, Origen could view the world through their organic eyes, the crystal nanites creating the necessary conduit to connect him with them.

With Origen's help, elven scientists created gates that connected points in the space-time stew based on the Wellspring prototype. Those gates allowed them to travel to any of the worlds Origen had mapped out and even explore those he had not. However, this gift carried responsibilities as well.

> 1. The races could only use time travel between Aeden and alien worlds, not on Aeden itself. Because new gates could connect the worlds at different points of the foreign time streams, we could coordinate and manipulate them using tachyon threads, enabling the gatekeepers to skip forward into that planet's future. This meant that one could spend time on another world and then return to Aeden as if no time had passed. Scientists could observe evolutionary patterns over eons before leaving work for the day.

> 2. Origen was adamant that Aedenians could not investigate the local timestreams. Aeden's past and future were effectively closed to us. The temptation to alter present conditions by changing the past would be too great, and such meddling could prove hazardous to the continuation of our species.

> 3. Once established, a time link between worlds was immutable. The two joined worlds would be locked into a synchronized dance until something destroyed the temporal bridge between the planets and severed the tachyon stream.

After the Wars, when Origen forced the races to exile humans to Gaia, both parties required amendments to their agreement. Origen required that the remaining races be held responsible for the habitat on Gaia in perpetuity. From his studies, Origen knew that the new world's biosphere was unstable. He didn't want any accidents to destroy what remained of the human population. He knew that many elves and pixies resented his intrusion into their affairs and feared such accidents might be intentional.

For their part, the elders requested that they be able to police the humans on Gaia. They didn't want any opportunity for the exiles to return to Aeden and renew the violence. For this, they required a police force, the Watchers, comprised of surviving soldiers from the Human Wars. The elders tasked these warriors with keeping humanity on Gaia for all time and created the Institute to coordinate their efforts.

Because the time-dilation effect between the two worlds made remote administration difficult, the council established fourteen archangels as the new world's overlords. They would have the final say in matters affecting Gaia and her relationship with Aeden.

Origen agreed and gave each archangel a gift – a ring. The jewel gave the archangel immense power, including the means to move freely, forward and backward, within the alien time streams. This gift came with a caveat, however. They could only use the time travel ability in an extreme emergency, the likes of which even Origen could not imagine. He tied the keystones within each ring to the individual DNA of its archangel owner so that its power would be useless to anyone else. Additionally, these stones could activate any gate, allowing the archangels to go anywhere or anywhen they required.

Chapter 3 – Actions and Consequences

Her hormone levels nearing normal, Kandi kicked herself for allowing the confrontation with the four elves to escalate to the point it had. After all, she was a Master Watcher, and those men were under her command. No matter the provocation's seriousness, she shouldn't have let her emotions take control. She replayed the scene in her mind, afraid she would discover a peaceful solution, something she had missed. Why hadn't the idiots backed down when they had the chance? If only that damn elf hadn't grabbed her!

Feeling guilty about delaying aid to the men in the gym, Kandi called the Institute's clinic as soon as her comm registered a signal. "Medical" was the only acknowledgment on the other end. The person on the line seemed a little bored. Probably the night shift, just waiting to leave. She instantly regretted the extra work she was giving them.

"Medical, this is Master Watcher Mehra. I want to report," she paused, "a training accident in the gymnasium involving some cadets."

Reception remained calm at the news, "Master Watcher Mehra, are you in the gymnasium now?"

Kandi responded, "No, I'm approaching my quarters." There was a pause on the line, "Master Watcher, you realize that instructors should remain with their students, don't you?" Kandi could hear the rebuke in the medic's voice.

Kandi tried to remain calm, "Yes. Normally, I would have stayed and called you from there, but the comms weren't working." Kandi proceeded to enter her quarters.

"Very well, Master Watcher," the medic's voice oozed disapproval, "We'll take it from here. There is a team on the way," and then disconnected the call.

Kandi felt relieved. With medical now in charge, she felt no need to return to the gym and her four would-be assailants. After all, once medics were in charge in the field, the soldiers could resume their regular duties. Kandi hadn't been at the Institute long enough to realize that rule didn't apply here.

Kandi chuckled just a bit as she reviewed the morning's events in her mind one last time. How could people like Dari and that bunch ever expect to be Watchers? They couldn't care for themselves, let alone be responsible for others! More importantly, how did they get through the screening process to be admitted to the program initially?

Kandi's adrenaline rush was practically gone, and exhaustion was beginning to set in. Part of her knew she should report the incident up the command chain and do a follow-up with the medical team, but the other part, the one that didn't care, won. She checked the time. *Besides, the Director's not in the office yet, and I desperately need a shower.* She carefully removed her tunic and battle armor, taking great care with the latter as she put the garment in the refresher. She felt another sore spot on her thigh where Sheda had landed a solid blow. *Going to be a nasty bruise there, but overall, a pretty good workout.* It's a shame that the cadets hadn't presented more of a challenge. She shook her head. No more second guessing; the boys had received what they deserved.

Her room comm rang while Kandi hummed a random tune in the shower, soothing hot water relaxing her stiffening muscles. At first, she ignored the steady buzz from overhead, but when the caller refused to give up, she turned off the water and shouted in an irritated tone at the comm, "Receiving." The comm beeped once. "What do you want?"

"Master Watcher Mehra, the Director needs to see you in his office immediately." Kandi recognized the voice as the Director's secretary—the same secretary who shouldn't be on duty for another hour. Kandi was immediately on her guard and answered much more professionally, "I just got out of the shower. I'll be there as soon as I can."

"Master Watcher Mehra," now the secretary did not attempt to hide his irritation. "He indicated that the matter was extremely urgent. You must come at once." He dropped his voice a little so no one could overhear. "The Director said, and I quote, to tell you to 'stifle any lame excuse and get your butt down here, now.'"

Kandi thought. *Well, Mehra, you really stepped in it now. Guess I should have called the Director when I first got back.* "On my way." She responded as she threw on a fresh tunic. The cloth absorbed the moisture on her body, but she would have to dry her wings later. With her dripping hair leaving little puddles in the hallway, she launched herself toward the office where the Director waited. She knocked.

"Enter." The response was more of a growl than an actual word.

Kandi went inside and instantly felt the awe the room commanded. She had been here dozens of times but always had the same reaction. The room was magnificent. Like all Aedenian constructions, it was grown and modified from a single crystal. Where the Director's office varied was the presence of clear crystal along one wall. From his vantage point, high above the valley, he could see across the entire city of Atlantia. The sight stunned even the most frequent visitor as it did Kandi now.

Even without the view, the imposing presence of this office's occupant would have been enough to make this room intimidating. Like Kandi, the Director was a pixie, but that was where the similarities stopped. Although he looked to be about Kandi's age, she knew better. The director was at least a century older than her. As an officer at the beginning of the Human Wars, he had seen the worst of the fighting. His story was a legend among the rest of the Watchers. Here at the Institute, the Director ruled. The only people on Aeden who could question his judgment were the Elder Council, and they preferred to leave him alone and keep the reminder of war far away.

"Master Watcher Mehra reporting as ordered, sir."

This morning, the man who controlled the fate of two worlds stayed silent for a bit, allowing Kandi to count the drops of water accumulating on the floor as they fell from her wet body. Finally, he spoke in a calm, measured voice, "I hear you had an exhilarating morning, Master Watcher Mehra!"

Now, Kandi knew she was in real trouble. Unlike cadets, the Director typically used first names in private conversations with senior officers. He only used full titles when he was angry. His red face, white knuckles, and restrained voice indicated that the Director was far beyond mere anger. As a rule, the softer the Director talked, the angrier he was, and right now, Kandi was straining to hear him.

"Master Watcher Mehra. Please tell me why a frantic medical corpsman needed to wake me in my quarters this morning?" The Director stood and began circling her like a predator about to make a kill. "She claimed that our gym had become a 'war zone' – her exact words, by the way. According to her account, bodies and blood were strewn all over three sparring circles in the facility."

The Director continued, "Naturally, I was concerned. When I asked what had happened, she claimed that you called the clinic and reported a training accident but that you had exited the scene before her team arrived. She quickly added that the scene in the gym reminded her of actual battle scenes during the war and not like anything she had experienced in a training scenario. Now Master Watcher, Corpsman Trence was present at Ragnarök. She should know a *real* battle when she sees one. Wouldn't you agree?"

The question was rhetorical. The Director allowed zero time for her response. His face was mere inches away from hers as he continued, "Nonetheless, I requested video footage from the scene. Please sense my frustration when she informed me that she couldn't transmit from the gym due to unexplained interference, so I had to wait, and you know how I hate waiting. When the footage finally arrived, I was stunned. I had assumed the corpsman was exaggerating the situation. Hell. If anything, she didn't do the scene justice," he flashed a picture of the gym floor on the main screen. Kandi cringed as she looked at the damage she had done. She didn't think it had been that bad. Somehow, the overhead view made it look worse.

The Director was on a roll; he didn't even breathe, "No sooner had I discommed from medical than I had the first of three calls from a very irate councilman. He claimed one of my senior officers had physically assaulted his son...." He quickly referenced his data feed. "...Dari. The boy had no problem naming you as his assailant, unlike two friends who had to have their mouths wired shut and could not speak. The fourth boy is in a medically induced coma while his body is healing."

The Director returned to his desk, "While listening to the councilman's tirade, I made my way to my office and scanned through the morning correspondence. Do you know what was missing?" Again, the Director didn't give Kandi a chance to respond as he uncharacteristically shouted, "I found no report from you, Master Watcher Mehra! There is no mention at all concerning the occurrence. I informed the Councilman that there had to be a mistake. I couldn't imagine Master Watcher Mehra involved in an incident of this magnitude without immediately filing a report with me!"

His gaze zeroed in on her, making her legs weak. "Master Watcher Mehra, you are a battle-hardened veteran – made a real name for yourself during the last years of the Human Wars. What could possibly make you believe that beating up cadets and abandoning them wounded on the gym floor was a good idea? What in Origen's name were you thinking? " He continued, "Fortunately, no one died, although they might wish they had with the damage you did. Medical treated and released two of the boys. The other two, including the councilman's son, must remain in the clinic for at least seven days and out of action for four to six weeks! There is some question if Dari will be able to walk without assistance even with the crystal nanites. "

Kandi remained rigidly at attention and allowed the Director's scathing tirade to course over her. Every word from his mouth burned into her soul. Yes, she regretted her actions, and she should've returned to the gym after reporting to medical, yet she could not find empathy in her heart for the foursome.

She should have expected nothing less from the Director, of course. Her actions after the confrontation were utterly out of line, on the verge of being irresponsible. She knew that and accepted whatever punishment was deemed appropriate, but she had at least hoped for an opportunity to defend herself. As for Dari, good riddance. Even with the Director's reprimand still scathing her soul, she assured herself that, under the same circumstances, she would protect herself the same way.

Kandi was getting antsy. She knew she deserved the berating the Director was leveling on her, but Kandi was also aware that he didn't have the whole story, and she wanted to rectify that situation sooner rather than later. Nonetheless, as much as Kandi wanted to interrupt him, wisdom kept her quiet. She realized her current situation would only worsen if she did. The Director was slow to anger, but once he did, his temper had to cool down before he would listen to what she had to say. Some minutes later, her opportunity appeared to have arrived.

"Sir?" she asked plaintively.

"What!" His answer came in the form of a shout.

Kandi thought, *Okay, maybe not as calm as I believed.* She continued cautiously, "Sir, with all due respect, you don't know everything about what happened this morning. Despite appearances to the contrary," pointing at the display showing the aftermath of the confrontation, "I was the intended victim here. Those four elves approached me during my pre-dawn workout for the sole purpose of raping me. They even admitted such when I questioned them."

The Director's face was flat and unemotional, "So, Master Watcher? Where is your evidence? Inexplicably, there are no video or audio recordings of what happened."

Kandi responded quickly, "I know, sir; Dari bragged about having the codes to reroute and delete the system audio and video. Said he got them from his father, the Councilman. He also installed the frequency scramblers, making the personal comms unavailable."

The Director's eye twitched as he half-heartedly laughed, "Interesting. Ironically, the cadets say the same thing, only about you."

Kandi was confused, "Sir?" Kandi had a brief flashback to Dari's threats if she didn't cooperate. Her heart began to sink.

The Director flashed legal documents on the screen, "The two conscious cadets have signed affidavits claiming you enticed them to the gym this morning with the promise of sexual favors. They claim you bragged about shutting down the video and comm links – for privacy." The Director added, "Which, by the way, is a function far above your pay grade. I don't know how to do that, and I would love to know how you accomplished it." He returned to his earlier thought, "They further swear that they were shocked when, instead of the liaison they expected, you went...." He paused to refer to his info display to get the exact words. "...you went 'psycho berserk' on them? Dari swore that they all feared for their lives."

As well they should have, she thought. *If I had known this would happen, I would have killed them and staged the scene. There would have been less paperwork.*

Kandi found herself again on the defensive, "Sir, with all due respect, that's not how things happened. Those four elves took me completely by surprise this morning."

"Again, you're a battle-hardened veteran! How do you expect me to believe that? Human intelligence operatives, trained in stealth, couldn't get by you, and you want me to believe these...four incompetents could?" he interrupted, never losing the stony expression on his face.

Kandi's anxiety increased, and tears began forming in her eyes. She had hoped the Director would believe her. "Sir, Dari bragged about his father giving him the security codes necessary to move and delete the video and audio data feeds. He also had possession of a field scrambler to turn off the comms in that section of the complex." She continued, "The four elves then admitted that they had planned to drag me into a sexual encounter – hopefully willingly, but there was no question, but, willing or not, they planned to assault me. After surrounding me, one of the elves made physical contact by grabbing me. At that point, I reacted. I felt I had no choice. I was acting solely in self-"

The Director raised his hand for her to stop and gave her his first kind look of the morning, "Kandi," She relaxed a little as he returned to her name. "I'd love to believe you; I really would. Between the war and the Institute, we've served together for more years than we care to admit. For what it's worth, because of our previous campaigns together, I DO believe you. Those four elves have been trouble since day one. Each of their instructors has filed dismissal papers to drop them from the program. If their parents weren't who they were... Let's just say I'm truly sorry they ARE who they are. I can't imagine a situation where you would violate your office and risk your commission over a fling with those four idiots. You have much better taste."

Kandi relaxed a little more as he continued.

"Unfortunately, it's your word against the four of them. Remember that one of those idiots has a Councilman father who isn't inclined to listen to any opinion other than his own and will definitely not admit to giving his son the codes you mentioned. Not just him, though; the other three have parents who sway a lot of influence in the Atlantean community – massive in the metals and crystal trade with Gaia. Without substantial physical proof, I had no option but to decide in their favor. That said, the Council and I have reached an agreement. I will demote you two levels and suspend you from the training corps until further notice."

"But sir..." Kandi was panicking now. What would she do if they sent her away?

"But nothing. The people on the Council don't know you the way I do. Dari's father wanted real blood – your blood, and he wanted you and the Institute flogged publicly. If he had his way, you would be court-martialed and then subjected to a public trial – a trial that would undoubtedly result in exile on Gaia with the humans and without Watcher protection." Kandi shuddered as the image flashed across her mind. "This outcome was the best I could do for you and the Corps."

He switched to a more conversational tone. "I've also decided that, until things settle down, I am giving you an off-planet project." Kandi groaned. Off-planet could only mean one thing: a return to Gaia. "What I'm telling you is in the strictest confidence." Kandi nodded that she understood. "Do you remember the near extinction event on Gaia ten Aedenian years ago?" She nodded as the Director continued, "To warn against a future catastrophe, we installed environmental monitor drones at various points around the planet. After the previous failure, we aimed to satisfy the Origen Pact's provision on maintaining a living environment on Gaia."

Kandi responded, "I remember them well. I was part of the installation team near Dorado Gate. They were supposed to monitor the biosphere, right?"

The Director nodded as he continued, "One of those drones has contacted the Institute regarding some troubling environmental changes there."

Kandi was confused, "Contacted the Institute? As I recall, the drones were programmed to contact the gate closest in proximity to their location."

The Director responded, "They were, and according to the data dump I received, the drone tried. The first beacon went to Dorado gate, but there was no response, which is noteworthy. The same happened on subsequent attempts to contact Atlantia, Asgard, and the other eleven gates. With no other options, the drone's protocols dictated using the backup tachyon link directly to the Institute, the link established when the drone was commissioned."

Kandi hesitated before commenting, "But, sir. How is that possible? The gates are in nearly constant use. Everything is working perfectly."

The Director frowned, "Now. They are working now. Unfortunately, the drone sustained some damage to its data cores, taking it offline for some time. Some sort of seismic event jostled it back into operation. If the data dump we recovered is accurate, this drone is communicating from an undetermined number of years in Gaia's future as relates to us – quite likely thousands of years."

Kandi had difficulty understanding what the man was saying, "Sir. If that is the case, we have a split in the timestream. I was told that was impossible. How could that occur?"

The director continued, "We don't know. According to its limited data regarding Dorado Gate, the drone went offline in our current time synchrony within a few years of our present. We did due diligence, of course. The drone in question is active in our systems and still reports data to Dorado. So, now we appear to have two drones with the same ID, one in our current timestream and one not, a potential paradox. We were shocked, of course."

Kandi remembered from her training that one of the trickiest things about time travel was how events unfolded might not make sense outside of that time stream: different places, different perceptions. Tachyon tags were the only way to keep from getting lost in the soup of time.

The Watcher Corps was thirty years into the fourth human exile. The first two failed because of radiation and atmospheric poisoning – an error in the planet's terraforming. The third occurred because of a human-caused environmental disaster ten Aedenian years ago. Kandi could remember the near-extinction event and the forced evacuation of the Gaian population that followed.

Aedenian scientists were convinced they had decades before the disaster befell the planet, plenty of time for the evacuation…" Kandi finished the sentence, "…but they erred. The catastrophe occurred less than two years after the initial prediction." The Director picked up the conversation, "Yes. In the resulting environmental collapse, not much survived. Hundreds of millions of humans, pixies, and elves died. Those that did survive became abominations as the number of mutations abounded, only discovered when we were ready to repopulate the planet. Thousands of years in its future."

Kandi was stunned. The Director was saying that disaster was again about to befall the humans on Gaia, and she knew that the Institute was honor-bound to try and stop it.

The Director continued briefing, "I've decided to send the same scientific team as before to investigate. They've learned a lot over the past ten years, and even if they hadn't, they are still the best we have. If the problem is similar to the last event, we might have a chance to mitigate some, even most, damage to the planet and to the life forms. We have used the tachyon stream attached to the drone to open a gate along the new timestream and have installed an AI in the human data network to gather information on the current state of human affairs. The analysis will be ongoing, but one piece of critical information stands out." Kandi waited for him to continue. "The current population of Gaia far exceeds last time – almost eight billion humans. Even if the environmental markers point to the same event as before, relocating the population would be monumental if not impossible."

Kandi spoke up, "Sir, I'm no scientist. I fail to see how I can help."

The Director smiled, "I need you and a team of Watchers to establish a physical base of operations for the mission with a permanently housed AI for support. Since we must still be concerned with cultural contamination, we will use Aedenian technology as a last resort. The mission AI has analyzed and encapsulated all the required information for you and your team.

"The AI has also done an in-depth study of the language in the target area, which the natives call English. I wish we could give you more than just the one, but humans have over five thousand distinct languages and dialects, and there is insufficient time to provide them all. Downloads should be available by this afternoon."

The scowl from her earlier reprimand still lingered on Kandi's face, but she was smart enough not to say anything aloud. The Director added, "Look, I know this isn't what you want to do with your career, but this is what you need to do now."

Kandi couldn't hold her emotions in check any longer. "Seriously, sir? You know how I feel about Gaia…and Humans in general. They are dirty, filthy creatures…and their air stinks." She tried to turn things to her advantage, "Besides, isn't this a bit above the responsibility level of my new rank?"

Her weak appeal did not dissuade the Director, "Rank aside, you're still the best person for the job. You would've gotten the call even before your little escapade in the gym this morning." He stared into her fiery eyes.

"Yes, I understand. You would prefer to destroy Gaia – or watch them destroy themselves. I fully understand what happened at Galadel, but your loss was not yours alone. The Human Wars cost almost half the combined populations of Aeden their lives. Tens of millions died in the carnage. I wasn't left orphaned like you, but I lost my spouse and children in the battle for Atlantia. I share your scars." Kandi hung her head as he continued, "Look, Kandi, all of us are still reeling from the aftereffects of that war. Who knows if we'll ever recover completely? "

She remained silent. What could she say?

The Director appeared to calm himself, "Kandi, you are just going to have to trust me. When this finally blows over, and it will, I will reinstate you. I promise you that. Meanwhile, having you out of sight on the other side of the galaxy is a good idea, especially when a Councilman is gunning for your hide."

Kandi sat rigidly in her chair as he continued. "There is another problem, even larger than the environmental one. The drones failed attempts to contact us tell us that in this future Gaia, our gates are gone – they vanished without a trace, and we have no idea what happened to them. Did we abandon them for some reason, or were they destroyed? The data feeds show many of our gate names now exist as parts of human mythology, giving the impression that whatever occurred on Gaia not only happened long ago but was significant enough to remain in racial memory. Our knowledge is insufficient. We are depending on you and your team to fill in the blanks. Aeden's survival might be at stake."

The Director stopped, letting Kandi know the meeting was over.

"Is there anything else, sir?" she asked.

"That is all, Watcher. You have your orders."

"Yes, sir. Thank you, sir. Might I add one thing about the incident this morning? Something I just remembered?"

The Director barely glanced up from his data feed. "I'm listening."

"Sir, there might be evidence of what happened in the gym."

Now, the person behind the desk looked up, his interest piqued.

Kandi continued, "Sir, I recommend checking the visual and audio cortexes of Sheda, my sparring partner. When she and I were interrupted, I paused the session but never shut it down. Sheda should have recorded all the events within her interfaces' range. You should find sufficient information in her logs to substantiate my claim."

The Director smiled, "Thank you, Watcher. I'll do that." He tapped on his data feed. He stopped to get in one last dig at his protege, "By the way, the latest reports indicate that Gaian air quality has diminished by 25% since the last time you visited. Every breath really stinks now. Dismissed."

Kandi grimaced as she left the room with the Director still chuckling under his breath. Despite everything that had transpired, she walked out with something resembling her customary swagger. The Director didn't notice. He was putting in a comm to AI support. Depending on the result, this day might be looking up.

The Last Time...Ten Years Ago, Aedenian Time

The screams of the dead still resonated in the hallways of the Institute. Multiple replays of events had shown that the end result was inevitable, but that didn't make the deaths more acceptable. Mistakes were made, and millions died as a result. Coming so soon after the end of the Human Wars, the additional sacrifice was even harder to take. Elves, pixies, and humans all joined in their mourning.

Environmental changes rarely happen quickly, more often taking thousands, even millions, of years to complete, so it was no wonder the scientists monitoring Gaia's biosphere didn't catch the problem at first. When the data came into the lab, they hardly believed what they saw. They repeated the tests multiple times, praying they were wrong, but each result was exactly like the first.

The news was not good. Gaia had developed a noticeable imbalance in its axial tilt, slowing the planet's rotational spin and thus reducing the strength of its magnetic field. This was unknown territory for the scientists. They estimated that, at the current rate of change, there was a real danger that Gaia could shift thirty to forty degrees on its axis within the next century. The gyroscopic effect of the planet's rotation would keep it from falling over, but the swings back and forth would be enough to be catastrophic to planetary life. What the wobbling didn't destroy, the increased solar radiation levels from the reduced magnetic field would. There was no way the human colonies could survive. The Council decided that the only option was to evacuate the human population before the event happened.

Unfortunately, the scientists' time estimates were flawed. They simply didn't have enough data to make an accurate assumption. Ultimately, they didn't have centuries; they had barely two years. When the collapse happened, and Gaia shifted twenty degrees practically overnight, the Institute had only managed to evacuate less than three hundred thousand humans to the Eastern Continent. The Event, as it became known, killed the rest.

With humans again on the Eastern Continent, time was of the essence. The longer they remained there, the more uncomfortable the elven and pixie populations became. The Council charged the Aedenian scientists to begin scanning forward on Gaia's timeline for a space-time when a stable habitat for humans on Gaia once again existed. They found such a time – one million years in Gaia's future.

Chapter 4 - Jonathan

Jonathan Martyr, renowned jewelry artisan of Boston, didn't feel so notable at the moment. The medieval torture chamber on the red-eye flight to Denver refused to conform to Jonathan's six-foot-two body. No matter what position he tried, comfort eluded him. He was already in a bad mood. First, the airline couldn't find his reservation. Then, he failed the security check three times before having TSA practically strip-search before allowing him to race to the gate, where he found the plane waiting on him - the last person to board. Even the flight attendant scowled as she launched a pillow and blanket in his general direction before hurrying down the aisle.

Jon gazed mindlessly out the window, thinking about the events of the past seven days. Only seven days? They seemed interminable. Images flashed before his eyes like a bad movie, only interrupted by the occasional wisp of cloud caressing the side of the plane. Nothing in those seven days seemed real. He couldn't allow himself to believe they were true. He tried to convince himself that he was living a bad dream and was bound to wake up soon.

Eight days ago, before the phone call, Jon's life had been predictable, bordering on boring. Even though he could afford better, his small, functional apartment in Braintree was more than enough for his needs, and his career as a jewelry designer in Boston finally showed signs of taking off on a national stage. Life had been good and was getting better – until seven days ago.

The phone was on its sixth ring when Jon answered, "Hello?"

"Is this Jonathan Martyr?" the voice inquired.

"Yes. Can I help you?" Jon didn't recognize the voice, but the style of speech was familiar – official, not casual or friendly. Commonly plagued by constant mass marketing calls, he fought the urge to disconnect. Something told him this call wasn't selling anything.

The unidentified voice continued, "Mr. Martyr, I represent the Shavel Law Firm in Boulder, Colorado. We're contacting you regarding your father, Stephen Martyr."

Jon was instantly on guard. He and his father had not seen nor spoken to each other since his mother's funeral three years ago, and what little relationship they shared before her death had always been more of a charade for Mom's benefit than anything real between them. When she wasn't around, they fought constantly.

The man on the phone seemed impatient, "Mr. Martyr? Are you still there?"

His voice shocked Jon out of his reverie, "Yes, yes, I'm here. I'm just confused. Why are you calling me?"

"Well...There is no easy way to say this. Your father passed away two nights ago."

Time froze.

"What? I'm sorry. I didn't quite catch that. What are you saying?" Jon's voice trembled.

"Your father suffered a massive stroke while at a charity gala. He died on his way to the hospital."

"My father...dead?" Jon found the very concept of his father dying incomprehensible. Stephen Martyr couldn't be dead! His body wouldn't have dared to fail him.

The lawyer continued, "Mr. Martyr, your father hired our firm to be the executor for his estate. As the sole beneficiary, we require you to come to Boulder soon. There are some sections of your father's will that you must handle in person. In keeping with your father's wishes, we have also begun making funeral arrangements. Would a week from Thursday be satisfactory?"

Jon heard himself agree even though he never felt his lips move.

"Very well. We can meet to handle the other business at that time."

Jon was in shock. He hovered over the table for a few minutes, phone in hand, unable to move. What the lawyer had told him was beyond belief.

His father was famous. His exploits as an explorer and archeologist resembled an action film character more than a typical academic. He was the indisputable best in his field – the gold standard of his profession. Jon could not allow himself to believe that he was dead.

The omnipresent shadow his father had cast had constantly hung over Jonathan. His parents were older when he was born, a miracle child his mother called him. Growing up, Jonathan often traveled with his father on digs. Everyone assumed he would take up his father's torch. After the elder Martyr's last discovery, the pressure on the genius' only son became even more intense. Jon didn't care. He knew he would never go that route. He was not his father's "chip off the old block."

Ultimately, to his father's dismay, he went a hundred and eighty degrees in a different direction. He studied art and later moved into designer jewelry. After finishing his studies, he found an apprentice job in Boston, just far enough from his parents in New York to blunt their interference in his affairs. There, he became his own man. Naturally, his father continued to insist that Jon was wasting his time – time that Jon could better spend pursuing great truths out in the world instead of playing with tiny tools and baubles.

Then, his father did the unthinkable. Still a relatively young man in his early sixties, with the archeological world at his feet and the mystery of his latest discovery still hovering over him, he left it all - the fame, his tenured position with Colombia, and the adulation of all academia. His peers stood in disbelief when he retired. His only comment had been, "I need to leave something for the rest of you."

Dad and Jon's mother, Janet, abandoned New York for a more sedate, almost monastic existence in the mountains west of Denver. Even out there, he found it impossible to escape his previous life. The dashing pair often appeared on the society pages in the Denver Post, supporting one charity or another – until cancer claimed her, severing the one link between father and son forever.

Jon stared blankly out the plane's window, watching as the lights of cities and towns slid slowly beneath him. There was no telling what awaited him in Boulder, but he would get through it. Martyrs always did. The quiet, darkened cabin and the past week's stress finally beat him into submission. Somewhere over the Blue Ridge Mountains of Kentucky, he slept.

At the funeral home, Jonathan came face to face with reality. His father was dead - wholly and entirely, no question about it, finished. Jon had seen his lifeless form in his coffin, his face twisted and made up into a caricature of the man he once had been. The funeral director explained that they had done their best. He told Jon that often, the face molds itself into strange shapes in heart attack and stroke cases, making restoration difficult. Jon assured the man that he appreciated what they had been able to do but then exercised his right to have the casket closed at the funeral. With Jon watching, the funeral director screwed the lid to the box with his father inside.

Jonathan stared unwaveringly at the ornate casket during the funeral, almost expecting the coffin to erupt and his father to step out in defiance of death. Jon was almost disappointed when the box stayed solid under his gaze. He looked around. The number of people in attendance surprised him. There were hundreds of people here paying homage to his father. Of course, he recognized few and knew none.

"Your father was an incredible person. I loved his work." One by one, the academics walked by Jon's place by the casket, streaming their platitudes.

"I played golf with your dad every week. He always spoke highly of you." Somehow, Jon doubted that. His father would have been more likely to praise his caddy than his only son.

Jon listened intently as each person echoed the one before.

"He died too soon."

"He still had so much to give."

"Are you in archeology too?"

"This must be very hard on you now that both of your parents are gone."

Jon feigned a smile and nodded agreement to each comment rather than state the truth that only he knew. His father was as much of a stranger to him as they were. Somehow, that realization made him feel even more empty inside.

At the cemetery, they buried his father beside his mother. Standing next to her grave, Jon felt lost - disconnected from life. He had loved his mother as much as he despised his father. In between those emotions, Jon had to find his way. Knowing no one in town and not wanting to find a bar and bury his feelings in a bottle quite yet, he decided to see his father's attorney. The bar would wait until later.

The firm's office was a modern building located in a suburban area away from most traffic and adjacent to a city park. As Jon entered, a pert, young secretary welcomed him and took him to a well-appointed office with a cup of coffee in his hand before he knew what was going on.

"Mr. Martyr..." the attorney began as he entered the room.

"It's Jon," he interrupted. "Mr. Martyr is no longer with us.

"Of course. I understand. Jon, it is." The attorney switched to a more conversational tone. "Please accept our sincere condolences on your loss. As I mentioned over the phone...Jon, your father left everything to you in his will, which shouldn't surprise you since you're his only child."

Jon thought, *I wouldn't have been surprised if he had given the whole shebang to some charity, sticking me with the bill for the expenses.*

Despite his inner turmoil, Jon maintained a steady gaze on the lawyer, who continued, "We have begun probate proceedings and will distribute his sizable assets to you upon their completion. We require you to sign these forms authorizing us to act as your agents."

"Of course. Thank you." Jon was on automatic pilot at this point. The secretary placed each page before him, pointing to where he should sign. His father would have been horrified that Jon didn't carefully read each one, but, at this point, Jon didn't care what they said. He just wanted this business done.

"There is one other matter which you and I must discuss alone. Miss Francis, would you please leave the room?" The attorney was suddenly all business.

The attorney continued after the secretary gathered her papers, removed herself from the room, and closed the door. "Jon, your father wanted me to give you this personally." He reached into a drawer and pulled out a ring box – a heavy ring box based on the way he handled it. He pushed the box and a sealed envelope across the desk to Jon, indicating that Jon should open the letter now. With trembling hands, Jon did so.

Jonathan,

The ring in this box is an heirloom passed down through our family for generations, longer than anyone can remember, and now, duty requires that I pass it on to you. There are a few things that you need to know about it, the same things that my father told me long ago. I wish I were across from you now to discuss them.

First, open the box rarely. The stone emits radiation – supposedly not harmful, but it pays to be careful. Legend says that the radiation is a signal for evil spirits or some such garbage. The box is lined with lead and is as old as its jewelry. The ring's purpose, whatever that might have been, was lost ages ago. It is, however, a beautiful piece that I am sure you can appreciate more than I ever did.

Second, despite its beauty, you should never wear the ring. I have no idea why, but my father was insistent about it, as he said his father and grandfather were to him. Family lore claims that putting the ring on your hand will result in the owner's death. Poppycock, I know, but sometimes there's truth to some curses.

What I suggest is that you think of it as a good luck charm. I did. Carry it with you as you make your way in the world. When I made the Jericho discovery, I had the box in my pocket, and that turned out pretty well. Hopefully, it will have the same effect on you.

Finally, I want to tell you I love and am proud of you. You don't know this, but I had a friend purchase one of your pieces when he was in Boston last year – a pair of cufflinks. I wear them everywhere and get jealous comments from all my friends. My stubborn pride kept me from ever saying it before. I know we never really bonded, but you were so annoying! Though, in truth, I guess I was too. I wish you the best in everything.

Whatever direction your life takes, always be true to who you are – a Martyr. Never settle for less than the best.

Love,
Dad

The note disturbed Jonathan more than it should. His father loved him? Really? The man certainly did not show it when he was alive. Why would he profess it here? A dying declaration that he couldn't take back? Jon picked up the box, startled by the heft. He pocketed it and asked the attorney about visiting his father's house. The man assured him that would not be a problem and provided him with the key. He also told Jon to feel free to take any personal items he wanted, so long as he kept a record for the probate. Jon thanked him, shook his hand, and left, promising to return the key in the morning before his flight.

Jon had visited the house in Seven Hills before, of course, twice a year on Thanksgiving and Christmas, but he never understood his parents' love for the place. The house was their pride and joy. Jon tried to reflect his mother's enthusiasm for her sake. Overall, they tried to keep the holidays cordial. His father kept his obvious disapproval under wraps most of the time. After all, Mother had insisted, and Mother always got her way.

Father saved his scathing tirades until late evening, just before they retired, usually after consuming too much Scotch. Mother excused herself early on those nights, leaving the father and son alone in the den. The nagging and nitpicking wore at Jon, making him feel more and more unwelcome – wishing he never had to return. When his mother died in October of the following year, he got his wish. He had not entered this door since her funeral.

Now, he hoped, he could put his demons to bed.

As he went inside, his body shivered as if shaking the weight of a lifetime from his frame. The first thing that caught his eye was the award sitting in its place of honor above the fireplace and the medallion displayed prominently at its center.

The British Academy is proud to award The Grahame Clark Medal to Dr. Stephen Martyr for his lifetime of work in the pursuit of archeology.

The award's eye-catching ability was not accidental. Stephen Martyr had carefully positioned the item on the mantle and installed special lighting so that the piece grabbed the attention of anyone entering the house. Jon smiled to himself. Father would never admit to the sin of pride, but he would not turn down an opportunity to showcase his award either.

The Academy failed to mention that Father's most recent discovery had cinched his being that year's recipient. The discovery had been a momentous one. Like most such things, rings in boxes aside, luck had come into play. While examining some ground-penetrating radar images, Father and his team found a slight inconsistency on the plateau above St. George Monastery just west of Jericho.

After confirming the findings, he assembled an expedition to investigate – no small feat considering the region's politics and religions. The dig uncovered an artificial seal a few feet below the surface. Behind that seal was...no one knows. Father and his team saw the contents, of course, but the authorities shut the dig down immediately afterward. The site remained closed while the powers determined who should have jurisdiction over the contents.

With so many governments and religions clamoring for possession, the same forces issued a gag order on the expedition. Jon's father was to make no public announcement, nor were any of his team permitted to discuss the find in public or private.

Father obeyed the rule. His only comment was a passing one that the cave was a treasure trove, not of gold, but of historical and biblical significance. He claimed the discovery would change the world. Jon chuckled to himself. Maybe that was the reason the world hid the secret away.

As Jon prepared to leave the house with his small box of mementos, including his father's cuff links, his hand brushed against the ring box in his pocket. He realized that he had not even confirmed the presence of a ring within. Feeling a sudden need to verify its existence, he removed the case from his pocket and opened the box in the light.

He gasped.

The stone made up almost the entirety of the ring. As Jonathan gently turned it over in his hand, he saw that the deep red of the jewel was unlike anything in his experience. A filigreed gold inlay encompassed the stone on the outside, leaving the gem uncovered on the interior, where it would set against the back of the hand.

He stared at the jewelry for a few minutes before reluctantly closing the box and putting it back in his pocket. He shouldered the small bag of possessions he had claimed, opened the door, and left. Over his shoulder, his father's award plaque shone in the spotlight created for it. Jon didn't want it. He had buried that ghost with his father.

Chapter 5 – Vermont Base

"Two months!" Watcher Mehra exclaimed to her people on the view screen; her frustration was apparent. The images of the people on the other ends of the call were seemingly frozen and silent, "The Institute allocated two months for this project phase. We've now spent five, and I'm not certain another five will be enough." The Watcher commander addressed her team via telecom at their various locations, and she was exceedingly unhappy.

"Watcher Mehra?" a timid voice dared to speak.

"Yes, Watcher Krone, do you have something vital to add to our discussion?" Vitriol dripped from her lips.

"Yes, Commander. Our biggest obstacle has been getting our science team through Gaian security. Originally, we thought that simple photo IDs would be sufficient, but we have since discovered our team would be discovered with little effort from the local governments. Other bypass attempts have shown that the Gaian authorities are incredibly adept at discovering subterfuge both in hardcopy and in their databases."

"You haven't told me anything I don't already know, Krone. You better not be wasting my time." The threat in the pixie's tone was sincere. She was not in the mood to tolerate fools today.

"What if we had a way to complete the preparations in only one month local time."

Kandi was suddenly interested in what the young Watcher had to say. "Krone, You have my attention."

"Yes, commander." Krone gulped audibly before continuing. "I have been researching something the Gaians call identity theft, particularly where a person assumes the identity of a deceased infant or small child. In those cases, the base data is already on file. All that needs to happen is to add our team member's information and invented background to the existing root record. There are quite a few documented cases where the illusion is quite effective. This process may allow us to integrate the science team into Gaian security protocols without setting off any alarms."

Mehra was impressed with Krone's initiative and noted to keep an eye on her in the future. She might be worth helping along in the program. "Interesting, and you believe you can complete this in a month?"

Krone responded, "Yes, that shouldn't be a problem, providing I have priority access to Sara for that time."

Kandi nodded, "Granted. Sara, you will assist Watcher Krone in her efforts. Her project will be the top priority."

Saraswati responded, "Yes, commander."

Watcher Mehra ended the meeting, "Very well. The remainder of the team will continue on your assigned plans. We hope that Watcher Krone succeeds, but we must follow our original plan as a backup in case she fails. Let us pray that she does not. Dismissed."

Watcher Kandi Mehra turned away from the telecom monitor and prepared tea in the kitchen. For some reason, this was the only Gaian beverage that worked for her. Many of her team members had become somewhat addicted to coffee, but tea hit the spot for her. Through the farmhouse's windows, she saw the first hint of Vermont fall. She hated to admit it, but sometimes Gaia was actually pretty. Only she and Saraswati, the team's AI, lived here, where the gate to Aeden and the tachyon link was located. The rest of the group spread across the continent with residences in Chicago, New York, Miami, and Los Angeles. The project required a lot of material, and Kandi feared that purchases in only one place might get unwanted attention from the authorities. Besides, they had established several secondary gates that could have all the team members moved to Vermont within seconds.

Kandi had selected rural Vermont for their base camp mostly because there was no shortage of isolated homes, and privacy was paramount. There were also personal reasons. The air here was a little cleaner, and although it was still stinky by home standards, it didn't smell nearly as bad as other points on the planet. The team's purchases of vehicles and other supplies from around the country were delivered directly to the house or picked up in metropolitan areas like Chicago, Miami, and New York, where they could drive them here.

True to her word, a month later, Watcher Krone delivered on her promise. Acceptable identities had been found and modified. Krone and Sara quickly added education, work experience, and credit history to the root records for all fifteen personnel. Kandi was impressed. They ran a test on the resulting documents and found they survived even in-depth scrutiny by the authorities. Finally, the preparation part of the mission was complete, and the base was ready to be assumed by the science team.

Of course, their multi-month delay hadn't affected the arriving scientists much. The months on Gaia had translated into only two weeks for them. The time variance would have been even less if not for the specialized Aedenian equipment required to complete the mission. That procurement took actual time away from the sending team. Gaian time wouldn't matter to them until they were a part of the local timestream.

While waiting for her team to reassemble in Vermont, Kandi had a rare moment of inactivity. She thought back to her past duty assignments on Gaia. In the current timeline, it was hard to believe those experiences were thousands of years ago. Life had been much easier for Watchers during Gaian colonization. There was no need to hide then. Watchers were recognized, known, and feared across the planet. They were the police and the wardens of the Gaian prison, and they rewarded disobedience with pain and death.

In the present assignment, that was not the case. Gone were skirmishes and crowd control – the things Kandi loved. Now, she was more concerned with finances and logistics – and gods, she hated logistics. All her experience as a soldier had done precious little to prepare her for running a business like the Aeden Corporation here on Gaia.

Kandi had accepted that a corporate identity was necessary, although she detested the time required to set it up and test it. Sara had approached her at the beginning of the assignment, advising that large amounts of money changing hands would raise red flags with local governments and banking institutions. Kandi had agreed but soon discovered that setting up a new corporation that appeared old was its own unique problem. Even a highly sophisticated AI like Saraswati needed time to analyze and navigate the intricacies of cash flows and corporate paperwork before she could finally establish a corporate presence. Then, she had to back-build a verifiable history for that entity. Still, as long as it had taken, Kandi was glad they had taken the time to do it right. Now, with a substantial line of credit with international banks behind them, the Aeden Corporation had no lack of financial resources at its disposal.

Now, at last, preparations were completed and, in Kandi's estimation, done as well as expected. Perfection was an elusive ghost, but the team had done their best to approach that lofty level. Kandi contacted the Institute via the tachyon thread connecting their two space-time points, "Control?"

A familiar voice replied, "Control here. Go ahead." The same dispatcher that sent the advance team was the one who responded, adding to the déjà vu of time-space travel. Kandi shook off the feeling and followed protocol, "This is Watcher Mehra at the Gaian Base. The prep team is ready to transit."

"Acknowledged, Watcher Mehra. The Director congratulates you on completing the assignment and regrets that you must stay as the scientists' liaison. He adds that things have not calmed down enough here for you to return."

Kandi sighed. Sheda's recording had been entered into evidence, proving her allegations of assault. That, however, did not mean that Dari and his father had acquiesced readily. Eventually, Dari and his cronies were dismissed from the corps, but Dari's father remained on the Council and had a very long memory. She and the director had decided she would remain here with the science team for the time being. She didn't like babysitting a bunch of civilians, but the Director insisted that Dari's father was still on the warpath. "Affirmative Control. Thank the Director for his sympathy. I will be fine."

Control chuckled, "Proceed with the transfer of the prep team when you are ready."

"Affirmative. We are proceeding now."

Kandi watched her team enter the portal individually, each seeming to vaporize as they contacted the crystal face. Kandi was genuinely saddened to see them go. Her sadness was only increased by not being able to return with them. Despite their differences, the team had built up a lot of camaraderie over the past months. Tonight, back on Aeden, they would party, celebrating their return, breathing the clean air of home. Kandi sighed. The stench of this world clung to her like a bad memory.

During the personnel transfer, Sara noted an abnormal signal – an unknown energy signature that set off an alarm deep in her programming. She immediately flagged it to be followed up when the transfer was complete and went back to the task at hand.

"Sara?" Kandi inquired.

"Yes, Kandi?" The AI's voice sounded from the audio pods.

"Prepare to receive the science team."

Sara did a quick check of all systems. "We are ready to receive."

Before Kandi could contact Control, the technician called her. His voice seemed different - tense – a touch of fear filtered into his voice. Kandi instinctively knew that something was very wrong.

"Gaia Base?"

Kandi continued to play it by the book, "We are here. Prepared to accept our science team at your convenience."

"Watcher Mehra, th-th-there has been a change in plans. Be advised that the Council has blocked all transits to and from all gates until further notice. We will keep you apprised as the situation develops." Control then terminated the comm before Kandi could ask a question. The room fell into a dull, vacuous silence.

Sara broke the spell, "This is highly irregular. Why would the Council put a stop to transits?"

Kandi knew that they could do so. The Council had emergency powers, giving them complete control over Aeden's gate network in case of a gate breach and subsequent human invasion. Something terrible was happening back home, and here she was in a backwater cabin on Gaia. Kandi couldn't feel more useless.

Later that night, an explosion rocked the base. Kandi was instantly alert and on her feet, running to the command center. "Sara. Status report."

"Running diagnostics now. The primary facility is intact, but there appears to be extensive damage to the portal chamber," Sara responded. "Luckily, the surrounding cave walls absorbed most of the shock. The house, power supply, and the remaining equipment appear intact."

Kandi sighed. The discovery of the cave adjacent to the home had been a happy accident. There was a long Watcher tradition of keeping the world portal outside the other facility. Accidents happened early in gate travel, and caution often paid for itself. Besides, constructing the gate chamber inside the cavity provided natural shielding, keeping the device's unique radiation from prying eyes. It would appear that the location of the crystal, quite by accident, just saved her life.

Kandi asked the dreaded question, "Sarah. What is the status of the crystal itself?"

Sara's answer confirmed Kandi's fears, "Sensors show that the intensity of the energy pulse shattered it. I have sent a drone to investigate."

The loss of the crystal was one of Kandi's greatest fears. Time seemed to stand still while she waited for the drone to arrive. "Looks pretty bad. Any chance of salvaging a part of it?"

Sara's answer was brief, "No. The drone reports what we feared. The detonation appears to have vaporized large portions of the crystal face. All that remains are small fragments. There is nothing to salvage."

Kandi began ranting, "Damn! This sort of thing is supposed to be impossible. I guess I knew that a crystal could overload and explode in theory. Back home, they had begun adding supplemental shielding on the gates as a precaution against such an accidental overload. An occurrence like this shouldn't have happened."

Protocol stated that Kandi should wait to hear from the Institute, but she felt the explosion warranted communication. "Sara, contact Control over the tachyon thread and advise them of our situation."

The shortest pause followed, yet a second was long enough for Sara to try the connection a hundred times. Sara responded. "Kandi, the tachyon stream is broken."

"What do you mean, broken?"

"Gone."

"Completely?"

"Yes. Disconnected from the Aedenian end."

Bad just became worse. The tachyon stream was Kandi and Sara's only tie to home. *Without that stream, no one can find us. We're lost, adrift in space-time.* She wondered. *What could have happened?* She also feared for her friends and companions back home. It was evident to her that someone had attacked the Institute, severing its connections to Gaia. She knew in her heart that this was no accident. This was deliberate sabotage.

Sara interrupted, "Kandi, I hate to disturb you, but I have followed up on an energy anomaly during the personnel transfer. If it is what I think it is, there may be a way for us to reconnect to the Institute."

Kandi was not hopeful in her reply, "Without a tachyon link, how would that even work? We know where we are but have no idea when we are in relation to home. Unless physics changed, a gate is adrift without the link."

Sara's voice was unstrained, "That isn't altogether true. Origen planned for something like this when he designed the rings. An archangel can initiate a connection. Time would still be variable, but I believe a ring could get us home reasonably close to when you left based on the last telemetry data received."

Kandi shook her head, thinking the explosion had damaged the AI, "Sara. At the beginning of the project, you and I scanned for any gate remnants, including archangel signatures. We came up with a few potential locations for crystal but nothing on the archangels and their rings. They are long gone. Whatever happened to them happened ages ago.

Sara continued, "At the time, I also believed that to be the case, but analysis of the anomaly indicates that it originated from an archangel's ring."

Kandi was incredulous, "Sara, the Institute's best guess was that at least two millennia have passed since the gates vanished here. No one, not even an archangel, could've survived for that long."

Sara countered, "I agree, but a person didn't send the signal. In this case, it appeared to be a distress call from an archangel's keystone, not the archangel himself."

Kandi stopped and caught her breath. *Was it possible? A keystone? Here? Now?*

"Did you get a reading on the keystone's location?" Kandi tried to remain calm. Sara had just thrown them a tenuous lifeline; she didn't want to lose it, no matter how great the odds against them were.

Sara continued, "Yes, the signal originated from the western quadrant of this continent near a town identified by Gaian GPS as Boulder, Colorado."

"I don't suppose we have any transit hubs in the area?"

"Negative. There's a large concentration of Gaian military in the area. We did our best to stay far from those bases. Besides, we could get everything we needed in our other host cities. The inventory shows we still have a few operational single-use portable field generators in stores. They should suffice for the trip."

Kandi had little hope that the signal was authentic, but with no other options available, she began preparing for the trip, "What are the transit parameters?"

"Destination time is ten pm." The team had long since decided to use local time rather than Aedenian standard. "The Gaian data feeds indicate that the area should be dark, dry, and calm. Be aware that GPS mapping indicates several homes in the immediate area."

Kandi acknowledged Sara's report. She changed into a black body suit to better blend into the night before going to the supply room and retrieving two transit projectors. Programming the first generator with Sara's coordinates only took a minute, and programming the second for the return took even less. She put the return unit on her shoulder and activated the first one, "I'll be back soon," she announced as she disappeared from view.

Transit using the portable generators was discomforting at best. Nausea and disorientation usually accompanied the trip, but the worst part was not knowing what would be at the destination when you arrived. Since there had been no time to do proper reconnaissance, Kandi could appear in a crowd, in the middle of a highway, or find herself submerged in a lake. She was at the mercy of Gaian technology, and she didn't like it one bit.

As the gate opened into the Colorado night, Kandi breathed a sigh of relief. No lake. No people. The area was dark...and appeared deserted. Looking up at the house in front of her, she quickly verified the address with the one Sara had given her: 276 Sunshine Trail.

A brief exterior scan of the home indicated no one was at home even though all the lights were on. She deftly picked the lock and let herself inside. She was not prepared for what she found. The main room looked like a bomb had exploded. Paper and household items were strewn all over the place. Someone had tossed a trophy onto the floor, shattering the frame into a thousand pieces, then, apparently, sifted through the remains. A medallion sat amid the debris.

The burglars also destroyed the furniture and picked it apart as if they believed something valuable might be embedded inside the frames. Whoever they were, they had done a thorough job. Although she had no idea what they were looking for, the presence of a keystone here only a day before seemed too coincidental. As quickly as the idea formed in her mind, she squelched it. Why would anyone else be after the crystal? After all, Gaia did not have crystal technology, let alone the capacity to know the uniqueness of the keystone – or how to use it. She wasn't sure herself how to get the stone to do her bidding.

Kandi took her time probing through the rest of the house, finding all the rooms in the same condition as the foyer and living areas. From her experience, unless the burglars had found their treasure in the last place they looked, they had come up empty. Finally, after exhausting the upper floors, she went into the basement, where she froze at the bottom of the stairs. There against the wall was a crude yet effective, incendiary device with a timer counting down from ten.

With no time to lose, she yanked the portable field generator from her back, thankful that she had programmed the return coordinates in advance. The countdown had reached two before she activated the transport and dissolved from sight as the bomb exploded.

Kandi's body flew through the opening to the Vermont house, followed by pieces of debris from the explosion. Sara was alarmed, "What happened out there?" Kandi, out of breath and visibly stunned, stumbled over to the overstuffed sofa in the living room of their safe house and sat down.

"Somebody wanted to guarantee that no one else took a look at that house," was Kandi's breathless reply. "They set an explosive near the gas intake in the basement. I barely escaped." She looked directly at one of Sara's video sensors, "I didn't find anything significant, no sign of the keystone anywhere. More importantly, the thieves sought something specific, considering how they trashed the place.

"Something like the ring?" Sara's voice sounded confused.

Kandi nodded, "I can't imagine how they would even know about the ring, but that would make sense. Besides, I hate coincidences. The ring was there, but now it's not, and the building is destroyed."

Sara asked the obvious question, "What do we do now?"

Kandi replied, "These developments support your feelings that the signal was real and that the owner must have a way of shielding the stone from detection. How long did the broadcast last?"

Sara was precise, "The crystal signature appeared for exactly two minutes and twenty-one seconds before the signal terminated abruptly."

Kandi pondered the problem, "The ring is broadcasting a distress call. The only thing that makes sense is that the possessor of the ring doesn't realize what they have and that they are keeping it in a container that blocks the signal. With those assumptions in mind, there is no reason for them not to expose the ring again. Our only choice is to wait and hope."

Chapter 6 – A Waiting Game

There was only so much relaxing a pixie could do, and Kandi was going stir-crazy between the waiting and the continued silence from the Institute. Kandi was a warrior, one of the best her world had produced, accustomed to using strength and agility to defeat physical foes, not sitting on her hands waiting for a call that might never come. Working out in the retreat's small gym helped somewhat, but she needed to get out and do something. She and Sara, the AI, had two boring weeks in the Vermont compound before their vigilance paid off. The alert came just as she was preparing her evening meal.

"Kandi? We have a signal." Sara announced.

Kandi held her breath, "Do you have a location?"

"Affirmative. The signal is strong. The stone is now on the eastern shore of this continent in the city called New York."

Kandi considered the name for a moment, "New York? Didn't we have a trade team there? I seem to remember several business dealings taking place. If I recall correctly, it's a major trade center for this area.

Sara responded, "Yes. One of our teams spent extensive time in the city arranging for various materials for the project."

Kandi became hopeful, "Sara, please tell me that we still have an active transfer terminus there."

"Checking...Yes, Kandi. We do. Actually, there is one not far from the signal location. It is in a semi-remote, forested area, part of something the locals call Central Park."

Kandi drilled further, "What is the proximity of the stone to the portal's location?"

"Triangulation puts the stone at nine-tenths of one of their miles away from the portal - a relatively easy walk. The terrain is flat and mostly paved with artificial stone. However, there could be a complication."

"That is?" Kandi had begun her preparations to go and wished her friend would hurry up and say what she needed to say.

"There is a risk that falls outside our normal operating parameters for such a mission. New York is one of the most populated areas on Gaia. We coordinated our earlier excursions there during periods of minimal cross-contamination with the Gaian populace. This time, however, you'll be traveling during the early evening while there is still ample daylight and significant foot traffic in the area. Sensors indicate that your route will expose you to potentially thousands of humans. You will need to go in a suitable disguise."

Kandi stopped her prep. "Recommendations?"

The AI quickly returned her suggestion, "Do you recall your trip to Chicago?" Kandi nodded, and

Sara continued. "I believe the ethnic clothing you wore there would be sufficient to mask your ears and give you freedom of movement."

Kandi remembered, "Ah yes, the hijab coupled with a flowing robe. As I recall, it did cover the ears nicely." With that, Kandi ran off into the back rooms of the house before returning momentarily wearing the headpiece and a long, flowing gown that neatly covered her body armor. She probably wouldn't need it, but her experience with the Colorado house had made her cautious.

Sara approved of Kandi's transformation. "I queried information about this faith group in the New York area. Data retrieved indicates that the city is known for its wide range of cultural groups, including people of this sect. Indications are that the general population should accept you without question. The Central Park node is activated and ready for transit."

Kandi acknowledged this by walking toward the portal face, thinking how fortunate they hadn't tied the planetary transmitters to the main crystal during construction. At the time, it was a matter of expedience, but had they done so, the primary portal explosion would have destroyed the planetary units also. Sara finished system activation, and Kandi exited the room into a beautiful New York fall evening. As she walked around the tree, headed for the park entrance, she nearly tripped over a young couple snuggled up in a blanket at the tree's foot. She heard the girl murmur, "Did you hear something?" The boy gave a typical male clueless reply of "No" before the two became utterly oblivious to external events once again. Kandi took a moment to get her bearings, noting the sun already setting behind the buildings to the west, before setting out toward where her quarry waited.

The Ring

Heroes are not bred or magically brought forth by unknown gods. They are usually ordinary people called to be extraordinary by events. If they survive their quest, they are heroes; otherwise, they are lost amid the trash heaps of history.

There had once been such a hero, a man, a protector, a leader of his people. He was set apart from other men. Rumors abounded about his misshapen ears and ability to fly like a bird. Outside his tribe, people discounted these rumors. There was no doubt he was a formidable adversary. After all, he and his people had defeated all comers for as long as anyone could remember. Inside his tribe, he was known as a good man, which was enough. He was married to one of their own and had several strong sons and daughters. He was one of them. It didn't matter that he wasn't human.

On his hand, this man wore a ring of power. Many times, he commanded it to save his people. During one such battle, the man was mortally wounded. He returned home with only enough strength to talk to his first-born son before he died.

The man told his son that his ring would loosen when he died. At that time, the boy was to take the jewel and put it into a lead box that the man had designed. He admonished the boy to keep the stone in the container – rarely to take it out and never to put it on his finger lest the world's evils devour him. The ring could sense the merit of the bearer, and only those seen as worthy could wear it. All others would die. The man instructed his son to leave the ring to his firstborn, who would then leave it to his firstborn. The pattern was to repeat until the ring's power was again needed and one of their descendants was worthy of the task. The boy swore to make it so. His mission safely completed; the man allowed himself to die.

Thus, it came to pass that years turned to centuries and, in turn, to millennia. The ring continued from one firstborn to the next. Occasionally, a chosen one would ignore the warning, open the box, and put on the ring; sure he was the one meant to command it. Although their lineage was true, the stone deemed them unworthy. They died within a month. That lesson would remind several future generations until one disobeyed again.

Chapter 7 - Showtime

The constant ringing at long last snagged Jonathan's exhausted body from the grasp of sleep. Wanting to stay in his warm, safe cocoon, he groaned, rolled over on his side, murmured a few choice words, and slammed his fist on the hotel's bedside phone, hoping to savor a few extra moments. Unfortunately, all he managed to accomplish was to shatter the phone's handset and possibly his palm in the process.

"Shit! Shit! Shit!" The pain coursing upward through his arm was intense.

A tinny voice came from the fragments on the tabletop, "Mr. Martyr? Mr. Martyr? Are you there? This is Joan with the gallery. It's six o'clock, and we were wondering where you were. Is everything alright?"

The realization came from the deep recesses of his mind that waking up was somehow…important. The reality followed shortly after that. "God, six already? Wait. No, that can't be right. I set my alarm for five o'clock! It can't be six!" he shouted at the plastic fragments littering the tabletop as his phone alarm began to sound in the background, announcing that he had not set the timer for five. The pieces of the handset didn't care. The microphone was in pieces; the girl from the gallery heard nothing, "Mr. Martyr?

Is everything alright?" Jon was already on the move, "Hell no! Nothing is alright!"

"Shit! Shit! Shit!"

"Why did this have to happen today?" he shouted at no one, "Today, of all days! I can't be late!"

Jonathan launched himself out of bed, snagging his foot on the bedspread, and fell flat on his face. His nose began to bleed.

"Shit! Shit! Shit"

Since early morning, Jonathan and the gallery staff had been working to ensure everything was perfect for tonight's opening. He'd only intended to return for a shower and a short nap but had been so exhausted that he'd opted for the rest first. *In retrospect*, he thought, as he caught a whiff of himself, *the bath would've been the better idea.*

His extensive vocabulary followed him as he extricated himself from the bedspread and stumbled toward the bathroom, attempting to staunch the blood with his left hand while his right hand was still pulsing with pain.

One glance at the grimy façade in the mirror told him he looked like crap, but at least his bleeding nose had subsided. His five-o'clock shadow would have to stay there; no time to shave. He snatched the damp washcloth from his morning shower, wet it, and scoured his face roughly, removing most of the dirt and blood. He saved two whole minutes by not brushing his teeth, instead relying on a hefty swallow of generic hotel mouthwash to do the job.

Jon's hair was a complete disaster. He slapped handfuls of water on his scalp, praying the liquid would hold his hair down long enough to be combed into a socially acceptable form when he got to the gallery.

Jon applied an extra-heavy dose of deodorant and cologne as he looked longingly at the shower. Cautiously, he took another whiff of himself and shrugged his shoulders in resignation. It would have to do. He threw on his dress shirt, realizing after he finished that the buttons didn't line up with the buttonholes. He decided he could fix them later. Then, he grabbed his suit from the closet, threw his coat on a chair, and attacked the pants, only getting two legs caught in the same pant leg twice in the process.

Still attempting to pull up his pants, he grabbed his jacket. A loud thunk stopped him as the ring box fell out of his jacket pocket and onto the floor. The box had been there since that night at the house...what was it, two weeks ago? He hadn't worn this suit since Denver, and truthfully, he had forgotten about the thing; there had been so many other things to focus on.

Without hesitation, he opened the box and placed the ring on his finger. "Sorry, Dad, I know you said that I shouldn't wear this thing, but you also said it was your good luck charm, and tonight, I believe I'll need all the help I can get." He took a moment to admire the ring. "and this baby has the bling." He would worry about his father's superstitious warnings another day.

He carried his shoes as he raced for the elevator, entertaining other riders as he jumped on one foot while putting the other shoe on. Somewhere in his subconscious, Jon registered surprise at how perfectly the ring had fit and how warm the metal felt on his hand, but, for now, there were far more pressing issues to address. Catching a quick glimpse of himself in the mirrored surface of the elevator car, he told himself, *The five-o-clock shadow gives off a kind of hipster vibe, right?* Somehow, he had his doubts.

As Jonathan exited on the first floor, he gave himself a mental slap. Despite appearances to the contrary, he was still one of the country's finest artistic jewelers. After attempting to break into the New York market for over three years, tonight, he would display his designs in a one-person show at the famed Blackstone Gallery near Central Park. Jonathan checked his watch – starting ten minutes ago. A pre-showing for favored guests accompanied by canapes and champagne began at 6:30. Mr. Blackstone, the gallery owner, had explicitly told him to be there no later than six to greet the early arrivals. *Way to make first impressions, Jon.*

Jonathan yanked his phone out of his pocket to call the gallery, only to get the device caught in his pocket lining. The phone slipped through his cold, damp hands and bounced across the sidewalk into a storm drain. Could things get any worse? Jonathan's mood and aspirations for the evening continued to sink. A quick scan of traffic on Columbia Avenue showed an endless stream of taillights sitting stationary. A taxi would be out of the question. Jon would have to run. Maybe he could still make the gallery before the official opening. After all, the venue was only six blocks away.

At 6:28, he stumbled and wheezed his disheveled form into the gallery. Special guests, already present, were swigging champagne and enjoying idle chatter. They froze to stare at the ragged stranger wandering in from outside. Jon had hoped to pass into the room unnoticed. That wasn't happening. The patrons had their eyes firmly focused on him, wondering what this homeless person was doing in this part of town. The owner, Mr. Blackstone, stood horrified. He couldn't believe his eyes as he scanned Jonathan from head to toe, his disapproving gaze speaking volumes.

Mumbling apologies and excuses as he passed, Jonathan quickly dashed to the Men's Room to do damage control and hopefully salvage some of his self-respect in the minute that remained. The owner's eyes followed him every step of the way. Jon could feel his eyes boring into the back of his head. The man shook his head, "Another prima donna," he muttered as he returned to continue chatting up his clientele.

United States Space Command
Cheyenne Mountain, Colorado

Formerly a NorthCom command center, the defense group released this part of the facility to the United States Space Force shortly after the newcomer's creation in 2019. NorthCom had enough room elsewhere in the mountain's immense artificial caverns to complete its mission. They could afford to be magnanimous. Buried deep within Cheyenne Mountain's frame, no windows indicated the passage of time outside the facility. That the room wasn't particularly large or impressive was beside the point. The sheer electronic muscle packed into it was enough to make up for its physical size. On one wall, an enormous monitor dominated the space, but the fifteen technicians, faces illuminated by their computer displays, were the ones who made the Space Force command center come alive.

"Colonel Forrester, we have another hit." Lieutenant Christine Fellows could barely control her excitement. She and the others had searched for another contact with the anomaly since the first blip two weeks ago. She had no idea what the contact meant, but she knew it was of vital importance. She couldn't believe her luck.

Forrester gave her his undivided attention as he approached her station, "Do we have a location, Lieutenant?"

Lt. Fellows struggled to calm herself and stay professional, "Narrowing it down now, sir. The contact is in New York City. Triangulation puts the subject on the island of Manhattan just off Central Park West. It is in motion...wait it's stopped. I'll have the address momentarily."

The colonel reached for his phone and called his superior, leaving it on speaker so the lieutenant could hear, "Sir, the item has been reactivated; currently at a stationary location within New York City."

The voice on the other end betrayed no emotion, "Excellent, Colonel. What resources do we have available?"

Christine was typing furiously on the command station keyboard to get the required answers. The colonel read them aloud as the results were listed, "We have a small detachment assigned to the NSA in Manhattan."

The voice didn't hesitate, "Let's get them on their way. How long?"

The Colonel looked back at the Lieutenant's display, which showed a real-time traffic map of Manhattan. The answer wasn't good. "At this time of day, transport will take at least an hour to arrive."

This time, the voice had an edge of displeasure, "That's too long. What about a helicopter?"

The colonel made a mental note to commend the young lieutenant. She had the information almost immediately. Forrester replied, "Even longer, sir. Anymore, air traffic in New York City is almost as bad as car traffic during rush hour. The only way we can get there quicker would be to declare a state of emergency and clear the skies."

The response from his superior was as he expected, "Damn. No, we don't want any unnecessary attention drawn to us right now. Any more word on the Martyr estate?"

The colonel silently instructed the lieutenant to send out the NSA team. He turned back toward the room's rear wall before responding, "Yes, sir. I just received the report a short time ago. Everything went to his son, a Jonathan Martyr."

There was a reflective silence on the line before the commander's reply, "Whereabouts?"

Forrester continued, "He has an office in Boston and an apartment in Braintree, Massachusetts, about twenty klicks south of the city. I sent a team from Hanscom to check them out. I was waiting on their report before contacting you."

The voice reflected a more positive mood, much to Colonel Forrester's relief, "Excellent, Colonel. Let's get that Manhattan team on its way and keep me posted on developments."

"Yes, sir." The colonel looked at Lieutenant Fellows, who nodded that she had sent the orders and received the team's confirmation. Forrester smiled. Now, all they had to do was wait.

Chapter 8 – Ships that Cross…

What a difference a few minutes could make.

Jonathan's calm facade contrasted greatly with the catastrophe he had been an hour before. His few minutes in the gallery restroom had transformed him into something like a neo-beatnik, artsy, quasi-counterculture look, which, according to overheard conversations among the clientele, indicated that they found him exotic and…quirky. At first, those comments bothered him, but then he found out that some of the clients seemed to like quirky. Who would've guessed? Now, he stood quietly gazing out the gallery window, engrossed by the mass of humanity passing before him.

Jon's fascination with the inhabitants of New York went back to his childhood here. His family had lived on Manhattan Avenue in a large two-story structure only a few blocks from where he stood today. Typically, a house like that would have been far out of the reach of a lowly professor, but his father's fame was such a feather in the university's cap that they allowed him to use a house that a well-to-do alumnus had bequeathed to them. This gift afforded his father a short walk to Columbia and made Central Park Jonathan's playground.

Over the past hour, Jon had completed the mandatory circuit of clients with Mr. Blackstone, smiling and shaking hands as the owner introduced him to people who made more in a day than he did in a year. There wasn't anything Jonathan despised more than rubbing elbows with the rich and pompous. They seemed so fake, so oblivious to the rest of the world. For that reason, he often avoided his Boston openings, usually faking illness, but, as the owner reminded him, people paying exorbitant amounts of money for objects d'art expected the artist to be there – and to be pleasant. The gallery's contract contained specific language guaranteeing his presence and demeanor for the opening, so he came, albeit a little late and ragged for the owner's liking.

As he made his rounds, there had been many oohs and aahs about his ring – including several generous offers for its purchase, which he politely declined. As he walked away from one would-be buyer, he overheard him comment that it was just like an artist to keep the best piece for himself. Jonathan just smiled. True to Dad's word, the ring had been a good luck charm, at least so far.

With his duty done, Jon allowed his mind to drift amid the swirling crowd outside on the street until his focus solidified on a single person, a young lady, standing in the middle of the sidewalk just outside the gallery door. Although she was dressed demurely in a hijab and long flowing dress, Jon knew immediately that she was stunning. The tan hijab draped tastefully over a bright pink gown presented the viewer with an ideal combination of aloofness and style. He assessed her as he would a fine jewel in his studio and found her flawless, petite, yet perfectly proportioned.

Her visible face indicated an age not much different from his own. However, something about her eyes betrayed her otherwise demure appearance. They were piercingly blue and suggested that there was something more to the woman than grace and beauty.

Ironically, her appearance wasn't what first grabbed his attention. It was that she stood still and allowed the rest of the world to spin like a dervish madly around her. As the masses of New Yorkers forged toward her, they parted, flowing around her, giving her a wide berth. It was almost as if they were afraid of accidentally bumping into her. She was an island in the middle of a frothing human sea.

Neat trick. Jon thought. *I wonder how she does it? If she comes to the show, I'll have to ask her.* Jon silently wished that she would and then laughed at the idea. What would I do if she did? Jon had a problem. He was insufferably shy around young women. He found speaking to the opposite sex tortuous at best, quickly becoming tongue-tied, especially if they were attractive. He would be positively catatonic if he came face-to-face with this beauty.

There had been a few relationships for Jon over the years, all ending badly. In every case, the woman was the one who initiated the romance and the one who ended it. Initially, they found themselves intrigued by his shyness, sure that it was temporary, perhaps thinking it was a clever ruse to lure them to him. Only later would they discover, to their dismay, that he was not pretending. He was who he was.

Verbal communication was useless. These relationships never lasted very long.

Talking to older women presented few problems, and neither did children, but a woman his age would leave him crawling for a corner in distress. Just thinking about the woman outside coming to his show raised Jon's anxiety to uncomfortable levels; sweat beaded on his forehead. *Perhaps*, he reconsidered, *she should stay on the street.*

A tap from Mr. Blackstone drew Jon from his reverie, temporarily relieving him from his conflicting emotions, "Mr. Martyr, I need you to come with me."

At first, Jon was disoriented. He stared at the proprietor briefly before finally responding, "Yes, What is it?"

"I hate to disturb you, sir, but we have a patron interested in the Firebird."

Jonathan's attention snapped into focus. The Firebird was the centerpiece of his collection, his prized work. The piece had taken years to complete and carried a hefty list price of $1.2 million, enough to dissuade a casual buyer but not too high for a true collector. Jon never expected the piece to sell in his first show. The purchase would be quite a feather in his and the gallery's cap.

Mr. Blackstone continued, "The lady is insistent that she discusses the piece with you before committing. I explained your 'laryngitis,'" a nod to his shyness, "but she insists."

Jon followed the man's gaze toward the gorgeous young woman beaming back at them. Jon lifted his champagne glass in her direction. *Naturally, she's young, rich, AND beautiful. This conversation was going to be very one-sided.*

Jon gulped and attempted a smile. "Of course. Lead the way." Jon whispered as he nervously scratched at the back of his hand. Looking over his shoulder at the street, he saw that the mystery lady had disappeared. The sidewalk was once again a solid flood of bodies. Jonathan sighed in regret.

Although Jon had met the woman briefly earlier, Mr. Blackstone made the introductions. "Ms. Fontana? May I introduce Mr. Jonathan Martyr."

The brightness of her teeth almost blinded Jonathan as he stammered his response, "A pleasure, Ms. Fontana," he squeaked, hoping to be heard as he took her proffered hand.

The lady's voice dripped honey, "The pleasure is mine, Jon. May I call you Jon?"

"Certainly, Ms. Fontana. That would be fine," Jonathan stuttered, sweat beading on his forehead and trickling down his back.

"Wonderful, Jon. My friends call me Susan. I would love for us to be friends, wouldn't you?"

Another short nod, "Yes, Susan. I would." *God! Is she flirting?* "I think that would be wonderful." New beads of moisture formed on his brow and upper lip, prompting a quick wipe on his coat sleeve.

The young Ms. Fontana seemed amused at her effect on him. She took his arm and walked over to the Firebird. "Very well then, tell me about this magnificent piece...."

After several minutes of small talk, smiling, gesturing, and minimizing his nervous reactions, the Firebird found a new home with the young Ms.

Fontana. She hadn't even blinked at the cost. The gallery owner and Jon were both ecstatic. The sale was incredible luck! Not only had she bought the piece, but she had also agreed to leave the Firebird on display for the show's two-week duration – with the caveat that the gallery listed her name prominently as the new owner. She wanted others to look on in envy at her purchase – bragging rights of the rich and famous. Jon and the gallery owner had no problem with that. As she took her leave, she gave Jon a short kiss on the cheek and handed Jon a card with her phone number. He nearly passed out.

With Jon's nerves at fever pitch, he desperately needed to hide in a corner and decompress. He spun around in an attempt to return to his window sanctuary, only to run headlong into the young woman from the street. Her piercing eyes stared into his, burning a hole in his brain. The conversation with Ms. Fontana had left him mentally exhausted. He couldn't handle this one, too. He was pretty sure there was no chance of anything intelligible coming out of his mouth. The young woman, on the other hand, had no such problem.

She grabbed his right hand, massaging it with her own. A quizzical look came over her as she dropped it as quickly as she had picked it up. "I need you," she calmly stated.

Of all the words Jon expected to hear from those beautiful lips, these were not them. He thought the words he couldn't say. *You need me? What the hell does that mean?*

His silence and reddening face prompted her to repeat, "I need you," much louder than before. This time, her statement garnered some idle interest from nearby patrons. Some guests appeared annoyed, while others smiled knowingly, assuming a lover's intimate conversation. Still, Jon remained frozen, unsure of what to say or do. She repeated herself one final time, nearly shouting, "I NEED YOU, NOW!" Every eye in the gallery was on them. A silence draped over the crowd in anticipation of what would happen next.

She grabbed his wrist like an iron vise and, with incredible speed and strength, began towing him toward the front door despite his feeble attempts to drag his feet in protest. By now, the commotion had the attention of everyone in the room, including the two off-duty police officers working security for the event. Running from opposite sides of the gallery, the guards intercepted Jon and the girl as they reached the main door.

What happened next was a matter of conjecture. Everyone in the room SAW what happened, but no one would have believed them if it hadn't been for the gallery's CCTV footage. One moment, the guards had the woman trapped between them, firmly in their grasp and attempting to extricate Jon from her. The next moment, the two men found themselves in a heap, mangled and barely conscious on the floor. The girl had moved with inhuman speed as she disarmed and disabled the two men – with one hand. She never let go of Jon.

The shock effect froze the gallery guests in their small groups and then quickly thawed. Nothing rattles wealthy patrons as much as proximity to violence. As one, the gallery occupants began moving toward the exit, acting as if nothing had happened. There was no pushing or shoving – that would be undignified, but no one wanted to be around when the police arrived. A police interview would, after all, hurt their plans for later. They evaporated from the room like smoke, merging seamlessly into the crowds outside. As to Jon and the girl? They vanished as well.

Chapter 9 – A Walk in the Park

Running with a beautiful woman through the streets of New York had once been a secret dream of Jon's, a scene from a romantic movie from his college days. But now, as he struggled to keep up with her breakneck speed, Jonathan felt more like he was in a waking nightmare than any fantasy. He swore his feet never touched the ground as he and the girl flew down the crowded thoroughfare. Pedestrians scattered as they frantically chose to get out of the way or be knocked down. Most chose to move. The others littered the sidewalk in Jon's wake. There was a lot of cursing going on, even by New York City standards.

What in God's name is going on? he thought. Verbalization was still beyond his grasp. *One minute, I'm standing in front of a beautiful woman who's telling me she needs me, and the next thing I know, there are bodies on the floor, and the same madwoman is towing me at warp speed away from the gallery.*

That woman hadn't said another word since grabbing him and showed no signs of slowing as she veered to the left, stepped off the curb, and jaywalked into the frenzy of the rush hour traffic flashing by in both directions. Jon cringed. New Yorkers barely tolerated people crossing in a crosswalk and were pretty unified in their disdain for those attempting the crossing in the middle of the street. Some of the more daring, or just ticked off, drivers might consider such lawbreakers fair targets.

Jon was confident he would die right there in the middle of Central Park West Boulevard, joined at the wrist with a crazy person. He closed his eyes and braced for a collision while imagining how they would write up his death in the newspaper, "Jeweler caught in lover's tiff." *Yeah. That would be how they'd spin it. It wouldn't matter that he had been forcibly removed.* He wondered if anyone would come to his funeral as he peeked between the fingers of his free hand. He couldn't help but be impressed as he watched the woman seamlessly navigate the traffic stream. The woman constantly adjusted speed and direction, allowing them to weave their way between cars unscathed. Her reaction time was incredible, especially with him in tow. That's not to say that they went unnoticed. Jon witnessed much honking, shouting, and middle-finger waving as they passed through traffic. The sound of screeching brakes enhanced the experience.

The woman didn't care about the chaos she was causing. She was a woman on a mission, and Jon began to wonder what she 'needed' from him. He tested her grip by again dragging his feet to slow himself down. Incredibly, she responded with an even tighter, more painful grip on his wrist as if to say, keep up, or I'll hurt you worse. Since his hand felt like it would fall off any minute, he did his best to keep up.

They were now on the 79th Street Transverse, moving into Central Park. With the fall weather so accommodating, people packed the park. Visitors scattered on either side as they flew through them; some had their phones out, capturing the moment to show family and friends later. Belvedere Castle, a favorite play area during his boyhood, loomed before him and passed just as quickly to his rear. He could swear he heard a Doppler shift as they flew past the gate.

Shortly afterward, the woman took an abrupt right turn at the weather observation station and ran headlong into The Ramble, an old section of trees. There, directly in her path, stood a giant oak tree. She paid no mind to its presence. In fact, the girl never slowed as she raced straight toward an inevitable collision with the tree. Jon knew that this was no contest - the oak would win. He squeezed his eyes shut, praying that not seeing would shield him from the pain.

Jon wasn't sure what happened next. One moment, the girl was hauling him headlong into a tree; the next, she wasn't. Instead of a concussion, Jon slid on his stomach, not across the leaf-strewn landscape he had left in the park, but rather across a hard, level surface that reminded him of – carpet? The air around him had changed also. He noted a clean crispness now that was missing from the urban odors in Central Park. His eyes popped open as his momentum stopped.

His mind couldn't fathom what he saw. He was lying on his stomach on the carpeted floor of a brightly lit room. At first, he was sure he was dreaming. None of this made any sense. Then he noticed the pain from the rug burns on his hands and his sweat-drenched clothing sticking to his body. Returning circulation caused his wrist to sting, bruise marks forming in the shape of a handprint. No, this situation, however inexplicable, was decidedly real. However improbable, instead of the forested area of a few moments ago, he now appeared to be in a living room – a living room furnished in Early American with autumn trees and fluffy clouds visible outside the large picture window.

There was a noise behind him. With some effort, Jon managed to roll over and see his kidnapper a short distance away, apparently speaking to the air in a language that simultaneously seemed familiar and strange. A glowing spot hovered in the air behind them and then disappeared from sight. He listened closer to what the woman was saying. His father had dragged him worldwide on expeditions, and, as a result, Jonathan had smatterings of several languages in his toolbox. Despite its familiarity, the source of this one evaded him.

Unaware or uncaring of his stare, the woman began to unwrap her blue silk hijab from around her head, revealing an unusual set of ears, elongated and thin with sharp points at the tips. Jon gasped at the sight, getting a sudden glare of hatred from the woman. As she returned to her conversation, she casually undid her gown at the neck and let the garment slide down to the floor in a heap. At this point, Jon stopped breathing altogether.

The ears were a big deal – he had never seen anything like them, but they paled compared to the naked form before him. He took some pride in realizing that his original assessment of the woman was correct – she was stunning. If Jon had been incapable of speech before, he certainly was now.

His inability to talk, however, didn't deny him the ability to look. Jon couldn't take his eyes off her, letting his vision take in every part of her body. Much to his dismay, he quickly realized that she wasn't naked, although she might as well have been. She seemed to have a semi-transparent bodysuit covering the length of her body from her neck to her calves. He allowed his eyes to continue moving over her body until she turned, and he found himself looking at the middle of her back, where he stopped looking.

There on her back was undoubtedly a pair of wings. Jon shook his head in disbelief, but they were still there. They weren't fake, either. They slightly twitched even as he looked. Jon was confident that he had gone insane. He thought, *What the hell! Did someone at the gallery slip something into my drink? This situation has 'bad trip' written all over it.*

He gave his forearm a hard pinch, which generated enough pain to make him gasp aloud. His mind raged, *OK, not a dream. Could still be drug-induced, though, right?* The young female – and she was definitely female – reacted to his sound and moved toward him menacingly. Jon sat petrified with fear, thinking she resembled the stereotypical angel of death as she approached. Unfortunately, instead of sitting quietly on the carpet, Jon chose this moment to regain his speech. He quietly stuttered the first words his confused mind could come up with, "A-a-a-re you a f-f-f-airy?"

Jon didn't understand what happened next. After all, he hadn't meant any offense. He was simply trying to make sense of an impossible situation. He had believed his question to be polite. He thought, *I mean, what else do you say to a nearly naked woman with pointed ears and wings?* However, despite his intentions, the woman's response was not polite; she reacted violently.

The fury in the young woman's eyes was almost feral– more animalistic than human. In the blink of an eye, Jon was no longer semi-sitting on the floor. Instead, he found himself lifted and then pinned to the wall by his throat, unable to breathe.

"Fairy?" she whispered with focused intensity. "Do I look like a fairy?"

Fortunately for Jon, the girl's grip constricted his airway, and he could not respond. Otherwise, he might have aggravated the situation. Frantically, he went over his comment in his mind: What did I say? I asked a simple question, and now she's strangling me! His eyes began to fog over as oxygen to his brain diminished. In his semi-conscious state, he imagined another woman's voice speaking in the same foreign tongue he had heard earlier.

"Kandi! Stop! You're killing him!" Sara shouted.

Whatever the voice said to the demon lady, the effect was immediate. The image of molten lava drained from her eyes, and she released her grip on Jon's throat, allowing him to fall to the floor in a heap, gasping for air. The release, however, was the limit of her compassion. She never looked at his bulging eyes or listened to his ragged breaths as she turned and strode purposefully out of the room.

Jon lay on the floor, afraid to move. His mind was jumbled and confused. *What did I do to deserve that!* he wondered. *I had been just standing there, minding my business at the gallery, when this girl came in from the street and grabbed me. Says she NEEDS me, for crying out loud. Does she think I'm wealthy because I make jewelry? My commission on the Firebird aside, I am not a rich man. Well, if she's looking for ransom, she is in for a rude awakening. Then this! She assaults....*

The second voice interrupted his commiseration, "Human, are you okay?" she inquired, this time in near-perfect English.

No, he wasn't. Jonathan was pretty ticked off and found himself spoiling for a fight. After being kidnapped, dragged through the city, and now almost strangled, he responded with as much sarcasm as he could muster, which came out as a strangled whisper, "Really? I almost died a minute ago, and you're asking if I'm okay?" He continued his rant as he struggled to his feet. "No, I'm damn well not okay! Stop pretending that you care one way or the other!" Jon's raspy voice struggled to get the words out.

The female voice continued in a soft, comforting alto, "I'm afraid I must apologize for Watcher Mehra. She gets 'excited' sometimes. Normally, I wouldn't have dared to interrupt her, but I was monitoring your vital signs. They were diminishing at an alarming rate, and I feared that, in her anger, she might not notice. She has damaged her sparring partners from time to time, and I was sure you would be permanently injured if I didn't intervene. Your death would have endangered the mission. "

"Damaged? She almost killed me! Is that your people's standard procedure when you kidnap someone? Try to kill them as well?" he said, trying and failing to salvage a part of his bruised ego with a showing of false bravado. At that point, Jon finally realized he was alone in the room, which prompted him to ask a more pertinent question, "Who are you, and why won't you show yourself?"

The voice seemed to come from all around him. "I am known as Saraswati. I am the Oracle for this outpost. In your world's terminology, I would be referred to as artificial intelligence, although I am far more advanced than the primitive attempts your world has created. Watcher Mehra calls me Sara. I would be pleased if you would as well. Since I have no physical form, I cannot show myself."

Great, a psycho and a computer. Fine. Dealing with a computer program that couldn't reach out and attack him sounded safer than dealing with the she-devil maniac. He decided that the best way to proceed was to play nice. The more he knew, the better. In a reasonably calm voice, he began. "OK...Sara, was it? Where am I? What am I to you? How did I get from Central Park to your living room? What is this 'mission' you referred to? Finally, what kind of creature kidnapped me, brought me here, and tried to kill me?"

Sara's voice continued in a calm, gentle way, "I'm sorry, Jonathan Martyr – may I call you Jon? "

Jon was immediately put on guard, "How do you know my name?"

Sara's voice never wavered, "I found your name in public records surrounding your father's death. Now, your questions are far from simple. A detailed answer would be far beyond your comprehension now, so I will attempt to simplify my response.

First, you are in a mountain cabin in your state of Vermont. This is our base camp. We became aware of you when we intercepted a distress signal from the ring you wear. You arrived via a teleportal using a temporary transmission site in Central Park, New York. That 'creature,' as you refer to her, has a name, Kandi Mehra. "

Jon laughed slightly at her name.

"Do you find something funny, Jon?" Sara almost seemed human in her response, putting Jon immediately on the defensive.

"No, just a chuckle over the irony of her name. I mean, Kandi indicates something sweet. She doesn't strike me that way at all."

Sara considered his statement for a second, "No, I can see where that would be confusing. In our language, Kandi would translate to 'crying.' The war orphaned her when she was very young. The trauma of watching her parents die erased all of her memories. She couldn't even remember the name her parents gave her, let alone anything about the attack. The head of her orphanage named her Kandi because she cried for most of the first year there. I strongly recommend not to laugh about her name in future conversations." Jon gulped at the implied threat.

"Regarding our mission, I think you should know that she did not kidnap you as a matter of choice. Her assignment was to recover the keystone embedded in the ring on your hand. Her attempts to remove the ring at the gallery failed. The metal seemed fused to you. Taking you was the only way to complete her mission and get the stone.

Finally, I assure you Watcher Mehra was not trying to kill you. She is a highly trained and decorated warrior. Had she wanted you dead, you would be dead. However, Kandi is very proud of her species and her warrior status. You called her a fairy – a grave insult to her kind. Kandi is a pixie, and, like all pixies, she is, shall we say, sensitive about fairy references."

"That's enough, Sara." While the two conversed, the woman, Kandi, had reentered the room via a hallway. Now, she was dressed in a flowing robe, making her seem less desirable and less dangerous at the same time. Despite her calmer outer appearance, Jon attempted to merge with the opposite wall as she approached. She took over the conversation.

"Human." She said the word with distaste like it was the worst curse imaginable. "I tolerate your presence only because I need that stone you wear," indicating the ring on Jon's hand with a passing wave. "If there was any other way to have the gem without you here, believe me when I say I would have followed that path."

Jon was becoming defensive and angry at her dismissive attitude toward him. He answered curtly, momentarily forgetting his shyness around women, "This was my father's ring. He left it for me when he died. What's the stone to you?"

Kandi continued, "I don't know what your father told you, but I assure you this isn't his ring. How the stone came into his possession isn't important, but that it exists at all is paramount. The ring was formed on a planet far from here and is vital for Sara and me to return there."

Jon's voice reeked sarcasm as he reached his left hand toward the ring, "Fine. This thing has brought me nothing but trouble. Take it!" Jon struggled to remove the ring as he spoke, but the object was stuck on his finger. No matter how he twisted and turned it, the metal refused to budge even a fraction of an inch.

Some perfect fit, he thought.

Kandi continued, "Convinced? I tried to remove it at the gallery this evening. I even considered removing your finger or hand but wasn't sure what the stone would do if I did. Archangel stones' are a closely guarded secret known only to the cadre of archangels alone. Some stories claim that the rings possess an intelligence of their own. Possibly, the metal has integrated into your person. I might well have destroyed it if I killed you. I am perplexed about this. The ring is supposed to attach to a single person's DNA, a non-human DNA. Its affinity to you isn't logical. At any rate, I only had one option – to take you along with the ring."

Jonathan could sense the frustration and disgust in her tone. He had little doubt but that the events of the evening had unfolded as she had described. Unconsciously, he rubbed his hand to reassure himself that his fingers were still attached. "Why is the ring so important?"

Sara answered, "That's the thing. It may not be. Rumors indicate an archangel ring can open a gate without a tachyon stream, something we currently lack. In simple terms, Kandi and I are adrift in spacetime. There is a chance your ring could allow us to go home again."

Jon replied, "And, without the ring, I'm…."

"Non-essential. As an entity, you do not matter at all." Kandi stated.

Chapter 10 – Later, at the Gallery…

The four black Cadillac Escalades screeched to a stop at the Blackstone Gallery just as the patrons began filing en masse onto the sidewalk. Something was amiss, and Agent in Charge Stephen Miller was bound to find out what. His orders were to find and detain one person on the premises, but indications were his orders might have changed in the interim. He would be lucky if his quarry was still here.

He ordered, "I want to know what happened here ASAP. Goins, Rodriguez? Take the back two cars and try to catch some of these people before they get lost in the crowd. I want statements!" Miller's group had heard the police call go out a few minutes ago, alerting all officers to a disturbance at this address, which happened to be the same address his boss had given him an hour ago. Miller wasn't sure what had gone wrong, but it must have been spectacular.

AIC Miller and four others searched for the suspect inside the building. Five people might have seemed overkill for a single suspect, but in his experience, being careful meant you got to go home that night. Initial inquiries with patrons indicated a single unarmed female attacker. Unfortunately, a thorough search showed neither the woman nor the man they were after were present. The only people remaining in the building were two semiconscious uniformed men groaning on the floor, the EMTs attending them, and the owner, Mr. Blackstone. Miller took the owner to one of the SUVs out front, guaranteeing that agents would secure his gallery in his absence.

Thirty minutes later, Miller's team compared notes. The answers were wildly unbelievable. None of them made sense, no matter how Miller looked at them. According to the owner and multiple witnesses, a single woman, a small woman at that, kidnapped the suspect and disabled the two guards – with one hand no less, before leaving the building while never letting go of the abductee who, at this point, Miller was certain was the initial target of his superiors. Miller began spewing out orders.

"Goins? Go with Mr. Blackstone and pull all the security tapes before the local police arrive. The rest of you secure the perimeter, front and back. A cockroach doesn't gain entry without my approval. Despite the conflicting evidence we've collected, this gallery is a crime scene, and I want it to be our crime scene. Understood?"

NYPD with their sirens blaring, appeared on the scene as the agents scrambled to begin their tasks. One of the perimeter agents briefed the newcomers, advising them, and later their lieutenant, that the interior was off-limits. This incident was a kidnapping and, thus, a federal case. AIC Miller smiled at the LEOs frustration. He'd been on the other side of this type of situation before. It never was pleasant, but the officers would get over it. He returned to the SUV alone to make his call.

"Forrester here." The man on the line had a no-nonsense tone to his voice.

"Colonel, this is AIC Miller in New York. We arrived at the gallery to a real mess. Witnesses indicate that a woman abducted a man who we believe to be your suspect minutes before we arrived. Local law enforcement just showed, and I suspect the media isn't far behind them."

Forrester was more intrigued that someone else was searching for Martyr than he was about the chaotic situation Miller was in, "Abducted, you say? Any clues as to who took him?"

The agent kept his narrative short and to the point, "Negative. The kidnapper disguised herself in a long gown and a hijab, making witness statements iffy at best. One thing they all agree on is that this lady is dangerous. We are currently pulling security tapes. I'll forward copies to you as soon as they are available."

Forrester wasn't ready to disconnect and continued to prod, "Was the kidnapper armed?"

"Negative, sir; the scene indicates she didn't have nor need a weapon. Every witness agreed on that issue - she was highly skilled in hand-to-hand combat. Sir, according to witnesses, she incapacitated two trained off-duty officers with one hand while dragging the suspect out of the building against his will."

Lieutenant Fellows signaled the Colonel to her workstation at the command center. The Colonel examined her screen and spoke to his agent, "Miller? The target is on the move in Central Park, traveling at a high rate of speed for someone on foot. I am sending coordinates and a projected trajectory ... Wait!" he redirected his comments to the lieutenant, "What the hell just happened?"

Miller heard indistinct voices in the background, followed by the colonel's angry tirade. The officer in New York was grateful he was not on the end of that rant. Finally, the colonel returned to the open line.

"Agent? I believed we had something there, but the suspect disappeared from our Central Park scans. We're going to reset our equipment and do another search. It should take about an hour. Follow up with your witnesses and get the CCTV video. Let me know if anything interesting comes out of it. I'll let you know when we have more."

"Affirmative, sir."

Goins approached to give Miller her report, "Sir, I've seen the video, and it's disturbing. The witnesses nailed it. A single, petite female approached the victim and exchanged words. According to witnesses, she claimed she needed him. When he didn't follow, she grabbed the victim by the arm and began to drag him outside. The two guards, off-duty officers with NYPD, moved to intercept. She quickly incapacitated both of them with one hand. Sir, she was so fast! I had to slow the video speed dramatically to see everything."

Miller looked at her incredulously, so she defended her statement, "Sir, I watched the tape three times at the slowest possible speed and determined that no other weapon was involved." She presented her boss with a data stick containing the file. Miller plugged it into his laptop as he reached for his phone.

"Colonel Forrester, we have confirmation that the assailant acted alone without any visible weaponry. I am transferring the video feed to you now."

Minutes later, the colonel watched the video and called Miller back, "Interesting and confusing. We widened the range for our scan and have just received confirmation that the signal has shifted to a farmhouse in upstate Vermont. We have a patrol at Hanscom AFB going to intercept. Continue your investigation at the gallery. Maybe something will come up."

The colonel's news shook Miller, "Vermont? How in the world could that happen?" Forrester's tone was flat, "That, agent, is the multimillion-dollar question."

Miller had barely disconnected before Forrester was on the phone with his superior.

"Commander, I just sent you the CCTV footage from the gallery along with our agent's assessment of what happened there." Forrester then explained the current situation.

"Excellent." The commander was already reviewing the tapes. "Have we sent a team to the Vermont location?"

"Yes, sir. But sir?"

"Yes, colonel."

"What is going on here?"

"Colonel, the technology we are building for the project is not unique to us. Others also are working in this area."

"So, you're suggesting the woman is a foreign agent with an operational portal?"

"So it would seem."

"That changes everything, doesn't it."

"No, colonel. That only makes things more interesting. Keep me posted."

The commander sat at his desk, freezing the video to look at the kidnapper. He recognized her immediately. "Well, well, well…" he said to himself, "Kandi Mehra. What are you doing here?"

Chapter 11 - Vermont

The pixie and Sara were deep in conversation as Jonathan sat cowering in the corner, talking to himself while trying to make some sense of his situation. Suddenly, an alarm became the focus of their attention. Sara explained, "Kandi, I set a bot to monitor the news feeds with an alarm if anything interesting popped up." Sara continued, "Jon's abduction generated a great deal of interest in him, as well as in the identity of his kidnapper." Sara's voice indicated more than a bit of tension. Almost immediately, an LED screen lit up over the bar.

Jon recognized the scene as the outside of the Blackstone Gallery. Police officers were huddled in clusters around the outside while people in dark suits guarded the door. The reporter continued her report. "Earlier this evening, this well-known Central Park West establishment was the scene of a bizarre kidnapping as an unknown woman forcibly removed Boston artisan Jonathan Martyr from the Blackstone Gallery, where he was staging a one-person show. Behind her audio appeared cell phone footage that someone had captured of Kandi entering the gallery, confronting, and grabbing Jon, and then moving toward the exit with Jon in tow. The quality of the video was excellent. It was apparent that her striking appearance had appealed to someone else besides Jon.

The video slowed as Kandi disabled the two security guards, then froze, and zoomed in on her face. The reporter added, "The FBI appeared within moments of this daring evening abduction." The unknown cameraman shifted focus to four black Escalades that pulled up in front of the gallery, each expelling a flurry of black suits within seconds.

The reporter shifted focus to a copy of Jon's gallery photo and the still of Kandi, "We are asking the public to stay alert as the police continue their investigation. If anyone sees either of these two individuals, call 911 immediately. Do not attempt to approach them. The woman, in particular, should be considered extremely dangerous."

Just as the reporter was going to send the report back to the station anchor, she noticed activity surrounding one of the Escalades. "Wait... I think there's going to be an announcement." There was a moment of rustling static as the reporter hustled over to where a young woman had just begun her briefing. "We wanted to get this information to the public as soon as possible," the agent stated, "Citizens have reported seeing the two suspects entering Central Park on the 79th Street Transverse near Belvedere Castle. We have dispatched NYPD officers to block all park entrances and search the area while removing civilians from the scene. We want to reiterate what we said earlier. Under no circumstances should you approach these people. The woman in question seriously wounded two off-duty police officers. Don't let her size and appearance fool you. She is extremely dangerous and should be treated as such." The video returned to the dual portraits before the studio anchor took over the broadcast.

Kandi seemed unnaturally pleased by the 'extremely dangerous' comment, which concerned Jon based on his personal experience with her. However, something else in the report bothered him even more.

"Something's not right," he muttered under his breath.

Kandi almost snarled her response, "What you consider right, human, is unimportant. If I require information, I'll ask. Otherwise, I'd strongly suggest keeping your mouth closed. "Jon meekly sat back into the sofa cushions.

As if daring Kandi to contradict her, Sara intervened, "I'd like to know. What bothers you, Jon?"

Jon's eyes returned to the pixie before continuing in a halting whisper, "It's the cops. Traffic was crazy when you pulled me out of there. There's no way the police could get there that fast, and those that got there first weren't even regular police; those were FBI. Normally, the regular police come first and then call the Feds if needed, not vice versa. What were they doing there?"

Kandi hated to admit it, but the human's assessment of the situation seemed correct. *How would the Federal officers know where to go?* she thought. *The human is accurate. The speed with which they found us was almost like they had a tracking device of some kind...*

"Do you have a phone or other transmitter on you?" The pixie threw the question at Jon like an accusation.

"No," he answered meekly, "I lost my phone in the storm drain as I left the hotel."

"Stand up," Kandi demanded. She proceeded to search him thoroughly and practically growled when she came up empty.

Her eyes widened as she gazed at the red glow on Jonathan's finger. "The ring? Could it be?" She directed the next question at Sara, "Is it possible that they are tracking the ring like we did?"

Sara replied, "That is unlikely. Gaian science is based on heavy metals, not crystalline forms. For them to have the ability to locate the stone is illogical. They shouldn't even know what to look for."

Kandi was unconvinced, "Sara, the ring is the only answer that fits. There is no other variable in play besides the human himself, and he appears free of any device. We had determined that a lot of time has passed since Aedenian Watchers controlled things here. The old restrictions against exploring crystal tech are no longer enforced. Human researchers must have made inroads in that area, and the ring must have set off some alarm as it did with us.

"Think about it, Sara. First, someone searched the house in Colorado. What were they searching for? They tore the place apart, burning the house to cover their tracks. Why the house? Why the gallery? What ties them together? The best answer is the ring."

Jon's ears perked up at the mention of his father's house. "What do you know about the fire?" The Boulder Police had notified him shortly after the house had burned. "I'd been told the fire was accidental – something to do with the heating system."

Kandi shrugged her shoulders, unwilling to communicate with the human directly. However, Sara took the lead and summed up Kandi's visit, including finding the incendiary device in the basement. Kandi then reluctantly finished the story, "The way the intruders placed the explosive, the fire would have looked like the furnace exploded, destroying all evidence. No one would be the wiser. Now, human. I need you to think carefully. Did you wear the ring inside the house at any time?"

Jon replayed his visit to the home in his mind and replied honestly, "No. My dad's attorney had just given it to me that afternoon. I had gone by the house to pick up some things when…Yeah, I opened the case for a minute to ensure the ring was inside, but that was all. I didn't wear it or anything. Afterward, I put the box away. Didn't open it again until tonight."

Sara commented, "Kandi, That would explain the short burst we received two weeks ago during the personnel transit. Do you honestly believe that the humans are tracking him?"

"Yes, yes, I do. I don't know how or why, but that is the only explanation that makes sense. More importantly, if the authorities tracked the ring in Colorado with such a short burst, they would have had a much easier time in New York when it was openly exposed." Kandi stopped talking as a realization came to her. "They won't stop. They will keep searching until they find him and us. "Sara, secure the perimeter and scan the compound for intruders. Also, begin monitoring all law enforcement radio frequencies. We need to know what's coming at us."

Sara was all business, "Yes, commander. I have bots monitoring all civilian, federal, and military frequencies and all CCTV in the immediate area. We should receive an alert as soon as something turns up."

They didn't have long to wait.

Sara's voice streamed from the coms, "Kandi, the CCTV at the main intersection in Morrisville just registered four SUVs similar to the ones on the television. They are headed this way."

Kandi didn't welcome the news. She knew there wasn't much out in their area. That was one of the things that had made this old farmhouse ideal – its isolation. She exploded in a flurry of language and rage. She wasn't speaking English, but Jon didn't need a translator to get the gist of what she was saying.

After the momentary outburst, Kandi was suddenly very focused, "Sara, can you modify one of the scientist's IDs to fit the human?"

Sara responded, "Yes. Why do you ask?"

"His existing ID will draw too much attention. We may need to get out of here in a hurry, and we will need to take him with us. "

Two IDs and background data appeared on the table only a moment later, seemingly out of nowhere.

Sara announced, "Here is Jon's new ID. I took the liberty of reprinting yours as well."

"Great." She said as she put her ID in into a pouch, keeping Jon's in her hand more news on the intruders?"

"Just now. Kandi, there is little doubt that we are the target. Our hidden camera, where Quarry

Road splits off the main highway, acquired them as they turned. I estimate their arrival at fifteen minutes, providing they maintain their current speed."

Kandi grabbed her ID and handed the modified one to Jon. He stared at the Saudi Arabian passport before him, with a fake name under what appeared to be his DMV picture. "Take it, human," she ordered.

Kandi's next order showed no hesitation, "Sara. Set self-destruct for fourteen minutes."

There was no question nor debate. Sara responded, "Confirmed. Self-destruct sequence has started."

Kandi hesitated slightly before issuing her following command. "Sara, prepare for immediate consciousness upload."

For a moment, the AI's voice was silent. "Kandi?" Sara was confused. Consciousness upload was standard procedure when there was a tachyon link to carry the data back to the Institute. That link no longer existed. She continued, "Kandi, there is no receptacle on-site to receive the upload and no connection to transmit the data."

"That isn't quite true. You have me," Kandi stated matter of factly. "Theoretically, AIs can upload their consciousness into the unused portions of an organic brain. I repeat; prepare to upload."

Sara's voice indicated concern, "Although technically possible, no one has ever tried to upload an AI consciousness to a sentient host. Such a transfer could cause you irreparable harm."

Kandi was resolute, "Sara. There has to be a first time for everything. We have been together for a long time, and I consider you one of my oldest and closest friends despite our physical differences. I've never left anyone behind on a mission, and I've no intention of starting now."

Kandi attached two electrodes to her temples as she sat by the console. They were standard issue when non-verbal communication with the AI was needed. This connection wouldn't be that different, she hoped. "Sara, this is a direct order. Commence transfer."

The pixie's body sat frozen in the chair for four or five minutes before finally pulling the electrodes off her head and staggering away from the console. The room was eerily still. The only sound was a clock on the wall ticking off the seconds, counting down to self-destruct. Jon was transfixed by what he was seeing. Although the pixie was incapacitated, the concept of escape never dawned on him.

"Light. Noise. Not enough. Need more data. Where are my inputs? What is happening?" Sara was at a loss to explain her surroundings. *"Unknown data feed. Malfunction. Abort. Abort."*

Sara's new host was not faring well either. Kandi was standing, holding her head, barely maintaining consciousness. Sara's confusion and panic threatened to override Kandi's sense of self. Sara guided their shared eyes up toward the human.

Jon? Looks different – distorted – video input inaccurate, resetting video cortex. Sara was beginning to panic.

Kandi's eyes blinked rapidly as her head turned back and forth in response to Sara's unspoken request, a request the AI had no way of interpreting.

Somehow, she had to slow Sara down. In her mind, she screamed, Sara! Stop! You are panicking!

Sara considered what her friend had said. *What is panic?* The definition of the word was instantly available. *Panic? This is illogical. Why would I panic? I am trained to deal with situations like this.*

Kandi realized that she was dangerously close to losing this battle. Sara's attempt to deal with a living body was almost as traumatic as Kandi's coping with a second person in her mind. The AI was winning the struggle for dominance, and the pixie felt herself slipping into unconsciousness. With all her will, she forced the darkness away one last time. She knew that she couldn't succumb. She had to get all of them out before the self-destruct detonation.

Kandi stood and stumbled over to Jon. She snagged him by the arm and stumbled toward the garage, using the human more as support than a hostage. She was thankful he didn't resist as he had at the gallery. She would have been helpless to stop him if he had tried to break away. Fortunately, his timidity kept him from attempting anything. She turned and faced him with as stern a face as she could manage under the circumstances. "Human, we need you to drive us out of here."

Jon's anger overcame his fear. He erupted, overpowering his reluctance to talk, "Why me? After what you have done to me, why should I help you?"

Kandi focused all her attention on Jon, staring him in the eyes. "Human, this place will turn into a fireball in about six minutes. If you want to live, you will drive."

Jon found her logic sound and nodded in agreement. Kandi grabbed his arm again, directed him toward where a blue Lincoln Navigator was parked, and thrust the keys into his hand.

Her voice seemed strained and weak, "Human, Listen carefully. Turn right at the end of the driveway. Drive two miles to where the road splits; take the left road. That will take you to Morrisville. From there…" Then, she collapsed against him.

Though he had many reasons to doubt her and her motives and more than enough reason to leave her on the garage floor, Jon never hesitated. He picked her up, surprised at how little she weighed, and gently laid her in the back seat of the Navigator. She looked so innocent lying there, unlike the vicious beast he had experienced earlier. Here, she looked more like a little girl.

Still conflicted about his motives, Jon did as the pixie had instructed. After all, getting to a nearby town sounded like a great idea. About two miles down the lane, the sky ignited behind them.

Chapter 12 - Fallout

"Woah!" Jon exclaimed when his rear-view mirror lit up. The light from the explosion turned night into day for a fraction of a second before throwing him back into darkness. Afterimages flashed over his retinas, forcing him to stop in the middle of the road. Just as his sight returned, the shock wave from the blast caught up with them. Even two miles away, the blast shook the car violently. He said to himself, "Damn! That woke a few people up. I bet the Feds didn't enjoy the show too much either."

Even as he said it, Jon soberly realized that the cops would have been uncomfortably close to the house when the explosion occurred. He hoped they were unhurt. They might not be his friends, but they were still people, and he didn't want any harm to come to them on his account. Kandi hadn't budged from her fetal position throughout the noise and excitement. Jon had to look over his shoulder to confirm she was breathing.

Silently, he continued down the back roads into Morrisville. A thousand scenarios ran through his mind, each raising a dozen questions for which he didn't have answers. Finally, his brain settled on what was undoubtedly the most important one.

"What in the hell am I doing here?" he announced to the wind, "I should be safely nestled in my New York hotel room, savoring the triumph of my big opening." He stopped briefly before continuing, "God, What if it wasn't a triumph?" He paused, "Who am I kidding? The artist is kidnapped an hour and a half into the event, and then the Feds show up a few seconds later. Those rich people would have been heading toward the door in droves. OK... not a triumph...closer to a disaster."

Jon's heart sank as he continued to wrestle with the first question. "Despite that, here I am, driving through the Vermont night – still no idea how that happened - with an unconscious young woman... OK, not a woman per se, a 'pixie' – the same one who kidnapped me only six hours ago. A pixie? Really? Jon, do you realize how stupid this all sounds? There is no way this can be happening! I must have had a nervous breakdown, or somebody slipped a hallucinogen into my drink. This whole thing is too incredible to be real." Jon smiled, "Yeah...Far more likely that I'm in a drug-induced coma at the hospital." Jon found the idea was the closest to making sense of any he had considered. "Yeah, that's what's happened." He smiled, not caring how his "plausible explanation" would be pretty bad all on its own.

He stopped and glanced over his shoulder again at the form in the back seat, her pointy ears reflecting the light from the dashboard, and pinched himself again – hard. "Ouch! I felt that! Can you feel pain in a coma? Hmm. I don't think so...OK, it's not an illusion then. Jon, old boy, let's assume everything is as it appears; the girl in the backseat kidnapped and nearly killed you. So, we return to question one. Why are you here, and why, in God's name, are you helping her? The gallery opening culminated years of work, which she stole from you! Now, here you are aiding and abetting – hmmm, can you aid and abet your own kidnapping? This business is getting way out of control. I need to find the closest police station and end this before things get any worse."

Jon began driving again, convinced he would locate the police in Morrisville and end this nightmare. Yet, something kept nagging at him. "Despite everything that's happened, why does turning her in feel wrong?" He visualized, courtesy of dozens of alien invasion movies, the probing and testing an actual alien would endure at the hands of the government. "What the hell! I'm actually feeling sorry for her! Lord knows she didn't feel sorry for me. Took me bodily from my show. Towed me through the streets of New York, and then – I have no idea what happened next. I'm suddenly in a cabin in Vermont, and then she tries to kill me, for God's sake! She kept saying 'human' as if it were a dirty word, and I was something she would scrape off her shoe instead of a living being. Hell, the computer showed more concern and compassion than she did."

Thinking about Sara reminded Jon that the computer was now living inside the brain of his captor, which made his head hurt even more. He had no idea how such a thing was even possible. Nonetheless, the pixie had risked her life in the attempt, an experiment that appeared to have succeeded. This action was a side of his assailant that Jon had not considered possible – love for someone, or in this case, something else, an artificial intelligence. Part of him admired Kandi for not leaving her friend behind to be destroyed. Despite what she had done to him personally, her attempts to help a comrade were reason enough to stand by her – at least for now.

Many questions still plagued Jon's tired mind, but the answers were locked in the skull of the creature asleep in the back seat, and it didn't appear she would be joining the conversation anytime soon.

Jon focused on the things he could control. Assuming he continued, against all logic otherwise, assisting his kidnapper and avoiding law enforcement, there were some things he could figure out by himself. Replaying the evening in his mind, he realized she was right about one thing. There was no doubt in his mind that someone in the government, for reasons unknown, was hunting him personally, and Kandi had given him the best guess of why – the ring.

In hindsight, every event this evening returned to the stone on his finger. The radiation drew the pixie to the gallery. Was it so hard to think that it also brought the government boys? Add that to the fact that the Feds showed up so quickly supported that hypothesis. Finally, the agents showing up at the Vermont house all but clinched the argument. He glanced at his right hand. The gem still cast its throbbing reddish glow, undoubtedly broadcasting his location to anyone desiring to check.

That realization hit Jon hard. "Someone else wants me, and I have no idea who they are or their motives." The pixie was sure the Feds were tracking the ring. If so, I must find a way to shield the stone. Maybe that would slow things down a bit so I can think. It's easier to think when no one is shooting at you or blowing things up. Later, I might turn myself in, but for now, I'll stay with the devil I know."

Just then, his car passed a sign announcing the city limits of Morrisville, Vermont. There was no traffic at this hour. The town seemed safely tucked in for the night. Only the streetlights and the neon sign above the local bar indicated any life. Not far into town, there was a different sign – both metaphorical and physical, pointing toward the local hospital. Jon smiled and headed in that direction. He suddenly knew what he had to do.

Morrisville was a relatively small community, so Jon only took a minute or two before finding himself in the parking lot of Copley Hospital. He checked himself in the mirror before heading to the emergency room entrance, attempting to straighten his suit as he went. Jon needed to look somewhat professional to pull this off, and his general appearance was far worse now than at the galley earlier that evening. For the umpteenth time today, he wished that he hadn't overslept.

When he entered the building, the ER was deadly quiet. There wasn't even anyone at the reception desk. Jon glanced around, finding a directional sign pointing toward Radiology, and headed off in that direction. He was halfway there when a female voice challenged him from behind. "Excuse me, sir, but can I help you with something?" she asked. He turned to find a young woman in scrubs, Martha Wall, RN, according to her name tag.

Jon attempted to ignore that she was a young woman and began the spiel he had invented only a few minutes earlier in the car, sputtering and stammering as he spoke. "Hello, Nurse Wall? I'm the radiologist on call, Dr. Hamm, from Burlington." He stuttered. "I received a call from the State Police. Something about an explosion in the mountains outside of town. They feared casualties and asked me to come down and get ready." He prayed that he had been right about this being an area-wide hospital.

The nurse relaxed and nodded. She, too, had received word of the explosion and the possibility of injured parties coming their way. "We are a small group here; Maddy will do. What happened to the regular guy? Sick?"

Jon continued with a sly grin that he hoped hid his bashfulness, "Just my luck, Maddy. He's on vacation. I'm the backup."

"Nothing personal," the nurse continued, "but what happened to you? You look like you were in an accident yourself."

Jon forced a laugh, "Believe it or not, I was at a party just down the road. Met someone, and...well, let's just say we were interrupted by the phone call." Jon shrugged his shoulders.

Sometimes, the simplest explanation, the one closest to the truth, is the best. Maddy seemed to buy his scenario without hesitation, commiserating with his bad luck. "That would explain how you got here so quickly. I just got the call a few minutes ago. OK, Doctor...."

"Please, call me Jerry."

"Fine, Jerry." Nurse Wall smiled for the first time. "Let me open the door for you. With such a small staff, we try to keep everything secured." She squeezed Jonathan on the shoulder, causing him to jump slightly as she opened the Radiology door. "I really appreciate your help."

"No problem." Jon closed the door behind her. The explosion had been immense, and he earnestly hoped there weren't any casualties or worse fatalities from the blast. He quickly began his search. Since he had no idea how long it would be before the actual radiologist showed his face, he needed to hurry. Luckily, he found what he was looking for right away - lead-lined gloves. Nice ones at that. Black that could almost pass for leather in the right light and not excessively heavy. He put one on over his right hand, waited a minute or two, flexed his fingers, and walked back toward the ER entrance.

This time, a kinder voice stopped him, "Where are you going now?" Nurse Wall was behind the desk. Jon was already sweating bullets from the cloak-and-dagger routine and didn't need the pressure of continuing his conversation with the nurse as well. Jon plunged his right hand behind his back and stuttered, "Things are in great shape. Just want to get some fresh air before the games begin." He flashed her a smile, walked out the door, and hurried to where he had left the car.

The pixie was still out like a light as he started the engine and headed out of the parking lot. Part of Jon wished that she would stay that way. Life would be so much easier if she remained in a coma. Then, he would have no choice but to report to the authorities and let the process take its course. His conscience would be clear. As it was, he knew he was way over his head, and he was only getting deeper with his performance in the ER. The stone's radiation signature would stop at the hospital, but his appearance and subsequent disappearance would raise questions. Eventually, the Feds would get the CCTV footage from the hospital ER and parking lot and then the make, model, and maybe even the car's tag number, depending on how good the hospital's cameras were.

Driving down the road, he knew he was now at a point where he needed the pixie's help to continue the deception. Unfortunately, she was still trance-like and not much good to anyone. He again considered taking her to the Morrisville Police and decided against it. He would wait for the next town. Perhaps she would be conscious by then, and they could talk things through. He hoped he was right.

WCAX News Report Burlington, Vermont

(Camera pans smoldering wreckage spread across a wide area along with firefighters still putting out minor burns on the perimeter before returning focus to the young reporter.)

> "This is Martina Cortez reporting from the scene of a home explosion about twenty miles outside of Morrison, Vermont. While fire and police haven't released any details, neighbors claim that a large propane tank might have exploded. As you can see, the resulting blast leveled the house and took most of an acre of forest with it.
>
> Four SUVs were tumbled and scorched by the blast. (Camera pans over to a vehicle upside down inside the police barricade.) Although we have two confirmed dead, we have no report on the status of the other person or persons inside the vehicles. Survivors were taken to Morrisville Hospital.
>
> (Camera pans back to a wide-angle perspective of the remains of the home in the background.)
>
> The house itself is a total loss. Sources within the fire department indicate that when the site cools, they will search the wreckage for additional bodies and possible causes."

Chapter 13 – A Meeting of Minds

When Kandi lost consciousness, her senses no longer functioned. Kandi was in no position to care, but Sara, locked within Kandi's brain, once again experienced the one emotion she was familiar with – panic. The total lack of input around her was unsettling. She was used to data bombarding her from all sides, a constant roar of information. The eerie silence of this information wasteland was unnerving.

"Kandi? Kandi?" Sara called for her friend as she felt her way through the coal-black hallways of Kandi's mind, but her friend didn't respond. "Kandi? Why is there no light, no sound? My audio and video inputs are not responding. Why is there nothing here? Kandi? Where are you?" The only thing more unnerving than her shout was the lack of echo; the imagined walls absorbed everything. Sara could not fathom a reason why Kandi wouldn't answer. She had briefly felt the pixie's presence alongside her after they merged, but how long ago was that? Sara's panic skyrocketed when she realized she couldn't remember her last contact with her friend and had no concept of the passage of time.

An unknown data impulse intruded into Sara's consciousness. *Curious*, she mused, *This data is unfamiliar to me. How did it get here?* Try as she might, Sara couldn't make sense of the strange input that had settled upon her. The sensation had nothing to do with logic, yet it reflected her concern about her friend's well-being. She wondered, *Was this another emotion? It seems similar to panic, but not quite. How exciting! I can't wait to tell Kandi...* The feeling became more intense and troubling. Comparing her reaction to those she had observed in her organic counterparts, she wondered, *Could this be the one known as fear?* That emotion quickly evolved into something else that Sara couldn't identify. She only knew it was different and had to generate a response. "Kandi! Where are you?" The empty hollows of the pixie's mind gave her nothing in return. "Kandi!" Sara's mental shout grew louder as her frustration and fear grew. "Kandi!" This one was a scream born of panic and fear.

"What?" Sara felt more than heard the pixie's groggy response. Relief spread through Sara's being. *Was this another emotion,* she questioned? *Had Kandi been injured during the transfer?*

Sara rushed toward the sound. Finally, the darkness weakened, and she "saw" a dim light with her friend at its center, lying on the floor.

"Kandi. What happened? Where have you been? I was considering the possibility that you were dead!" Sara launched her questions at her friend as she hugged her tightly.

Kandi still felt like her brain was about to explode, and Sara's mental shouts were not helping. "Slow down, Sara. I'm fine – I think. I must have blacked out. So, I guess the upload worked, huh? We'll have something to tell those researchers when we get home." Her response grew stronger as she talked.

Sara had no idea what Kandi was talking about. "Kandi, What is blacked out?" Unwilling to wait for her friend to respond, Sara took a guess. "Did you experience a system reboot?" she asked.

Kandi paused and briefly reflected, "Actually, that's not a bad analogy," the pixie slowly picked her bruised psyche up from the floor of her mind. "For lack of a better word, reboot works. The conflict between you and me occupying the same space caused an overload. That's what caused me to black out – reboot. Sara, having us both in my mind will create unique situations. There is no wonder we are confused. I think we should establish some ground rules for our new relationship."

"Certainly. What do I need to do?" Sara was more than willing to do anything that would make sense of this alien existence around her.

"For now, I need you to do nothing; say nothing unless I ask. Accept what I do without interruption or interference. This will help both of us. You need time to adjust to my organic body and the limitations that form puts upon you, and I have to adapt to the reality that my thoughts are no longer mine alone. Do you understand? Can you do that?"

Sara was pensive in her reply, "You are asking me to restrict access to information. I am not accustomed to holding back what I perceive as vital input. The idea goes against my primary programming."

Kandi thought before responding, "Okay…I get that. How about this? We'll use a notification protocol. You 'say' my name once and then wait for my response before communicating or doing anything. Will that work?"

"Yes. That's not much different from our existing working relationship. Uh, Kandi?"

"You have a question?" her friend replied.

"Yes. I experienced unusual inputs a short time ago. The experiences were unknown to me. Based on my observations of team members, I have processed one of the signals as the emotion known as fear, but I'm not sure of the other."

"Describe the sensation to me."

"What I felt, if felt is the correct word, was not unlike an intensive data search with short, defined time requirements."

At first, Kandi couldn't understand her friend's confusion, but then the truth hit her, "I think I see. I believe I can help you with that one. We organics refer to that as anxiety."

"Is that also an emotion?"

"Yes, one slightly more complex than fear."

Sara continued, "As I continued my search for you, the input increased in severity until I was concerned I might shut down. Is that normal as well?"

"Yes, it is. Sara, emotions are tricky – things I've spent my entire life attempting to adapt and control. You haven't had that luxury. This transition…this learning period will take time – not nanoseconds, but weeks and months to adapt. Talk to me when these inputs appear. I will do my best to explain them to you."

"Thank you, Kandi."

"This discussion brings up a different issue. You no longer have mechanical data inputs. You have no cameras and microphones; the physical attributes of my body are your data feeds. My eyes generate all the video. Audio comes from my two ears and my mouth, olfactory from my nose, and touch from my epidermal layer of skin. If what you sense seems illogical, it is probably due to the interface change. Don't react to inputs without talking to me first. Any response you make will translate into a physical movement for me, and I can't have my body doing things I don't anticipate. Understand?"

Sara reflected on what Kandi had said, "Yes, I believe I do."

With that problem covered, Kandi added, "Speaking of physical movement, I believe I'm feeling well enough to wake up. Our physical self may still be in danger, and there is no telling what mess that human has gotten us into."

"Kandi?" Sara almost shouted the word.

"What?" Kandi replied.

"You said to tell you."

"What, Sara."

Sara continued, "I just experienced a powerful invalid input when you thought about Jon."

Kandi's mental façade hardened at the mention of the human, "That one would be hatred."

"I don't understand. Why would you hate Jon? What has he done to you?"

"He is human. I need no other reason."

United States Space Command – Cheyenne Mountain, Colorado

The young lieutenant hesitated as he approached the door to the Colonel's office. He was new to the team, and this was his first time delivering a briefing to his commanding officer. He stopped at the nearby men's room to straighten his tie, comb his hair, and check his overall appearance before knocking with what he hoped was some degree of confidence.

"Enter," came the terse command from behind the door, almost causing the young man to run in fear. The lieutenant swallowed hard and went in to find the steel-blue eyes of Colonel Forrester focused directly on him. The young man stood frozen like a deer in the headlights, unsure what to do next. The Colonel finally grew tired of waiting, "What is it, lieutenant? I don't have all day."

Lieutenant Jeffries's voice stuttered just a bit, "Y-y-yes, sir. We tracked down the owner of the Vermont house. It was quite a task. The purchase had been buried in four shell companies and…"

"Get to the point, lieutenant." Forrester was not the patient type.

"Yes, sir." The young officer continued, "The Aeden Corporation made the purchase six months ago."

The Colonel replied, "What do we know about them?"

Jeffries continued, "Sir. That's what's really strange. An in-depth analysis showed that Aeden Corp didn't exist as an entity until six months ago, just before the purchase. The paper trail on the corporation stops there. However, once we investigated their banking accounts and those of their subsidiaries, we found other purchases the entity has made since then – cars, furniture, electronic gear....."

A telephone call interrupted the briefing, "Good work, Lieutenant. Compile a detailed list of all purchases. We may need to track them down." Jeffries quickly took the sheaf of papers in his hand and placed them in front of the Colonel, "Here they are sir." His job done, Jeffries saluted and made a hasty retreat from the office.

"Forrester here," the colonel practically shouted into the phone. The man on the other end of the line spoke hurriedly. Forrester had sent a backup team from Hanscom. The first team had gone silent as they approached the Vermont house, with no communication since. The news was worse than he had imagined. He raced to the commander's office, scattering staff in his wake.

"Sir, the backup team from Hanscom just sent their report." Colonel Forrester stood at attention, his outward bearing giving no hint of his internal turmoil. As much as he hated bearing bad news, he didn't want to entrust this to an underling. He had browsed the material list from the audit on his way.

"Status?" the commander sat quietly behind his desk, drumming his fingers on the polished wood.

The colonel continued, "Bad, but not as bad as we had feared. Two of our people are dead—four more are in critical condition. They'd already exited their vehicles at the time of the blast. The remainder of the team arrived a few seconds later. That, the vehicles' armor-plating and bulletproof glass probably saved their lives. Still, the explosion sent the cars end-over-end for about a hundred feet down a hill and into a ravine - banged the team up quite a bit. Medics transported them to a local hospital for evaluation. We will evac them later.

The commander cradled his head as he considered the colonel's words. *How could something so simple go so wrong?* "Status of the suspect? Did he survive, or was he killed in the blast?"

The colonel cleared his throat, continuing, "We don't know. The area is still too hot to go inside and look for bodies. We are assuming the man escaped, probably with his captor." The colonel anticipated the next question, "Unfortunately for us, the explosion generated an expansive energy field that created a communications dead zone. When that finally dissipated, we caught a brief flash from the stone near Morrisville before the signal went dark. We've continued to monitor, but there has been no other contact. I sent a recon team to the town to do routine interviews. Maybe we'll get lucky."

"Colonel. We make our luck. Do we have the vehicle information from the Aeden Corp audit?" The colonel nodded. "Good. Access Morrisville CCTV and look for any comparable cars. Any other transportation listed?"

Forrester took a moment to refer to the report, "Yes, sir. The report indicated they leased a yacht, *The Voyager Templar*, out of the Bahamas."

"Where is the boat right now?" The commander was very intense.

"Our people report it in a slip at Boston harbor."

"Excellent, have your team track the vehicles and put the yacht under surveillance immediately. By the way, we still have a team monitoring the Martyr residence outside of Boston, correct?"

"Yes, sir."

"Advise them to be ready. I don't think the two suspects will go there - far too risky, but recent events will have turned their plans upside down. Anything is possible. Dismissed."

As the colonel left the office, the commander was already deep in thought. He considered all the existing data and came to the only conclusion he considered possible. He said to himself, "They have discovered we are tracking the ring and have found some way to shield it - very unexpected. I mustn't underestimate them again."

Chapter 14 – The Desperados

The blackness in the rearview mirror and the nothingness at the end of his headlights gave Jon ample time to continue stewing over his dilemma. He had left Morrisville in his rearview mirror over an hour ago, and the pixie had shown no signs of recovery. He'd convinced himself that surrender was their only option when he was startled by a quiet moaning from the back seat. He had mixed feelings of relief and fear at the pixie's return to consciousness.

Jon called back to her, "You okay back there?" He didn't detect any motion, but she groaned again. Jon took the sound as a positive sign, "Glad to see you've returned to the land of the living." He tried to sound chippier than he was.

The pixie rustled around some more before responding in a groggy yet somehow still snarky tone, "Where are we, human?"

Jon thought, *"So, how are you, Jon? Everything going okay? Tell me again, Jon, old boy, why we didn't turn her butt in at the police station in Morrisville?"*

When his brain didn't give a satisfactory retort, he answered her question. "We are about ten miles outside Lancaster, New Hampshire, looking for a car to steal."

"Steal a car? Why? "The pixie was suddenly very alert. She sat up quickly, instantly causing her head to feel like it would explode. Sitting back in the seat, she asked, "What's happened? Are we in danger? Has something happened to the vehicle...." Kandi stopped her rant as her vision returned, and Jon's hands on the steering wheel became focused. "What are you wearing on your hand?"

"Oh, this old thing?" Jon waved the glove in her direction. "I acquired this magical glove at the hospital in Morrisville. Lead lined – blocks the radiation from the ring. It also happens to be why we need a new ride."

The pixie reflected before responding, "OK, retrieving shielding was a surprisingly good idea. But I don't understand why your glove mandates a change in vehicle." Kandi crawled over the center console and collapsed into the front passenger seat.

Her voice had an edge, giving Jon the impression she was still in intense pain. He lowered his voice before responding. "If what you told me back at the house is accurate, and logic aside, I believe it was, the people looking for us will eventually follow us to the hospital in Morrisville where I acquired this glove. The charge nurse will dutifully tell them about the mysterious radiologist, Dr. Hamm, who disappeared not long after he arrived just before the REAL radiologist showed up. One look at the security video, and the Feds will know it was me.

Our trackers will then check the parking lot cameras. Assuming they know the make and model of the car we have, and we must assume they have, they will match it with the car I drove into the hospital lot. They will get the onboard anti-theft GPS information from the manufacturer and have us. At that point, they will know exactly where we are and have the information necessary to turn this beast into a lump of stationary metal - unless we ditch the car. I figure we have two, maybe three hours."

The pixie was quiet for several miles as she assimilated Jon's information. He was thankful. Her silence gave him time to think and let his adrenaline levels go down. To the best of his recollections, in the past twenty-four hours, Jon had abetted an attack on federal agents with a probable battery charge – if not murder, thrown in for good measure, and he had impersonated a doctor – not a bad night's work for a guy who'd never had even a parking ticket before! Who knew what else might happen before the end of the night? The party appeared to be just getting started.

"You awake over there?" Jon decided to break the silence.

"Yes," was the curt reply.

"We need to change cars pretty quickly. I have an idea, but I'll need your assistance."

At first, Kandi was not interested in helping the human do anything. "Who do you think you are suggesting plans and thefts? You are a jeweler. I am the warrior. I should be the one to make plans."

Jon was immediately on the defensive, "Fine! What great plan do you have?"

After a short internal conversation with Sara, Kandi realized she had no idea what to do next. The AI's integration into her neural network still had all her senses on overdrive. Her most immediate need was to rest her aching head. No matter how bad the human's idea was, it had to be better than her nonexistent one.

Kandi attempted to maintain her dignity, "I am willing to entertain your idea. What is it?"

Jon took the small victory and smiled, "There's a resort a few miles from here down Highway 5. My parents used to take me there during the summer on vacation. Dad enjoyed golf, and Mom and I did everything else. Today being a Friday – well, early Saturday now, weekenders out of Boston will have packed the place. We can grab a car from one of the long-term guests and have an excellent chance of it not being missed until at least Sunday afternoon."

"What is my part in this plan?"

Jon explained, finishing just as the sign indicating the turnoff for Mountain View Grand Resort and Spa appeared. He drove around until he found a semi-vacant backlot with older cars and pickups. Figuring that this must be the employee lot, he found an open spot among the other cars to park their SUV. Now came the hard part. The pixie had to feign drunkenness to lure the lone desk clerk away from his station where the valet kept the residents' keys. Kandi wasn't concerned. She was, after all, a soldier and had enjoyed many off-base leaves. Jon wasn't as sure.

Who knew? Apparently, when a beautiful girl staggers into an empty lobby, people could care less about acting ability, regardless of the planet. The pixie, having arranged her clothes to be dangerously close to falling off her, stumbled into the foyer, singing at the top of her lungs. The words weren't English, and the tune was literally out of this world, but that didn't matter. The bored desk clerk came running around the desk to help. He was so focused on Kandi that he never spotted Jon, who managed to slip in behind her.

Even though Jon had seen her in action, Jon was still impressed by how fast she executed a sleeper hold and let the clerk drop to the floor. The clerk's head made a solid thump as it hit. Jon winced. He hated hurting the boy, but the clerk had to feel a little pain when he woke up for the con to work.

Jon ran to the valet box.

"Damn. It's locked! See if he has his keys on him," he shouted at Kandi.

Still annoyed at taking orders from a human, the pixie nonetheless went through the man's pockets and located his keys, which she tossed to Jon. After several failed attempts, he opened the box and looked for purple tape. During his boyhood visits, the valet always put purple tape on his father's keys. That was how they identified long-term guests so they could park those cars farther away. Fortunately for Jon, that tradition continued. He grabbed the keys to a Lexus, locked the box, and had the pixie return the key ring to the man's pocket.

This next part of the plan was crucial. The clerk had to believe the story they spun.

Jon had the pixie sit on the couch, slumped over as if she had passed out. He then kneeled next to the desk clerk, gently tapping him awake.

"Hey there, buddy. You OK?" Jon asked.

"Hmmm...What happened?" the clerk slowly responded.

"You were helping my wife inside when you tripped and fell. Popped your head right on the floor."

The clerk rubbed his head as he looked at the pixie and smiled, "Yes, I remember her. She's quite beautiful. You are a lucky man."

You don't know the half of it, son. Jon thought.

"Are you going to be alright?" Jon feigned concern.

"Yes, yes. I'll be fine. Thanks."

"No problem. If you are sure you're OK, we'll head to our room."

Jon helped the pixie up and began steering her toward the elevator. He stopped halfway there to pat his own pockets.

"Damn. I left my wallet in the car!" He turned with her back toward the door.

Still rubbing his forehead, the concerned clerk offered to watch Jon's wife while he went out.

Jon quickly replied, "Nah. You need to recover from that fall. Besides, fresh air might help sober her up a bit. Thanks anyway."

With that, Jon and the pixie exited and headed toward the valet parking lot, where a late model Lexus ES was blinking in response to his unlock request. Before long, the lodge disappeared into the darkness behind them.

Jon turned down a side road several miles down the highway and stopped. Kandi seemed genuinely confused as he pulled over. Had the human seen something she had missed? "What's wrong? Was there something on the road?"

"No," was his unexpected reply.

"Then, why did you stop?"

"We need to talk," was all he said.

His answer was unacceptable, "We do not have time to talk." Kandi grabbed his wrist with her other hand. They both knew that she could break his arm like a twig if she desired, and right now, she desired a lot. Again, Sara's intervention stopped her from maiming the human. She released his arm and slammed her fist into the dash, denting it in frustration, "We should continue, human. We are wasting time."

Jon was unapologetic, "Look, I've broken numerous laws tonight, and I can't identify a single reason to justify why I did. I need answers, and before I get in any deeper, I think now is the time to ask." His voice seemed shrill and uncontrolled. Exhaustion and stress were taking their toll.

She yelled, "Who do you think you are to demand anything?"

"Right now, I'm the guy helping you, and I'm not going anywhere until I get some answers."

The temptation to bash his head against a window and return to the road with him unconscious was strong. Again, Sara proved to be a calming influence on her host.

"Kandi?" Sara asked.

"What! "Kandi's anger startled the AI.

"Kandi, let me talk to him. You said it yourself; we can't return to Aeden without him, and he can't help us if he is dead. Being physically violent with him whenever you don't get your way is not logical."

Kandi slowly calmed to the point where she could reluctantly see some wisdom in what Sara told her. "OK. We'll try it your way. You do the talking."

Jon noticed a subtle difference when Kandi spoke next. The voice was the same, but the inflection was different. The tone was calmer and more focused than before.

"Jon, I'll tell you what you want to know."

Now Jon was confused. "What's going on here? You seem different."

"This is Sara, not Kandi."

"This is weird."

"Trust me when I tell you the situation is much worse for us. Now, what do you desire to know?"

"Let's start with who are you?"

"I am Sara, and she is Kandi..."

Jon interrupted, "Not your names! Who are you? Where do you come from?"

The pixie's mouth gave an uncharacteristic laugh, and her lips turned into a grin, "Oh. We are from the city of Atlantia on the planet Aeden."

The answer, though expected, was still hard to take, "OK. That makes sense...I guess. Those wings of yours kinda set you apart from the crowd." He continued, "Your English is excellent. Why is that?"

"We had a monitor AI that processed the nuances of your spoken and written language for several months of your time. The Institute downloaded that information into the team's memories shortly before we arrived."

"The Institute?" Jon inquired.

"That is a long story in itself. Let's say that the Institute is responsible for ensuring your planet and its inhabitants remain safe and, more importantly, remain here, far away from Aeden."

Jon was blown away. "Why are you here – in Vermont?"

"We were part of an advance team for a group of environmental engineers."

Jon shook his head, "That still doesn't answer my question. Why are you here?"

The pixie's body shook violently. When she stopped, her physical posture and her persona changed. There was no question that he was now speaking with Kandi.

"You want to know why we're here, human? You think you are ready for that?" Jon nodded. Kandi took a deep breath before continuing. "Fine, start driving and get comfortable. This isn't a short story."

Over the next hour, the pixie related how humans were Aedenian exiles, relegated to Gaia after losing the war between humans and the other races. As part of the treaty ending the conflict, the pixies and elves assumed the responsibility of ensuring Gaia against anything jeopardizing the humans' survival there. She also told him how past planetary upheavals had affected Gaia. She finished with how only the intervention of Aeden's scientists could save the human population in the face of the coming reckoning.

Jon gathered his wits, trying to take in all she said, "Look, we know our planet is in trouble. Our experts are on top of the situa..."

Kandi interrupted, "Your current attempts at mitigation are woefully insufficient. Your world is headed toward a total collapse of the biosphere."

"So, the Eart...Gaia is going to get hotter?" Jon asked.

Kandi chortled, "Global warming is the least of your worries. Other changes are far more troubling. Some of these changes are a natural progression of the planet, but the largest contributor is humanity. You have nearly depleted the massive water deposits in the aquifers and collected much more in artificial reservoirs. That redistribution of water combined with melting the ice packs at the north and south poles will result in a variance in your planet's axial tilt. Humanity will learn that actions have consequences."

"I don't understand."

"I am not a scientist. I was only here to establish security for the group, but from what I do grasp, the redistribution of so much mass has helped shift Gaia's center of gravity. The planet has always had a wobble, but now your magnetic north pole is hundreds of miles from where it was only a century ago. So far, the change has been only slightly greater than Gaia's normal tilt, but an exponentially greater variance will occur in the coming years. Soon, your global ocean currents will be affected, causing irreparable harm to the hydrosphere. Combined, these changes will alter the rotation patterns of the planet, which will, in turn, degrade its magnetic field. Your magnetic field protects life from the deadly aspects of your sun's radiation. Entire species will be eliminated or mutated. If left unchecked, organic life will cease."

Jon was skeptical, "I don't believe you. Such a thing is not possible."

Kandi continued, "I know it's possible because all of this has happened before. Your scientists have found evidence of humans going back close to a million years, correct?"

"Yes."

"Those oldest specimens are the mutated remains of the poor creatures left here over one million of your years ago. At that time, our scientists felt the same way as your people do now. They could treat the symptoms, and life would return to what it had been. A planet was too large to tip, so they never entertained the consequences of an axial shift. Even as the problems escalated and the reality of biosphere collapse was upon them, they felt we had hundreds of years to evacuate everyone. Instead, the collapse happened in days. We were able to save thousands, but billions died before we could get to them. We are not allowed to let that happen again."

Jon was still confused, "That's interesting, but you have made little doubt about your hatred for us. Why help us at all?"

The pixie sighed, frustrated as if talking to a small child, "Yes, human, I hate you and everyone else in your race, and I am not alone in that assessment. Your ancestors killed my parents and millions of my people during the Human Wars. I will never forgive you for that. I would have exterminated your race if the decision had been up to me.

"However, I am a Watcher, one of a corps of elves and pixies charged with policing humans on Gaia while ensuring that humans never find their way back to Aeden. Our pact with Origen states that my people will do everything possible to see that your race survives."

Now it was Jon's turn to interrupt, "Wait. Who is this Origen?"

"Origen is an intelligent being made up entirely of crystal. He brought stability to the non-human races long ago, and now his lifeblood runs in the veins of all Aedenians in the form of crystal nanites. Origen knew that this world was unstable. He insisted that we implement controls, or he would pull out of the symbiotic relationship we enjoy. That is not something we wanted to risk."

"So, you are part crystal?"

"Living crystal. Its presence in our blood allows us to live longer and gives us greater physical strength than our bodies would normally have."

This discovery forced Jon along a different path, "OK. The war lasted for over a hundred years, right?"

"Yes."

"How old are you?"

Kandi didn't hesitate in responding, "I am just over one hundred and fifty Aedenian years old."

That revelation blew Jon's mind. He had no trouble accepting that this young woman was deadly – he had seen and, unfortunately, experienced her skill, but over a century old? He remembered seeing her outside the gallery window and thinking she was his age. Wow!

His next question hit home, "So... If you had this planned out, why aren't your scientists here instead of me?"

The pixie's voice dropped. "Something went wrong. Everything was on schedule one minute, and the next...." She shook her head, "Something destroyed our transport and severed our communications. We have not heard from the Institute since. Human, something terrible has happened on Aeden. They're in trouble, and I must help them."

"So, where do I fit in your plan? Why am I important?" Jon asked earnestly.

"You are not, but the stone in your ring has, or at least had, the power to initiate gates between worlds. Without a temporal connection to Aeden, you and your ring may be our only chance to get home again, save my world, and in the process, save yours."

She continued, "I realize that I must sound like a lunatic, but everything I've told you is true. Although I was not alive when Origen announced his presence, I was around the last time your planet's environment collapsed. For Gaia, more than a million of your years has passed since that event – on Aeden, barely ten." The pixie fell silent.

Jon didn't know what to think; "Gates between worlds? Time streams? Savior of the world? How is any of this even possible?"

As Jon quietly attempted to absorb the science fiction novel he was now living, they continued driving down Highway 5. Her story was incredible, on the verge of unbelievable, yet she seemed genuine in her revelations despite her violent nature and apparent hatred for him. Violent outbursts aside, he hadn't caught her in a lie yet.

They had gone a few miles farther before she spoke again, "So, where are you taking us?"

"Boston."

Chapter 15 - Boston

Throughout the early morning hours, Jon zigzagged over county and state roads in his approach to Boston. Kandi was impressed. The human seemed genuinely worried the authorities might be looking for the car and wanted to avoid capture. She silently applauded him for his caution but wondered why he was so helpful. Was he leading them into a trap? Was he genuine in his aid? Kandi had to know. She asked, "I've told you why we are here, but why are you here - helping us?"

The resulting silence was deafening in the close confines of the car. Finally, Sara mentally asked, *Why is he being so quiet?*

I have no idea.

Finally, Jon spoke, his face twisted as if in conflict with itself, "Truthfully, I don't know. There isn't a logical reason for me to help you. I find your explanations for your actions confusing, upsetting, and implausible; however, I also find the actions of my fellow humans disconcerting. Everyone seems to want this thing," waving his right hand before him, "and I'll be damned if I know why. I need to figure out my situation. From what you have told me, somewhere in time, one of my ancestors was one of your chosen ones. I need to know more, and I think I have the best chance of learning more with you."

Jon's response was not the answer Kandi expected, but his reasoning rang surprisingly authentic. She had never considered he might be a descendant of an archangel, but now that she heard him say it, she realized that had to be the case. The rings used DNA for activation, and there was no way he could interface with the ring without it killing him, but why was it still flashing the distress signal? If the ring were this man's to control, the ring should have terminated the warning.

The sun was pulling itself out of its Atlantic bed just as Jon pulled into Boston traffic south of Concord. Saturday traffic was nothing like what it would be on a weekday, but Kandi was impressed anyway. User-operated vehicles were non-existent on Aeden, and although she had been practicing for months, she would never have attempted this drive. She asked Jon, "Where do we go now?"

Jon laughed, "I have no idea."

Kandi was stunned, "No idea? Then why are we here?"

Jon was honest, "I know this town. It's familiar. If someone is hunting me down, I want to be on my turf."

Kandi's experience had shown that familiarity with a place was always a plus. They were fugitives, and a familiar base could only help. They needed food and shelter, and thanks to the base's destruction, they had neither. Sara had reminded her to be the Watcher, the guardian, and put her personal feelings about Jon aside. Kandi knew she was right, but with the unknown status of the Aeden gates, her distrust of humans was running exceptionally high. Playing nicely with Jon would be very difficult.

Nonetheless, she tried to sound friendly when she spoke, "We're going to need food and a place to stay soon. A change of clothing would be good as well. Any ideas?"

Jon reflected for a second before replying, "A few. First, I want to dump the car somewhere it won't show up for a few days. Then, we'll need some cash to get the food, clothes, and shelter. I have a safety deposit box where I've stashed some money for a rainy day – seems like it's pouring right now, agreed?"

Kandi was confused. There wasn't a cloud in the sky, and the human was talking about rain. "Are you feeling alright? There is no rain."

Jon laughed a little heartier this time, "Sorry. That is an expression we use. It means to save something for a bad time, like now."

Kandi wasn't convinced, "I see, but won't the authorities be monitoring your bank?"

"Probably not. It's not my regular bank. I bought the box when I had an account there years ago and kept it when I moved out of the city. Hopefully, that will put the place off the Fed's radar. Besides, I don't see where we have any other choice."

Kandi agreed they needed the money, and other alternatives to the bank involved breaking additional laws and drawing even more attention to themselves. She nodded her assent. "Where are you taking the car?"

"We're taking it to the one place in Boston where a car sitting abandoned for a few days will get zero notice – the airport. We'll leave it at one of the remote parking facilities. Then we can take the "T" to my bank."

"The 'T'?"

"That's what we call the Boston mass transit, the 'T.'"

"Won't mass transit's security program recognize us? Kandi wanted to show that she knew some things about Gaian security measures.

"We'll keep our heads down at the stations and while on the train. The cameras are generally looking for a different kind of lawbreaker. We'll just blend into the background." Jon grinned, "Don't worry. Many people travel during the day, even on Saturday. If we don't draw attention to ourselves, no one will give us a second look." Jon tried to sound confident, but his insides were squirming.

The airport drop and bank stop went as planned. Jon had found a backpack in the rear seat of the Lexus, which now held the contents of his safety deposit box. Afterward, he guided Kandi down the street to the Goodwill store to see about improving their wardrobe. With hijabs, jeans, and shirts filling a couple of bags, Kandi asked the obvious, "We still require food and shelter. Do you have a source for those as well?"

"Unless you have a better idea, we need to see a friend of mine."

Kandi reacted vehemently, "No! Involving other humans is an unacceptable security risk. Besides, your government is undoubtedly tracking your known associates."

Jon nodded, "You're probably right, but I doubt they've had time to track a guy I do trivia night with once a week. Look, we need help, and I trust Marty. Okay?"

Begrudgingly, Kandi agreed. They arrived at a nondescript apartment building near Goodwill a few minutes later. Jon and Kandi ran up the steps and pressed the buzzer for Apartment 3.

"Yo! Who's this?" Marty's voice had that strained "just woken up on a Saturday morning" tone.

Jon tried to sound normal, "Hey Marty! It's Jon. Jon Martyr. You got a minute?"

Marty was now very much awake, "Jon? What the hell, man? You, my friend, are big news. Can't turn the telly on without hearing your name. Half the world is looking for you, and you show up on my doorstep? Aren't you supposed to be dead or kidnapped or somethin'?"

Jon attempted to sound nonchalant, "Look, buddy. Slow down. It's a long story, and I need your help. Can I come up? I promise to explain everything."

"Sure." The door release sounded, allowing Jon and Kandi to go inside and up the stairs, where a very confused Marty Sullivan was standing outside his apartment door.

"Hey! Jonny boy! So, what..." Marty stopped cold when he noticed Kandi, "Whoa, who's this pretty little thing? She is major league!" Marty whistled in appreciation.

Jon laughed the comment off, "She's mine, buddy. Hands off." As if to support his statement, Jon pulled Kandi close, hoping to appear as a romantic gesture rather than to protect Marty from aggravated assault. Her muscles felt like coiled springs. "This is my friend, Kandi. Kandi, this is one of my pub quiz friends, Marty Sullivan." Jon began to fear that neighbors might see them. "Marty? Can we come inside?"

"Sure. Kandi? Really? I only thought strippers used that name!" Marty laughed at his joke, and Jon felt compelled to join in. Meanwhile, Kandi's grip on Jon's arm was reaching the point where Jon wasn't sure he would ever get full use of that hand again.

Marty continued in the living room, "So, does this mean you are over that whole 'shy among the ladies' routine, or were you ever? I always wondered if that was just a thing you used to pick up girls." He hit Jon in the shoulder as he laughed again.

Jon's face became suddenly serious, "Look, Marty, we need to talk about that stuff on the news. This may be hard to believe, but Kandi and I staged the whole thing in New York as a publicity stunt to draw attention to my show. Things sorta got out of hand. First, the cops showed up way too early. Then, the media blew the whole operation out of proportion. Finally, all that attention made the guards we hired pretend that Kandi overwhelmed them for real, as if this little girl could seriously hurt two grown men, right?" Jon winced as the pain in his hand and arm increased. "The whole thing was fun and games until the damn Feds got into the mix." Jon looked at his friend seriously, "Look, Marty, I was hoping you could put us up for a couple of days. We need the heat to cool off some and get a good lawyer before we can even begin straightening this mess out, okay?"

Marty's face reflected Jon's new mood, "Sure, no problem. You're in luck. My roommate's out of town. You can use his room."

Jon replied, "Perfect. Uh, Marty, I need you to forget we are here for a bit. Absolutely no one can know. Got it?"

Marty nodded, "I get it, Jon. Mums the word until you break the news. Hell, this is the most excitement I've had for years. If you need anything else, I'm here for you."

Jon began to relax, "Thanks. That's it for now. If you don't mind, we'll go back and get settled in."

Once behind closed doors, Kandi spoke, "I hope you aren't under the impression that I will follow you with adoring eyes. That is simply not going to happen!" The sarcasm dripped from her lips.

Jon caught himself chuckling, "No, of course not, but I can't have you killing my friends either. I had to play along, or he would have sensed that something was up. I assume I have Sara to thank for you not going ballistic back there."

Jon's supposition was correct, but Kandi ignored it, "He saw us. He knows we are here. That alone makes him a danger to the mission. What's to keep him from talking to the authorities or the media."

"His word, which should buy us until early next week. Once he's back at work, he'll probably let it slip. I doubt he'll be able to keep his mouth shut. Marty does love a good story, not to mention he seemed to like you a lot, and he could never resist talking about a pretty girl. Anyway, the story I told him *could* be true. Marty's talking can't hurt us. The story can only help – especially with the local media and police."

Kandi quieted, still angry but able to see some reason behind the ruse Jon had told. She never confirmed Jon's suspicions but was thankful Sara had calmed her while the two men talked. Sara and Kandi's mental conversation had likely saved Marty's life and Jon's arm. She thought, *Hard to believe that an AI who had never had any could teach someone to control their emotions.*

While Jon showered, Kandi took the opportunity to investigate the pack's contents. Inside was a lot of cash – several thousand dollars in hundreds, five VISA Travel Money cards, and a small leather pouch. When he returned from the shower, she asked, "What are these?" waving one of the cards.

"They're prepaid debit cards. I put five thousand dollars on each. Whenever I travel overseas, I use one. That way, I never have to convert currency in the countries I visit. They also have the benefit of being untraceable."

Kandi nodded, "This is a lot of money. I'm surprised you have so much readily available."

"Yeah. I'm afraid that's something I picked up from my father. Often, he had to travel on a moment's notice. Having the cards and some loose cash made that happen easily. The urgency is not as great for me, but the convenience is wonderful."

"And this?" Kandi held up the leather pouch.

Jon took the bag from the pixie, "Dad also taught me to keep a toiletry kit in the box. It has a shaver, some soap, and deodorant, all the trappings of civilization for those times when you didn't have time to pack well."

Kandi nodded and headed off to the bathroom. While Kandi enjoyed her shower, Sara was in awe of the experience. Everything about the shower was new to her. She delighted in the sensation of water flowing over her. The wings fascinated her the most. She had admired them via video input on many occasions, but to be able to flex them with a mental command was a heady experience.

Jon was sitting at a small table watching TV when Kandi returned. He casually turned toward her, "About time you finished. I'm surprised there's any hot water left for the rest of the building...." He stopped speaking when he realized his companion was utterly naked, beating the air with her near-black wings. Jon sputtered and choked, whipping his head back toward the television. His face was beet red, and he couldn't speak, causing Sara to communicate with her symbiotic host.

Kandi?

Yes.

I am sensing that Jon is uncomfortable.

Kandi was mildly amused. She had been observing the scene and knew precisely why Jon was uncomfortable. *If you want to talk to him about it, go ahead.*

Sara managed to move her eyes to where they focused on Jon before speaking, "Are you alright? Your face is flushed, your heart rate is elevated, and you appear to have breathing problems. You may be having a seizure."

Jon accidentally turned toward the voice and immediately returned attention to the TV before choking out a reply, "I'll be fine. Could you please put some clothes on?"

Sara didn't understand. "That would make no sense. Clothing would inhibit our ability to dry our wings properly."

Jon still stuttered in his discomfort, "Look. I am unaccustomed to having a naked woman, wings or no wings, in my room, and I find the situation disturbing."

With a bit of impishness in her voice, Kandi switched places with the confused AI and replied, "Please excuse Sara. She is still naïve and has no concept about species-specific mores. Nudity is not an issue on Aeden. Often, males and females bathe together comfortably. This bathroom is too small to extend my wings. I'll need to stand behind you until they dry." Kandi still seemed amused, whereas Jon found this anything other than amusing. "Human? I must ask. Have you never talked to a naked female before?"

Jon's response came easier knowing where she was, "Actually, before Friday, I had trouble even talking with a clothed female."

His response confused Kandi, "Until now, you haven't had a problem with me. Why is that?

Jon was slightly sarcastic in his response, "I don't know. Maybe because you aren't a human woman, or maybe because you tried to kill me; both are new experiences for me."

Sara was confused, so she asked, *Kandi?*

Yes.

What just took place?

Kandi mentally chuckled. *I believe our human companion finds my body sexually stimulating.*

Strange. Jon should be old enough to control that, shouldn't he? I've heard that elves and pixies do.

Appearances can be deceiving; they may look the same, but elves are generally older. Keep in mind that humans only live about seventy years. Besides, even elves mature at different times. Kandi remembered Dari and the incident that landed her here. Sara gasped as she captured the memory as it passed. She had no idea such things could happen, especially on the Institute grounds. Kandi was mildly shocked that Sara could "see" her memories and admonished herself to be more careful in the future.

Their conversation was interrupted by the appearance of Kandi and Jon's headshots on the afternoon news program. "...No further information is available on the abduction and disappearance of Mr. Jonathan Martyr of Braintree. Mr. Martyr, a noted Boston artisan, was in the middle of his first Manhattan showing when this unidentified woman took him bodily from the scene." The screen switched to CCTV footage of Kandi dragging Jon out of the studio while single-handedly dispatching the two guards to dream time. After repeating the encounter with the guards in slow motion a few times, the anchor continued, "Authorities quickly traced the pair to a point in Central Park where the trail went cold. A lengthy search has revealed no additional information. Central Park remains closed to all visitors while the investigation continues."

The screen changed to a mountain scene with a large crater in the middle of it. "In other news, a mysterious explosion at a mountaintop retreat has perplexed local and federal officials as they search for a possible cause. People heard the blast fifty miles away while the shock wave rattled windows ten miles away in Morrisville, Vermont. Authorities have confirmed two dead at the scene and three others seriously injured. More on this developing story later."

The newscaster droned on as Jon turned the TV off, reflecting on what he had heard, "Two federal agents are dead? Damn! This day just keeps getting better and better! Wonder how much time I'll get for just hanging around?"

Kandi put her spin on the event, "Two are dead. If they weren't looking for us before, they are now."

Jon nodded his agreement and added, "…with a vengeance."

Kandi's eyes shifted to the one thing that would give them away – the ring. She caught her breath when she realized the glove was no longer there. Jon saw the panic in her eyes and quickly intervened, "Don't worry. That damn glove was getting hot, so I cut it down to size while you were in the shower. See? The ring is still covered." He flashed his hand, which she could now see had a black strip around the fourth finger where the ring was. He continued, "Look, right now, we're safe. No one knows about our involvement in the Vermont thing except the Feds, and for whatever reason, they aren't talking about it. The best thing we can do is get a little rest. Then, we can talk about the next steps."

Marty had gone when they exited the room but had left them a key to the apartment along with the passcode for the street entrance downstairs. Jon led Kandi to a pub down the street, whose shadowy interior would hide them from inquiring eyes, and thought about what came next.

Near the end of the meal, Kandi asked, "Okay. What does your plan say we do now?"

Jon finished the last bites of his hamburger before replying, "Nothing. I'm an artist, not an action hero. I took the lead today because you looked pretty wrecked after your experience with your computer. It was fun, but my experience with this type of operation is limited to watching too many James Bond movies. In other words, my bag of tricks is empty, and we must start fresh. You said last night that the future of my world depends on you getting back to yours, so I am vested in your success. What must we do to make that happen?"

Kandi reflected for a moment. *Having the human here violates every part of my Watcher oath. How much should I tell him?* Then, she quietly responded, "I need to find a salvageable gate crystal, and if I could do this without you, I would, but I can't.

Jon paid the tab and walked with Kandi toward the door before asking, "What can I do?"

Kandi shook her head, "Maybe nothing. Maybe everything. I'm not sure. When we established Gaia as a human colony, the rumor was that Origen had designed the archangel's ring to power a gate and go anywhere or time. Your role will be to test that rumor, use your ring, and activate our way home. Sara and I have estimated that the best chances of finding one are at locations on the other side of the Atlantic, so that is where we shall go."

Jonathan tried his best to grasp the scope of what she was implying, "Seems that you are putting a lot of trust in my ability to command this thing," shaking his ring hand in the air, "So far, this jewel has been nothing but a nuisance. What if we find this gate, and nothing happens?"

Kandi whispered, "Then, I have failed; Sara and I will be exiled here for the rest of our lives, and both worlds will be doomed."

Jon said, "So...no pressure then. Of course, we must first find a way to get out of the United States while everyone in the country is looking for us."

Kandi offered him a small smile, "I think I may have a way."

United States Space Command
Cheyenne Mountain, Colorado

Colonel Forrester hesitated for just a moment before knocking on the door of his superior.

"Enter"

The colonel's hands shook slightly as he opened the door.

"Yes, Colonel?"

"Sir." Even though the man in the chair was not military, Forrester always felt that he needed to add the 'sir' when speaking to him. "You asked to be kept in the loop on our search for the Martyr boy and his companion."

"And?"

"Unfortunately, there is no news, sir. None of the radiation scans have spotted anything. He must have shielded it somehow."

"I agree. Have you read the report from our Vermont detachment?"

Forrester nodded that he had.

"Very thorough. Our Mr. Martyr apparently impersonated a doctor at the hospital the night of the explosion."

"That is what I understand, sir."

"Why?"

"Why, sir?"

"Yes, why? Here is a man on the run in the company of a woman who kidnapped him. Why go to the hospital in the first place? No one was injured; at least the emergency room staff saw no one. Only one nurse even spoke to him. Most importantly, no one spotted his kidnapper anywhere. Why? Why not turn himself over to the authorities if he were alone?"

"I don't know, sir. We know he was present at the Vermont house because of the signals from the stone. Perhaps he was afraid of what would happen to him. Maybe he feels responsible."

"Possibly, but I don't think so. Our team leader had the hospital do a complete audit of equipment and supplies. Do you know what they found?"

This time, Forrester was in the dark. "No, sir."

"A single lead-lined glove was missing from the radiology department, the same department our Mr. Martyr was supposedly the replacement doctor for."

Forrester did a mental head slap, "He's hiding the ring under lead gloves?"

"I believe that is a safe assumption."

"In that case, we won't be able to find him."

"Only one pathway is closed. We need to depend more on standard surveillance techniques now. They are slow but can still get the job done."

"In that case, I'd better get my team moving. Is there anything else, sir?"

"No, Colonel. You are dismissed."

Forrester left the room, closing the door quietly behind him. His face was reddened by the encounter, both by embarrassment and shame. Once the door closed, his supervisor got up from the desk, locked the door, and walked over to a blank wall. He considered, *Of course, there is another possible answer."*

He reached out and found the hidden stud, which, in turn, opened a secret room. This room had caused numerous questions during construction. The costs were excessive, but he ultimately got what he wanted: a small lead-lined chamber. He entered and waited for the door to close behind him.

Inside, there was only a tiny table and a small gold box on top of it. The commander heard a satisfying click as he opened the case, revealing twelve glowing red rings, with space for one more at the end. His thoughts continued, *Yes, that is a possibility that I cannot ignore. The ring may have accepted him. Unlikely, but if so, the situation has decidedly changed.*

The commander spoke to the air, "Well, Michael. I feel that you may have been a naughty boy. Of course, I knew of your liaison with the human woman, but I would never have believed that you, of all of us, would sire a child with her. Even so, the odds against one of your physical descendants possessing the ring after all this time are astronomical. Fortunately, your heir is clueless about what the ring does, isn't he? Too bad you couldn't pass that information down as well."

The man closed, locked the box, and reopened the door to his office. He glanced down at his right hand and smiled. The ring on his finger glowed blue.

Chapter 16 - Hope

After returning to Marty's apartment, Jon gave Kandi a quizzical look, "What do you mean you think you have a way?"

Kandi said, "Our mission plan included transporting scientists to the continental ridge between North America and Africa to do core studies. To facilitate that, we rented a boat."

The change in Kandi's vocal tone was apparent as Sara interrupted, "...it's called the *Voyager Templar*, a one-hundred-and-eighty-foot 2011 Heesen with a cruising speed of 13.7 knots."

Kandi flashed a mental jab at her companion, *Sara. You promised not to do that!*

Sorry.

"You have a what!" Jon exclaimed.

The pixie was shocked by the intensity of his response. She felt that he should be pleased, not angry, although she had no idea why she cared one way or the other. "We leased a boat and crew for six months, and since Boston was the closest port city to the house in Vermont, we positioned the boat in a harbor here for when we needed it."

Jon was still skeptical, "Boat? From what Sara described, this is a hell of a boat!" Kandi forgot her promise to use Jon's name, "Human, we needed a boat for fifteen scientists and engineers. What would you have suggested?"

Jon laughed, "I would have probably hired a cargo vessel for half the cost, but I get it. You couldn't have used a ski boat, could you? So, where did you stash this 'boat'?"

"The Boston Yacht Marina, slip three."

Jon whistled, "Of course you did. Only the swankiest place in the harbor." He began gathering belongings and putting them in one of the bags they had bought at Goodwill. "Okay, I guess we had better go and fetch our ride."

Kandi motioned him to stop, "I believe we should check out the marina first. We don't want any more surprises."

Jon wasn't convinced there was a need, "Why? No one knows we are here. If they did, they would've already collected us?"

Kandi was adamant, "True, they may not know about this place, but I am not taking the chance that they haven't connected the house in Vermont with the yacht. We only had time to establish a single line of credit to buy everything for the mission – house, supplies, cars…yacht."

Jon nodded, beginning to see where she was going with this.

Kandi continued, "Sara and I have underestimated your police several times on this mission. Fortunately for us, you did not. I don't want there to be a chance of making a similar mistake this time. We need to check out the boat. Is there a place where we can covertly observe the marina?"

Jon thought, then nodded, "Yes, a city park a short distance away should afford us a clear view of the marina and the pier, and it's not that far from here, an easy walk."

Jon left Marty a note indicating they were meeting with a lawyer and would probably be late. Kandi didn't understand why Jon needed to lie, and he didn't want to take the time to explain plausible deniability to her.

Jon noticed a pair of binoculars on the end table and grabbed them just in case, "Ready to go check out a marina?"

Some minutes later found them casually walking north on Atlantic Avenue toward the park entrance. Their heads were touching, and they looked like a young couple in love, taking advantage of a stroll in the moonlight, not a couple of conspirators hatching a plot.

Jon nudged her into turning right onto the park path. The foliage-covered trellises stretched the park's width and would lead them to the large open area opposite the pier and marina. About two-thirds of the way along the pathway, Jon guided Kandi onto a beautiful lawn overlooking the bay currently occupied by several couples oblivious to anyone else except each other. To their left were the lights of the pier and marina, where the yacht sat in its berth. The night was gorgeous. There was little wind, and the bay reflected the full moon in all its glory. Under other circumstances, Jon admitted that it would be a very romantic setting.

Together, they sprawled on the grass while Kandi and Sara analyzed every aspect of the pier, from the offices near the jetty to the Boston Yacht Haven Marina, where the *Voyager Templar* sat in slip three. After a few minutes, Kandi rolled over and talked to the sky before rolling over and talking to Jon. "We've got problems. Sara and I spotted several anomalies. Eight late-model cars are on the pier, each with a person standing outside. Additionally, I counted at least seven people walking back and forth on the pier at random intervals, but never less than four strategically placed near the boat's berth at any time. That can't be a coincidence."

Jon nodded, hating to admit that the pixie had been right in her suspicion, "I agree. So, what do we do?"

"A frontal assault is out of the question. I could probably handle the people with my body armor, but I lost that in Vermont. If I were alone, I would take the chance anyway, but I can't risk getting you killed or captured. After all, you are my ticket home. We need to find a way on board. Our luck will not hold much longer."

Jon leaned into her, "Even with the Saudi passports, that isn't going to be easy. The media has plastered our faces all over television. No matter how good our IDs are, the port authorities won't even check them; they'll lock us up until the Feds come and take us off their hands."

Suddenly, the main park entrance behind Jon caught Kandi's eye, particularly the police cars assembling there, lights ablaze. "Jon? We need to go. We need to leave now!"

A dozen patrolmen entered the lawn on the far end from where Jon and Kandi sat, pausing to check each couple against a photo the officers carried. Jon panicked, "How in the hell did they find us?"

"That doesn't matter. What matters is that the police don't capture us," Kandi responded, "Act like you haven't seen them. Get up slowly, and we'll walk away toward the marina."

"Won't that be just walking into the Fed's hands?"

"Possibly, but I'm certain the local police have covered all the entrances to the park from the south." They slowly picked themselves up and moved away from the officers. "Once we reach a cross street, we turn away from the water. Sound good?"

Jon was unsure, "Hell, no, it doesn't sound good. I don't know if I can do this."

Kandi remained calm, "You'll be fine. Just keep putting one foot in front of the other."

Just as they thought they had gotten away, a shout came from behind them. Kandi didn't even look. She knew that the yell was meant for them, "Run!"

Kandi was in far better shape than her companion and quickly had a commanding lead. Jon tried calling her but was already gasping for air, and nothing came out. He didn't know how much longer he could keep this up. Suddenly, he didn't have to worry. Jon's body wasn't his own anymore. Nothing worked. His arms and legs spasmed with pain, and what had been forward motion was now a face plant on the lawn. Jon had been tased.

Kandi didn't stop until she reached a building whose shadows covered the street. Only then did she look behind her, just in time to see the police lift Jon from the ground and help him toward a waiting police cruiser. Despite her efforts, Jon was in the hands of the authorities. What was she going to do now?

Chapter 16 - Captured

Jon was still twitching in the back seat, suffering the after-effects of being tased, which made the ride to the police station a quiet one. The officer in the front seat didn't even attempt to converse with him – way out of his pay grade. Besides, any conversation with the prisoner might complicate things with the detectives at the station, which wouldn't bode well for the patrolman's future. He wasn't sure what this guy had done, but his running when told to stop meant that the man had probably done something against the law. If not, the officer figured that vomiting in the back of a squad car was reason enough to take him to the station.

The night had been quiet in the precinct, so Jon's booking took only a few minutes, and the next thing he knew, he was in a cell alongside a couple of hookers and drunks who only gave him a sidelong glance. The only uncomfortable moment was when the booking officer attempted to remove his ring, to no avail. The officer wasn't happy but had no choice but to allow Jon to keep it.

Jon looked around the cell. He figured that with everything that had transpired, he should get comfortable. Once the police discovered everything he had been up to, they would probably decide to throw away the key. Jon's world changed when a detective walking past the cells happened to glance his way and did a double-take. After that, things got pretty exciting.

Suddenly faced with tasing a well-known victim rather than a perpetrator, the officers fell over themselves, apologizing for the incident, hoping and praying that there was no fallout. They escorted him from the cell to an interrogation room, giving him free access to a bathroom and refreshments. Then, since kidnapping fell under federal jurisdiction, they alerted the FBI about Jon's surfacing in Boston. At first, Jon was confused about the change in his situation. What about all the things he had done over the past two days? Why was he being treated so well?

Slowly, Jon realized the truth. Boston PD had no idea about his connection to the Vermont cabin, which allowed him to breathe a little easier. From their perspective, he was still the victim here. Suddenly encouraged by his change in status, he asked when he could go home, only to be told the FBI wanted to talk to him before he left. The girl that escaped had several charges pending – kidnapping as well as assault and battery. They were sure that Jon would want to aid in her capture. What could he do but agree?

About an hour later, the FBI arrived with a thousand questions about his kidnapping in New York and how he had come to Boston. Jon made several noticeable mistakes when cross-examined by the agents and realized that the ruse he had given to Marty wouldn't work with skilled investigators, so he opted to tell the truth – more or less.

The next questions were easy, "Mr. Martyr, had you met this woman before the gallery showing?"

"No, I had never seen her before."

"Jon, may I call you Jon?" Jon nodded his assent. "Several witnesses overheard the woman telling you that she needed you. Was that true?"

"Yes. K..." Jon stopped himself before saying her name, "She approached me out of the blue and said she needed me."

"Why?"

Here, Jon had to lie a bit. "I don't know why. She never told me."

"We were able to trace you from the gallery to Central Park, where we lost your trail. Where did you go from there?"

The lies got more extensive, yet surprisingly more believable, "I have no idea. We got in a car, and...she must have given me something because I was in Boston the next thing I knew. She demanded that I get her money." He related how he had emptied his safety deposit box on Saturday morning, which he knew they could readily verify. Jon believed he was home free when a knock on the door and a short argument out in the hallway abruptly terminated the interview.

Jon's relief was short-lived as two new men entered and presented themselves as NSA agents. Jon's anxiety skyrocketed as he looked at the newcomers. These guys looked like they were chiseled out of stone, not to mention they probably knew a lot more about current events than the two FBI guys. Their superiors would have fully briefed them about the happenings of the past twenty-four hours. Jon paled as he realized they might even have known the guys involved in the cabin explosion.

The two agents got down to business. They closed the blinds to the hallway and turned off the camera and microphone. Whatever they discussed here, there would be no permanent record. As Jon expected, the conversation shifted immediately from New York to the house in Vermont.

"Mr. Martyr. I want the truth – all the truth. No lies: trust me, I'll know if you are lying. Understand?"

Jon willed his head to nod yes.

"Excellent, Mr. Martyr. Now, I'm not interested in what happened in New York. I'd like to know what happened after your portal transfer to the cabin?"

Jon was visibly startled. Do they know how he got there? There wasn't even a bit of hesitation in the agent's voice; he just accepted the fact. Jon answered, "I'm sorry; what's a portal transfer?"

The agent smiled slightly, "Mr. Martyr, don't waste my time. You went from Central Park to upstate Vermont in less than a second. Do you honestly expect me to believe you didn't ask your captor about that?"

"OK, but…"

"Mr. Martyr. How you got there is not the question. What we are trying to determine are your movements afterward. Most importantly, where your accomplice is right now."

Jon was shocked. The agent talked about portal transfers as everyday occurrences, yet it appeared he and his associates didn't use them. They still used vehicles to get around. They still required time to do so. What shocked Jon more was the agent's use of the word accomplice to describe himself.

"Look. I wasn't her accomplice. She kidnapped me!" Jon tried to sound confident, but the words came out in a squeak.

The agent smirked and continued, "My apologies. What alerted your...abductor to our pursuit?"

Jon carefully told him how Kandi had been watching the news and was spooked by how quickly the police showed up at the gallery and about the cameras in town and on the road. Afraid of being captured, Kandi set the self-destruct and forced him into the car. He intentionally omitted the parts about Sara and the pixie merging and then losing consciousness. He didn't see any reason to complicate matters more than they were.

The agent sat back in his chair, "See? That wasn't so hard. Now, why did she stop at the hospital in Morrisville?" The agent asked the question like he knew the answer, so Jon stuck to the truth as much as possible.

"The woman figured out that there was some kind of locator in my ring. She stopped at the hospital so I could go in and steal a lead-lined glove."

"Why did you go inside alone instead of both of you together?"

This part of the story was a little more difficult to side-step. "The woman told me she was afraid to be recognized. She said she would kill everyone inside unless I did as she said. I had seen the house blow up. I was afraid. She seemed crazy." Jon tried his best to sound convincing.

The interview continued tracking his movements up to his apprehension at Columbus Park. That, too, Jon blamed all on Kandi. He insisted that he feared for his life the entire time until the point when she ran away from the authorities. He pointed out the bruises on his neck and arm where Kandi had grabbed him as proof.

The questions stopped. One of the men exited the room, phone in hand. When he returned, he told Jon, "Mr. Martyr. I have just spoken to my superiors. We agree that your life appears to be in imminent danger. Your presence as a witness to these events makes it imperative that you remain in protective custody until this person is apprehended."

Jon could tell they were lying; call it what you will; he was a prisoner, a canary in a gilded cage.

As the agents escorted Jon out the precinct doors, a swarm of media people came out of nowhere and swamped them. Microphones sprouted like weeds in spring as cameras flashed and TV mobile studios broadcasted live. Apparently, someone at the police station had leaked the news, and even in the middle of the night, the return of a high-profile kidnappee demanded immediate attention. The cameras flustered the agents, who shielded their faces as they pushed Jon through the crowd and into the waiting vehicles. The agents packed him into a waiting SUV and sped off. In their haste to leave the swarm of reporters behind, they hadn't noticed the small sedan that followed them at a discreet distance.

United States Space Command, Cheyenne Mountain, Colorado

The commander was at his desk when the call came, "Yes?"

"Sir, this is Colonel Forrester. Boston just notified me that we have the man in our custody. What are your orders?"

The commander attempted to hide his excitement, "Excellent, Colonel. Do you know if he is still wearing the object?"

The colonel smiled, "Yes. I had our people check. Although attempts to remove it have still proven unsuccessful."

The commander understood, "Yes, I would imagine they would. Did your agent happen to report what color the ring was?"

"No, sir. The agent didn't want to remove the ring's cover. He claimed Martyr got pretty agitated." Forrester wondered about the point of the question.

"Interesting. Colonel? Who caught him?"

"Local Boston PD. They were doing a sweep through one of the parks for an armed robber and his accomplice. The man and his companion were spooked, believed they were the targets of the search and started running. BPD tased him. She got away. Once they identified him, they contacted the FBI. One of our people in the Bureau contacted us right away."

The commander stroked his chin absently, "Hmm. Too bad the locals caught him first. It would have been much simpler if we had. Now, we have to play by their rules. There is no reason to detain Mr. Martyr. He is still considered the victim, after all. We know of his connection to the whole Vermont affair, but we don't want that public now, do we?"

"No, sir."

"Alright, let's do this. Tell the locals we have reason to believe the woman brainwashed him and that you're going to put him in protective custody until we capture the girl. I'm sure they will agree."

"Yes, sir. Consider it done."

"Thank you, Colonel. As always, keep me posted."

"Sir?" Forrester dared a question.

"Yes."

"Why is the girl important? The man was our target, wasn't he?"

"The girl represents an unexpected shift in the case. A wild card if you will. Her importance has risen so that her very existence threatens our project."

"I understand. We'll get her, sir."

"I know you will, Colonel."

Chapter 17 - Aftermath

Kandi slumped to the alleyway pavement, dazed and confused. Adrenaline flowed through her veins, making every sound and movement something to react to. She replayed the last hour in her mind, trying to find something she had missed that had led to the colossal screw-up surrounding her. One minute, she and Jon had been calmly discussing options on retaking the yacht from the Feds, only to be surrounded by police before they finished. Then, the desperate exodus from the park. She had sworn Jon was behind her, never dawning on her that his physical condition was not up to the task. Now, he was gone, captured by the very police they had been so careful to avoid.

Kandi wallowed in self-pity. Her chances of success, finding a gate and making it operational, had never been good, but now, with Jon in the hands of the authorities, her and Sara's odds of ever getting home and setting things right were virtually nonexistent. She realized she had no idea what to do next. Her mind, known at the Institute for its tactical wizardry, was a jumbled mess.

Sara also experienced anxiousness over the recent turn of events. She, too, analyzed every detail of tonight's operation as only an AI could and found no logical error in their process other than Jon's lack of stamina...unless Jon's friend had sold them out.

She passed her suspicions on to Kandi. They realized neither had seen Jon's note, so they had no idea what he had told Marty. Did Jon tell him where they were going? The inference was damning. Despite Jon's assurances, could Marty have turned them over to the police? There was insufficient data to support the accusations, but the circumstantial bits were pretty convincing, so she decided to find out.

The electronic keypad at the street entrance to the apartment wasn't a problem. Sara had seen the slip of paper that Marty had left and remembered everything on it, including the codes. They were inside within seconds. Access to Marty's apartment, however, was another story. Jon had Marty's spare key, and Kandi didn't want to alert anyone inside to their presence by knocking. She solved the issue by slamming both fists into the door, splintering the frame, and propelling it across the room and against the opposing wall. She was not in the mood for subtlety and didn't give a damn about showing what she could do.

A rattled Marty peeked in from the kitchen, not knowing what to expect. At first, he was relieved when he saw Kandi standing in the entryway, "Kandi? What in the hell's going..." Marty never knew what hit him. Moving at the inhuman speed she had displayed in the gallery, Kandi slammed him against the splintered door, pinning him with one hand while putting the other over his mouth to ensure his silence.

She tilted her head toward the back of the apartment, "Is there anyone else here?" Marty, who earlier had looked at this woman with desire, now had only fear in his eyes as he shook his head no. Kandi continued, "I don't have any time for nonsense. If you lie to me, you will die. Do you understand?" This time, Marty frantically moved his head up and down in the affirmative. Kandi relaxed her grip just a bit, "Good. I will keep this short since I'm certain your neighbors have already called the police, and I'd imagine their response time is about four minutes. Why did you turn us in?"

Marty was confused. "I don't know what you're talking about! I just got home a few minutes ago and found Jon's note." Marty gestured at the paper on the end table. Kandi scooped it up, scanned it, and returned it to its place. The note only indicated that he and Kandi were meeting an attorney – he didn't mention the location. Kandi relaxed a little more. If Marty wasn't the leak, then....

Trying to recover, Marty stuttered, "OK, Kandi, what gives? Why the third degree? How did you do that to my door? Is there a problem? Where's Jon?" The rapid-fire list of questions only enhanced his anxiety.

Kandi relaxed her grip, "We don't have time to discuss. Suffice it to say that our situation is more complicated than Jon indicated. Telling you the truth would have put you in extreme danger. Jon wouldn't risk that, and neither would I. Eventually, the authorities will trace us back to you. The more you know, the more danger you will face. So long as they see you as 'just innocently helping a friend,' you should have no problem. Now, I am afraid that I need your help. I must find him, and I have no idea where they might have taken him."

Marty paused momentarily while rubbing his throat, "Where were you when they caught him?"

Kandi answered, "I believe it was a place called...Columbus Park?"

Marty continued, "OK. If they took him from Columbus Park, the nearest precinct would be A-1. It's about four blocks due west of the park on Sudbury." Marty proceeded to give directions to the station, surprised that Kandi wasn't writing anything down.

When Marty had finished, Kandi looked him in the eyes. "I will need your car." Kandi's tone of voice left no room for argument. Marty handed the keys to the crazed woman before him, "It's a white Honda Civic parked down the block on the street." Marty continued, "Look, Jon's case is pretty high profile. A little publicity can't hurt. I've got a buddy who works for the local TV. Do you want me to give him a call? It might create a diversion for whatever you have planned."

Kandi could see where a little confusion might help her free Jon at the station. Since she had no plan, any interference could be helpful, so she nodded her assent. Marty made the call and turned back toward her. "Made his day. Newsrooms are terrible with secrets, though. Spies from other media outlets are everywhere. Something like this will spread like wildfire. So, what happens now?"

Kandi looked at him apologetically, "Jon was right. You are a good friend. I apologize for what I must do, but this must look real." She then walloped him, slamming his head against the wall and knocking him unconscious. Then, almost as an afterthought, she ran to the back room, recovered their backpacks of cash and clothing, and ran down the street to where the little car waited. Had she looked in the rearview mirror as she sped away, she would have seen flashing lights as they topped the hill.

Chapter 18 – Midnight Extraction

The cookie-cutter room at the Holiday Inn Express on I-95 wasn't the Ritz by a long shot, but Jon had stayed in a lot worse, and it was undoubtedly a giant step above the jail cell he had recently vacated. The two goons outside his door looked military, formidable even in civilian clothing. Although he hadn't seen any others, he was sure his captors weren't taking any chances and had others scattered around the complex. He knew that 'protective custody' was a ruse. This was a trap, and he was the bait. They wanted Kandi.

Outside his twelfth-floor window, traffic moved like ants down on the interstate. Jon hoped that Kandi and Sara were far away from here. Still, he couldn't help but wonder how they were and what they were doing. Were they working out a plan to succeed without him, or were they sitting in a jail cell? Jon thought, *No. Kandi wouldn't allow herself to be captured. She would kill herself first.* He looked down at the ring on his finger, the black glove fragment hiding its glow. He knew that if she could, she would be back for him. Kandi would move heaven and earth to get the stone, and he and the ring were a package deal.

While Jon was musing over her fate, Kandi stood in the shadows below beside Marty's car, looking up at the Holiday Inn Express. She had found the police precinct by following a patrol car going back to base only moments before the agents plowed through reporters and put Jon in an SUV. Even though the agents took action to hide their trail, Kandi found it child's play to follow them to the hotel.

Observing the building from the outside, Kandi could see two agents by the front door, probably one or two outside his room. Sara figured a high probability of other agents covering the other exits and the lobby. Kandi stared at the wall of windows in front of her, wondering where Jon's room would be. A few seconds later, Sara matter-of-factly stated, "He's on the twelfth floor."

Kandi was confused, "How can you be so sure?"

"Look at each floor and tell me what you see."

"Room lights, and...Oh!"

"Exactly. Every floor has multiple rooms illuminated except the twelfth. There, only one room has any lights at all."

"Sara, you are amazing." As a security precaution, it made perfect sense for the agents to clear the floor where Jon was.

Sara continued, "Now, we must figure out how to get to him. With all the exits covered...Kandi? ... You understand there is only one logical reason to keep Jon in Boston, right? They want to catch you."

"Yes, Sara. This game has become much more important to them than the ring alone. I'm afraid there will be significant resistance to my taking Jon."

Sara agreed, "Yes. The probability of physical violence involving serious injury and loss of life is 98.4%."

Kandi grinned slightly at the possibility of doing some serious damage but then calmed herself. "There is another option other than a frontal assault. They have my picture, so they know what I look like, but there is a good chance that, even if their superiors know the truth, the agents don't know WHAT I am. Being a pixie gives me options others wouldn't have."

A short time later, Jon sat in front of the television, not watching, just letting the noise wash over him and maybe dozing a little, too tired to stay awake and yet too wound up to go to bed. In his semi-awake state, he heard a soft tapping at the window. At first, Jon ignored it, but the sound persisted, its volume increasing until Jon finally turned toward the glass. Outside in the night was something that convinced him he was dreaming. A naked Kandi, wings fully extended, hovered one hundred and twenty feet off the ground, just outside his twelfth-floor room.

Jon was transfixed, his mind refusing to accept what he saw– he had to be dreaming. Although, he had to admit that, as dreams went, this one was pretty darn good. Her body was exquisite, more perfect than he had imagined it that evening outside the gallery or even her earlier brief exposure in the room at Marty's place. Now, her wings had to be fifteen feet across, like black lace, moving effortlessly back and forth to keep her afloat. *Too bad she's on the other side of the glass,* Jon mused.

The pixie, however, watched Jon's reaction and was not amused. She slapped the glass hard, shaking him out of his reverie. Kandi motioned him to move back from the window toward the door. When he had complied, she backed up, built up speed, and rammed the glass, shattering it across the room's interior while she followed behind, wings compressing along her back as she entered. She immediately grabbed and held him tightly to her chest. A second later, she leaped from the window, wings expanding as the agents outside beat on the door before breaking in with their weapons drawn.

Kandi didn't have time to worry about the men and their guns. She had a bigger problem to deal with. Jon was heavy! Kandi had known humans lacked the hollow bone structures of her people but had no idea that he weighed this much. Her wings could easily carry her weight plus about sixty pounds, but Jon was at least three times that.

She banked her wings toward where she had left the car before realizing they wouldn't make it. With Jon on her chest, there was no way a ground impact wouldn't hurt or kill him. Then Kandi saw the dumpster off to the right. Making a minor adjustment, she waited until the last instant to release Jon, his trajectory landing him safely in the mostly full container. Then, Kandi put on the brakes, fanning her wings frantically in an attempt to slow her approach. She almost made it. At this speed, there was no way to stop in time. Kandi simply couldn't bank her wings enough. A large brick building rose in front of her. At that point, she was still moving at a fair clip, and, as tough as she was, she was no match for the wall. The pain of impact was diffused by her loss of consciousness.

Kandi awakened to find Jon driving the white sedan along I-95. "Hey, girl! Good to see you back with us. I was beginning to get worried. I'd checked your breathing before I put you in the car but wasn't sure about any other injuries. You do have a few cuts and scrapes, though." Adrenaline coursed through his veins.

Kandi looked around, "How did you...."

"I recognized Marty's car." Jon paused, "He's OK, isn't he?" Kandi nodded while checking for broken bones with her hands. "Cool. Anyway, I found your clothing in the back seat along with the keys, and here we are. By the way, nice save back there. Watching you hover outside the window was amazing."

"What about the agents at the hotel?"

"From over your shoulder, I saw them standing slack-jawed before the broken glass. It wasn't until you dumped me that I saw them raise their weapons. I don't remember them ever firing. So, what's the next part of the plan?"

"There isn't one."

"What? The whole plan was to crash into the hotel and steal me away?"

"Yes. I honestly believed we would both die in the process."

That statement sobered Jon up in a hurry. He had never even contemplated that the two of them would die. "Well, I'm glad we didn't go out in a blaze of glory. How are you doing? Anything broken?"

"No, but I think I left a significant part of my skin on that building back there."

"You'll recover. By the way, your body heals fast! Most of your bleeding had scabbed over before I got you to the car. Is that due to the nanites?"

Kandi nodded, "They greatly speed up repairs to our bodies. Unfortunately, they do nothing for the pain."

He said more soberly, "Sorry that you hurt, but we need to do something other than drive down an open road. I have an idea if you are open to it."

"I will consider your suggestion," She groaned.

"First of all, the matter of getting off the streets. Hookers and druggies frequent some no-name motels on Boston's south side. They always make the news, but so long as no one dies, the cops pretty much leave them alone. We can hide there for a few hours while we plan."

Jon didn't take long to find such a place – The Snooze Lodge. It was perfect for their purposes as the parking lot was behind the building, away from the street. As promised, this was a pretty dingy place. The guy behind the desk never looked up, exchanging a key for a hundred-dollar bill – no registration needed, questions asked, or change offered. In his mind, couples like this were best not remembered. That suited Jon just fine.

Just after nine the following day, Jon wandered over to a pawn shop they had passed going to the motel and bought a used laptop and a pre-paid phone, so happy that Kandi had thought to grab the backpacks before leaving Marty's place. Then, outside the North End Branch of the Boston Public Library, Jon and Kandi connected with the library's free Wi-Fi.

While Kandi typed, Jon asked, "Are you certain the captain will check his email?"

Kandi looked at him, "No. Nothing about humans is certain, but when we rented the yacht, we established this email account to use in case of a change in plans. He is supposed to check that account every day at noon. Since we are several days late, he should be checking daily."

"Perfect. Tell the captain that the ship must leave at tomorrow morning's high tide. He can tell the port authority that his clients are no-shows, and he has another charter."

Kandi smiled and typed the email as he had said. When she had finished, he took over the laptop and connected to the Norwegian Cruise Line website, where he ordered two tickets for tomorrow's sailing to the Bahamas. He used their forged Saudi credit cards and when asked, submitted pictures of their passport info taken with the computer's camera. Now, they just had to go back to the hotel, wait for the morning, and pray that Marty had not reported the car as stolen when the police had shown up. Neither he nor Kandi liked the plan. There were just too many ways it could fail and very few where it would succeed.

United States Space Command
Cheyenne Mountain, Colorado

Colonel Forrester was visibly agitated as he marched down the long hallway. His call last night from the team watching the Martyr boy was infuriating. The fact that Martyr escaped could be dealt with, but the possibility it could have been avoided was another thing altogether. Forrester had anticipated the woman would somehow locate Martyr and attempt a rescue. After all, that was his plan. Capture the girl when she made the attempt. Where he failed was assuming she would need at least a day to locate the holding area and plan her assault, which she didn't. Even with the accelerated timeline, his people should have been able to subdue her at one of the hotel entry points. Even then, it was the manner of the assault that infuriated him. They hadn't enough information to predict her point of attack. Hell, he wasn't sure he believed what the girl had done.

The colonel was now standing in front of his superior's office. Without knocking, he barged in to find the commander calmly sitting at his desk like nothing was wrong. "Sir, we need to talk," Forrester demanded.

The commander seemed non-plussed by the officer's brash entrance, "I'm sorry, Colonel. You have me at a disadvantage. What do we need to talk about?"

"Sir, the female suspect launched a successful aerial assault on the hotel last night."

"Yes. I received the report of the Martyr boy's escape. Unfortunate." The commander was infuriatingly calm.

Forrester allowed his aggravation to creep into his voice, "Sir, you don't seem surprised by any of this, while the rest of us were shocked as hell. What was that creature who flew up to his room last night because it sure wasn't a human female?"

"Ahh, right to the point. Tell me, Colonel, how much do you know about our project?"

Forrester relaxed slightly at the change of topic, "Only that it carries the highest security clearances. Even then, information is on a 'need to know' basis. From what I've been read in on, it will completely overturn our preconceptions about space exploration. If all goes to plan, it will allow us to go to another world without using rockets or thousands of years to do so."

The commander smiled, "Good. That's enough for starters. Colonel, what I'm about to tell you must be kept in the strictest confidence. Telling anyone outside this room would be an act of treason. Do you understand?"

The colonel nodded his assent.

"That woman last night was a being from such a world."

Colonel Forrester couldn't believe it. "Are you serious? An alien, here, now?"

"Colonel. Don't act so surprised. After all, we are building the foundation to send people to other worlds, possibly hers. Why shouldn't we assume that other civilizations could potentially send their people here?"

Their conversation continued for several minutes while the commander gave Colonel Forrester a briefing on Aeden and its life forms - pixies, elves, and, yes, even fairies.

Forrester took a few minutes to respond, "Sir, how did you come by this information?"

The commander replied, "Space Force accumulated the data from micro drones sent to the their planet during the infancy of our portal project. We wanted to know as much as possible before proceeding."

The colonel wasn't sure he believed all of it, but the commander's explanation went a long way toward making sense of what his men had reported. He shook his head. A pixie had taken Martyr from the room, possibly the same person who had taken him from the gallery. As the colonel stood there, the commander reiterated, "Colonel. No one else on your team has a need to know, understood?"

"Understood, sir."

Later that evening, Colonel Forrester was attending a party at the Air Force Academy when his phone rang using the tone reserved for emergencies. Excusing himself, he walked out onto the veranda and answered.

"Forrester here."

"Sir, we have a hit on the fugitives."

"I'm listening."

"They have booked passage on the *Norwegian Pearl* out of Boston. The liner leaves in the morning for the Caribbean."

"Are you certain that it's them?"

"Yes, sir. The cruise lines require all international passengers to upload a copy of their passports to speed up departure proceedings. Facial recognition picked them out right away."

"I see."

"Also, sir, Boston Port Authority notified us that the *Voyager Templar* is returning to Bermuda in the morning. The yacht's Captain claims his client failed to show up and has another waiting. Of course, we can't verify if that is true. AI projections show a high probability that the pair intends to meet up with the yacht there."

"Okay. Advise the team on the pier to go down and inspect the yacht – stem to stern. Have the agents present themselves as customs personnel following up on a smuggling tip. Tell them to pull up every deck plank if they think it's necessary. I want to ensure our targets aren't trying to pull a fast one. If the yacht checks out, station three people near there and send the others to surveil the Norwegian departure area. Understood?"

"Yes, colonel. I'll see to it, sir."

The colonel disconnected the line, smiled, and returned to the party. The alien and her pet human had made a fatal error in thinking the false IDs would fool him. He would leave the party shortly and take a private jet to the east coast. Tomorrow was shaping up to be a great day.

Chapter 19 - Leaving

Jon and Kandi had many plans for the next day, none involving a Caribbean cruise. They first drove Marty's car to Massachusetts General Hospital, where they parked it in the tower garage. With the constant coming and going of patients and visitors, Jon felt it would take days for hospital security to find it, let alone report it to the police. Eventually, he was confident they would connect the car to Marty and return it. Jon reminded himself to give Marty something nice for Christmas.

The "T" trip to South Station and the subsequent bus ride to the Boston Cruiseport went without incident. As Jon had hoped, vacationers in brightly colored clothes packed the bus headed toward the *Norwegian Gem* and the warm Caribbean waters in Bermuda. Their excitement was contagious. Jon almost wished they were going along. As he and Kandi reached the Trade Center stop, they firmly pushed their way toward the exit. Then, as the door opened, they ducked and slipped away unseen.

A short walk later, they arrived at Fan Pier, where Jon was delighted that the water taxi he ordered was docked and ready to go. "Hey, skipper!" Jon forced his voice to sound happy and carefree as he addressed the sole occupant of the small boat in front of him. "I think we're your 9 o'clock."

"Good to see ya," the skipper replied, putting his cigarette in a bucket of sand. "I'm Jack Ferguson, cap'n of this wreck, and you are…" He checked his appointment slip, "…Michael and Julie Anderson. Nice to meet you." Only a few passengers traveled this early on a Sunday morning, and the taxi's skipper felt lucky to be hired. "So, Where we headed, Mike?"

"Going up to Sargent's Wharf," Jon said as he paid the fare. The destination was just past the marina, where the yacht was. If the yacht's captain had been successful, his boat would be just now leaving on its way downstream, and Jon and Kandi would be able to see them soon. At that point, Jon would negotiate a change in destination with Captain Jack.

The skipper had barely begun his spiel about the historical significance of the harbor before he realized his passengers weren't listening. Their interest seemed to be on the other side of the taxi, away from the city proper.

Kandi's eyes were far better than Jon's, even without Sara's AI-enhanced abilities, and she carefully scanned each boat in the downstream channel. Several boats were taking advantage of the tide and making their way to the open sea. She knew they would only get one shot at this – no time for mistakes. Soon, she nudged Jon with her elbow and pointed upstream. "There's our ride."

The taxi's skipper watched as the man, Mike, made his way to the helm. "What can I do for you, son?" he asked warily.

Jon replied quickly, "Cap'n, how would you like to make extra money on this fare?"

Now, the skipper was no fool. From the beginning, he had deja vu about these two. He knew them from somewhere, but the 'where' was evading him, "What did you have in mind, Mike? I'm not a rule freak, but I'm not into smuggling or anything too illegal. Hell, I'm too damn old to go to jail, so if it's somethin' like that, you just put that idea out of your head, and we'll pretend you never said anything."

"No, sir. Nothing like that. What I'm asking might be a little strange, but not illegal. You see that yacht up ahead off the starboard bow." Jon pointed toward the *Voyager Templar*. The skipper nodded but said nothing. Jon continued, "Well, the missus and I must get aboard that ship. The crew is expecting us. We're not talking hijacking or anything like that; however, others don't want us there and would do anything to keep us away. I was wondering if I could convince you to pull up on her port side and drop us off on her stern? We could make the side trip worth your while."

Now, the skipper spoke, "And if I don't."

Jon replied with a steeled voice, "I'll be honest with you, Jack. We're pretty desperate. If that is your decision, we'll have to tie you up and steer the taxi ourselves. After we meet up with the yacht, we'll set you adrift and hope you don't crash into anything." Jon caught the older man looking at him as a possible adversary, "Oh, don't question our ability to restrain you. I assure you that we would have no trouble doing exactly that."

The skipper looked at Jon and then at Kandi, thinking over his options. "Well, now. So long as you don't tell me what you're up to, I don't see anything that would be illegal. Just two folks going to visit some friends, right?" A sudden flash of recognition hit the skipper. He knew where he had seen them before, "Of course, with your faces plastered all over the news the past few days, I could be wrong."

Damn, Jon thought; *I was counting on him not being into the nightly news.* Kandi moved to the captain's side, ready to restrain the man if necessary. The skipper was impressed by the way she moved. He realized that the woman had done this before. He had looked at the man as a possible adversary. He realized he would have been wrong.

Jon jumped in before the situation got out of hand. "Look, everything is fine. The news has the story all wrong." Jon gave him the thirty-second version of the lie he had told his buddy, Marty, including the part about lying low for a few days. At the end of the tale, the skipper looked up at him, "Okay, I'll take you. Your problems are your problems, and I don't need to be involved. You made mention of a "tip" for my services?"

A few minutes later, five-hundred dollars changed hands as the water taxi pulled up parallel to the stern of the *Templar*. Close up, the yacht dwarfed the other boat, with the fantail being the only thing close to the same height as the taxi's deck. The *Voyager Templar* slowed, and the taxi reversed her engine as they approached each other. In the two-second gap when the two boats matched speed, the fugitives tossed themselves and their bags over the gap between the vessels. They rolled across the deck, shielded from the shore by the railing. The taxi pulled away as if nothing had taken place.

Jon and Kandi crawled off the open-air fantail to the relative shelter of the aft salon and into the legs of the yacht's captain, quite amused at the activity on his deck but carrying a Beretta in his right hand just in case. "Captain Roger Stilman, at your service."

Kandi and Jon stood, cautious of the windows in the salon. The captain commented, "The glass is one way. They can't see inside. I have found my clients prefer it that way. Kandi smiled nervously, "Hello. I am Aisha Noor, and this is my husband, Ahmad." She handed him the Saudi passports they carried. "We wanted to thank you for allowing us this unusual boarding. Is the weapon necessary?"

Something about the two bothered the captain, but he buried his reaction behind his rehearsed smile, "Your email indicated that you had your reasons, and you knew the agreed-upon security codes. That was enough for me. U.S. Customs did an unannounced inspection of the vessel about two hours ago - they were very thorough. I was afraid the *Templar* wouldn't be seaworthy when they were done. Might I assume that their presence had something to do with your change of plans?"

Kandi continued, "That would be correct. Agents of the United States Government are actively looking for us."

Jon was shocked. *What the hell! Why is she telling him that?*

The captain, however, was not bothered by the revelation; in fact, her honesty convinced him to lower his gun just a little. "I see. When you contracted with us, your representatives indicated something like this might occur, but I had been told the odds were quite low. I also believed we would have fifteen passengers, not two."

Kandi never batted an eye, "We have to adapt to the times. When you first contracted with Aeden Corporation, you indicated that you weren't beneath bending a few laws. Has that changed?"

The captain smiled, "No, Mrs. – Noor. Nothing has changed. You paid twice our normal rate – more than enough to ensure confidentiality and a certain degree of "flexibility." I'm going to assume we aren't participating in an act of terrorism."

"No terrorism. No smuggling unless you count the two of us. There is, however, a change in destination. The original plan was to go to the mid-Atlantic rift for scientific observations. Now, we need to go a bit farther. We will, of course, compensate you and your crew for your trouble."

The captain's smile disintegrated, and a severe façade replaced it as he leveled the gun once more at his guests. "Where do you need to go?"

"You will set course for London via the Isle of Skye."

Not seeing anything threatening in the request, the captain lowered his gun again. "A little late in the season to be sightseeing, isn't it?" Something about the pair seemed very familiar, which bothered him more than the cloak-and-dagger routine. "London will take about two and a half weeks. We have plenty of fuel, and since we planned for a much larger complement of passengers, food and water shouldn't be a problem."

Kandi nodded. "Good. Additionally, don't be surprised if you are boarded and searched by the U.S.

Coast Guard again before we enter international waters. The people looking for us are single-minded in their attempts to find us. I'm sure they will try again. Would you have a space on board where Ahmad and I could hide – perhaps a special place they didn't discover on their last visit?"

The captain often accommodated clients desiring to be invisible to the authorities. He smiled, "The Coast Guard and the *Templar* are old friends. She has just the place for you. Please, follow me." He led the way to a stateroom near the bow of the boat. The room was plush. One wall was composed entirely of sliding windows, allowing full access to the deck.

The captain didn't waste time showing them the cabin but instead walked to the opposite wall. Finding a notch in the paneling, he pressed it, revealing a hidden closet – a well-appointed closet complete with comfortable chairs and a wet bar. The captain continued, "As you can see, you are not the first passengers to need 'special handling. I will alert you as the Coast Guard makes its approach. Once they depart, I will see you are notified personally."

Chapter 20 – Aboard the *Norwegian Gem*

First Officer Alex Denisaw was making his final inspection of the *Norwegian Gem* before allowing the passengers to board. He smiled. The clear, crisp air and blue skies made this the perfect fall day to set sail for the Caribbean. He allowed his gaze to take in the lido deck below him. Every deck chair was placed just so, and he was confident that no stain was present to interrupt the whiteness of the group. He was proud of his boat and her crew. Every rail gleamed in the morning sun; every carpet was spotless. Everywhere, freshly cleaned glass sparkled, just waiting for someone's nose to press against the shimmering pane – leaving a streak that would magically disappear before the next day. The *Gem* was like her name – a jewel beyond price, and it was his job to see it stayed that way.

His inspection tour continued flawlessly until he arrived in the passenger reception area, where he spotted Activities Director Jane Sunderland in what appeared to be a heated conversation with three men in black suits. Alex straightened his jacket and stepped forward when their voices began to get loud enough to attract attention from the gathering passengers in the lounge.

"What is the meaning of this, Miss Sunderland?" The first officer inquired, obviously irritated at his perfect morning being interrupted.

"Sir, these gentlemen are federal officers. They insist on speaking with the captain. I've explained that the captain can't be disturbed during departure preparations, but they won't listen. They claim to have information that they can only share with her."

Alex addressed the men, "Gentlemen, I am First Officer Denisaw. Whatever the problem is, I'm sure I can assist you with your inquiry."

The two men were unhappy with the situation, but time was short. One of the men stepped forward, "Mr. Denisaw, I'm Special Agent Smithson from Homeland Security. We have received word of a potential terrorist attack on your vessel."

Alex recoiled at the agent's use of the t-word, "You have my attention, Agent Smithson. What is the nature of this threat, and what can we do to assist you?"

Smithson continued, "I was instructed to only talk to the Captain, but speed is of the essence. We are searching for two people." He flashed the pictures of Jon and Kandi to the first officer. "They are responsible for detonating an explosive device in Vermont as they attempted to escape. Two of our people were killed in the blast." Denisaw nodded. He had seen the news about the unexplained explosion. Smithson continued, "Our intelligence indicates that they are targeting your vessel. We intercepted their registration under false identities last night. We don't believe they will do anything in port, preferring to wait until you're at sea where they can escape unseen.

To mitigate the threat, we must subject all passengers and crewpersons boarding the ship to a full search of their persons and belongings along with everything in the cargo hold."

The first officer tried to answer with a hint of his bluster from earlier but found himself rattled by the agent's words. Instead, he whispered, "Agent Smithson, do you know what you are asking? We're supposed to have a full complement of passengers on this trip – that's over 2,000 people. Our departure time is completely dependent on the tide. Any major delay would mean missing our window and losing a full day." Alex's morning was suddenly not as sunny as it had started. He envisioned the adverse reactions from the passengers to the delay, not to mention the response from the captain and corporate. He looked at the federal agent expectantly, hoping the man would offer another solution.

Agent Smithson's expression never changed as the first officer stated his case. When, at last, Denisaw finished, Smithson's response was direct, "Officer Denisaw. How do you think a bomb going off at sea with dozens, possibly hundreds of casualties, would play with the shareholders? You need to think of the safety of your passengers and crew, not your timetable. This process will take as long as it takes, and it will only grow longer while we stand here arguing." The agent gave the first officer a dismissive look as he reached for his ringing phone.

Alex realized that there would be no further discussion, just as he realized that the boat would not make its departure window. After checking his watch for the umpteenth time, and with no other way past the problem, he headed for the bridge to notify the captain – not a conversation he wanted to have.

Meanwhile, Agent Smithson, aka Colonel Forrester, focused on a call from his commander.

"Yes, sir."

"Colonel," the man on the other end said, "I'm tying you in on a conference call with Coast Guard operations. They have informed me that the *Voyager Templar* has signaled a change in destination. They appear to want to go to London now."

"Do we have a way to verify that, sir?"

"No. Not without dealing directly with the Bermuda courts, and that would take far too long."

"Can I assume that you think the targets are aboard?" Colonel Forrester asked.

"I think we need to be positively certain they aren't. Don't you?" He redirected his attention to the Coast Guard officer on the line, "Commander, can the Coast Guard intercept the *Voyager Templar* before they reach international waters?"

"Sir, if we have a valid search warrant…yes, we can do that. The *Trident* is one of our fastest cutters." The operations officer began to realize he was way above his pay grade.

"Get your boat underway, Commander. I'll fax the warrant to your bridge within ten minutes. I also need you to dispatch a helicopter to the Cruiseport to pick up the Colonel and deliver him to the *Trident*. Colonel, I want you to lead the search."

"Yes, sir. What about the *Norwegian Gem*?"

"The cruise ship, yes. Nothing has changed. Those two could be present among the passengers and running the yacht as a red herring. Have your

men continue the inspection process. Check everything. Leave no stone unturned."
"Yes, sir."

Chapter 21 – The *Templar*

Less than an hour after leaving Boston harbor, the radio on the *Templar* sprang to life.

"Attention, *Voyager Templar*. This is the United States Coast Guard Cutter *Trident*. You're hereby ordered to stand down and prepare for boarding." The radio call echoed through the small control room that served as the bridge on the yacht.

The captain of the *Templar* smiled. His first mate had notified him of their approach ten minutes earlier when he spotted the cutter on the ship's radar, and Stilman had been anticipating the call. He killed the engines and told the deck crew to drop anchor. Then, he nodded for the radio operator to acknowledge the call.

The launch from the cutter came alongside a few minutes later. An officer and two enlisted disembarked with another man who looked very out of place in his black suit.

"Welcome aboard, gentlemen." Captain Stilman's voice belied his stress, "To what do I owe the pleasure of your company."

"Good afternoon, captain. Lieutenant Monroe of the Cutter *Trident*. We have orders and a duly executed warrant to search your vessel for contraband," he said as he produced the document authorizing the search.

The captain glanced at the document before setting it aside, "Certainly, Lieutenant. We are always ready to assist the Coast Guard. I'm a bit confused, though. Customs searched us before we left Boston. We've had no contact outside the boat since."

The lieutenant responded, "Be that as it may, Captain. Someone thinks you are carrying something you shouldn't. I'm just following orders."

The captain had to laugh, "Be my guest." He gallantly swept his hand across the span of the ship. "By all means, search away."

Three hours later, Lieutenant Monroe presented himself on the bridge, "Captain, I'm pleased to report that we discovered no contraband during our search. I apologize for any inconvenience this delay has caused you." Looking over the young man's shoulder, the captain could see the other men by the launch. The man in the suit made no attempt to hide his displeasure.

"Excellent, lieutenant. You didn't take that long. We should have no problem making up the time."

"I'm glad to hear it. One question, if you may. Before you left Boston, you indicated that you were returning to Bermuda, and then a short time later, you amended your destination to London. Any particular reason why?"

Stilman laughed, "No secrets there, lieutenant. The answer is cold, hard cash. We received a communique from a client in London specifically requesting the *Templar* for a trip to New York. Said that they had used us before and were impressed enough that they would be willing to pay our fuel bill both ways. In our business, that's an offer we can't refuse."

The lieutenant smiled, "Sometimes, I envy you guys in the private sector. You go where and when you like and get someone else to pay for it. Pretty sweet."

"Not always, lieutenant," the captain said, "Sometimes we just sit on our hands praying for a contract."

The lieutenant smiled as he saluted, "I guess. Looks good to me, though. Calm seas, captain."

"Same to you, Lieutenant Monroe."

Captain Stilman maintained his friendly demeanor until the launch had departed and was well on its way to the *Trident*. He told his first officer to resume course and speed before heading to the stateroom where his guests were stashed. He had a reason for not delegating this task to a crewmember. While the Coast Guard had been doing their search, he remembered where he had seen his passengers before.

"All clear, Mr. and Mrs. Noor," he announced. "Safe to venture out." Jon and Kandi stepped into the stateroom.

The captain continued, "We're entering international waters soon, so I don't expect any other interruptions before we get to London, but I was a little concerned by a strange man on the Coast Guard launch, a tall man in a black suit. Looked official, and he wasn't happy when the search came up empty."

Jon spoke, "I believe we've encountered some of his friends already. We fooled them back in the harbor, and I imagine that unhappy would not begin to describe what he was feeling."

"Look. Your situation is none of my business. You have paid for our discretion. My crew and I have a great deal of experience dealing with confidential clientele, but I need to know what's happening before I can handle potential obstacles. First, we're expecting a complement of fifteen men and women. Instead, we get you two. Not just any two, but two people who have dominated the news for four days. You," he said, pointing at Jon, "are supposed to be a kidnapped jeweler – Martyr, was it? And you," pointing at Kandi, "are supposed to be the person who snatched him, dispatching two of New York's finest to the hospital in the process. Now, here you are, posing as husband and wife under assumed names. That doesn't make much sense to me. I need an explanation. After all, you are only one charter, and I intend to have a business when this is all over."

Once again, Jon pulled out the tried-and-true lie about how he and Kandi had staged the kidnapping as a publicity stunt gone awry and then had no way of backpedaling out of the firestorm it created.

The captain remained silent throughout the entire story. "Bullshit," he said.

Jon looked startled, "Sorry?"

"I said bullshit! Aeden Corp commissioned this boat six months ago as a scientific expedition leaving Boston three days BEFORE you disappeared in New York. We even received a shipment of supplies consistent with the scientific mission.

Suddenly, you two show up instead. I'm unsure who you are, but you are decidedly not scientists.

Also, you are no more an Arabic husband and his wife than I am your father. Don't get me wrong; your papers are excellent, but they're still fakes, and your backstories are practically non-existent. That tale you just told is so full of holes...tell me why I shouldn't restrain you and call that cutter to return."

The captain's rant caused Kandi to tense up, and Jon was afraid she would react to the captain's hostile voice and perceive it as a threat, so he responded as calmly as he could. "Captain. I apologize. You are right about us. We aren't married, and our papers are false. We have only known each other since New York. We have no weapons and mean you no harm. I'm afraid I can't go into more detail, but I promise that we pose no threat to you or your crew."

The captain calmed slightly as he glared at Jon, "Look, your business is yours, but whoever you are, I'm sure you are not an innocent jeweler. Over the years, the *Templar* has had several clients who needed anonymity for various reasons, some legal and some not. You hid your faces when you boarded, so the rest of the crew has no idea who you are, and I intend to keep it that way. I will tell them you are two celebrities seeking a quiet trip to London. We deal with those types all the time, so they won't question the isolation. "The daily routine will be like this. The crew will announce themselves when bringing your food and fresh linens. You will exit the area when they do so. Otherwise, they will afford you complete privacy. That is the best I can do. If you require anything, I am at your disposal." With that, the captain turned and returned to the bridge.

"We can't trust him," Kandi's focused voice was as sharp as a razor.

"We have to trust him," Jon stated matter of factly, "We have to hope he's a man of his word. After all, he hid us from the boarding party. We just have to hope he won't notify the authorities now that he knows everything. "

Kandi acted as if she hadn't heard anything he had said, "I would have no trouble dealing with his crew."

Jon gulped. He remembered how she had 'dealt' with the security guards at the gallery and the explosion in the mountains. "We'll keep that as a last resort, okay? As of this minute, we are not in danger. Besides, my background has not prepared me to sail a yacht across the ocean. How about yours?"

Kandi hated to admit that he might be right, "No, my training was limited to combat, not logistics. Sea-going vessels are far outside my personal experience. Perhaps you are correct. I shouldn't deal with them yet."

Jon was visibly relieved. "Sounds like a plan. Now that we're not committing piracy, what will we do about our IDs? The captain is right; our faces don't fit the names. Besides, I burned them in Boston when I reserved that cruise. Every port and transit facility in the world will have them flagged."

Sara volunteered a possible solution, *Kandi. One of our contingency plans on the original mission involved the possibility of having to modify IDs mid-*

project. For that eventuality, I included a document generator in the ship's cargo allotment.

Kandi replied aloud much to Jon's confusion, "Sara, that is perfect." Encouraged by her alter-ego's comment, Kandi pulled her hat down further over her ears to hide them from prying eyes and headed toward the lower decks. Jon had no idea what her comment referred to but decided to join her, nonetheless. They passed by crates and crates of equipment, a veritable treasure trove, some of which Jon could identify, although there was a lot that he had no idea of the purpose. Guided by Sara's knowledge of the manifest, Kandi located a medium-sized crate and headed back upstairs with Jon struggling to keep up, gasping for breath and feeling like a little boy trying to keep up with his mama.

Once upstairs, Sara took over Kandi's body, setting up the equipment and creating IDs based on data she had stored in her memory. They were now Tom and Chelsea Smythe-Walker, tourists from Great Britain, a much better fit, especially considering where they were going. The original couple of that name had died thirty years ago. There would be no digital footprint to confuse the authorities.

IDs assured, they discussed how to make the most use of their time aboard. Sara suggested that Jon might benefit from learning a bit of the Aedenian language. She reasoned that being able to communicate in a language that absolutely no one else knew could have its benefits. They could then share information without being intercepted by casual listeners. Surprisingly, Kandi agreed that was a good idea and designated her alter-ego to teach him during Kandi's rest periods.

The ship was massive, half the length of a football field, and every square inch was designed to keep her wealthy occupants busy. Kandi's eyes gleamed when she noticed the small room affectionately called 'gym' on the ship's map she had found in the room.

The gym would suffice for weight training and treadmill runs, but for the rest...she looked out the window onto the upper deck fantail overlooking the ocean. Yes, that would do nicely for sparring practice. Of course, she couldn't use a crew member as a partner, so Jon would have to do – a role she was sure he would regret. Kandi smiled inwardly. The mental imagery of throwing him around a little sounded like fun.

United States Space Command Cheyenne Mountain, Colorado

The commander's office was darker than usual, adding to the mystique of its occupant sitting behind the desk. The room's sole light seemed focused on the officer standing at attention.

"So, Colonel. Have our fugitives surfaced?" The commander was succinct but not hostile in his question.

"No, sir," Forrester replied, "The ocean liner was a dead-end, as was the *Voyager Templar*. The two suspects are completely off the radar."

The commander leaned into the desk, "What does your gut tell you?"

The colonel replied immediately, "I still think they're on the yacht, but I have no idea how they hid from our search team. We were very thorough."

The commander continued with his questions, "What is your evidence?"

"It would be easier to show you." Forrester pulled up a video on his phone. "One of my agents shot this as the *Templar* left dock. The yacht doesn't show anything unusual but look at the smaller craft approaching from downstream." The commander moved to get a better viewpoint, "If you look carefully, you can see three people on that boat. They were too far away to get faces but look at the same craft after it passes the *Templar*." The commander could see Forrester's point. The smaller craft only held one person as it moved away from the yacht.

The colonel continued, "What are your orders? We have a fix on the *Templar's* transponder and could easily blow them out of the water or possibly do a drop with one of the airborne teams."

"Easy. Yes, except for the fallout from the politicians. The State Department is already giving us grief about the cruise ship. No one will give us authorization to blow up or commandeer a foreign vessel on the high seas and doing it without permission would be considered piracy. Washington and the U.N. would have a field day. They are only two weeks out of London at their current speed. We'll wait for them there."

"Very good, sir," The colonel said before leaving.

Again, alone in his office, the commander mused, "Well, Kandi. Looks like your luck has run out. I'll see you soon."

Chapter 22 – Sweet Dreams

Kandi tossed and turned, tangling herself in the covers of the king-sized bed. Despite the room's chill, beads of sweat formed on her arms and face as her body thrashed wildly against unknown attackers in her sleep. Other than an occasional moan or grunt, no sound came from her lips as frantic scenes flew through her mind.

Repressed images of the Human Wars accounted for most of the torturous visions. Having lived it once, she was forced to watch again as battles raged and people, many of them friends, died. The number of dead far outweighed any chance of traditional burial. Consequently, the bodies were piled up regardless of race. Pixie, elf, and human in a single heap and then set aflame. There was no honor here, no prayers for the dead, just expediency. Burn the bodies before their decaying corpses created a greater death in the form of disease that not even the crystal in their veins could counter. Kandi could smell the burning pyres as they gave off an overwhelming stench as bodies turned to ash.

Over the crackling flames, she could hear ephemeral wisps of conversations from disembodied speakers – never loud enough to understand what they were saying or even what sex the speaker might be. She tried to move toward the perceived voices, but they distanced themselves with every step.

After the war scenes, her past lovers returned to haunt her. These were not pleasurable memories of love and want. Each depiction was a caricature of the actual relationships. Kandi had never searched for anything more than something casual – a fact she stressed to each of her partners from the beginning. Still, some refused to let go when her attraction for them faded, and she moved on. Those jilted suitors returned to her now, outraged, and distraught, chasing her through the caverns of her mind, looking for ways to avenge their damaged egos and take revenge upon her. These were no longer lovers; they were predators seeking retribution.

Then came the final scene in her dreamscape – the most damning. Kandi stood alone on a hilltop overlooking Galadel. Below her, the tree-top city of her birth still gleamed in the morning sun, red hues shimmering over the crystalline forms. She was only three when she escaped but now appeared fully grown, wings unfurled in the warm breeze, and battle armor in place. As she watched, the skies darkened as malignant creatures – human creatures came from the land, sea, and sky, murdering and burning everything in their path. She watched, unable to act, as her family – her mother and father were butchered in front of their home while she stood helplessly on the hillside.

The urge to do something was overwhelming. Kandi broke through her invisible restraints and flew toward her parents, readying her weapons. She had to defend them - keep this travesty from happening once again. Try as she might, every movement slowed as if her wings were plowing through thick mud instead of air. Her mother's eyes were fixed on Kandi with hands outstretched, the word "help" indelibly etched upon her face as she suffered in agony as she died. The dream ended with her village in ruins and her mother's screams echoing through her mind.

Kandi woke, gasping for breath, her body shaking; the bedclothes, wet with sweat, stuck to her. Her matted hair was pasted to her head. Breath came in deep, ragged gulps, and her heart threatened to explode inside her chest. Shakily, she rose from the mattress and went to the shower, forcing the stream on full force – cold. There she stood, shivering against the temperature, forcing herself awake, forcing the demons to be gone.

Kandi? Sara sounded frightened as she called.

Yes, Sara.

What was that we just experienced?

I'm not sure. This has never happened to me; although I have heard that elves and humans have such night visions, there is no record of pixies experiencing them. The whole thing was highly unsettling; The images were so authentic, yet scattered and fragmented... Kandi's blood was still racing in her veins.

The last part...on the hill? Sara prompted.

Yes.

I recognized Galadel from images captured before the war. Was what we saw true? Is that how the attack happened? Was that how your parents died?

I wish I knew, Sara. I was only three at the time. I vaguely recall Mother screaming for me to fly away, to get out of the house and hide in the forest up the hill. I have some memories of smoke and an awful smell, but honestly,

I'm not even sure what my parents looked like, let alone if that was them.

So...the vision?

I have no idea what the images mean, nor why I can't see everything that happened – why I can't see the faces of the people who did it.

The brutality was horrific. I can't understand how one race can be so cruel to another. I can see now why you hate Jon, although I don't believe he's like the monsters in your vision.

Perhaps not, but the same blood runs in his veins. Before Galadel, we made the mistake of thinking humans had changed and that they could be our allies. We were wrong. For now, Jon's still the enemy. He has been helpful, but I will require much more than that before I dare to call him "friend."

The two women remained awake, conversing in their shared minds for the rest of the night. Neither slept nor mentioned the visions for fear of them returning.

Meanwhile, Jon was on a personal quest. His hand itched, and he had to do something about it. In retrospect, there were a lot of things that could have gone wrong. He knew Kandi would be against him proceeding and irritated that he did it without her permission, but that didn't matter. The more he tried to ignore the irritation, the worse it became – enough was enough.

The yacht had a small infirmary, including a small portable X-ray machine. Jon drifted down there after midnight when he was sure the crew was on minimal staff and not likely to wander below the main decks. Next to the x-ray was a lead apron, just like his dentist used. Before changing his mind, he placed his hand under the apron and removed the lead-lined glove fragment covering his albatross – the ring.

The area around his finger wasn't pretty. The fragment had irritated the skin around the ring to the point that it now more closely resembled raw meat rather than the digit he remembered.

What took his attention away from the damage was the ring itself. From the time he had laid eyes on the jewel nestled in the box in his father's living room, the stone had an internal luminance, a definite red luminance. Now, peeking under the apron, he was surprised to see an iridescent blue color had replaced it. Like the red, the radiance wasn't an overpowering glow. A casual observer would have believed the aura only reflected light, but the ring glowed steadily in the darkened area under the lead apron.

Jon wondered what the change of color meant. He would have to ask Kandi or Sara tomorrow. For now, though, he decided to take a chance and not put the piece of glove back on his finger. His hand hurt! NSA, FBI, and Coast Guard be damned. If they wanted to find him in the middle of the ocean, so be it.

Chapter 23 – The Reality

Jon lay on his bed, the dark North Atlantic dancing in the moonlight through the large windows of his stateroom. The undulating movement of the ever-changing sea fascinated him. He could stare at it for hours and never tire of the waves. Of course, with the preparations for their departure, he hadn't much spare time to enjoy the simple things, making times like this even more special. The only thing that would improve it would be if he were out on a deck chair to breathe in the sea air. Alas, the North Atlantic's outside temperature in early November was never over sixty degrees in the heat of the day, and this was a particularly frigid night. Jon decided that the inside-looking-out view was just fine.

Jon shifted his gaze to the shades of blue radiating from the jewel on his finger. As he had predicted, Kandi was incensed that he had removed the protective covering, sure that the authorities would attack the ship at any moment. Unfortunately, neither she nor Sara knew what the change of color from red to blue meant. Sara cobbled together a device from the Aedenian supplies in the hold to register the distress signal from the ring; however, the device remained silent. For whatever reason, the ring appeared to have adopted him.

The past two weeks had gone by quickly. Having Kandi and Sara work with him on language and basic defense skills had been a godsend. He was finally getting his head around the reality that two radically different individuals inhabited one body. He could now quickly determine which person was in charge of the body at any given time. Freud would've had a field day.

Every morning, Kandi would push him to the edge of his endurance, leaving him panting and exhausted in the gym while she sauntered off, not even breaking a sweat – except for the past couple of days. Jon smiled as he remembered she had seemed a bit more tired lately. Jon was pleased that he was at least giving her something of a workout for his pain.

Sara would tutor him after lunch on the Aedenian language. He quickly remembered why the speech had seemed so familiar to him that first night in Vermont. While Jon was accompanying his father on a dig in Pakistan, he picked up a smattering of Urdu from the local villagers – enough to make himself understood anyway. Urdu's similarities to Aedenian were striking. Sara wasn't surprised when Jon told her that Urdu evolved from Sanskrit, one of the oldest human languages. The similarities were making his assimilation of the language go much quicker than the process might have otherwise. Like Kandi, though, Sara seemed a bit more distant as the voyage neared its conclusion on Skye.

Jon and Sara also took the opportunity to talk about her home world of Aeden. Kandi never discussed her world, treating him with suspicion whenever he asked. Sara was far more open. He discovered that Aeden circled a red-giant star. The lower radiation from their sun, along with the planet's orbit and two moons, gave Aeden a mild climate year-round. Also, Aeden was huge. The Eastern and Western Continents exceeded the area of Earth's continents and islands combined. Even so, the gravity on Aeden was barely ten percent more than on Earth, er Gaia. Jon constantly reminded himself that his planet had another name that his two companions used exclusively.

There was one piece of her history that Sara could not describe since she had no hard data to authenticate it. There was no point of origin when the hatred between humans and the other races had begun. Its outset predated recorded history. In all the oral legends and lore describing the early times, humans were already anathema to the others.

Sara did know quite a bit about the last Human Wars. She explained how the humans' surprise attack on Galadel had been vicious and destructive and how Kandi was one of only a handful of survivors. The brutal attack on the defenseless village set the war's tone. There could be only total victory – no prisoners taken, no mercies shown. Every battle and raid became a fight to the death. Jon began to understand the depth of Kandi's hatred for humans, for him.

Jon glanced around his room. He was going to hate leaving this place. Everything was heavenly. Unfortunately, heaven was scheduled to leave tomorrow. That was when he and Kandi would leave the boat's safety for the Isle of Skye, a place Jon had never heard of until this trip. He had asked Kandi why Skye. She told him, "There was a fourth race on Aeden, fairies. They were unapologetic pacifists, and since they couldn't support the common war effort, they left Aeden and established a colony on Gaia. Later, we discovered their refuge on Skye during the last human settlement. They still wanted little to do with the rest of us, which was fine. We just let them be, bypassing the island altogether. I've been thinking that they would have taken all their crystal stores with them since their trip was one way. We hope that some of those artifacts remain." Jon replied, "That's unlikely, though, right? From what you've told me, at least a thousand years have passed since the gate collapsed. What are the odds anything useful survived?"

The voice shifted as Kandi returned. She stared at him, "May I remind you that you wear such an artifact? Your ring seems to have survived just fine."

Jon's face flushed red. Just then, a voice over the ship intercom spoke.

"This is the captain. We will be approaching Skye tomorrow night. You should be ready to depart then."

As Jon continued to muse about the morning's discussion, he noticed a larger-than-normal shadow on one of the deck chairs. Considering the captain's ban on the crew being in the passenger areas, this could be only one person - Kandi or Sara, depending on who was in charge. *What in the world is she doing out there?* He thought.

Curiosity got the better of him. He put on a jacket borrowed from the ship's stores and ventured outside. Not sure which personality currently possessed the pixie, he approached cautiously – like he would a wild beast, at once apparent and, at the same time, non-threatening.

"Hi. Everything OK?" Jon asked, raising his voice so the sea wouldn't drown him out. Kandi didn't respond.

"Kandi? Sara? Wake up! What're you doing out here?" Jon noticed that she was only wearing her nightclothes. "What are you thinking? You'll get hypothermia without a coat or at least a robe." Even though he was speaking louder, the girl in the chair showed no sign of hearing him.

"OK. You're starting to scare me a bit." He cautiously moved his hand to shake her. She didn't react. "Kandi," he shook her more strenuously. "You don't want to sleep out here on the deck. It's damp and cold. Come on inside." Then, she gave her first awareness of his presence, a quiet moan, barely audible over the sea noise.

At that, Jon threw caution to the wind, grabbed her hand, and threw her over his shoulder, her cheek flush with his own. "You're burning up! We need to get you to your cabin." She was still unresponsive. He would have felt better had she slugged him or thrown him down on the deck for daring to touch her. The lack of response and the heat radiating from her body scared him.

Once in her room, he struggled to recall his Boy Scout first-aid training for treating high fevers. He ran a cool bath and removed her clothing. As her flesh hit the cool water, her moans became more audible.

After ensuring she was not in danger of drowning, he went to the ship's infirmary for some ibuprofen and clean cloths for compresses, not caring if any crew members were there. He considered contacting the captain for assistance but decided to see how his home remedy worked first.

Returning unnoticed, he raced to the bath with the pills and some water. He forced open her mouth and inserted the tablets, following them with the liquid. He then held her mouth closed until she swallowed. A thermometer, snatched from an infirmary shelf, indicated the matter's seriousness–106.7 degrees.

Not knowing what else to do, Jon kept vigil by the tub, placing cold compresses on her forehead and neck while staying alert for any sign of the fever breaking. He had no idea how ibuprofen would work in her physiology. Sara said that humans, elves, and pixies evolved from the same original species, but there had been a lot of evolution taking place over the years between then and now.

He reconsidered contacting the captain about her condition but quickly rationalized that the captain could do nothing more than what Jon had done. *Very few emergency rooms out here, Jon, old boy,* he thought. Besides, her ears and wings would create more problems than getting the captain involved would solve.

Hours later, Jon slumped into sleep with his head resting on the side of the tub. Jon had no idea how long he had been out, but when he woke, he became painfully aware of a dripping wet, pissed-off pixie standing naked before him.

Kandi got right to the point, "Human! What is going on? Why are you here!"

Jon responded nervously, "Look. I found you passed out in a deck chair about," he checked his watch, "six hours ago. You were unconscious with a high fever. Since I had no idea how you treated things back home, I treated you like I would a human...sorry."

Kandi completely dismissed his explanation as fantasy, "Fevers are impossible. My crystal nanites protect from any infection and adapt rapidly to new variants. None of my people have been ill for millennia. I couldn't have had a fever. Try again, human!" Even in her weakened condition, she appeared formidable.

Jon quickly grabbed the thermometer lying on the floor. The device reflected her earlier temperature, which he showed her, "I beg to differ. Unless your body differs from ours more than I think, you were in bad shape. Completely incoherent. Scared the hell out of me."

Kandi stared at the device in disbelief. She had a hard time accepting what she saw. She couldn't have been ill. That didn't make sense.

Jon continued, "If you don't believe me, ask Sara."

Suddenly, Kandi realized that she had not heard from her alter-ego.

Sara?
Sara?
Sara!

Chapter 24 – Time to Go

Sara was still gone the next evening when the time came to leave. There was a gaping hole in Kandi's consciousness where the AI had been, but no sign of where she might have gone. Kandi was frantic with worry. *Could the "impossible" fever have killed her? The human claims that the disease almost killed me. Was the stress too much for Sara to endure? Just the idea made the emptiness that much more pronounced.*

During preparations, Jon and Kandi had barely exchanged three words. Sara's absence meant a lot to discuss, but neither wanted to speak, as if they feared talking about her would make the situation more real. In their hearts, they knew that all the talking in the world wouldn't change the fact that Sara was gone, and in all probability, Sara wasn't coming back. Tears combined with sea spray as they each grieved their lost friend.

Jon wasn't sure why the AI's death affected him so strongly. He had only known her for a few weeks. Yet, Sara's optimism and emerging, almost adolescent, personality had been contagious. Jon would have loved to have known her better. Now, though, he was here with Kandi, cold, calculating Kandi. *Why couldn't she have died, and Sara lived?* He quashed the thought as quickly as it came. He had come dangerously close to losing them both.

As they stood by the launch, ready to depart, Kandi finally spoke to the Captain. "You're going to be in Portsmouth."

The Captain was concise in his response, "Yes. We'll be at Gunwharf Quays Marina. As discussed, we'll wait until December 15th. If we haven't heard from you by then, we'll consider our contract completed and be free to accept another charter – preferably somewhere warm. Nothing personal, but I'll be ready. Damn cold up here, unusual even for this time of year." He briefly smiled, then allowed it to vanish when he saw no one else considered it funny.

A cold rain started just as the shuttle left the yacht, first a drizzle, then mounting to a full-blown downpour, adding to the overall depression of its passengers. Fortunately, there was little wind, leaving the seas relatively calm. The crewman piloting the boat never looked back at his passengers. He had his orders, but he couldn't help wondering why two high-profile guests would be out on a night like this and decided that they must be the kind of "celebrities" he would be better off not knowing, the kind that could get a man killed if he asked questions. He beached the small craft in a cove north of Dunvegan Castle, allowing his passengers to silently depart.

Jon looked up at the castle as the launch returned to the yacht, and he and Kandi shouldered their gear. Dunvegan was one of the reasons Kandi had led them here. She told Jon that it was the ancestral home of the MacLeod Clan, and the many myths and legends surrounding the place and its owners made it especially interesting for her search. One such legend involved a former Laird of the castle who had fallen in love with the fairy princess Titania. The story went that they loved each other deeply, and despite her father's objections, they married and had a son. After a year, Titania's sire returned for her, forcing her to leave her grief-stricken laird alone with the child.

Another part of the legend was of particular interest to Kandi. The legend pointed to a bridge not far from the castle where Titania's transition back to the land of Faerie supposedly took place. The tale was undoubtedly bogus, tainted by hundreds of years of telling, but Kandi was grasping for any hint of where the fairies from Aeden had settled, so here they were. Jon, for one, thought they were on a fool's errand. What evidence could possibly remain?

Before she had been lost, Sara had snagged a map of the area from the castle's Internet site. Neither Jon nor Kandi had thought of that. It was just another example of how much the AI would be missed. On the document, she found a well-worn path up from the shore that would lead them to the main gate and the road beyond. Since Kandi wanted to avoid any human interactions, they would follow that road north toward a private road leading east.

As they left the cove, with the cold rain still pouring down, Jon decided to chance breaking the silence. "Do you want to talk about it?"

Kandi answered unemotionally, "Not particularly. What is there to say? Sara's gone."

Jon became exasperated, "Kandi, she was your friend – a long-time friend. You shared so many life experiences. You must be feeling something."

"Don't tell me what I MUST be!" Kandi exploded with pent-up emotion. "You have no idea the range of feelings going through me. Do you want to know how I am feeling? I am numb inside but also burn with rage, and right now, I have no one to vent that anger on EXCEPT YOU!" She accented the last two words and then fired a cold, hard stare in Jon's direction. Even under cover of darkness, he paled in fear as she continued, "Do you know how many friends I have lost in my career, human? I have seen a hundred years of war. Counting those who survived would be far easier than numbering the dead—any tears I may have had for fallen comrades dried up long ago. From what I can tell, my world is again at war, this time with an unknown foe. Wars have casualties, and I am afraid that Sara is only one of many." She lapsed into silence, and Jon joined her.

They slogged over the muddy path to the main entrance. Jon was again thankful that the captain had insisted on them raiding the ship's stores for the parkas and boots. Kandi showed no deference either way. In her current mood, Jon was sure she would be fine trudging naked in the rain.

According to the map, the bridge was only a four-mile walk; however, the journey was interminably longer once adjusted for the misery index, a combination of cold, rain, and pitch blackness along with the hills they had to slip and slide across. What cover the trees had given by the shore quickly disappeared, leaving no shelter from the icy drops. The private road was little more than a cow path and soon transformed into pools of thick, sucking mud.

Through it all, Kandi trudged onward, apparently unaffected by the miserable weather. How she deftly maneuvered the quagmire convinced Jon that her alien eyes could see through the blackness around them. She never wavered, stumbled, or fell, and Jon began to hate her for it as he fell into every hole. What seemed an eternity, but actually, less than two hours after setting off from the castle's main gate, they stood by their goal just as the dawn began to break, the sun only offering a lightening of the sky in the east.

Jon slumped down and sat on the side of the bridge. He almost wished for the night to return. The rising sun had not made their surroundings any more appealing. The area around the bridge was desolate. Gray sky met with gray earth, the semi-dormant vegetation adding little color to the mix. The bridge was in the center of this morass, a slightly darker brown than the surrounding area. Jon was noticeably underwhelmed.

"This is the portal to the fairy realm?" he asked sarcastically.

Kandi tried to appear optimistic but was similarly taken aback by the bridge's plain appearance, "All the legends point to this being where Titania was taken by her father, leaving Laird MacLeod standing on this side." Kandi's response was simply a statement. There was no emotion in her speech. She peered over the top of the bridge and then dropped into the stream to inspect the underlying structure thoroughly.

Jon was wet, cold, and angry as he shouted to her, "What are you hoping to find here? According to the story, this bridge is at least a thousand years old, yet someone has obviously maintained the structure. Heck, they've probably replaced the entire thing more than once. There's no telling what has happened here since the time of Titania, if she was here at all. Kandi, you must face the possibility that what you seek may no longer exist."

There was no response to his taunt. After a moment, Jon peered over the side of the bridge to see his companion face down in the water. His heart jumped into his throat as he raced to her side, turned her over, and started CPR. After only a few seconds, he felt the warmth of her breath on his cheek, but consciousness didn't follow.

"Oh no, not again. We're not going to do this right now. Get up!" Jon exclaimed as a flashback to the events from earlier in the week flashed before his eyes. He maneuvered the pixie out of the ditch and onto the nearby roadway. Kandi was in serious trouble and had no idea where to get help.

Even though the main road was only a quarter mile south, getting her and the packs there would be difficult. In the end, Jon made two trips – one for the backpacks and one for the girl. He picked her up gently and tried to maintain his balance on the wet roadway. He set her down at the intersection with the single-lane main road and covered her with the two parkas. Now they waited, hoping that someone would pass by - and be willing to help.

Chapter 25 – The Other Side of Nothing

Sara was alone. All that had existed before the fire had consumed Kandi was gone. Everything was buried in darkness. No light. No sound. No inputs could penetrate the black wall that surrounded her. The nothingness absorbed her screams. Her fists bounced from the surface. Where was she? What had happened? Where was Kandi?

Her last memory in what had become her real world had been waking up with Kandi's head on fire. The visions racing through her mind were incoherent, chaotic morasses of light and sound, searing her eyes and tormenting her ears, far worse than the ones a week ago. Her alter ego, Kandi, was unresponsive, unmoving, and seemingly dead. She had tried taking over Kandi's body, hoping to get Jon to help, but the physical form resisted her attempts no matter how hard she tried. Her erratic movements only brought her as far as the deck chair outside his window. She decided to rest there before continuing.

While she rested in the chair, the attack resumed. Deep pain assaulted her from every direction. Then, a shadow passed amid the lights and sounds. The darkness slowly gained form, and as it did so, it became a figure, not a person exactly, more of a construct attempting to appear human. The dark thing grew closer to her, deflecting, possibly absorbing the light and sound as it approached, until both decreased to the point they disappeared, leaving an empty echo of the former chaos behind. For a second, Sara basked in the relief that the onslaught of sight and sound was over.

Her relief was short-lived, however, and quickly turned to terror as the still faceless creature reached for her, pinned her arms to her side, and began pushing her back farther and farther into the recesses of Kandi's mind until she found herself here. The pretend man blocked her way out, devolving into the surrounding walls. The beast-man had eased her discomfort only to isolate her entirely from her friend.

The emotion Kandi had identified as fear crept upon her. *What was this place? What had happened? Was she dead? Was this what waited for her at the end of her existence, nothing? What about Kandi? Did the fire and light kill her as well?* In her despair, she called out again for her friend.

Kandi?
Kandi?
Kandi?

There was not even an echo in response.

Chapter 26 – Time Stands Still

Jon's wait seemed endless. Paint drying would be more enthralling than doing nothing. The other side of the tedium coin was worry. Kandi was still unconscious, and Jon felt he should be doing something - anything, to help revive her, but what? Even if he had a clue which direction was best, Jon knew he couldn't carry her very far, so he sat on his pack, watching his companion breathe and praying that she wouldn't stop. After an eternity, an ancient, rusted Peugeot sedan approached from the west. Jon frantically waved the car down. Thankfully, the driver stopped.

A middle-aged man rolled down his window and commenced yelling, "Be ye dunderheads, ya? What be ya doin' roaming about on a day like this? The two of ye will be lucky ifn ya don't catch your death...." At that moment, he noticed that the man stood with his head down, and his companion hadn't moved at all. He spoke to Jon in a softer tone, "Be there a problem, boy?"

Jon responded as courteously as possible, "She just collapsed, sir. I've been trying to keep her warm, but she's not responding." Jon sounded as worried as he felt.

The man jumped from the vehicle and ran to where Kandi lay. Jon had covered her with as many of the packs' contents as possible. The stranger checked her vitals with what appeared to be a practiced hand. Then, without hesitation, he scooped her up and bundled her into the car's back seat. He looked over his shoulder at Jon, "Well, what ye waitin' for, laddie? Get ye stuff in the boot, and let's go!"

Jon was so relieved that someone was taking charge besides himself that he found the relative freedom exhilarating. He loaded their things and barely had time to close the door before the man took off down the road as fast as the vehicle would take him, slick surfaces be damned.

They were still careening down the one-lane road when the stranger noticed Jon's fists clenched on the door handle, "Sorry for the rush, lad. Yer wee lass is in a bad way, and I need to get her to the clinic sooner rather than later. I'm Tom Yarrow, the nurse practitioner servin' these parts. I be based at the hospital in Portree, south of here, but I spend a day or two a week takin' care of folks in Dunvegan and Edinbane. Ya was lucky that today was my travelin' day. Traffic be sparse on a Sunday, especially in this kind of weather."

Despite his relief at their rescue, Jon wasn't sure that Kandi would like a professional medical person looking at her, but that ship had sailed as soon as they had gotten into the car. "Where is Edinbane?" He asked.

"A few miles. Be there before ya know it."

Shortly after, the car parked in front of a building with Gesto Hospital emblazoned above the door. A smaller sign next to the door read Edinbane Clinic. Tom answered Jon's unspoken question, "The hospital closed back in '06. NHS decided keeping the place going wasn't worth the time or money. Makes a perfect location for our clinic, though." Tom opened the car door and said, "I'll open the front door. You get your lassie and carry her inside."

Jon wasn't sure how Kandi would have reacted to "your lassie," but she wasn't responding to anything right now. He was doubly glad of her comatose state when he accidentally hit her head on the edge of the car door as he pulled her out. *Ouch! She's gonna kill me if that leaves a bruise.* Secretly, he prayed that she'd get the chance.

He followed Tom to a small examination room and laid Kandi down as gently as possible. "Tom, there is something you need to know...."

Before Jon could get the words out, Tom had already removed Kandi's parka and hat, revealing her ears. Jon forgot to breathe. "Hmmm," the nurse began, never losing his calm, "She's a fairy, but I've never seen her before."

Jon stuttered, "Actually, no. She's a pixie."

At that, Tom turned toward Jon, looking genuinely surprised. "Pixie? I've only heard tales...never expected to see a live one. Wings?"

Jon nodded, still stunned by the lack of shock in the nurse's demeanor.

Tom removed the rest of her wet clothing and turned her over, revealing her iridescent display. "Impressive. I've always felt it a shame the fairy lasses lost their wings over the years. Best we keep her on her tummy so they can dry."

Jon finally found the courage to speak, "Pardon me, Tom. This situation doesn't bother you at all?"

Tom laughed as he continued his examination, "This is Skye, laddie. I've seen a lot of things. Would take more than this to surprise me. Speaking of which, you're human, right, not elven?"

"Yes."

"And you two are traveling together?"

"Yes."

Tom laughed, "See now, lad; now that surprises me. A pixie in the company of a human? The stories I've heard said humans are the only things a pixie hates worse than fairies. The fact you are alive is a real shocker."

Jon dismissed the slight to his humanity, "What about her? Is she going to be OK?"

"Physically, she's exhausted and dehydrated. I'll give her an IV to get some fluids inta her, and then we need to get her somewhere else for more specialized attention."

Jon's heart stopped. "Where are you planning on taking her?" One mention of taking her to the authorities and this nurse would have a fight on his hands.

Tom replied in a calm voice, "Relax, lad. Her secret is safe with me as it will be with those where we be going. I'm gonna take her to me ma's place in Ulg. Ma can help her far more than I can." He checked his watch. "We'll need to get a move on, though. The drive to Ulg will take a fair bit, and I have to get the clinic here opened in a couple of hours."

A short, uneventful drive later, Tom deposited the two travelers in a cozy, warm sitting room in Ulg in the company of Fiona Yarrow and her daughter, Barba. Kandi had responded to her IV and antibiotics. She was conscious and could walk a little, but not much more than that.

Although Kandi was still weak, she was acutely aware that her hat was off and someone had changed her clothing. Jon, for his part, was more concerned with their new acquaintances. Both were beautiful women who looked more like sisters than mother and daughter.

After getting comfortable, Fiona frowned slightly and asked, "So, lass, what be a pixie such as yerself be doing on Skye?"

The woman's blunt comment stunned Kandi, who stammered, "Pixie? What would make you think I'm a pixie?"

"Well, first of all, ya got the ears and the wings for it. Plus, yer laddie here," pointing toward Jon, "told me boy, Tom, everything." Fiona saw anger flash in Kandi's eyes and quickly moved to calm her. "Don't fret none, lass. The boy did what he had to. Saved your life, he did. Besides, yer secret is safe with us." Then Fiona continued, "So then, little pixie, why are ye here?"

"You'll think I'm crazy."

"Crazier than a pixie poppin' in fa afternoon tea? I think not."

"I...I'm looking for remains of a fairy colony from long ago."

Fiona seemed relieved and visibly relaxed, "Oh! Is that all?" She laughed. "Well, now that ye found us, what can we do fer ya?"

Fiona's announcement left the room silent. Jon stuttered, "What do you mean? The colony would be thousands of years old. Are you telling me that you two are..."

Fiona, still laughing, interrupted, "No, silly boy, the original colonists are long gone, but we are a part of what remains – their descendants." Jon took note of their human ears and commented on them. Fiona answered, "Ye may ha noticed that Skye is pretty sparse regarding people. No pure-bred fairies are left, but most everyone in these parts has at least a wee part fairy in em. Tom be part fairy as well, although, being a man, his bloodline dinna matter. That was how he knew to bring you here. He saw the lassie's ears and wings and knew right away she would need, shall we say, more focused care than he could provide. Among other things, Barba and I are local healers dealing in more, hmm, homeopathic remedies. Many date back to the colony's beginning, others only to Queen Mog and Princess Titania."

Kandi's head was spinning. This was so much information all at once. She was shocked at the revelation of the fairy colony's continued existence, which created another problem. The history between fairies and pixies was checkered at best. The two races hadn't spoken since the beginning of the Human Wars. The fairies on Aeden had been healers, as Fiona claimed she was here, but they ran from the fight the humans brought to their shore and escaped to their haven on Gaia with no word of where they had gone.

For Kandi, that was an unforgivable stain on the race, almost as bad as the one on humans. Would the fairies be able to put their differences aside? Would she? The two women seemed pleasant enough, even after discovering her true origins. After all, even though the dispute was recent for her, it was centuries in the past for these women. She perked up, sat a little taller in her chair, and said, "So, Titania existed? The legends are true?"

Barba responded, "There be so many stories. Which legends be that you speak?"

Kandi recited the tale, "That, as a young woman, Titania married Laird MacLeod and bore a son before being brought back to Fairie by her father."

Barba giggled, "Now, dinna believe evre'thin you hear. Be no doubt; there always be a wee bit of truth in evre'thin, and the story you've heard be partly true, aye, but there is a lot of difference between the legend and the real truth. First of all, Titania and the Laird never actually married, but yea, they did have children, twins, a boy, and a girl."

Kandi was confused, "But the legends only tell about the boy staying with his father. What happened to the girl?"

Barba replied, "She returned with her ma, of course. Later, in the course of time, she became Queen herself."

Kandi was confused, "OK. I don't understand. Why did she take one child and not the other?"

Barba gave her a compassionate look, "Now, Kandi, as me ma hinted, men can't be a part of faerie. The energy dinna work with them. Only women can belong to the colony."

Her face reflected even more confusion, "But what about the king, Titania's father?"

Fiona giggled, "Aye, that is the other lie in the legend. Dang humans have always been misogynistic. Twas never a king of faerie. Never has been. Titania's ma, Queen Mog, fetched her back after Titania's wee laddie was weened. Only women can rule here. Always have and always will. Men are needed only to continue the race."

The room became strangely silent as its newest occupants considered the information they had received. Finally, Fiona broke the spell.

"So now, you dinna come here for a history lesson. Tell us the real reason why you come searching for us?"

Kandi told her story. When she finished, she concluded, "So, I'm trapped here. Something happened on Aeden, something bad. I need crystal – specifically, the types used for gate structures- to attempt to go back. I had hoped that you closed your gate after setting up the colony and that some crystal might still exist here."

Fiona shook her head, "Well, lassie. Not to say those crystals don't exist, but they sure don't exist here." Kandi's face fell. "We did have quite a few at the time of the collapse, but then them scavengers from the East, Yodin, and a bunch of his thugs from that icy wasteland of theirs laid siege to our land and only spared our lives when we agreed to give them what crystals we had."

Fiona's comments caused Jon to speak up, "Wait! Yodin? Odin? Are you telling me that the Norse Gods are also real?"

Fiona looked back at Jon, "Laddie, we know nothin' of gods. Yodin was a real elf, a Watcher at that, as were his cohorts, but gods? Nay. They were as mortal as you or I. That encounter with Yodin was when we fairies decided we could no longer afford our peaceful ways. We had to learn to defend ourselves against whatever came next. Years later, we heard rumors of battles between them and other Watcher groups from the Southlands. We assumed that those clashes destroyed pretty much all the remaining crystal."

"Battles? What kind of warring took place?" Kandi's interest was piqued.

"Just rumors, yanno? Tales told by wayward ships and all. Word was that Watcher Commander Zeus, from the Atlantia gate, along with the bunch from Gomorrah controlled things along the southern sea between them. Then, in the far southern continent, Amon, Ra, and their bunch were also making some noise. That's about all we heard here."

Kandi was surprised at the fairy's comments, "That's still pretty detailed information, Fiona. I remember Yodin and Zeus very well. Yodin was one of the Watchers stationed at Asgard gate, but that was long ago in Gaian time. How can you possibly know about them if the collapse was so long ago."

"The histries child – the histries kept by every queen since the colony began 22,346 years ago."

Kandi gasped, shaken by the information. 22,346 years? She'd had no idea so long a period had elapsed since the collapse. *How could anything have survived?* Then the truth slapped her, "Wait, are you saying that…you're the queen?"

"Aye, Kandi. I am truly the 200th queen of this colony, a direct descendant of Queen Mog and Princess Titania and all the queens before and after them, as is my daughter and heir, Barba."

The two newcomers took another moment to assimilate this information. There was a lot to comprehend, and Kandi grew ever more confused. She had come looking for ruins, a place where a colony had once existed, perhaps a hidden chamber if they had been lucky. Never in her wildest dreams did she ever consider that the settlement might have survived.

Jon piped up, "So, when did the gates fall?"

"Two-hundred and twenty-three years after our founding. Dinna affect us, of course. The pixie is correct that yon gate was disabled right after we arrived. Dinna want nor need those Aedinian bastards tellin' us what was what." She glanced at Kandi, who looked startled, and quickly added, "No offense, dearie. Still, when the collapse happened, we felt it in our bones – crystal to crystal, as if somethin' ripped the fabric of life itself.

Hard times followed – for everyone. Humans, elves, pixies, and fairies – we all suffered. Faerie fared better than most since we were self-sufficient and had built our colony without outside interference. We had always tried to stay as far from crystalline technology as possible–staying close to the earth was our motto."

They continued talking until the shadows turned to night. Then, Fiona took a deep breath, signaling the end of the conversation, "Well, the time be getting' late. Tomarra be another day for jawing and the recounting of tales. Best we retire and pick this up in the mornin. Barba will sleep with me. You two can have her bed."

Jon responded quickly, shouting, "No!" which startled the two fairies and got a stern look from Kandi. Jon added, "I mean, no, thank you. We aren't a couple."

"Oh? Sorry, boy. My mistake. Just assumed a handsome lad and a comely lass traveling together be bedmates. No matter. We can make ye a pallet on the floor while the young miss can take the bed."

The house stilled as its residents turned in for the night. Later, in the wee hours of the morning, a blood-curdling scream came from Barba's room, waking everyone in the house. Jon jumped off the floor and ran to the top of the stairs, where he found Fiona and Barba already standing by the side of Kandi's bed. Kandi, herself, laid still; her lost eyes were open and fixed on something no one else could see. Sweat was beading up on her lip and forehead. She screamed once again, followed by a shout.

"Kandi? Kandi? Kandi!"

Fiona sent Barba downstairs to fetch something; Jon couldn't hear what, while she directed him to hold the pixie down to keep her from hurting herself.

Great, Jon's mind wandered as he did as Fiona asked. *What will keep her from hurting me, and why was she screaming out her name?*

Barba returned with a glass of water and some powder, which Fiona deftly poured into the drink, stirring the two with her index finger. Then, with Jon's assistance, she forced the potion down Kandi's throat. Despite the sputtering and strangling sound coming from the pixie, most of the liquid went into her, and a short time later, she calmed.

Fiona looked at Jon, "She'll sleep for a bit now. Was this be what happen' on da road when Tom found ye?"

Jon nodded, "But not this bad; there was another time on the boat that was more like this." He described the earlier instance and what he had done to counteract it. Fiona nodded as she considered what he said.

With Kandi calm, Fiona took Jon by the arm and led him downstairs to the parlor room, leaving Barba sitting with Kandi, "Aye, ye be a lucky one. Not all human remedies work on Aedenians cause of the crystal in da blood." Jon looked frightened that he might have made Kandi worse. Fiona shook her head, "No, lad, you probly saved her life. High fevers are a bane for all of the races. Surprised her nanites didn't take care of it, though." She took a chair and motioned Jon to the other opposite of her. "Now, since we are up and not likely to sleep again anytime soon, let's talk more about the young lass and what ails her."

The two of them sat in the dimly lit room as Jon told her everything, the whole story, from the time he received the ring in Colorado to his and Kandi's arrival on the Isle of Skye and their chance meeting with Tom. The fairy listened quietly and respectfully but gasped when he recounted Kandi downloading Sara into her mind before listening patiently to the rest of his tale.

Fiona remained silent for a few minutes before speaking, "Well, Jon, that is a worthy tale, and I do not doubt its truthfulness." She pointed to his hand, "After all, a ring of power is hard to ignore. I assumed you would share your story when you were ready. An archangel's power tis great. Wha do ya know of it?"

Jon spoke quietly, "Little, I'm afraid. I never knew it existed until my father died. He left a note telling me what he knew about the ring, which wasn't much." Jon looked Fiona in the eyes, "I do know that he was afraid of it – that generation after generation had passed the stone down and never put the ring on their finger."

Fiona nodded sympathetically, "Aye, the burden of the archangel's ring isn't for most. Still, I'm surprised that the mystery tempted no other, or maybe they were, and the stone failed them. Only a direct descendant can wear the thing, and only then ifn the ring accept them. Those not accepted would die a horrible death."

Jon trembled at that news as he looked at his hand and the chance he had taken back in New York, "How do I know if I'm accepted?"

Fiona reached over and patted his hand, "Well, ya be alive. That be a good sign." She laughed as she looked at Jon's troubled face, "Don't fret, lad, you be fine. The ring shows its acceptance when the stone glows blue."

Jon added, "The ring did change. There was a red glow before."

Fiona nodded, "Aye, red be the sign of distress at being separated from its owner. The stone was callin' out for another archangel to help. Course twas no one left then. Know ye who your ancestor be?"

Jon shook his head, "No. The note my father left didn't say. Kandi told me there were fourteen of them in the beginning. That's all I know."

Fiona gazed into the empty room behind him, "There is precious little I can add to that, I'm afraid." She looked back at Jon, "The histries tells us that the rings draw from the same earth power as fairies. The crystal at the ring's heart is said to be from Origen hisself. There is much power in such a stone."

Jon felt comfortable talking to the fairy and continued, "Does the ring have a plan for me?"

Fiona laughed softly, "Nay, laddie. The ring is not a god, only a tool to help the archangel in his daily work. The stone is sentient like an AI, yanno?"

"How do I know what to do with the thing?"

"Aye. Someday, I feel certain you'll figure that out, but we have more pressin' things right now. You said that Miss Kandi downloaded an AI into her mind?"

Again, Jon nodded. "Yes. Her name is Sara. They rushed the transfer. Sara had already activated the self-destruct, and Kandi only had a few minutes to do everything. Fiona, there has to be something you can do – some way to help her."

"I be thinkin' I see what may be the yon lassie's problem." Fiona grew even more severe, "Jon, me thinks I can help her, but the power I'm drawing on has a cost. She can't agree, so the burden falls on you. Are you willing to pay?"

Jon was confused but never hesitated, "Yes. Whatever I can do to help her, I will gladly do."

"Very well. The price will not cause you physical harm, but it will not be without consequence, understand? "

"Yes." Jon was resolute in his decision.

"Good lad. I canna do the cure here. I need to take her to the Castle."

Jon nodded his understanding, "The Castle, you mean Dunvegan, where we landed?"

"Nay lad, that one's just for show. We need to go to the Fairy Castle, Ewan, up in the hills next to a place the tourists call the fairy glen. We laugh about that. The glen is pretty enough, but we never took to the place much. Still, it's great fun to watch them doodle around, lookin under rocks and such." She called up the stairs, "Barba, get the car ready. Jon, I need ya to help me with the girl."

As they headed up into the hills, Jon reflected on the number of times he had relied on the kindness of strangers on this trek. *Of course*, he thought, *If I hadn't been kidnapped...* Then he looked down at the pixie lying with her head in his lap. *As much as she has done, how can I care so much about her welfare? How can someone so deadly look so innocent?* He remembered the last sparring session on the fantail of the yacht. She had mopped up the floor with him. He still had muscles that complained every time he moved them. He glanced up just as they passed a car park off the side of the road; Fairy Glen Parking was displayed on a small sign barely visible through the deepening fog.

A short time later, Barba pulled over into a passing place, ignoring the "No Parking" sign posted there. "From here, we hafta walk. No road to Ewan. Mum, wanna grab a torch from the boot?"

Jon picked up Kandi and waited, all the time shivering from the cold and dampness. Kandi showed no reaction to the external conditions at all. Her face remained frozen in the same position as her last scream.

The two fairies led the way, with Jon stumbling along behind them. Even with a torch shining directly before him, the deepening fog made walking treacherous. Fortunately, the winding trail wasn't too long, eventually ending up at a rock formation that, even in the mist, looked every bit like a doorway.

Fiona whispered, "Alright, Jon, now comes the tricky part. Any tourist can get to this point. They looks up an sees rocks in a castle shape, right? They mights even climb the bugger. Then they goes home. Now, watch this."

She gathered herself up until she appeared much taller than she had only a moment before. A radiant aura surrounded her, getting brighter with each passing second. Finally, she reached out and allowed the glow to contact the slab of rock. The result was like nothing in Jon's experience, nothing short of spectacular.

Where the hill had been, a castle – a real castle, now stood with its door open for them to enter.

"Now, Jon," Fiona continued, "I not be sure what will happen next. If you be a normal human male, the castle will reject ya immediately, but I be thinkin' that the stone you carry might allow you safe passage. Just in case I'm wrong, I'll put the torch at the gate and the car keys in your pocket. If the castle denies you entrance, go back and stay warm."

Jon seemed confused, "Why would the castle refuse me?"

Fiona looked at Jon with faint bemusement, "You be male, ya daft bugger. Like Barba told ya, faerie is a land for women only."

Jon was still confused, "How will I know?"

Fiona turned toward the entrance and laughed, "Trust me, you will know."

Jon continued, unwilling to let this go, "But won't you need me to carry her back to the car?"

Fiona began walking, "If this works, she can carry herself."

Jon stopped, "And if the treatment doesn't work?"

Fiona turned back toward him, compassion in her eyes, "Then...Sorry to be blunt, she'll die. That is the whole of it."

Jon went numb after hearing the fairy's words. *Kandi, dead?* As much trouble as she had caused him over the past weeks, he still couldn't imagine her dead – he didn't want to imagine her dead, especially so soon after losing Sara. The four of them began walking to the inner doorway. Almost at once, he felt a feeling of dread come over him, a sense of despair so strong that if he didn't turn back, the power would utterly crush him.

Fiona noticed his hesitation on the castle's threshold and was impressed by his intention to continue. She quietly, almost apologetically, said, "Me thinks Barba and I will have to manage from here, hey?"

He choked out a reply with tears in his eyes, "I'm guessing so. Bring her back to me, okay?" The fairy looked at him sympathetically, "Oh, laddie; you do love her, don't ye?"

"No...no...I...it's...complicated."

Fiona smiled. *Aye, laddie, love always is.*

The two fairies turned and proceeded down the brightly lit hallway, struggling under the dead weight of the unconscious pixie, keeping their eyes focused on the room at the end. Behind them, the heavy door closed, leaving Jon in the cold.

"Pray tell how this creature can fly?" asked Barba innocuously.

Fiona laughed, "Mighty strong wings be my guess. Besides, could be we are a wee bit puny, heh?"

Barba laughed, "Go'n all the way to the main hall?" She nodded forward.

"Yep. The lass is pretty far gone. If there be a chance of savin' her, we need to pull out all the stops."

The well-lit hallway seemed impossibly long. Earthen energies made that happen, of course. What appeared as a ruined castle facade on the outside stretched hundreds of meters under the hill. This place had been the site of the original colony's ring of power, drawn from deep within the planet itself, the same energy used by the fairies today.

Finally, half spent, Fiona and Barba maneuvered Kandi to their destination, the central hall of the castle, an impressive space illuminated by light emanating from the walls. Shelving ringed the room, each ledge hewn out of the rock itself. On each one sat rows of jars with labels written in an ancient script. In the center of the room was a large, roughly carved stone table, the only furnishing the room had or needed.

The two fairies lifted Kandi onto the table and rapidly gathered their needed books and materials. There was no time to lose.

"This not be a simple healin'. I be guessin' that one of us needs to go in?" Barba asked, even though she knew the answer.

"Aye. The poison runs deep inside the pixie's mind. What's killin' this lass isn't on the outside fer sure." Fiona talked as she compounded the contents of several jars from around the room. She stopped and looked at her daughter suspiciously, "Not you, though. I be the one to do it."

Barba held her ground, "Nay, ma. I canna let ye. You be the Queen, after all, and the people need ya. Let me go."

Fiona took a moment from her compounding to look Barba in the eye, "Nonsense, child. Like I would let you die before you can reign? I've had a good run of it. If this be my time, our folk will sing well of my life. You be a good daughter, Barba, and ye will make a fine queen yerself. I must be the one to go, and part of ye knows it."

The compound finished; Fiona walked to where a small stream flowed across the floor and pooled in a basin near the far wall. She took some water and mixed the liquid with the powder in the bowl. Then, she carefully carried the potion to the table, pouring half of the contents into the pixie's half-open mouth.

Fiona turned back to her daughter, "Barba? If this mind-merge I be about to try dinna work, the fate of our colony be in your hands. You be the queen. Among other things, that means no more messin' around. Ye need to find yourself a male and get thyself an heir. I saw you fancy yon Jonathan. Methinks highly of him, too. He has also claimed ownership of the price of this magic. Think about it."

Barba was shocked as the seriousness of the situation sank into her consciousness, "Ma, you be scarin' me now. Don't be talking crazy. You're gonna be just fine. You both are." She tried her best to hide the tears forming in her eyes.

Fiona gently set the bowl on the table and crawled up beside Kandi. Holding the potion in both hands, she quickly downed the contents. "Damn, that be foul stuff there," the fairy laughed as she set the bowl down and laid down next to the pixie. She began chanting in an ancient tongue, not elven, but something even older - faerie. Somewhere in the middle of a phrase, she joined Kandi in sleep, a sleep that could only conclude if both participants wanted to wake, and Fiona had no guarantee that would happen.

From her post beside the table, Barba watched her mother drink the potion and begin saying the words that would tie her mind with the girl beside her. She knew this to be high magic, the earth magic brought from Aeden centuries ago and now fed by Gaia, their adopted world. Her mother had trained her well in its use, and she prayed that the power didn't fail Fiona now.

Chapter 27 – A Meeting of Minds

Fiona had joined minds many times during her reign as queen. Often, the afflicted person would be dealing with grief or abuse. A few times, the illness was more profound, a psychosis that required finesse to ease the personality back into balance. This time was different; the joining would be unique. In all her years and all the histories, there was no reference to a shared mind, two complete personalities existing within one body. She would have to tread delicately or risk losing herself in the process.

The entrance to Kandi's mind was a flat gray tunnel with no visible imperfections. Entering a person's subconscious was a lot like being born. In both, a person moves through a channel, leaving safety for the uncertainty of the undiscovered country ahead. This part of the journey was familiar to the fairy. The mystery within the pixie's mind was what concerned Fiona. That lay in the unknown before her.

At the end of the tunnel was a dark, not entirely black, room. Fiona took a moment and allowed her eyes to adjust, not her physical eyes, of course, but the inner eye she would need here. She found herself encased in a room – a stone room. Fiona ran her hands over the walls, feeling the coolness, the dampness of the hewn rocks. She investigated the space around her and found it empty. This was a bad sign. She had to hurry; time was short.

Feeling her way around the walls, Fiona began to despair when no openings presented themselves. Was she already too late? As a last resort, she shouted at the top of her lungs, "Kandi! Are ya here, lassie? It's me, Fiona, come to fetch ya out." There was no response, "Lass, ifn you can hear me, let me know!" No sound returned to her, but she got a feeling, a vibe, leading her to a spot on one of the walls that looked like every other.

Pressing against the stonework, she called upon the powers of the earth to aid her. As before, her form began to glow. Her aura merged into the wall and dissolved the stones where her hands touched.

Fiona was impressed with the intricacy of the construct. *Methinks, whatever created these barriers was more powerful than the lass or her AI friend. Somethin' else is at work here.* Finally, she melted enough stonework to see inside a second room. There, curled in a fetal position on the floor, was Kandi.

Fiona crawled through the hole, thankful that, in her present state, she didn't have to suffer through her arthritis as she did so. She embraced the pixie, allowing her aura to fill her and to seek out the source of Kandi's affliction. She was progressing when startled by another voice, "Why are you here? The pixie isn't for you."

Fiona spun around to see a dark shadow of a man in the light of her aura. "What do ya mean, not fer me?" she asked.

In a robust and steady voice, the creature explained, "This one belongs to my master. He claimed her long ago when he planted me in her mind. She is for him alone, and he has decided she must die."

Fiona prepared to fight, "Ya thin so? Not ifn I have a say, tis not."

"I am not for you, witch. Do not vex me. There are powers at work that you cannot understand."

"Oh, I understands plenty. You wanna this child. Well, laddie, you are gonna be disappointed there." With those words, Fiona gathered all the power she commanded into her person and threw herself onto the dark form. She managed to catch the creature off-guard. The fairy drove it back toward the wall. Yet, the construct quickly recovered, countering her move and pushing her back toward Kandi.

During that first contact, Fiona became instantly aware of what kind of creature she fought and how its power came not from within itself but from the pixie herself. As long as this struggle continued, Kandi would weaken until, at last, she would die. Fiona also became painfully aware of who had created the beast before her. *How had the pixie gotten herself involved with that one....* She allowed her mind to wander before refocusing on the task at hand. There was only one thing to do. She would plunge into the darkness to destroy the parasite from within the lass. This move would most likely kill her but might save the pixie. She glanced at the helpless girl on the floor and made her decision. *So be it.* She focused on the immediate threat. *Ifn ya gonna die, Fiona, go out with a bang, heh?*

Fiona threw herself entirely into the fight, attacking the creature at its source, hoping that the intensity of the attack would conquer the beast before it could kill the girl. At first, the battle seemed hopeless. The creature mirrored every trick she tried, throwing them back on her with equal or superior force. She had the beast's full attention now. It began to focus on her as a source of power instead of the girl. *Good.* The fight seemed endless, and Fiona knew she was losing. Her defeat was imminent, a defeat that would mean death for both women and a victory for the only person she knew who could have designed this abomination – the Archangel Iblees.

The power of the dark force seemed jubilant as it battered her, absorbing all the energy she could muster. Fiona was ready to give up, her body slumping toward the mind chamber floor. Content that she had given her best effort, she was shocked as another being joined them in the room.

At first, Fiona feared Barba had disobeyed and entered the fight, but a second look showed that this was not her. The form of the newcomer's aura was so strong that Fiona's vision of it was of intense light, and no fairy could equal it. However the newcomer came to be, it was welcome. The light creature joined in the battle without hesitation. It grabbed Fiona, embracing her and supplementing her strength with its own. The new creature's power was immense, far greater than anything the fairy had ever experienced, but she had doubts that power alone could quell the darkness threatening the pixie's life.

Her answer came soon enough. The brilliant light grew in size and intensity until it encompassed the dark man. Try as it might, it could not escape the aura surrounding it. It twisted and turned under the attack, wailing his doom before issuing a primal scream that echoed through Kandi's mind chambers in defeat. The dark form vaporized, and with its exit, the chamber's walls fell into a thousand blocks that dissolved into nothingness, revealing yet another room similar to this one. Fiona smiled as she realized what this latest revelation meant.

"Kandi!" The newly released being sprang from her former prison and ran to embrace her friend. At first, the pixie did not move, but as the new person hugged her intensely, sharing her aura, an eyelid fluttered, a cheek twitched, and a slight smile appeared.

A weak voice rose from the still form, "Hello, Sara. About time you showed up."

Chapter 28 - Acceptance

Jon awakened in a cold sweat, still in the car with the engine running. The nightmare had been so vivid and clear, yet he couldn't explain what had happened. He knew that Kandi had been there with him, as had Fiona. Some dark creature was threatening the two women. He had somehow saved them, destroying the creature in the process. *There you go, Jon. The only way you play the hero is in your dreams!*

Still upset, Jon could wait no longer. He had to find out what was happening in the castle. He flew out of the car and up the path, soon regretting that he hadn't brought the torch. Unsuccessfully trying to force his eyes to see in the dense fog, Jon slipped and then tripped over the rocks. As he picked himself up, feeling foolish, he looked up and saw Barba and...Kandi? He almost shouted, "I've never been so happy to see anyone!" He ran to their sides and gave Kandi the biggest bear hug he could manage. She didn't return the gesture, of course. He was just happy she didn't use him as a sparring dummy. He held on until Kandi whispered, "Human? Let go of me or die." "Oh...I see you really are back then," he responded, "Haven't mellowed much."

Barba interrupted the reunion, "Jon, I've got Kandi, but Fiona be still sittin' by the castle entrance. Would you be a dear and fetch her? She be needin' a wee bit of help herself."

Jon nodded his assent, "Meet you back at the car."

No longer needing to run to the rescue, Jon slowed his pace, which made the obstacles on the path easier to see. Before he knew it, he was standing in front of the castle and the huddled figure beside what should be the door.

"Fiona?" The figure pushed the hood from her face and looked up at him. Jon gasped. She looked terrible! What did Kandi's recovery cost her? "Hey, I'm here to help you back to the car. Can you walk, or do I need to carry you?"

"I can manage ifn I have a strong arm to lean on," was the weak reply.

Jon gently helped the fairy to her feet and cautiously led her back to the car. Fiona took advantage of their slow progress to ask some questions of Jon. "Tell me, boy. Didya stay in the car the whole time?"

"Yes, ma'am. I stayed put. Honestly, though, I did drop off for a spell."

Fiona's voice seemed stronger as she asked, "Did ya now?" Jon nodded. "Now, that's interestin'. Did you perchance dream?"

Jon shuddered, "Don't think I'd call it a dream. More like nightmares."

Now the fairy was intrigued, "Was there anything or anyone you remember?"

Jon told his story, "Yeah. You were there. Kandi was, too, but she was on the floor of some ancient room, old stones on all sides. She seemed to be unconscious. There was someone else there as well. I couldn't distinguish his face, but he seemed like a bad dude. You and it were fighting, and, no offense, the fight wasn't going your way. Anyway, I ran over to see if I could help. As soon as I touched you, I felt something...energy, maybe. The power seemed to flow out of me and into you. Together, we beat the bad guy. Now that I think about it, I guess I've had worse nightmares."

Fiona turned toward him earnestly, "Twas no dream, laddie."

Jon tripped over his own feet. "What do you mean? I had to be dreaming. I woke up at the end and was still in the car."

Fiona sighed, "You joined me in Kandi's mind. Somehow, ya sensed her danger and flew to be by her side. Good thing ya did, too. You weren't imaginin' anything. I was losing. Without your help, we couldn't have survived the assault. You saved our lives. Ya be a hero there, laddie."

Jon was thoroughly confused, "I still don't understand. How..."

Fiona shook her head in disbelief, "The ring, ya idgit! The ring! Ya sensed the danger, and the stone projected ya inta the scene. Now, there be no question that the bloody thing's adopted ya, and the stone has begun to respond to yer needs. Ya see?"

Jon was still skeptical, "I'm not sure I believe all this; an ancient ring that responds to me?" Jon paused before continuing, "Fiona? If this was real, who was the dark man?"

Fiona spoke honestly, "I've no idea. I've never met anything like that monster, but I'm sure of one thing. Someone made that beastie, and I'm pretty sure there's only one creature capable of making something that evil."

"Who?" Jon asked.

"He was a nasty breed of elf, the Archangel Iblees. He was evil through and through. Over the centuries since the collapse, his name changed. You probably would know him as Lucifer."

Jon couldn't believe his ears, "Lucifer? As in the devil? Are you trying to tell me that the devil did this?"

Fiona continued her tale, "Aye, but he is far more powerful than your devil ever dreamed of being. I had hoped he'd died in the collapse along with the others, but this creature inside the lass tells me differently. Ifn he was truly dead, the earth energies he'd conjured up would have left with him, and this power was most decidedly alive. One other thing about Iblees; he isn't one to give up when he fails. Not sure when he planted the dark fella back there or why, but one thing for sure, he wanted the little lass dead and out of the way." She turned to face Jon, "Pays to be prepared."

As they approached the car, Jon asked Fiona not to mention his involvement until he was more comfortable with what had happened. The four were silent all the way home, where they drifted into a deep sleep.

Sometime during the night, a form joined Jon on the pallet in the living room. A nude form pushed herself against him, a decidedly female form. "Kandi?" he murmured. "Nay, Jon," she murmured, "Tis me, Barba," the woman responded.

In his near dream state, Jon still had the presence of mind to ask, "What…why are you here?"

The fairy responded by gently kissing him on the lips, "Enough talk for now."

The following day, Jon awoke from yet another fantastic dream.

Chapter 29 – The Prodigal Returns

What a difference a day makes. Jon stretched lazily as he awakened to a beautiful day. The sun was out, and the sky practically sparkled with happiness. He and Barba prepared breakfast, with Jon finding her closeness very distracting based on last night's dream – a perfect dream, but a dream nonetheless.

After eating, Fiona commented, "Jon, There is something important you should know." She gave a look in Kandi's direction. "I believe you should do the honors."

Kandi nodded. Her demeanor seemed more reserved as her voice and facial muscles shifted slightly. "I'm back too, Jon."

"Sara?" Jon couldn't believe it, "Sara, is it really you?"

"Really me. Guess you can't get rid of me that easily."

"Sara, what happened to you?"

Sara retraced the events on the boat—the fever, the visions, and finally, the man or beast. Jon shuddered as he recognized the figure as the one he had battled in his "dream" last night. Gripped by Sara's story, Barba blurted out, "How awful!" Fiona nodded her agreement with the sentiment.

Jon stood there with tears in his eyes, "Thank God you're back."

The facial mien of the pixie changed once again. The bearing and demeanor of the girl gave no doubt that Kandi was back in charge. She spoke with their hostess, "Fiona, so much that happened last night is a blank; most of the rest is a blur of color and emotions. What happened to me?"

"Ah, lass. At first, I was certain ye was reacting to Miss Sara sittin' in your subconscious. Possession will do that from time to time. Once I got into ye head, though, I realized your situation was far more serious. For lack of a better term, a demon had his hooks inta ya."

Kandi laughed, "I'm sorry. I don't believe in demons."

"Dinna matter what ye believe. This demon was real. The beast had the name of its creator attached to it. I thinks you will recognize it – Iblees."

Kandi blanched at the mention of the name and became strangely withdrawn.

"So, who is this Iblees?" Jon asked, attempting to be unaware of what had transpired the night before.

Even though Jon directed his question to Fiona, Kandi quietly responded, "The Archangel Iblees was in charge of the University of Babel when the Institute assigned me there as his guardian."

Her response prompted a follow-up question from the human, "And that's important – why?"

She hesitated in her response. Jon had never seen her look so vulnerable. "Iblees was a very handsome, powerful elf with a mesmerizing personality. I had completed several assignments since the war and was given this as a reward for my efforts. After working together for a while, Iblees and I became – involved."

Jon inquired sheepishly, "So...You were lovers?"

"We were intimate, but the relationship wasn't purely physical, at least on my part. I was madly in love with him and wanted to be his soul partner, and he gave me every indication that he felt the same." Kandi was unnaturally sad as she spoke, "I felt that the world was perfect when we were together."

Jon dared another question, "So, what happened?"

"Not a what, a who. Her name was Mara. She was a new intern at the university, where she assisted in the physical sciences. She was beautiful, young, naïve, and not tainted by the stink of war like I was. She was a tantalizing morsel for Iblees to possess. He dropped me in a heartbeat. I had gone from the 'center of his world' to 'I didn't matter anymore.' I was crushed and requested an immediate transfer back to the Institute."

Now Fiona took time to speak. "I be pretty sure that during one of your trysts, he planted that mind drone in your subconscious. Methinks he didn't want you telling stories, yanno?"

"But that was long ago, even in Aedinian time."

"Aye. For whatever reason, the drone malfunctioned. It dinna seem to activate until you gave Miss Sara here a home in your noggin. I'm a bettin' that was the trigger."

With trepidation, Kandi asked, "Is it...is the thing gone now?"

Fiona smiled, "Aye, child. We destroyed the drone. The beastie dinna trouble ye no more." Fiona glanced at Jon and nodded, acknowledging his involvement without saying anything. "Now, lass. Tell me true. How be ye feelin'?"

Kandi's voice belied her words. "A bit weak, but I think I'm OK."

"Good. I recommend plenty of rest for the next couple o' days. Yer future can wait a bit."

Chapter 30 – Aboard the *Voyager Templar*

The time was well after midnight, and most of Gunwharf Quays Marina was quiet. At the far end of the mooring area, a bachelor stag still raged, but where the *Voyager Templar* sat berthed, nothing stirred except the gentle lapping of the Channel waters against the hull. Like the other yachts around her, her windows were dark, and with no duty assignments, her crew slept. Unlike military vessels, no one would be on security watch. Why would they? There could be no danger here.

For that reason, no one witnessed the five men in wetsuits climb onto the fantail. They silently and efficiently stripped off their air tanks, masks, and flippers while recovering their weapons from a side pouch. Using hand signals only, the one who appeared to be the team leader directed them in the assault. One by one, the team awakened the sleeping crew and herded them into the yacht's salon at gunpoint. Soon, all fifteen groggy crewmen were safely gathered. The only one missing was the captain.

Captain Stilman had awakened a few moments before the boarding and was out on the bow of the *Templar* smoking a cigarette to calm his nerves. He wasn't sure what was bothering him, but something didn't feel right, and he was confident that 'something' involved his former and possibly future passengers. He flicked his unfinished smoke into the water and headed toward his cabin.

"Didn't expect to find you out here, Captain," a quiet yet intense voice stated.

The noise unsettled the captain. He knew that voice. He was sure he had heard the man before, but where? He decided to play along. "Didn't expect to be looked for." Only then did the captain see the silenced Uzi in the man's hands and realize this was more serious than he could ever have imagined. He gestured toward the gun, "Mind telling me what's happening here?"

"My men and I are going to have a friendly chat with you and your crew. If I like your answers, we will let you go; otherwise...." He nodded toward the weapon in his hand.

"So, you are commandeering my vessel?" the captain retorted.

"This is no longer your vessel. Your ship is under my command now."

The captain decided to take a chance. As he walked past the man with the gun, he stumbled, drawing the man's attention away for just a moment. The Captain took advantage of the situation by reaching over and grabbing the man's weapon, pulling the pirate off-balance. The Uzi slid across the deck, leaving the two men in hand-to-hand combat.

The Captain was retired military and had kept himself in good physical condition. Usually, he would be able to get the upper hand on just about any assailant, but the adversary he faced was special forces, stronger and faster. Despite his best efforts, the attacker quickly subdued him, beating him even after the captain lost consciousness. The man got up, recovered his weapon, and returned to the still form on the deck. He fired two silenced shots, leaving two small holes in the Captain's forehead.

"Well, this just got messy," the man said before returning to his companions in the salon.

"Where's the captain, sir?" one of the invaders asked.

"The captain won't be joining us."

"Very well, sir." No questions were asked.

One of the *Templar*'s crew, the helmsman, commented, "Hey, I know you. You were that suit on that Coast Guard cutter that stopped us out of Boston!"

Colonel Forester smiled. "Very good, young man." *Even if the captain hadn't sealed their fate, this one would have.* He continued to address the crew, "Gentlemen, I am certain you are all intelligent men," Forrester started, "I hope that we can resolve our differences quickly and efficiently."

"Where's the Captain?" one of the crewmen spoke up.

"Your captain elected not to resolve our differences."

"You mean you killed him? Right?"

"Your Captain did not demonstrate the intelligence I am sure you possess."

"You can go screw yourself!"

"Apparently, you do not possess that intelligence either." A short burst from the Uzi silenced the crewman forever. "Anyone else care to comment?" The room was silent as Forester changed clips for the weapon. All the crew's eyes focused on the still form on the floor. "Very well. Here is what I need. There were two passengers on board when you left Boston." Only silence was his answer. "You can answer my questions, or I can kill someone else. Your call."

The ship's cook spoke, "Yeah, a couple of people got on board in Boston, don't know who. They wanted their privacy, right? The captain told us to steer clear of them. I even had to call to schedule their meal deliveries. None of us ever laid eyes on them except the captain."

"Very good, young man. What happened to these travelers?"

Another sailor raised his hand like he was back in school.

Forrester was amused, "Yes?"

"Captain had me use the launch to take them to shore a few nights back. They stayed there."

Forrester leaned in toward the sailor. This was getting interesting. "Where exactly?"

"We were sailing through the Little Minch. We did a dead stop, dropped anchor, loaded the launch with their stuff, and took them to the Isle of Skye."

"Any idea where you landed?"

"No, sir. The lady was the one giving me directions. Not sure where we were …no, wait, I remember a silhouette of a castle outlined against the sky."

"Nothing else."

"No, sir."

Forrester went on to interrogate the crew for another hour. One of them gave up the presence of the secret room where Martyr and the woman had hidden when the Coast Guard visited. The space was empty now. He addressed one of the men, "Rig the boat, then have the team assemble on the fantail."

"Yes, sir."

A member of the yacht's crew asked, "Rig the boat? For what?"

Forrester smiled as his Uzi spoke and sprayed the crew members with bullets. The room stank of gunpowder and blood when he finished.

Their mission completed, the team eased themselves back into the water and headed toward Old Portsmouth, where their vehicles waited. Once they were safely on their way back to London, the colonel nodded at his demolition expert, and the *Voyager Templar* erupted. Fiery hull fragments, cabins, and crew flew hundreds of feet into the air before settling onto the sea and surrounding ships. What little remained of the yacht quickly sank.

Forrester grabbed the sat phone and made an encrypted call. "Sir. Our quarry made a side trip to the Isle of Skye for unknown reasons. Do you have any idea why they did that? No, me either. Anyway, we know they landed on the island's west coast near a castle of some kind. I'll get my people on the problem and see if they can narrow the location down more than that. I'll contact you from the island."

The man behind the desk hung up the phone and slammed both fists into the polished wood. *Damn!* he thought. *Isle of Skye? What could be there for them? What do you think you are doing, Kandi Mehra?* He sat silent for an eternity, pondering over the problem.

Suddenly, an improbable answer came to mind. *Wasn't there a fairy colony on Skye once?* He gave the idea further consideration; *Yes, there was. The damn fairies had found their way there before the war started, light years from the pixies and elves that caused them grief on Aeden. The Institute discovered them later, somewhere on the island's northern end – away from the human colonies in the south. There would be no way for the settlement to survive this long without being noticed. Nothing of importance could possibly remain. Could the fairies still be the connection? An artifact, perhaps? I'll have Forrester check it out.*

United States Space Command
Isle of Skye

Colonel Forrester and his unit made a side trip before going to the Isle of Skye. The island offered only a few covert landing sites that would be suitable. Besides, they would need a land vehicle once they arrived. He instructed the pilot to set course for Kinloss Barracks on the northern tip of Scotland. There was an American contingent there who would have the items he needed.

Kinloss was remote – about fifty kilometers northwest of Inverness and spitting distance to the North Sea, with only small towns and villages surrounding it. Two days passed while the team performed the resupply, and Forrester pared his team down to five members. *Five would be more than enough to handle this problem.* He thought.

Based on the crew of the Templar's statements, the crewman had dropped the pair off near a castle on the island's western side after the captain dropped anchor in the Little Minch. According to Forrester's map, that left only one real option, Dunvegan Castle, located on the Loch of the same name.

The latest correspondence from his commander indicated the fugitives were searching for something on the Isle. Forrester had no idea where his intel came from or the target of their search, but that didn't matter. What mattered was that his quarry would be asking questions to find the answer to their quest. The castle proper would be an excellent place to start.

The team arrived at Dunvegan only to find the gates locked and darkness rapidly falling. Forrester and one of his men scaled the wall and approached the castle on foot. Continuous beatings on the door eventually revealed an unkempt caretaker scratching his head. Forrester asked pointed questions and showed the man pictures of the two fugitives. The man denied ever seeing them. He claimed that the Colonel and his assistant were the first two people he had seen since the castle closed for the season in October.

The night was upon them when the pair returned to the rest of the detachment. He was irritated that the caretaker was a failed lead, but even a lack of data was still information he could use. He directed his men to camp inside a car park across from the castle's entrance.

Later, as he ate his MRE, Forrester walked through the scenario. He was sure his adversaries were not in the castle; the caretaker was far too simple to lie about their presence. Forrester remembered passing a restaurant a couple of klicks down the road. He smiled. A public gathering place would be an excellent place to start.

Chapter 31 – Things that Go Bump in the Night

Jonathan awoke to his heart pounding in his chest and a cold sweat trickling down his forehead. The dream had been the same every night. He was in a dark canyon, surrounded by shadows, when an even blacker figure approached him, taunting him into doing battle. There was no turning around and fleeing. There was no method of escape available. Jon's only option was to fight the creature, a fight he sensed he was predestined to lose. The dream's end was always the same - him lying broken on the floor, waiting for the creature to finish him.

Barba had felt him jump and curled up beside him, soothing his pain with her gentle touch. He calmed as she reached into his psyche with her fairy healing and watched him as his breathing and heart rate returned to normal.

"The same dream, Jon?" she asked.

Jon paused before replying, "Yes, the vision has been identical every night since Fiona cured Kandi at the castle. It must mean something, but I'll be damned if I know what."

Barba was concerned, "Jon, it's been a week now. Ya need to talk to ma about this."

Jon nodded. He hadn't wanted to bother Fiona. Even now, Kandi needed her help far more than he did, but he could see that Barba was right, "Yeah. I guess it's time. I'll talk to her in the morning." Barba settled beside him, her breathing gradually sinking into sleep, but sleep was not for Jon this morning. Closing his eyes meant that the monster might return.

The darkness during the night was the only part of Jon's life that wasn't perfect. Everything else was like paradise. He smiled as he remembered his first dream encounter with the fairy princess, Barba, a week ago. He had assumed the encounter to be a vision until she approached him the following day.

After that, their affair evolved into a full-blown relationship. They were inseparable - like teenagers, giddy with the heady aroma of first love. They couldn't seem to keep their hands off each other. They hid it from the others, of course. This was something private between them.

Fiona and Barba owned several holiday cabins in Ulg, and Fiona encouraged Jon to move into one. She claimed she didn't like him having to sleep on the floor in the living room. That solution worked for Jon and Barba fine. They found themselves inventing reasons to run errands, allowing them to escape to their secret love nest where their amorous behavior wouldn't distract the others. Jon was hopelessly in love and felt the young fairy was as well. Even after so short a period, he could easily envision a permanent life with her and couldn't imagine one without her at his side.

The only thorn in his otherwise perfect life was his traveling companion, Kandi. Jon was having mixed feelings about the pixie. Part of him feared her, and rightly so; she had tossed him around like a rag doll that first night in Vermont, almost strangling him to death. Still, her dogged pursuit of what she perceived as a duty to Aeden and Gaia filled him with admiration. Then, there was the thousand-pound gorilla in the room. Was he in love with her?

Jon glanced over to where Barba was sleeping peacefully. How could he entertain being in love with someone else when this beautiful creature was right here? Still, Fiona's comment as she carried Kandi into the hidden castle echoed in his memory, "Oh, laddie, you do love her, don't ye?" Then he had said, "It's complicated," which was more or less still the case.

For her part, the pixie made no secret of her hatred for him and the rest of humanity. He wasn't sure she could love anymore, especially since her former lover, the Archangel Iblees, had just tried to kill her. He shook his head in an attempt to convince himself. *No*, he thought; *She only needs me for the ring. Once I open the gate, she will leave me in a heartbeat. Why am I worried about her anyway? I have a beautiful fairy woman who loves me, and I love her. What more could I ask for?*

Later that morning, Jonathan and Barba found Fiona sitting beside Kandi's bed, watching her sleep. "Ey Jon? What do yer need?" Jon quickly related his recurring nightmare, the words spilling out in a torrent, the memory alone enough to elevate his heart rate and cause him to sweat. When he had finished, the fairy queen looked him in the eyes, "Yer was right to bring this to me. The same vision every night?" Jon nodded. "Ah, laddie, this is Iblees scrying for ye."

Jon looked a little confused, "I'm sorry…scrying?"

Fiona managed a tired smile, "He be lookin' for ye, lad. Iblees be lookin' hard."

Confusion was still written on Jon's face, "Why me? What would he want with me? It was Kandi he wanted to kill, right?"

Fiona nodded, "Aye, he aimed the mind drone at her, but that was long ago. He probly dinna even remember setting the beasty until it went off in yon lass' skull. I be guessin' that your timely intervention in his plan caught his attention. Musta picked up on yer ring's signal during the fight. Findin' a stone such as yers alive and well probly bothers him a great deal more than yon pixie lass. He wanna know more about ye; most importantly, he wanna know where ye be."

Jon was deadpan, "So, I'm leading him here?"

Fiona replied, "Aye, but scrying is not that precise. He may know ye are on Skye but not where. Though Skye is small, there are still many places to be."

Jon gave a defiant look, "So, what do I do now?"

Fiona pushed herself out of her chair, "I can give ye some potions that will hold the visions at bay for a while. Then, I'll teach ye some mind tricks to keep him out fer as long as ye need. Ne'er ye mind Iblees. You're a match fer his like."

Jon appeared relieved, "So, I won't have to see him again?"

Fiona turned deadly serious, "Nay, Jon. I dinna say that. Iblees will nay give up until he finds ye and the two of ye do battle."

Jon blanched, "So, I'm going to die?"

At that, Fiona laughed, "Relax, Jonnie boy, we'll have ye prepared. Ye won't havta face him until ye are ready to do so. He canna harm ye less you invite him inta ye."

Chapter 32 – The Impending Storm

The following day, Colonel Forrester and his team headed south toward the Fairy Glen Café in Dunvegan. Logan McCubbin, the proprietor, was friendly and, more importantly, talkative, eager to please a prospective customer. Forrester put on his best folksy façade as he asked his questions.

"So, sir. Do you remember serving a young man and woman traveling alone about a week to ten days ago? Would have looked like tourists."

"Nay," Logan responded, "Out a'season. Dinna get many visitors this time of year, yanno. Only locals. Strangers would've stood out like a sore thumb. What ya need em for?"

Forrester flashed his government ID. When the official document sparked fear in the proprietor's eyes, he followed with a smile to settle the man's nerves, "Just need to talk to them about an incident on our side of the pond. Pretty important that we find them." He handed Logan a card and scribbled a local number on it. "Give me a call if you hear anything?"

"Aye, aye, I will." Logan pocketed the card in his apron.

Forrester had turned to leave when Logan's voice stopped him. "Nay…nay…just wait a minute." Forrester half turned back toward the man. "I just remembered somethin'. The nurse practitioner from Portree came in for a bite a few days ago. We got ta talkin' bout how quiet the island was with the tourists gone, and he started jabbing bout a couple he picked up on the high road. Pretty sure he said twas a boy and a girl."

Forrester attempted to mask his excitement, "And where would I find this nurse?"

"Aye, yer in luck there. Today is the day he holds a day clinic in town. Only here for half a day, though." He checked the clock on the wall. "Should be getting' there about now." Logan smiled, quite pleased with himself for remembering the information.

Forrester clapped the man on the shoulder in a sign of friendship, "Hey, Logan, that's great. Appreciate it. We'll go check in with the nurse. Thank you for your time."

The Dunvegan Health Centre was easy to find. The village only had one thru road, and the clinic was prominently identified with a sign out front. As Forrester approached, a middle-aged man was pulling files and equipment from his car's boot. The nurse asked, "Aye. Canna I help ye? Not quite ready for patients. Just getting ready to open up. Give me a minute, and I can see ya."

Forrester and his men followed the nurse inside. The colonel was all business as he flashed his ID at the nurse. Tom Yarrow initially panicked but calmed himself before replying, "Yer a long bit from home, sir. What can a poor soul like me do fer ya in this backwater of the universe."

Forrester inquired in a calm, even voice, "I believe you can be a tremendous help. I understand you met two strangers on the high road about a week ago."

The panic returned to Tom's eyes. He attempted to maintain his composure. "Ya know, sir, I meet loads of people every day. You'll need to be a bit more specific."

Forester pulled out the pictures of Jon and Kandi. "Boy was tall, about six-foot-two, the girl a lot shorter, barely over five feet." Forrester passed the photos of the two fugitives for the nurse to examine.

"Strangers, ya say? Don't get many of them this time of year." He shook his head, "No, I'm sorry. Dinna see anyone like that."

One of the team members closed the door to the clinic and turned the sign on the door from "open" to "closed." Forrester continued, "Well, that would be most unfortunate. You see, we have information on good authority that you did. Seems you told a whole café about them just a few days ago at breakfast."

Tom was trembling now, "Ol' Logan told you this tale? Sorry, friend. Old Logan canna keep a story straight from one day to the next. Loves to add things he feels make the story more interestin'. I be thinkin' he was just pullin' yer leg, yanno?"

Forrester's voice became lower and more intense as his eyes focused tightly on the nurse. "No, Tom. He seemed very alert and aware to me." The colonel subconsciously cracked his knuckles and his neck. "Now, are we going to do this the easy way or the hard way?"

Tom was now shaking with fear, and his voice trembled, "I dinna know what you mean? I dinna know the two?"

Forrester's lips curled into an evil smile, "The hard way then."

Chapter 33 – The Best Laid Plans…

Fiona's furrowed brow seemed out of place on her usually happy face as she looked at Jon and Kandi. "I hates to say this, but I need ya both to leave – right now."

The comment startled them, "What's happened?" was Kandi's first reaction, followed by, "Is everything okay? You gave me the impression that you wanted me to rest for a few more days. Where would we even go?"

Fiona's troubled face attempted a smile, "Look, Barba and I would love for ye to stay as long as ye desire, but circumstances have changed. It is not what we want but rather what is best. My Cousin Bram works at yon castle, the one where you landed. He calls this mornin' and tells me some Yanks came by lookin' for ye, lookin' for ye real hard ifn ya know what I mean."

Kandi looked at Jon, "NSA?"

Jon nodded in agreement as he whispered, "Or one of the other alphabet agencies. We do seem to be in demand." They had found them. He hated that his and Kandi's presence in Ulg was putting the fairies at risk, especially Barba.

Fiona continued, "As far as where to go…I be thinkin' ya need to be lookin to Norway. Way back when Yodin took all our crystals, he probly helped hisself to others' crystals too." She pulled a blank sheet of paper from a box on the shelf and began drawing a remarkably detailed map of a fragmented coastline at an unfathomable rate of speed.

"This be where the Valhalla gate was way back then," she pointed to an area just inland, "There be a waterfall, big un. Look for it. Twas big then, probly huge after all this time. Used to be a cave behind the falls that, in olden times, connected to Bifrost – the rainbow bridge to Asgard. I assume the big mess destroyed the gate and probably the bridge, but maybe some crystal remains."

Fiona pointed at a location on an inlet near the southern end of the map, "Today, this be whar Oslo be. Look for large waterfalls. The cascade's source is a huge plain, very unusual accordin' to the histries. Yodin and his bunch called the area Ragnarök after the battle site on Aeden. Them bein close together should help ya narrow yer search down. I ken that it's not much to go on, but I dinna know anything more."

Just then, the telephone interrupted her. Fiona excused herself. Kandi looked over at Barba, "Can I ask you something?"

"Of course. Anything." Barba was afraid that the question dealt with her relationship with Jon.

"Something has been troubling me. Why did Fiona think my problem started with Sara, and how did she know how to treat it?"

Barba sighed, "That's easy. The histries tell us of such things."

Kandi continued, "But when did Fiona consult the histries? I don't recall...." Suddenly, Kandi's face lit up with recognition. "Unless the histries are with you all the time. That's the answer, isn't it?"

Barba shyly replied, "Aye, lass. Long ago, when our AI's power be dyin', the queen did as ye did and downloaded the histries into her mind from it. Since then, the queen has shared a copy of the histries along with her experiences with the next queen. Over the centuries, we have encountered a few problems with the process."

Kandi began to understand, "I see. Problems like what I experienced?"

"Aye. Like that."

"So you..." Kandi looked at Barba intently.

Barba nodded, "Aye. Ma gave me the histries when I reached maturity a few years ago. Ifn she'd died in yer head, I was prepared to be queen."

Fiona, looking troubled, came back into the room. "The problem be more urgent than I first believed. We need to git ye on yer way immediately." She looked at her daughter, "Barba, darlin', I need fer ya to get these two into the car and down to the ferry landing at Armadale. The boats be the best way to avoid prying eyes."

Now, Barba was getting worried, "Ma? What's happened?"

"That were Cousin Ewan on the phone. He saw a bunch of men at the clinic stuffin' poor Tom into their car. Said they took off in a terrible rush – headed north, not east, toward Portree. Said Tom looked to be in a rough state. Don't take a genius to figure they be a comin' here." Fiona directed her attention to her daughter, "Barba, gather all their things and get goin'. Be fast. Ya need be long gone before they get here."

Kandi had other ideas, "No. We stay. There is no way we are leaving you here alone against these men. There is no telling what they will do if they don't find us here and discover you aided us. After all of your kindness and help, we won't leave you."

Fiona smiled, "Ah, dearie." She chuckled as she continued, "You not be wantin' to leave a poor, defenseless old lady, heh? I appreciate the sentiment, but sweetie, I be neither – not old nor defenseless. Never ya mind about me. I can more than handle this bunch. Now get on. I be fine."

Kandi was adamant, "Fiona, the fairy folk are famous for their non-violence. I used to hate your kind for that. How do you expect to defend your people against men without respect for such things."

Fiona gave Kandi a stern look, "Like I told ya before. The fair folk you remember so fondly are long gone. We've changed over millennia; we are not so pacifistic now. Living on Gaia gave us a new perspective on the cruelty the races incur on each other, especially after the collapse."

Kandi began to protest again, but Fiona raised her hand as a sign that the argument was over. They all had things to do, and Kandi and Jon needed to go. Reluctantly, the two gathered their things and loaded them into the car. As Barba drove down the single-lane road to Portree and points south, she smiled knowingly, "Dinna ye worry about Ma. She's got this."

Jon's frustration got the better of him, "But, we could've helped. Together, we could've stopped them."

"Never ya worry. Ma needs no help to stop the likes of them."

Not sure how they should respond, Jon and Kandi continued silently down the road.

Barba made excellent time getting to Armadale, mainly thanks to the lack of tourists. Even in Portree, one of the largest towns on the island, there was little to slow them down. On the way, she chattered at the others, pointing out sights and wishing they had more time to stop and look. No one would have believed she had abandoned her mother to face a terrible threat alone.

When they arrived at the ferry terminus, a small frame building perched out on the pier, the ferry had just arrived and was disgorging cars and people. Kandi said her goodbyes and went inside to buy their tickets while Jon lingered inside the vehicle. He broke the silence, saying, "Barba? I want you to know I'll be back after this ends."

A look of sadness crossed Barba's face as she caressed his with her palm, "Ah, Jonnie. I hates that it happened this way, but this is how it was always gonna be. There be no happy ever after for the likes of us."

"What do you mean?" Jon was confused by her remark.

"Jon, we had a bit of fun, but that was all it could ever be. You are a wonderful man, but I am a fairy princess, and I couldn't love ye the way you need. I required an heir, which you have lovingly provided me."

Jon was slow to register what she was saying, "Barba? Are you saying you're pregnant?"

"Aye, even after a short time, fairies can tell such things. More importantly, ye have blessed me with a daughter."

"Then I must stay and let Kandi go on without me. I have to protect you and our daughter. We need to get married."

"Nay. Ye haven't been listening, Jon. There be no marriage in me future with you or anyone else. Jon! Look at me! I am like Titania of old, and I will never marry. Don't ya see? Men canna be a part of faerie. Those women of the colony who do marry canna be of the royal house."

Jon was crestfallen, "But...Titania had a year..."

Barba started crying, "Aye, Jon, and I wish our time together had been longer, but that be not our fate. After t'day, neither me nor the bairn will see ye again."

"That's not right!" Jon blurted, "There is no fairness in this."

Barba's following words were a reminder, "Jon. Do ye remember saying you would pay the price of magic? Well...this be the price. I will always remember ye, Jon, and I can faithfully promise ye there will be no other man in my life. Now, get movin'. Ye need to go and get on that boat. There be yer destiny." She kissed him passionately, a fitting last kiss, and then drove off, leaving Jon crying in her wake.

When Kandi came out, she saw Jon's distress and was genuinely concerned. "Do you need to talk about it?" she asked. Jon was a little surprised at the question, "You knew?" She smiled, "Jon, I'm pretty sure everyone on the island knew. You two were not doing a great job of hiding things. So, what happened? She break it off?"

Jon nodded, "Apparently, all she wanted was an heir. I meant nothing to her."

Kandi looked at him, a hint of compassion crossing her face, "Don't sell yourself short, Jonathan Martyr. Fairies are a prickly lot, but they put much consideration into who sires the royal heirs. You had to be very special for Barba to choose you."

The ferry ride was a little rough but otherwise uneventful, and the five-minute walk to the train station was a welcome exercise for muscles left unused for too long. They put the mission away momentarily and relaxed as best they could. Unspoken, Fiona's fate hung heavy over them.

Jon and Kandi were not the same people who had blundered into the fairy colony. Kandi now had a stronger sense of her mortality, while Jon experienced a different kind of death. They had a couple of hours before the train to Glasgow, so they decided to wander around town, looking into shops and feasting on fish and chips, looking every bit the part of a young couple on holiday.

As Jon swallowed some of the fries, "So, any ideas on how to move forward? I know our destination is Norway, but how are we supposed to get there?"

Kandi looked up, shook her head, and smiled, "Have you forgotten that we chartered a boat? So long as we get to Portsmouth and claim her in the next...what day is today anyway? I've lost a few days, and Sara is even more lost than I am."

Jon smiled, "Today is November the 30th. Even though it seems longer, we have been traveling companions for only a little over a month. Providing the captain told the truth, we have about two weeks to make our way to London. Shouldn't be a problem. We'll take this train to Glasgow, and from there, we should be able to catch another one to our destination."

Kandi shivered as a gust of north wind hit her, "South. Will the weather be warmer there?"

"Not much. This time of year isn't high tourist season in these parts for a reason. People tend to stay indoors more. I don't know if I should say this, but Norway will be worse." They made their way to the train and bundled into a couple of seats. A blessed sleep soon followed.

Jon knew they had returned to civilization when the train pulled into Glasgow Central. The architecture might have been from the 19th century, but all the amenities belonged to today. Though most of them were closed, dozens of shops dotted the galleria. Television monitors announced train arrivals and departures. Sadly, the increased presence of technology also meant more enhanced CCTV coverage, which they tried their best to skate around unseen or at least unnoticed, challenging to do with so few people in the area.

The monitor above the waiting area seats was fixed on BBC News, blandly rotating through the day's top stories. Jon had spent most of the past month without television, and he found himself staring intently to quench his video addiction. Suddenly, the broadcast had their complete attention. There, on the overhead screen, was the nameplate from the bow of the *Voyager Templar*, obviously charred around the edges.

"This is Conlon Smythe reporting live at Gunwharf Quays Marina in Portsmouth." Historical footage played behind the commentator. "We are following up on events of two days ago when this peaceful spot was home to a grisly crime. As you may recall, the *Voyager Templar* exploded down the pier from where I'm standing. The police now tell us that the retrieved body parts were shot multiple times with a military-type weapon."

"Police are actively looking for the whereabouts of two Saudi citizens, Ahmad and Aisha Noor, as persons of interest in this crime. According to the yacht's charter company in Bermuda, they were the last to charter the craft." A copy of Jon and Kandi's Saudi passport photos graced the screen. "If you have seen these people or have any evidence of their whereabouts, contact the authorities immediately."

Jon was in shock. Kandi spoke first. "The captain must have sent our passport info when we boarded in Boston."

Her comment prompted a response, "That's what you are wondering about? Not about who shot them and blew up the boat?"

Kandi remained calm, "I'm simply saying that it is unfortunate to have our pictures on the news again. As to your questions, I don't know who's responsible, but I would be surprised if the agents who have been tailing us somehow weren't involved. We're fortunate that Sara could generate new IDs while going to Skye. The old ones," pointing at the screen, "will be doubly burned now."

Jon nodded in agreement, "Being Tom and Chelsea Smyth-Walker with British passports would be very beneficial. You do realize that this changes everything, right? There is no need to go to London now. How do we get to Oslo? Planes are still risky, especially with our photos on display."

Kandi mulled over the problem. *Sara, do you have any ideas?*

Sara responded quickly to Kandi's request. As an AI, she tried to consider all circumstances and delighted in anticipating her team's needs. *The United Kingdom has some of the highest levels of civilian surveillance of any country. Their use of CCTV alone is extensive. Still, their resources are limited, and they must concentrate on high-travel areas and modes of transportation. I agree with Jon. Air travel from Glasgow is far too great a risk. The authorities will also be monitoring trains between large cities. A bus or ferry would be the best....*

Kandi hadn't requested a dissertation, so she interrupted her silent partner. *But where do we go, Sara?*

While Kandi and Sara silently communicated, Jon was distracted by the crowds forming for the morning trains, questioning who might recognize them from the morning news and, as a result, sound the alarm. He jumped when Kandi finally spoke aloud, "Aberdeen."

The answer Kandi gave needed a question to go with it, "Aberdeen? What? Why?"

Kandi filled him in on the situation, "Sara tells me there is a bus station about a half-mile down the road. She advises that our best chance is to catch a bus to Aberdeen and then a ferry to Lerwick in the Shetland Islands."

Jon was still confused, "What?"

Kandi continued, "The buses to Aberdeen run regularly, indicating that they are normally full. As a rule, CCTV in the bus stations will be visible and easier to avoid than the airport."

"And Shetland?"

"Sara feels the ferries are less of a security risk, and the government will monitor them less diligently. When we get to Lerwick, we have no choice but to take a plane. Sara suggests we fly from there to Bergen, not Oslo. Bergen appears to be closer to our final destination based on the map overlays she has done. She is confident that a small airport like Lerwick will offer the lowest odds of someone discovering us."

Jon whistled, "I have to say that is impressive. How did she come up with all that in the past five minutes?"

"Even though she resides in my head, Sara is still an AI. As such, she is very observant and remembers everything she sees. As we entered the main concourse, she saw a poster for the bus depot along with the Aberdeen departure schedule. A little farther down, she spotted a flyer on a tourism desk for the Aberdeen ferry."

Jon considered the implications of what Kandi told him, "OK. That makes sense, but where did she find a map to overlay?" Kandi replied, "She is not completely positive, but based on maps of Scandinavia shown during an earlier BBC broadcast, she is 80% sure that she knows the general area we are going to, and Bergen would be the best landing site. Let's get going."

Jon, however, put the break on any quick move. "Look, let's not rush off." Kandi looked confused as he continued, "Kandi, we need to slow down. People are actively searching for us, and we will make mistakes if we continue at this pace. We need time to think, plan, and prepare.

"I'm no geographer, but these places we're talking about heading are pretty far north, and we are already well into November – gonna get nothing but colder from now on through Spring. We're simply not outfitted for the winter weather they get up here. I suggest we find a hotel for a day or two and resupply. Then, if you two still think the Shetlands are the best bet, we can head north." Kandi wanted to argue and say that time was of the essence, but part of her knew he was correct. Reluctantly, she nodded her head in agreement.

The same tourist desk where Sara had spotted the ferry flyer gave up another for a youth hostel a short walk away with space in a dormitory room for them. The nice thing about hostels was that they only do a cursory check of IDs and preferred cash in payment. This was the perfect place for a couple of desperados such as themselves to lay low for a few days.

The next day found Jon and Kandi going to some used clothing stores near the hostel, and soon they had collected all they would need for a venture into the northern parts of Europe in winter – at least, Jon hoped they did. A local travel agent was more than willing to give them a map of Norway, a brochure, and a promise to "make them a great deal" when the time came to travel. Shopping done, Kandi relinquished control, allowing Sara and Jon to talk on the way back.

The afternoon sun had already disappeared behind the buildings of downtown Glasgow, and long shadows haunted the streets. Kandi and Jon had chosen to travel down the back roads and alleys to avoid government surveillance, so it made sense for Jon and Sara to return the same way. They were so engrossed in their conversation that they never noticed how dark the alleyway had become or that they were no longer alone.

Five men came out of the shadows behind them. One stunned Jon with a small club, dropping him to the pavement. Two other men swallowed Sara in a suffocating embrace, one holding a switchblade to her throat, daring her to move, the other ripping the shirt from her body. If Kandi had been in control, her instincts would have taken over and made short work of them, but this was Sara, still wet behind the ears Sara, in charge of a body she couldn't control well. In her panic, she wasn't mindful enough to allow Kandi to regain command. She stood there frozen in place while her alter-ego screamed for release.

Jon struggled to get up, only to have his attacker kick him in the head, "Better stay down, kiddo. Ya can watch the show from down there."

There was no question about what "show" he was talking about. Kandi, desperate now, hammered at her friend's consciousness. *Sara! Sara! Let me out! Let me out now!* Whether it was the mental pounding or the men's groping, Sara finally snapped out of her fear. There was a shudder as she released. The men hadn't noticed any change, but Jon had.

Kandi took her time and assessed the situation with a warrior's eye. Mere seconds later, she glanced at Jon bleeding on the cement. Then, with a "ready or not; here it comes" look, an impish grin snaked across Kandi's lips, echoing a similar grin from the gym on Aeden over a month ago. This was going to be fun.

The five attackers never knew what hit them. They were in control; then they weren't. Kandi struck first at the man holding the knife to her throat. He had been so sure that she was helpless that he was unprepared for the fury she released, forcing him to drop the blade and paralyzing his hand. Kandi stomped on his instep, delighting as the small bones in the foot gave way. A kick caught the second man in the groin, doubling him over in pain, and a sharp uppercut put him down for good.

Kandi never saw him hit the ground. She was already working on the next two men. The guy watching Jon became distracted, allowing Jon to get up. Jon was still woozy, but he wanted to get in the fight. His training on the yacht had more than made him the match of a single distracted thug. He threw his attacker off balance with a foot sweep, tumbling him to the ground, where Jon incapacitated him quickly.

In less than a minute, all that remained of the group of would-be-attackers were bodies scattered across the alleyway. Someone must have called the police because they could hear a far-away siren getting steadily closer. Jon and Kandi picked up their packages and hurried away. Neither noticed the person on the third-floor landing with a cell phone in his hand.

Chapter 34 – The Battle of Ulg

Around two o'clock in the afternoon, Colonel Forrester's SUV pulled up in front of a nondescript white two-story house in Ulg. As his men exited the vehicle, he asked, "Are we sure this is the place, Corporal?"

"Yes, sir. We extracted this information from the nurse before he passed out. He was tough; I'll give him that. Not many would have lasted as long as he did. Ultimately, he told me everything – picking up the two people, the girl's illness, and delivering her here for his mother to treat. I'm certain that he wasn't lying. This is the place."

"Very well. You and the others fetch our guest while I make his mother's acquaintance."

"Yes, sir."

Fiona answered the door just in time to see the soldiers carrying her son out of the back of the SUV. Bruising had already begun on his face and his bare upper body. She shuddered as she made her way down the walk toward the road. "What have ye done with me boy?" she demanded. "What have ye done with me boy!"

Forrester spun her around by her arm as she attempted to pass by. "Now, now. Let's just relax. We'll bring your boy inside for you. There is no need to bother your neighbors." He looked around, but none of the neighbors were around to take note.

"Come with me." He firmly guided her back into the house, sat her in a chair in the living room, and poised himself over her from a perceived position of power. "Ma'am, your son made some bad decisions this morning, and we had to convince him to reveal information about some very dangerous criminals he assisted. I'm hoping you will be wiser and more forthcoming."

Fiona attempted to appear frightened, "What criminals come to these parts? We be a peace-loving folk."

Forrester gave her a reptilian smile as he showed her the pictures, "A man and a woman, both in their mid-thirties. Among other things, the United States wants them for murder and treason. Your son claims the woman was ill, and he brought her here for special treatment."

Fiona laughed as she feigned ignorance, "I dinna know what you are sayin'. Me boy, Tom, hasn't been here in over a month. As for the man and woman? Well, we get precious few strangers in these parts after the tourists leave. Yer mistaken."

The smile disappeared from Forrester's face, "No, ma'am. We are not mistaken. I have no doubt your son was telling the truth. He was in a lot of *discomfort* when he gave us this information. I don't think lying was something he was even capable of doing. To his credit, he put up with a lot of pain before caving in. I hope you don't make the same mistake your son made. There is no need for unpleasantness between us, but be there no question that I will do whatever I need to get these two into custody. Now, we can do this the easy way...."

Understanding where this conversation was going, Fiona smiled an otherworldly smile, one not too different from a pixie's grin. She looked at her son crumpled on the floor and then looked back at Forrester, at the evil that seemed to emanate from the man. There wasn't any hesitation in her voice as she said, "Ah, Colonel. I fears twill be the hard way, yanno? Ya dinna cause my boy this much pain for it to be otherwise."

No sooner had she said the words than she closed her eyes. A sharp wind seemed to come from everywhere all at once, slamming the windows and doors closed. One of the men tried to force the front door open but found the portal unyielding to his efforts. Two of his cohorts joined him with no apparent effect. When they failed with the door, they turned to the windows, first trying to open them, and when that failed, attempting to break them with the butts of their weapons. The team couldn't understand; the doors looked like old, weathered wood. The windows looked a hundred years old and sat skewed in the wall, but they reacted to the soldiers' efforts to open them like they were welded shut.

Forrester glared down at the woman in front of him and instinctively reached for his sidearm, only to have his weapon fly across the room while contorting itself into a twisted lump of metal. The other guns in the room suffered a similar fate. The men grew silent. They could handle any enemy on the planet, but what was happening here was not in their training. The hunters had become the hunted, and a deep fear set in on the group.

Forrester shattered the moment by trying a frontal attack, assuming that hand-to-hand combat could succeed where weapons had failed. He reached for the older woman's frail neck, believing he could snap it in half before she could finish whatever she was doing. She was only inches away as he threw himself forward – he never bridged the gap. The metamorphosis of the weapons was nothing compared to the damage that same energy did to the human body. The rest of the men cringed in fear as they watched Fiona dismember the colonel before their eyes. They whimpered when she finished with their commander and turned her attention toward them. Loud cries and the sound of breaking bones filled the room as Fiona wreaked her vengeance upon them. When the chaos she had created was complete, only silence remained while bodies littered the floor.

Unbothered by the damage she had created, Fiona went to her boy, her Tom. Cradling his head in her lap, she could see his shallow breathing. He stirred a bit in her arms. *That be a good sign*, she thought. She spoke to him as tenderly as she would a newborn, "There, there, laddie. Ma's got you now. The bad mens not goin' to harm you again." At that, Tom's body seemed to relax, and though unconscious, he smiled.

Subconsciously alerted by the queen, the rest of the fairy colony came quickly. Fiona's cousins, nieces, and assorted other relatives made quick work of the mess, allowing her the time to attend to Tom upstairs. They knew what they needed to do.

The villagers put the bodies of the men in the garden behind the house. The women then gathered in a circle, hands joined. An aura surrounded them as they focused the earth energy they required. Starting slowly, the decomposition process gradually sped up, spurred by the fairy magic. The bodies faded into the dirt, leaving only the bones that soon became brittle and dust themselves.

That only left the soldier's car. One of the men, a mechanic from Portree, disabled the onboard GPS. Two others drove the vehicle to Loch Leathan, a deep lake north of Portree. The SUV made its final trip there as it sank beneath the waters.

Chapter 35 – Back in Colorado

Captain Felix Masters raced down the brightly lit corridor, almost forgetting to knock before entering. One should not equivocate his speed to excitement. Instead, the man was frightened out of his wits. The man in the office before him would not welcome his news. The captain prayed that the commander didn't shoot the messenger.

"Enter." To the captain, the voice had the ring of death.

The captain took just a second to straighten his tie before opening the door and entering. "Sir. We have received some disturbing news concerning our patrol on Skye."

"I'm listening." The tone of the commander's voice made the captain's knees weak. *God, this isn't going to go well.*

While interested in what the captain had to say, the commander already knew the news was terrible. When Colonel Forrester failed to report and did not respond on his satellite phone, the commander sent a backup team from Kinloss Barracks to check on them. He assumed this was their report.

"Sir. The colonel and his team were following up on a lead in the northern part of Skye. At that point, they disappeared. No trace of them anywhere. We attempted to find the nurse Forrester interviewed, but the hospital in Portree claims he is on extended leave somewhere in Europe. The colonel's last message indicated they were going to Ulg to interview the nurse's mother. The person doesn't appear to exist, and the address leads to a vacant house. Seems no one had lived there for a long time. We're at a dead-end."

The commander focused on the captain, who was sweating bullets before him.

"S-s-s-sir?" The captain again felt his knees beginning to buckle. He only remained standing by sheer force of will.

The commander continued, "Captain, the idea that Colonel Forester would disappear without a trace is impossible. Someone is lying to us. Did our team find anyone to corroborate the story?"

The captain's sweat began soaking through his armpits, "Yes, sir. The owner of a café in Dunvegan remembers the team. Said they were lost and wanted directions to Portree. No one else recalls them at all."

"Captain, I don't buy the story. These were highly trained military professionals with the latest satellite communications and GPS. They would not have stopped for directions. Have they recovered the vehicle?"

"No, sir. The last reading from their onboard GPS was in Ulg, where the nurse's mother purportedly lived. Nothing after that."

The commander slammed his hand down on his desk. The captain instinctively jumped back.

"Damn it! You're telling me a group of highly skilled special forces disappeared while interviewing a little old lady?"

The captain shuddered under the onslaught before giving the rest of the bad news, "Sir, there was something else."

The commander's eyes were bright with rage, "And?... Don't make me ask every time unless you want your lieutenant bars back."

"Yes, sir. Sorry, sir. The BBC just broke the news about the cause of the *Voyager Templar* explosion. Local authorities are circulating pictures of our suspects' Saudi passports. They are considering them persons of interest."

"So, Colonel Forrester got sloppy and left incriminating evidence. Anything in the team's ordinance that might come back and haunt us?"

"Negative, sir. Everything was standard terrorist or gang issue. There is no connection to us or any other government."

"Well, that's something. If our prey were going to Portsmouth, that plan would have changed now. There is no escape point for them anymore. Circulating their pictures is a good thing. Having an entire country look for them can't hurt."

"Agreed, sir." The captain allowed himself to relax a little.

The commander calmed himself and focused on available information, "With what happened to Colonel Forrester's group, I think we can assume our quarry has left Skye. Where might they head?"

The captain didn't know if the commander's question was rhetorical. He took a chance and responded with more than a bit of fear, "Sir. There is no commercial air service on Skye. Their only way off the island is by bus or ferry. In that the closest airport of any size is Glasgow, my money is that's where they'll go."

The commander began barking orders, "I agree. Get with the Brits and ask them to share their CCTV with us, everything they have. Give them the standard National Security excuse."

The captain responded quickly, "Yes, sir."

"Captain, while we're at it, have someone monitor social media in the Glasgow and Edinburgh areas. It'll be a long shot, but we might get lucky."

"Yes, sir." The officer remained standing at attention.

"Well, get after it. Dismissed."

The captain caught himself saluting, then quietly closing the door as he left.

The commander sat quietly at his desk before standing and walking over to the bar inset into the far wall. Fixing himself a scotch and water, he raised his glass to Colonel Forrester and his men. He had genuinely liked the man. The colonel's single-mindedness and willingness to use any necessary method made him perfect for the commander's purpose. The commander also realized he would probably never know what had occurred to his team on Skye, but he had his suspicions. Now, the pixie and the human were off his radar, and all he had were guesses of where they went.

Chapter 36 - Northward

Traveling by bus had just become Jonathan's least favorite method of transport. To call the three-hour trip from Glasgow to Aberdeen loud and raucous would have been a gross understatement – living hell would be a better assessment. One of the young men onboard was getting married in Aberdeen this weekend, and Jon was confident that the entire male population of Glasgow was going with him to the celebration.

Considering the state of most of the young men, the party had started some hours ago, possibly even last night. Some of the 'gentlemen' had collapsed into a drunken slumber, loudly snoring as they draped across the seats; however, the party seemed to be just beginning for the rest. Jon and Kandi, especially Kandi, were offered multiple bottles of questionable liquors in hopes they would join in the festivities. Kandi was not taking the attention well and looked like she could slit all their throats. It was all Sara could do to keep a lid on her, undoubtedly saving a wedding in the process.

Once they arrived in Aberdeen, Jon and Kandi quickly gathered their packs and headed toward the ferry dock. Their destination was only a half-mile away, an easy walk, or so they believed. The temperature here was the same as in Glasgow, but it seemed much colder with the wind unobstructed between here and the North Pole as it coursed over the North Sea. The half-mile walk seemed more like a marathon, and they felt nearly frozen by the time they arrived at the ferry terminus.

Jon left Kandi huddled in a chair while he went and checked them in for the sailing to Lerwick. When he returned, she was still shivering in her parka and boots. He wondered if he should tell her Lerwick would probably be worse and then decided against the idea. They were already going to be sharing a cabin. That in itself would be stressful enough.

"Hey," Jon attempted to be jovial, "How are you warming up?"

Kandi's reply was caustic, "How do you people survive like this? No living creature should have to endure these conditions."

Jon bit his tongue as he again considered telling her about his expectations for Lerwick and Norway, then responded, "After you get used to it, it's not so bad. Look, I saw a little café over in a side area; let's get some hot tea to warm you up." Jon thought, *Of course, your people are the ones who sent humans here to begin with.*

As they sipped at their tea, Kandi attempted to cover her earlier weakness, "I only saw three cameras when we came inside. One aimed at the ticket window, and the other two on opposite sides of the boarding gate. Our coats and head coverings should be sufficient to block us from view."

"I did my best to keep my chin down as I was talking to the attendant," Jon had also seen the cameras. He was more than a little proud of that achievement. Kandi showed no appreciation for his efforts as she continued to talk. "So, fifteen hours on a boat, right?"

"Yeah, it's an overnighter. I booked a cabin. I figured that would keep us away from any cameras in the main salon and any inquiring eyes that may have noticed us on the television the other night. The less we are in the public eye, the better."

Kandi agreed, "If someone had told me a month ago that I would be sharing a cabin with a human, I would have killed them for thinking it." She made the statement nonchalantly. Jon was pretty sure she wasn't kidding.

The accommodations on the ferry were bare bones but serviceable. Jon unconsciously turned on the small television as he flopped himself down on his bunk. The national news was in progress.

"...from Skye," Jon's ears perked up when he heard the name, as did Kandi's. "You might recall the disappearance last week of five American servicemen. Search and rescue called off their search today after finding no evidence of the men's presence on the island's north end. Assumptions are the men have left Skye and gone AWOL in Scotland proper. Authorities continue to monitor all transit in an attempt to find them."

Jon and Kandi looked at each other. They didn't need names to realize that these were the same men who had followed them from Boston. One thing was sure: these men wouldn't be following them anymore. Jon wondered what Fiona had done to them, realizing the little fairy queen was not as frail and helpless as they had feared.

Neither Jon nor Kandi slept the rest of the night. They continued watching television in case further news presented itself, but none did. They worried about Fiona and Barba. Jon felt a pang of regret that he hadn't been there to protect the woman he loved and the unborn child he would never see. The men were gone, but at what cost? They also took the opportunity to compare the map they got in Glasgow with the one provided by Fiona. Looking at the two maps, Jon realized how uncannily similar they were.

With little difficulty, they could identify Ragnarök, now called Hardangervidda, a large plateau that looked out of place against the swath of mountains surrounding it. Several waterfalls cascaded down to the river gorge below along one edge of the immensely flat area. For a moment, they wondered how they would choose where to start their search. Then, Kandi noticed a winner, Vøringfossen Falls. This cataract was almost six hundred feet in height, more than satisfying Fiona's requirements. Vøringfossen was where they would go.

With their destination finally settled, they leaned back in their respective bunks. Kandi looked at Jon and asked, point blank once again, "Jonathan Martyr. Why are you here? I will not accept the story you gave me in Vermont; why are you here?"

Jon was quiet for a bit before replying. "The story I gave you in Vermont is still true. I had no reason to lie then; I don't have one now." Kandi scowled as he continued, "Other than that, I have no idea why I'm here. This whole string of events reads more like a bad science fiction book than anything I would ever do in real life. I mean, really? I was the guy who always played his life safe, and here I am, trekking across the globe in the company of an alien pixie and her AI companion. I've seen firsthand what you can do when provoked, and your abilities frighten me. I've also seen what my government is willing to do to stop you – stop us. In short, I don't have anywhere else to go.

"The people on the *Voyager* were good people who didn't deserve to die, and I do not doubt that...," Jon pointed at the television, "...those men, my government, were responsible for their deaths. I also stand by my earlier statement that, even though I don't necessarily like what you say, you haven't lied to me, and because of that, I fear for my planet's future. You said that you needed me and this ring to fix things," holding his hand up, "It and I are a package deal. We're here to help where we can."

Kandi was uncharacteristically civil, almost tender, as she answered him. "Your motives seem admirable, but I'm not confident that will be enough. Jon, I appreciate your honesty, so I need to do the same. We could very well be on a fool's errand. Finding the fairies on Skye was a fluke, a stroke of luck, not a plan. I had no idea they were still around, let alone that their queen would hold the answer to my illness. Now, I'm headed to Norway, searching for a renegade Watcher team that, over millennia, seems to have become legends, gods of all things.

"Of course, I doubt if any of them are still around. I mean, seriously, Jon, it's been over twenty-five thousand years! From what Fiona said, they were pretty keen on bullying people for what they wanted. They probably went out in a blaze of glory, exhausting any remaining crystals in the process.

If…when the trail ends in the Norse mountains, I have no idea what to do next."

Chapter 37 – In Search of Norsemen

The ferry disgorged a bundled-up Jon and Kandi along with the other passengers, vehicles, and cargo at 0730 the following day onto the frigid pier at Lerwick. Both travelers were looking rough as they walked down the exit ramp.

"Thank God for Dramamine," Jon said softly.

"Agreed," Kandi added, "Some of your Gaian remedies are very useful indeed."

"Admit it. The heavier clothing was a good idea, too, right?" Jon had to blow his own horn here.

Kandi gave him a disdainful look, "I suppose, but I'm still freezing."

"It's your thin pixie blood." That comment earned him a slap that he would remember for quite a while.

The steward on the ferry had pointed them to a hotel just across the road from the dock that would take early arrivals from the ferry. A short time later, they settled in their room and eating breakfast in the hotel restaurant. The traditional Scottish breakfast was a little heavy for Jon's liking, but Kandi dug into hers with gusto.

Watching the pixie eat was disgusting. Despite her petite, feminine appearance, her eating habits were definitely more "soldier in the field."

They ran into one snag when it came to getting a flight out. The carrier didn't fly to Bergen daily; the next flight would be Saturday. They would have to lay low for a few days before moving onward.

Saturday morning, the sun appeared in the sky over Lerwick for the first time, and the temperature rose to a point where their heavy coats were more comfortable over their shoulders than on their bodies. The village took on a completely different mien. Suddenly, a dull, dreary place became a colorful, wonderful spot. Hotel check-out was at 1100, and their flight to Bergen didn't depart until 1430, so Jon and Sara took the opportunity to walk with the locals before taking a taxi to the airport.

Of course, Kandi was always in the background but tried not to intrude on their conversations. Despite her efforts to discourage Sara, she knew that the AI was infatuated with Jon, much like a schoolgirl crush. Sara hung on to every word he said, making her social development proceed faster than if Sara remained in Kandi's shadow.

For his part, Jon needed Sara too. He was still hurting from the loss of Barba. Having Sara's company was good for him. Besides, Kandi knew that the relationship wouldn't go too far; she wouldn't allow that to happen.

Compared to the other legs of their journey, the ninety-minute flight to Bergen was just a hop. Jon quickly exchanged his British pounds and American dollars for Norwegian kroner, and the two of them headed out toward Eidfjord, a town not far from the falls but still six hours and two bus transfers away.

Kandi was not impressed with the village. "This is a miserable place. I'm cold, wet, and hungry. Why do humans bother living in places like this?" She said to no one in particular. Jon casually responded, "Well, since a third of the planet's land mass is like this, people adapt to the conditions. Don't you have snow where you're from?"

"No. Our two continents are completely in the Aedenian temperate zone. We don't have a volcanic history, so our hills and mountains are not tall enough for snow. You can only find weather like this on some outlying archipelagos in the northern ocean. Elves and pixies never settled there, only humans."

"Well, only humans are living here now." Jon grinned, liking that his race was hardier than their cousins. Kandi only scowled in response.

Jon gave a casual examination of his surroundings. If Lerwick had been the size of his neighborhood, Eidfjord would have been more like his apartment building. The small cluster of wood frame homes and businesses with smoke curling out of chimneys was more reminiscent of a Currier and Ives painting than a real place. He took a deep breath, relishing the cleanness of the air.

The real question was, now that they were here, what did they do next? They hadn't anticipated that Eidfjord would be this small and that there wouldn't be an infrastructure to support "lost" tourists like themselves. Of course, the fact that they were here in late November instead of mid-June may have had something to do with that. The size of the bay and dock at the end of the main street indicated cruise ships often made port there, but, of course, none were there now. With no better idea, they shouldered their bags and headed toward the sea, hoping they could find someone to help them.

With the departure of the cruise ship came the departure of the temporary workers who looked after them. Those that remained in the small village could speak a little English, but not enough to be conversant. After a disastrous attempt at communicating with a clerk at the corner grocery who had obviously been absent from her English classes, Jon turned toward his companion. "Kandi? She doesn't speak English, and I don't speak Norwegian. Ideas?"

"Are you certain the problem isn't that she is a young, beautiful female?" Kandi's smirk indicated mild amusement.

"I'm getting better at that....fine, I stammered at first," Jon had been painfully aware of the young lady. It seemed he was only immune from his affliction with non-human females. "Yeah, she's cute, but that has nothing to do with our lack of communication."

Kandi replied, "No, I regret that we didn't include Norwegian in our language download, but it wasn't considered critical to our mission. No one envisioned this scenario. I'm afraid I'm also at a loss."

Discouraged, they were ready to leave and try elsewhere when Sara spoke up. *Kandi? I want to assist in communications. I have been examining the speech patterns of the locals, and I believe that I have found a possible basis for the language in the Asgardian standard dialect from the northern islands. The form has changed dramatically over the centuries, but I would like to try it.*

Kandi told Jon what Sara had said and what she was attempting to do. Then, as Sara, she turned back to the clerk.

"Need place." She said in her pigeon Norse.

The clerk was understandably confused, "Place?"

"Place sleep."

"Ah. Sleep." The clerk smiled in understanding.

The clerk then took out a tourist map of Eidfjord left over from the summer and put an X on a corner, "Here." She pointed to the store and then to the map. She then moved the pen down a block or two and put another X. "Sleep."

"Thank you!" Sara was delighted with herself.

As they walked toward the X, she told Jon, "I should be able to observe the locals and quickly improve my knowledge of the language structure and vocabulary. The more I hear Norwegian conversations, the faster my ability to translate will come."

Jon asked a question he had been thinking about, "So, Kandi indicated this was Asgardian standard. I believed all of Aeden spoke the same language?"

Sara was happy to clarify, "We do, but as you have your dialects in different areas, so do we. Some are so severe that they could be considered a different language. That is the case with Asgardian."

They quickly made their way to the inn, Sjel og gane bar og restaurant, according to the sign on the side of the building. Jon wasn't sure what all the words meant, but the name included bar and restaurant, so he was ready to go inside. Today had been long, and he was ready for food and drink.

They entered the main door only to be shocked by the number of people crowding around the first-floor room.

"How will we ever find the owner?" Sara asked curiously.

Jon said, "In my limited European experience, the owner almost always is the guy behind the bar."

He was correct; the bartender was the inn's owner, and although not fluent, he was at least aware of basic English.

"What can I get ya?" The man had the unique ability to make you feel that you were the most important person in the room, even when a hundred others were milling around you.

"Two lagers and hopefully a room," Jon answered.

The owner was very accommodating, "The two pilsners I got. Room too. Not much of one, though."

"I'm sure the room will be fine. Would you know the best way to get to Vøringfossen from here?"

The owner laughed, "With snow like this, no way good. A bus goes by in the morning and returns in the evening. Work for you?"

The news uplifted Jon's mood, "Yeah, that works. Internet?"

"Laptop?"

Jon shook his head no.

The owner scowled and then led them toward a small room to the side of the bar, where he pointed to a desk with a computer. "Internet. No porn. Understand?"

Jon nodded vigorously in agreement. Meanwhile, Sara was already typing away, looking for a way to get to the bottom of Vøringfossen and the hidden chamber they hoped was hidden behind its veil.

Chapter 38 – Giving Chase

Captain Masters wasted no time in getting to the commander's office. He didn't even wait for permission before flying through the doorway.

This lack of protocol made the commander visibly upset, "Captain? What's the meaning of this?"

"Sir, we may have a lead on Martyr and the girl. The captain played a cell phone clip of a fight two floors below in an alleyway. The light was terrible, and discerning faces was almost impossible. This video showed up on social media in Glasgow yesterday."

"What makes you so sure this is them?"

"Wait for it, sir."

At first, the scene appeared to be a group of five to six young men attacking an unfortunate couple carrying bags. The assailants incapacitated the man with a blow to the head while forcibly mauling his companion.

Suddenly, the video seemed to move at double speed. The "helpless" female began tossing around her assailants like they were nothing more than the bags of clothing she had been carrying. The male recovered enough to incapacitate his attacker as well. The entire exchange took less than a minute.

"I see your point, Captain. These two would appear to be our targets. I will have a team meet you at the airport. You leave for Glasgow within the hour.

I'll clear you with the Brits. Despite our deniability, we are getting a lot of unwanted blowback from Colonel Forrester's activities on Skye. There would be hell to pay if they knew we were responsible for what happened to the yacht. We'll play this one by the book."

"Yes, sir." The captain was shocked. In one instant, he had gone from glorified messenger to field commander. He smiled as he left the room. There was no time to get jet lag on the trip to Scotland. The commander had arranged for a modified SST commissioned by USSF to travel from Peterson Space Force Base to the NATO-run Campbeltown Airport in Scotland, the only airport in the area able to accommodate the still experimental craft.

The good news was that the transatlantic crossing had only taken three hours. The ground team shuttled the team to a waiting G600, fueled and ready for departure. The afternoon sun was beginning to sink over the horizon as they arrived at Glasgow Airport, where a liaison officer with Glasgow police met them.

"Captain Masters?" The police detective showed his badge. "DCI Knowles, Glasgow Constabulary. My boss leads me to understand that you may have information about our little problem here."

Masters smiled sheepishly, "Not sure how much I can help you, sir. There were similarities between your attack and one in New York a month ago. We have been trying to track these two down ever since. Would you mind taking us to see the crime scene this evening?"

"I don't see a problem with that, Captain. Gather your gear, and let's get you and your group to your hotel, and we'll go by the scene. Have to tell you that I have mixed feelings. Part of me wants to arrest the lady, and the other part wants to give her a medal. Those were nasty blokes she hospitalized. Had about a dozen outstanding warrants between them."

USSF had made the team reservations at the Airport Holiday Inn Express. In keeping with the commander's wishes, they did everything by the book. After they checked in, DCI Knowles escorted Captain Masters and his lieutenant to recon the area where the video placed the suspects. They found the site preserved with police tape still surrounding the scene and a 24-hour guard posted for security, but other than the markers where the police had found the bodies, there wasn't much to see.

Masters looked up to the third-floor fire escape where an unknown individual had shot the video. "I don't suppose you found the person who took that footage, did you?"

Knowles shook his head, "Nah, bugger's probably long gone by now. They definitely won't own up to shooting the video even if we did find them. The gang wouldn't be too happy about the publicity."

Masters laughed, "Yeah, probably not too good for your tough guy images to have a couple of tourists beat you up – and one of them a woman! Say, do you have a map of the area I could have?"

"Aye, have one in the boot of the car. Seen all you want here?"

"For now. Let's head back to the hotel."

DCI Knowles parked the van and joined them inside, where Masters and his team had commandeered a small meeting room and spread the Glasgow map across the table in front of them.

The captain began his briefing, "There wasn't much in the alley to help us, but we know two things for certain. One, they were carrying shopping bags, so they were coming from one of the local stores. Secondly, the attack happened in the late afternoon, so they were probably headed to where they stayed for the night."

"Captain?" Corporal Barnes spoke up.

"Yes, Barnes."

"I don't understand. Why were the suspects even in the alley? Wasn't that just inviting trouble?"

"Well, Barnes, one might think that our pair of desperados are a wee bit camera shy, and the main streets around here are filthy with CCTV."

Corporal Barnes ducked his eyes. In retrospect, the answer to his question was obvious. The rest of the crew quietly chuckled at his expense.

Masters was paying them no mind; he had already moved on to the next step. He had a straight edge and a pencil and was deftly drawing lines that would intersect with the alleyway. Knowles observed, chiming in where needed. "Right there," pointing to a small street, "is a cluster of used clothing shops. The bags they were carrying were pretty large."

Masters made a note to have one of the men check out the stores in the morning. "What about the other direction? Hotels?"

"There are two or three in that direction, but one that comes to mind is a youth hostel about three blocks from the scene. We checked the place out after the incident but didn't have a clear photograph of the two to share. Might have better luck now."

SST or not, the time difference alone was wearing on the group, and they needed to be sharp in the morning. The Captain decided they should hit the sack. Knowles told Masters that he would be back at 0800 and said goodnight.

The following day, Knowles found Captain Masters and his team already hard at work. The youth hostel turned out to be a good call. The desk clerk clearly remembered the pair, "Yah, them two was here—room 216. Twern't no trouble. They spent two nights. Paid cash. Said they were English. Girl was quite a looker."

Captain Masters thanked him for his time. He had just turned to go when his phone rang.

"Yes, lieutenant?"

The young soldier spoke in a rushed whisper, "Sir, we have three shops about two klicks from your location. They remember our quarry very well. They seem to have bought a good deal of cold weather gear."

"Interesting. Thank you, Lieutenant." He closed the phone and turned toward his Scottish aide, "We may be searching in the wrong place. We assumed they would head to London from here. That may not be correct. Have we had any luck with the CCTV?"

"Nay. Airport's clean. So's the trains."

"What about buses?"

"Ah, coverage at the bus station isn't that good. Too many people and too few cameras in use."

"Still, I think we should check, don't you?" Captain Masters was not pleased.

"Aye, we'll check." The DCI felt that this was turning into a fool's errand. The two criminals had given the Yanks the slip, and now they were looking to blame him for their failures. "Ya comin'?" The captain nodded his assent.

Three hours later, the two men stared over their coffee and tea at the screen. The DCI spoke first. "We've been over this twice, and no sign of your pair. They weren't here."

Captain Masters wasn't so sure. He started thinking like an operative in a foreign country rather than a glorified cop. "Bear with me here. Let's take one more look. This time, look for people, any people, who seem to always be just out of the camera's view."

Knowles seemed confused, "I dinna understand. What be we lookin' fer?"

The captain focused on the display, "I'll know it when I see it." Less than thirty minutes later, he spotted them. "There they are."

Knowles was not so sure, "Where? I dinna see anyone."

"That pair with the hats pulled down just enough that their faces are partially hidden. See how they never look up and always seem just outside the camera's primary focal area." Knowles nodded his agreement, "Aye. Would've missed that for sure."

The two men watched their prey until the pair exited the terminal. The Captain quickly noted the time on the station clock and the CCTV timestamp. "Let's get down there and find out where they went."

At the station, they discovered only one bus left from that side of the terminal on that day and time, the 8:40 to Aberdeen. The captain smiled. "DCI Knowles. What's the fastest way to Aberdeen?"

The inspector smiled, "That little G600 of yours would probably get you there the quickest."

"I agree." The captain got on the phone and called the lieutenant. "Get the team and everything out of the hotel and meet me at the plane. We're traveling." He was glad that he left standing orders for the plane to be prepared to take off with little notice.

Less than an hour later, they circled Aberdeen International Airport, preparing to land. Captain Masters called his group together. "Lieutenant Connors, I want you and Corporal Jones to go to the airport CCTV center and scan for our fugitives. I doubt they would be foolish enough to fly, but we have to cover all the bases. To that end, you can tie in the Cognizance software from HQ." He received a questioning look from his subordinate. Cognizance was still classified – need-to-know stuff. "I know the security ramifications, but Command insists that this mission warrants the risk." The lieutenant signaled acceptance of the order.

"Sergeant Jackson, you and Corporal Barnes do the same with the train depot. Scan everyone and everything going in or out, understood?" He received an additional verification from the sergeant. "DCI Knowles and I will stay at the bus depot and look for them here. Any questions?" His was met with silence just as the wheels touched the ground. "Very well. Keep me posted."

As the patrol scattered to their respective assignments, the idea that the fugitives had escaped by sea never crossed anyone's mind; after all, why would they go farther north?

At the end of a long and disappointing day, Captain Masters and his men had nothing to show for their time. They reviewed all the CCTV footage at their various locations, scrutinizing those that Cognizance indicated warranted special handling and paying close attention to outliers who seemed to be always intentionally out of view. Even though Cognizance managed to identify several bad players from the CCTV, which DCI Knowles was very excited about, their two suspects remained unidentified. The only reported contact came from the bus depot, where Cognizance flagged their departure from the building but failed to see them ever return. Frustrating indeed.

The team had arranged for rooms at a small hotel near the bus depot, and while they were on the way there from the train station, Corporal Barnes casually looked out the cab window and noticed the ferry port. "Say, Sarge?"

"What is it, Barnes?" The sergeant sounded bored, tired, and ready for a drink before dinner.

"I was just thinking. What if they left by boat?"

The sergeant's head spun around like someone had hit him with a haymaker. "What was that again, Barnes?"

"What if they took a ferry?"

The sergeant turned his attention to the cab driver, "Change of plans, bud. Take us to the ferry terminal." Turning back to Barnes, "Corporal, you may get a promotion out of this."

Sergeant Jackson immediately called the Captain, "Sir, it's probably nothing, but Barnes here had the idea of checking the ferry terminal. That be OK with you?"

Masters mentally slapped himself, *the ferry!* "OK? No. Excellent idea? Yes. Barnes may have just found their way out."

Jackson pushed, "Are we approved for Cognizance there as well?"

"Affirmative. We will wait to hear from you."

They didn't have to wait long.

The report came back within an hour. CCTV showed the two fugitives getting on a ferry – to the Shetlands of all places! That was three days ago, giving them a sizable head start. The captain was furious! They could be anywhere by now.

He took a moment and asked himself, *What if this was where they were heading all along? What could be in Lerwick? Why go there of all the places in the world?*

DCI Knowles was unaware of the conflict in the Captain's mind and was already on the phone with his counterparts at Lerwick Constabulary. They would contact local hotels and charter fishermen and inquire at Sumbergh Airport about possible sightings. Although Lerwick could be their final destination, they had to consider that the village was only a way-stop. Besides the ferry and the airport, there was no other way for them to leave the islands. Within an hour, his inquiries paid off.

"They dinna stay in Lerwick," he announced, disturbing the Captain's concentration.

"How do you know?"

"I just got off the phone with the constabulary there. The two of em registered at a local hotel as Mr. and Mrs. Smythe-Walker. Stayed there fer three days. Airport search shows they left on a direct flight to Bergen, Norway this morning."

"Bergen? Why go all the way to the Shetlands to get a flight to Bergen?" the captain asked him.

The DCI nodded, "Pretty smart, actually. The Lerwick airport is pretty remote. If yer weren't lookin' for 'em, ya wouldna find 'em, ya no?"

The captain smiled, "So, we've managed to cut their four-day lead to two." He looked over to his sergeant, "This is good news. Get the jet ready. We're headed to Bergen as soon as possible."

DCI Knowles walked over and shook the captain's hand. "This be where I get off. No jurisdiction in Norway. I can make some calls and get ye a liaison there iffn ya like."

The captain smiled. He was going to miss the DCI's company. "That would be wonderful. Thank you for all your help."

"No problem there. When you catch 'em, dinna forget the two of 'em need to answer for things in our neck of the woods, too."

"We will," although the captain was confident that the two fugitives would never see the light of day again after their capture.

After everyone left, Captain Masters reported to his superior in Colorado Springs. As he recounted the past two days, the Commander sat quietly, assimilating all the information.

"Thank you, captain. Excellent work."

"Sir."

After they hung up, the commander frowned as he tapped his chin with his index fingers tapping on his chin. "You are proving very resourceful, Watcher Mehra. What are you up to this time?"

Chapter 39 – Vøringfossen

Jon and Kandi were the only passengers on board the 933 bus to Vøringfossen. Sara discovered a trail leading to the bottom of the falls that was popular with tourists during the summer. The popularity of the route concerned Kandi. *How was the secret kept if hordes of people were constantly walking around?*

When they boarded, Sara asked the driver, "Vøringfossen trailhead?"

The driver nodded that she understood, "No go there this time. Weather bad."

Sara was insistent, "Must go. How get there?"

This time, the driver reluctantly smiled. These two must be crazy to hike there with snow on the ground and the rocks coated in ice, but what could she do? "Will stop."

The bus did indeed stop at a deserted spot on the highway – the proverbial "wide spot in the road." The driver waved for them to get off and then pointed at a sign indicating where the trailhead was. "Will be back this afternoon, yes?"

Jon thanked her and said that they would be there.

As the bus drove off, leaving them stranded, Jon and Kandi questioned what they had done. Here they were, standing on the top of the Hardangervidda plateau, the large plain that supposedly Master

Watcher Yodin had named Ragnarök from Fiona's map. In the distance, they could hear a dull roar that could only be Vøringfossen.

Although the wind had blown much of the snow off the plain, they feared the descent to the bottom would be far more treacherous. Still, what choice did they have but to continue? In this quest, leads were hard to come by, and right now, this was their only one.

At first, the path was an easy walk down an old roadway pitted and worn down by the weather. Then, the trail led toward the edge of the plateau and then downward toward the river. At this point, the path was treacherous and steep, with patches of ice and snow clinging to the rock faces.

Tired and covered in cuts and bruises, they finally reached the bottom of the gorge. Unfortunately, the conditions had turned what would have been a one-hour hike only two months ago into a four-hour trek today. Time was running short if they wanted to make their bus.

At the bottom, the sound of water hitting the rocks was deafening. The sound echoed off the canyon walls, adding to the overall effect. They screamed at each other to be understood and, when even that failed, tried to use sign language.

The last stretch of the trail involved a pedestrian suspension bridge comprised of weathered wooden planks and wire completely coated with snow and ice. They looked all around, but there was no other way to cross the river before them.

Jon tied them together with some rope they had brought. He rationalized that if one fell, the other could pull them back. Kandi considered it equally likely they would each end up in the water but said nothing. Finally, cold and wet, they stood at the base of the tallest waterfall in Norway, only to discover they would have to cross a pool of water at the bottom to get to the falls themselves.

Their hearts fell. There was no way they could manage such a trip. They didn't have sufficient supplies, and their strength was running low. Their only option was to return tomorrow with additional equipment to accomplish the task. Disappointment sat heavily upon them as they began returning to the top.

Fate did not smile on them, and the return took a lot longer – six hours. The tiredness they had felt at the bottom was nothing compared with their complete, total exhaustion when they arrived at the pick-up point. They almost collapsed when there were only fresh tracks in the snow where the bus had been an hour or so earlier.

Jon spoke first, "We are in serious trouble here. The sun is setting, and we cannot return to the inn. If we stay out in the open, we'll freeze, and I don't see any likely shelters around here. Any ideas?"

Kandi shivered and shook her head no.

Jon continued, "I'll try moving some of these larger rocks to make a windbreak, but I don't think that will make much difference."

Just then, lights appeared coming down the road toward them. *What luck!* Jon thought. He turned toward Kandi, "Surely, they wouldn't leave us stranded out here, right?"

He heard the pixie's response, "But we have no idea who they are?"

Jon held her closer, "It doesn't matter. We know we'll freeze to death if we stay out here all night. Hurry!"

Jon ran, dragging Kandi behind him, until they stood in the center of the road, waving their arms wildly. If the driver didn't stop, they would hit them. Either way, they wouldn't freeze on the top of the plateau. Fortunately, the truck stopped.

Jon gulped as a mountain extricated himself from the driver's seat. Mountain wasn't much of an exaggeration, either. The man who stood before him was easily seven feet tall and looked almost that big across—more of a wall than a mountain. The man stood next to Kandi, making her appear to be a small child in comparison. "You lost?" was all he said, but he said the words in English.

"We missed the bus," Jon answered.

"I know. Berta call me. Said two fools hiking to the waterfall in winter. Tells me you not here when she returns. Ask if I look for you."

Jon tried to be jovial as he stomped his feet, trying to stay warm, "Well, here we are! Thanks for coming out to check. I don't suppose we could trouble you with a ride into town?"

The man looked hard at Jon as he mulled the question, mentally translating the statement into Norwegian.

"No town. Too far and too late. Take you to my place. Catch bus tomorrow." He saw that Kandi was having difficulty walking, so he picked her up like a doll and returned to the truck.

Jon grabbed their packs and raced after him, "Sounds good."

Sitting in the truck's cab with Jon in the middle, Jon sensed a reluctance in the pixie's demeanor. "What gives?"

Kandi whispered her response, not wanting the man to hear, "I know him."

Jon worried she was delirious but responded in a whisper anyway, "What! How can you possibly know him?"

"Not him personally, but him as a people. He is jötunn, one of the island giants of Aeden."

Jon knew she was hallucinating, "Kandi, that would have been over twenty-five thousand years ago. This man can't be one of them."

Jon turned his attention to the driver, "Hi, I'm Tom Smythe-Walker, and this is my wife, Chelsea."

The driver grunted, looked toward Jon, and said, "Halvar Olsen," then said nothing else. The weather was getting worse, and the snowfall was thickening. A few minutes later, the man pulled into a large complex. A front placard announced they were at the Fall View Hotel.

The lack of cars in the snow-covered parking area got Jon's attention. "Say, Halvar? Where is everybody?"

Halvar answered, "Hotel closed. Construction."

Well, that answered that question but then opened another. "Do you work here?"

Halvar's monosyllabic reply was short and sweet. "Family own. Live here."

Wow! Jon thought. *The big man has big bucks.*

Halvar took them to one of the rooms the workers hadn't gotten to yet. The lack of plastic sheeting over everything was a dead giveaway. He pointed to the door, "Stay here. I get food ready."

Kandi and Jon entered a well-appointed room with a view of the waterfall far below. Kandi, who had been uncharacteristically quiet, spoke up. "I realize that my earlier statement is impossible, but that man IS one of the jötunn or one of their descendants. We can't trust him."

Jon was about fed up with her attitude, "Why? Because of something his ancestors did over six hundred generations ago? Do you hear yourself? People change? By that same rationale, you shouldn't trust me either."

Kandi responded bluntly, "Who said that I do? I'm beginning to see that you are unlike the humans I knew, but I don't trust you completely either."

Jon was slightly disappointed in her response but continued, "What does Sara say? As an AI, she would be more dispassionate."

Kandi shrugged, "She agrees with you."

Jon was almost triumphant, "There you go, then. The whole jötunn thing is all in your head." Jon walked over to a large wardrobe against the nearby wall, "Hey, look! Robes! Let's get out of these wet things and see what's for dinner."

Chapter 40 - Secrets

Dinner consisted of a hearty Lapskaus, or stew, accompanied by some delicious potato dumplings and a delightful mousse with a strange berry taste. Trying to be sociable, Kandi asked their host, "This desert is wonderful; what kind of berries do you use?"

"Lingonberry," was Halvar's curt reply. After they had finished dinner and the dishes were clean, he asked, "Where you from?"

Jon answered between bites, "England."

Halvar laughed, "Nah, no talk like Brits. American?"

Damn! Jon thought. *Caught.* He and Kandi had been so careful to use their accents until today. Sara quickly said, "You're close; we're Brits who have lived in America for ten years. Lost a lot of accent on the way."

Halvar nodded his acceptance, "What you want at the falls?"

Kandi remarked, "Just sightseeing. We heard the falls were magnificent, and we were not disappointed."

The giant smiled, "You no lie well. No one comes during snow. Why you here?" The smile disappeared from his lips, and a look of fierce determination replaced it.

Now Jon took a turn. The truth had worked for them on Skye; maybe a straight story would also work here. "OK, you caught us. We heard stories about a hidden room behind the falls, a gateway to magnificent treasures. We were curious. We're only here for a week and wanted to find out if there was any truth to the stories." Kandi nodded her agreement.

Halvar was amused, "Hah! Hidden room? Looking for Odin's gold, ya?" The big man laughed heartily, and Jon and Kandi enthusiastically joined him.

While they were distracted, Halvar reached across and moved Kandi's hair off to the side just a little. His suspicions were confirmed; his mood went from light to dark, "Now, tell Halvar what elf is doing here, heh? No more lies."

Kandi, who had jerked her head back as soon as the giant touched her. She was incensed and held nothing back, "Not elf, you jötunn. Pixie." She stood proudly defiant and was secretly delighted by Halvar's shocked response to her statement. "We search for the crystal Yodin stole from Skye's fairies."

Halvar almost appeared contemplative, "Hmmph. You think treasure behind Vøringfossen? You wrong. Nothing there."

The pair of adventurers initially displayed disappointment at his comment, but brightened as he continued, "Norse government use Vøringfossen for electricity now. Also, very popular with tourists. Cave too exposed, not safe. Moved here when hotel built."

Kandi's reaction was one of shock, "Here? The crystal is here?"

The giant laughed again, "Nah. Entrance here. Get dressed. I show you."

Their clothes were still damp, but they didn't care. Kandi was excited beyond words as she quickly dressed and impatiently waited for Jon to follow. "Can't you move any faster?"

Jon was intentionally slowing her down. He knew from his jewelry work that a combination of speed and excitement was a recipe for mistakes, "I'm going as fast as I can. About an hour ago, you believed Halvar was the reincarnation of a devil-giant breed of humans. Decide he's OK now?"

Kandi replied, "He claims to know where the crystal is. More importantly, he wants to take us there. That's all I care about. Besides, you tell me that your people have changed. Who is to say his didn't as well."

Jon wasn't as sure. Something about the way the giant behaved was beginning to concern him. He was starting to think twice about the man's offers of help.

When they returned to the dining room, Halvar was patiently waiting. He said nothing, headed for the kitchen door and toward the wine cellar. When Halvar reached the end of the racks, he stopped and pulled a dusty bottle from the shelf. Like a scene from a bad spy movie, that section of shelves pulled back from the wall, revealing a niche. Halvar gestured for them to follow him inside, and the shelving slid silently behind them.

The niche led downward into a gradually opening cavern burrowed into the stone. A muted light lit the space from some unknown origin. At this point, Jon and Kandi were practically running to keep up with the giant's normal gait across the floor's uneven surface. Just as Jon approached Halvar to ask him to slow down, a large hand reached out from the giant's side, grabbed Jon by the throat, and tossed him into the wall, rendering him unconscious. Halvar's other hand was already immobilizing the young pixie with a strong, suffocating grip. Try as she might, Kandi's strength and agility were no match for the giant's raw power. Halvar had caught her off-guard; her years of training had betrayed her.

With Jon no longer a factor, Halvar used both hands to secure his prize and headed for a door at the end of the corridor. He carried her across the threshold. One second, they were in the hidden cellar room; the next, they weren't. Instead of rock walls and a musty smell, she and her captor were looking out onto a snowy, barren landscape from a castle's parapet.

Once clear of the transfer portal, Halvar dropped Kandi unceremoniously onto the floor, where she recoiled into a defensive position as she decided what to do next.

"Relax." Helvar was calm in his statement.

"Relax? You kidnapped me and probably killed my husband." Kandi tried to put up a false bravado to counter the giant.

Helvar spoke matter-of-factly, "He isn't your husband, nor is he dead."

Something in the man's bearing had changed. Kandi said, "Your English has suddenly gotten much better."

"I found the situation amusing and expedient for you to think I was unfamiliar with your language."

"What is this place?"

"The ancients named the structure Himinbjörg, the castle of Heimdall, the owner of the flaming sword. Himinbjörg was where Bifrost, the rainbow bridge, connected to Asgard. When the gate collapsed at the far end of the bridge, the blast destroyed Bifrost, leaving this castle isolated and relatively unscathed."

Kandi remembered how the rock cave below the Vermont safe house had shielded them from the collapse of the gate; distance would probably provide the same protection.

"When did all this happen?" Kandi was desperately vying for time.

Halvar shrugged his disinterest, "Ages ago. Told now only through the walls."

"Walls?" The pixie was surprised by the answer.

"This castle holds many secrets."

Kandi returned to the current situation, "So, what happens now?"

Halvar laughed, "Ah, excellent. I like how you approach a problem head-on. I'm afraid this will be your last stop on your journey."

Kandi and Sara both reacted, "You're going to kill me?"

The giant stared at her intently, "No...not right away. You will live here until you die here. How long a time is completely up to you."

The pixie tried to remain calm, "You can let me go. I wouldn't dream of telling anyone." Kandi had maneuvered herself into a crouch while she spoke.

Halvar was distracted while he searched for something on the floor, "Empty promise. You knew too much when you went to the falls in winter. The writings are clear. You cannot leave. Besides, you are of one of the evil races, the ones who imprisoned my people here long ago. There are many legends of how untrustworthy your people are."

"And how are you going to stop me?" Kandi asked as she was already flying at the giant's head.

Her move sounded good in her head but, in practice, lacked something. Helvar demonstrated a speed that belied his size as he swatted her like a mosquito and watched her piteously as she fell to the floor in a heap. "You can't win against me, little girl. Your strength is impressive, but mine is far greater. Did you ever wonder why my ancestors were so hard to defeat on the home world?" He quickly chained her to the wall before she recovered.

Dazed, Kandi remembered the stories of elven and pixie armies in combat with these beings and the casualties that had resulted from those skirmishes. "So, you are just going to leave me here to starve? I would rather die a warrior."

"Nah, I know the death you prefer, and I intend to deny you that. I will return each day to provide you with food and water. You won't starve. The bucket on the floor will take care of your other needs." He smiled evilly.

Kandi struggled against the chains on her hands. "Don't wear yourself out. That isn't normal steel. I cannot break them. Neither can you."

"What are you going to do with my husband?"

"You insist on continuing that charade? He isn't your husband. He is human, your kind's most hated enemy. The odds of you forming a life partnership with a human are beyond calculation. He will die as soon as I return. Too many people know you came to the falls. They will expect to find a body. His will do nicely."

Kandi was strangely affected by the giant's cavalier attitude toward Jon, "He is innocent. Why should he be punished?"

"Innocent? I care not for innocence. Dedicated to you? Definitely. Doesn't matter. As I said, the authorities must find a body. Because of your attributes," pointing at her ears, "yours would be unacceptable. No, the investigators will believe the story I show them. There was a terrible accident during your descent over the icy rocks. I will say that I found his body wedged between two of them – crushed. They will assume that your body swept farther downstream. Of course, they will search but not find you." Halvar began moving back to the door. "For now, I must say goodbye. I will see you again after I take care of your friend."

"Why leave me alive?"

Halvar turned back toward her and smiled evilly, "You are quite beautiful. Even a giant has needs."

"I will kill you."

"You will try."

Helvar smiled as he left her struggling against her chains.

Chapter 41 – Catching the Scent

The fugitive's trail from Bergen had been easy to follow. They didn't know the language, and they weren't familiar with the area. In effect, they were tourists – tourists visiting a site not known for having a lot of wintertime visitors before the ski season started. The big draw in Eidfjord was the fjord and the waterfall, and they were best in summer.

As they walked into the corner store, Captain Masters walked beside Politibetjent (Sergeant) Erik Nilsen of the Norwegian police. *Fortunately, the man preferred to use first names and not titles*, Masters thought. They had spoken to many people to no avail. While they were paying, Erik noticed the clerk was not the same person they had spoken to earlier. He casually asked the girl if she had seen either of these people, flashing a picture on the counter.

The young woman was happy to cooperate with the handsome sergeant, "Yes, I remember them. They came in yesterday evening looking for a place to stay. They were funny; they only knew a few words in Norse. I sent them to my uncle's inn, Sjel og gane bar og restaurant just toward the docks and around the corner to the left."

Erik thanked her with a smile while the captain paid for the food. They exited the store and then beelined toward the inn, the food tossed in a bin outside the store. As they walked, Masters phoned the rest of the team, telling them to establish a perimeter around the hotel. He didn't want his prey to escape this time.

Cautiously, Master's eyes scanned the room as he approached the man at the bar. He and Erik placed their NATO and police credentials on the counter. He asked his questions slowly so Erik could translate, "Good evening, we are looking for a pair of Americans. Would have arrived yesterday." He placed the pictures of the fugitives alongside the credentials on the counter. "Have you seen them?" knowing full well that he had.

The owner of the inn was sweating profusely. *What is going on? What did these people do to get the authorities after them?* he thought. "Yes. They came in for a room last night, did a search on my computer, and then left early this morning."

"Did they say where they were going?"

The owner tripped over himself, trying to be helpful, "Ya. They were going to Vøringfossen waterfall. A bus went to the trailhead this morning, but they missed the bus back. The bus driver came in after her route for a bite to eat. Said she had told them the climb was foolhardy this time of year, but they didn't seem to care. When they didn't appear for the return trip, she called the manager of the Fall View Hotel and asked him to keep an eye out for them."

"Did he find them?"

"That I don't know. Halvar's been coming into town to pick up building supplies for the hotel remodel. Usually, he comes in for a drink before heading back, but I haven't seen him."

"You're sure he hasn't slipped in?"

The man laughed, "Ah...yeah. Halvar Olsen doesn't just slip in anywhere. The man is huge. Built like a wall, he is."

"Fine, how do I get to the Fall View?"

"Tonight, you don't. We just got word that another snowstorm is headed this way—a big one. The weather has been crazy this year. Police have already closed Highway 7 to the south. Afraid you are stuck here for the night."

"Wonderful," Masters tried to hide his disappointment, "Might need a few rooms then. How many do you have available?" Masters called his men inside while the innkeeper made the arrangements.

After getting the number of men needing rooms, the owner confided, "Sir, I am afraid I'm a room short. The young lady and gentleman rented the only other room I had."

Now the man had Masters' attention, "Wait. They didn't clear out of their room?"

"No," the man answered casually, "They paid for a week."

"We'll take their room as well as a possible crime scene. Take me there, now."

The innkeeper felt his knees would give way as he climbed the steps. Tentatively, he opened Jon and Kandi's room. "Here we are. He had never had trouble with the police, and now he had an armed NATO patrol under his roof. "I have their passports downstairs in the safe if you are interested."

The captain became incensed, "You what! Is there anything else you aren't telling me?" Masters was almost shouting at the poor man.

"Nnnnoooo, sir."

Captain Masters turned to his sergeant, "Jackson? I need you and Jones to accompany this man downstairs and retrieve the passports. Jones? I need you to check the computer and see if anything useful appears in the search history. We may not be able to go anywhere this evening, but by God, we will still get things done."

"Yes, sir!" the men shouted as they headed downstairs. The captain then contacted his superior, "Sir, we are very close. Unfortunately, the weather situation is deteriorating even as we speak. There is no way to get to the target tonight."

"What do you require, Captain Masters?"

"They have closed the roads already, and the innkeeper says he's pretty sure they'll still be closed through tomorrow morning. What I need is a helicopter outside the door first thing tomorrow."

"I'll have one there for you."

After hanging up, the Commander called in a favor with the Secretary of Defense. She, in turn, reached out to her counterpart in Norway, who then sent the necessary order to Gardermoen AFB, about two hundred miles east of Captain Masters' position. Immediately, the base commander assembled a helicopter crew and told them to prep their chopper. The flight team obeyed their orders; they would be in Eidfjord by morning, even if the mission meant flying through this storm.

Skiing accidents sometimes brought medical helicopters to Eidfjord, but a military cargo copter was a rarity. As the Norwegian Air Force copter landed on the new snowfall on the morning of the

22nd, the town came out to watch. Masters had been impressed when the commander had called him and told him to have his men ready at first light but had questioned the reality of the helicopter traveling across the mountains in a storm at night. Yet here it was.

The trip to the Fall View Hotel took little time by air. The road was still impassable even though they could see the snow plows working furiously to open it up. They landed in the nearly vacant parking lot where only a single four-wheel-drive pickup sat.

Captain Masters exited the chopper and churned through the fresh snowfall to the front door. No one answered his knocks, but the door was open, and the entryway beyond was dark. He entered cautiously, flanked by his team on either side, weapons out and ready. Erik was beside him shouting, "Politiet! Politiet!" but an echo was the only response. The building appeared deserted.

Masters wasn't happy, "OK, we need to do a room-to-room search. Each team takes a section of rooms. Search them all. I need to know if our fugitives are here or if they are lying dead at the bottom of the canyon. Also, keep an eye out for the caretaker. The innkeeper told me he's huge, so he shouldn't be hard to find."

"Yes, sir!" The men went about their assigned duties.

The Captain turned toward his Norwegian escort, "So, Erik? What do you think happened here?"

The sergeant shook his head, "Well, we know the bus driver contacted the caretaker, who indicated he would go to the trailhead and look for the pair, but...."

Captain Masters finished the sentence, "But his truck is still here. He wouldn't have walked to the trailhead, so we must assume that 1. He never left to look, or 2. He found them and brought them back here."

Erik nodded, "That's what I think as well."

The two men soon had their answer. A shout came out from one of the side corridors, indicating something interesting. Masters and Neilsen ran to the room, finding two packs containing climbing supplies and a half-dozen pre-paid Visas lying on the bed. Erik looked at Masters and smiled, "Seems the caretaker found them." Masters nodded, "But where did they go?" He gathered the team and gave them an order, "Tear this place apart. If you don't find them, I better get some leads about where they went."

Despite the veiled threat, a thorough search of the building and the grounds came up empty, and Captain Masters made a much-dreaded phone call back to base.

"Yes, captain?" The Commander seemed almost relaxed.

"Sir. We followed our lead to the Fall View Hotel, where it ran cold. The caretaker and our suspects have vanished. The man's truck is here. The fugitives' supplies and money are here. The people, however, are nowhere to be found."

A hint of anger crept into the Commander's voice, "That is disappointing indeed, Captain. No leads at all?"

The captain gulped and began to sweat as he continued, "No, sir. Unless something else comes up right away, there is nothing else we can do here. I will make the necessary arrangements for the return to Colorado."

"Yes, yes. I suppose that would be best. Brief me completely upon your return. Hopefully, I can see something you might have missed." Masters flinched at the demeaning tone his superior was using. "Also, Masters, put out an Interpol alert for our suspects and the caretaker."

"Yes, sir."

"That is all, captain." The line went dead before Masters could begin to say goodbye. He could tell that the old man was really pissed, but for the life of him, he had no idea what he could have done differently. Well, he had a transatlantic flight to come up with something. No SST this time. The trip would take a full ten hours. Masters dutifully called Interpol and sent the descriptions of the now three people the United States had an interest in finding. Maybe something would come out of the inquiry, but he had doubts.

The commander, sitting in his Colorado office, sat deep in thought. *What are you up to, pixie? What have you and your pet human come up with now? Is it possible that some of the Asgardian materials were there somewhere? No, I don't think so. The captain may not be perfect, but crystals like those would stand out anywhere. Somehow, you escaped death again, but I know you will surface somewhere.*

Chapter 42 – When One Door Closes...

Jon regained consciousness far below where the captain searched for him. The dimness of the cavern made focusing difficult. Where was he? What had happened? He felt something wet on his temple, and he pulled back blood when he reached up to touch the spot. Groggily, he sat up, his head spinning with every move. He knew where he was, but not how he was injured, and definitely not why he was alone.

What the hell happened? The giant's attack had been so quick and unexpected that Jon had no recollection of the assault. Instinctively, he looked up to see if he had clobbered himself on a rock outcropping, but nothing like that was even close to his location. Gradually getting to his feet, wincing with each flash of lightning that blasted from behind his eyes, Jon looked painfully for Helvar and Kandi. No one was there.

Jon shouted, "Hello!" *God, that hurts!* Despite the pain pulsating behind his eyelids, he persisted, "Hello, anyone there? Helvar? Kandi? Sara?" No other voice responded. The only replies to his calls were the echoes of his voice sounding back from the cavern walls. Although the room was still spinning around him, he became aware of the small door at the end of the cave.

That door appeared to be the only way out besides how they entered, and Jon doubted they would have backtracked without him. *That must be where they went. Without me? Kandi was anxious to find the crystals. Maybe she was afraid I'd slow them down. Figured they would pick me up on the way back or something.* Something about that line of reasoning sounded false to Jon. No, something was wrong. He had been unconscious and bleeding. Despite their differences and Kandi's instinctive hatred of humans, Jon didn't believe she would desert him for a minute. He knew for sure that Sara wouldn't.

Jon stumbled over to the stone door, looking for a way to open it. None was apparent. There was no handle to pull, and pushing with all his strength did absolutely nothing. *Well, isn't that special? A door that won't open.* He put both hands on the door and leaned in, resting his hurting head against the cool surface of the stone.

Suddenly, he sensed a warmth running through his right hand. He glanced up to see the stone glowing a brilliant blue, the aura seemingly feeding itself into the door. The door dissolved into nothingness without warning, forcing Jon to stagger into a hidden room beyond.

A wave of nausea and vertigo caused Jon to drop to his knees. At first, he was concerned that he had a concussion. Then, he was struck with the déjà vu of the experience. What he was feeling were the same things he had experienced arriving in Vermont from Central Park. Realization hit him. Something had transported him to another location.

Still reeling from his head wound, he gradually became aware of voices off to the left – angry voices. With some effort, he identified the speakers as his traveling companions. Whatever was going on, Helvar and Kandi were really going at each other.

Jon's initial reaction was to rush to Kandi's aid, but something held him back. Kandi was far more capable than he was at self-defense. Jon wasn't sure what he could do to aid the pixie. As he contemplated his options, Jon again became aware of the warmth in his hand. This time, the stone seemed to pull him – away from the angry voices. He fought the feeling at first. He needed to help Kandi, not run away. Still, the feeling was so persistent that he finally relented and followed where his hand led, finally coming to rest in a small, empty alcove in a dusty old room with massive runes etched into the stone walls.

His hand, seeming to have a life of its own, forced his palm flat on the wall. As with the first door, the blue light radiated into the wall, revealing a hidden doorway that swung open at his touch.

What is this? Before him was a large room with unusually shaped items made from opalescent crystal. He grabbed one of the spiral tubes in front of him. The material seemed strong and fit over his arm well. There was even a place to grip the device with his hand. He struck the tube against the wall with all his might, but the substance gave no inclination of shattering. *I have no idea what this thing does or once did, but the surface appears strong. It might give my punch a little more zing.* Jon ran back to the voices down the hall.

As he got closer, the voices became more defined. Jon identified Halvar's voice, saying, "For now, I must say goodbye. I will see you again after I take care of your friend." Somehow, his tone of voice in "taking care of your friend" wasn't encouraging. Neither was Kandi's response. "Why leave me alive?"

Jon could hear the lust in Halvar's voice as he replied, "You are quite beautiful. Even a giant has needs."

Kandi was defiant, "I will kill you."

"You will try," the giant answered with disdain.

The giant was still chuckling at his joke as he left the room, turned the corner, and saw an angry Jon standing in his way. Halvar quickly moved into an attack position, "Well, I guess you recovered from the little tap I gave you."

Jon, still hurting from the 'tap,' refused to show weakness. "Yeah, was that the best you could do?"

His taunt incensed the giant before him. "No matter, little man. You will die now." He swung his fist at Jon with a speed that belied his size. Jon barely had time to block him, and still, the force of the blow sent Jon reeling back to the wall. The tube around his arm absorbed most of the impact.

Halvar taunted him, "Where did you find your little toy? There shouldn't be any around anymore. The giants called it Thor's Hammer in the old days and feared it like nothing else. Of course, the power within has long since died. The thing is useless. Strong as it is, that piece of glass won't be enough to save your life. Give up. I'll make your end quick."

"I'd rather not." Jon felt in his heart that this was the end. He tentatively lifted his right arm and pointed the end of the tube at the giant before him like a spear. He gripped the crystal for all he was worth, concentrating as if mental power alone would end his nemesis.

Once more, the blue light streamed from the ring and infused the crystal around his arm. In front of him, Halvar's face went unnaturally pale just before the object launched a blast of energy into his chest. Halvar fell back momentarily, shook his head, regained his footing, and charged at Jon again.

The tube flared again, hitting Halvar in the chest and pushing him back against the parapet.

The giant took a little longer to recover this time, shaking his head as if waking up. Jon barely had time to reposition himself before Halvar rushed at him again. Jon leveled the weapon toward the giant's head and again squeezed his hand against the crystal. The blue aura filled the device. Halvar's face seemed to glow briefly before flashing out of existence. The blast's force thrust the giant's body over the parapet and onto the snow drifts far below.

Jon was stunned. Thor's Hammer indeed! After a few moments to fully realize what he had done, he pulled himself off the floor and ran into the room behind the giant's body. "Kandi, Sara?"

"In here! I can't believe I'm saying this, human, but I'm happy to see you. What was going on out there anyway? How did you survive the giant's attack?" Only then did she notice what Jon wore on his arm.

"Jon? What are you doing with that? "Kandi was startled and slightly frightened to see such an item on a human hand.

Jon tried a little false bravado in his response, "Just a little something I picked up on the way. Halvar called it Thor's Hammer. That seems to fit pretty well. It blew Halvar back to his version of hell."

Kandi tried to remain calm, "That, my human friend, is a force-three phase disruptor, one of the most powerful hand weapons developed on Aeden and one of the few that could take down a giant. Now, would you please take that thing off? I don't feel right watching you swing the tube around like that. I wouldn't want an accident to happen."

Jon reluctantly complied and then picked up the keys to Kandi's manacles lying where Halvar had dropped them on the floor, "Now, the question is, where is here?" He looked over the parapet at the giant's body in the snow, "I would say we're pretty far from the hotel."

Kandi spoke, "Agreed. Wherever this castle is, the Asgardians would have placed the structure in an unexplored part of the northern wilderness for security. How did you get here?"

"I opened a portal door using the ring."

"Do you think it would let you return the same way?"

Jon was less than optimistic, "I can try, but I've no idea how I opened the door before, let alone how to repeat the trick. Besides, are we certain that's the best option. Even if we do get back, people WILL be looking for him," pointing down at Halvar's corpse.

"Some worker at the hotel will need authorization for something, or the bus driver who called him about us will be checking in. Someone will report him missing, and we will be the ones the authorities will look to for answers."

Kandi agreed in spirit but countered, "Jon, that gate might still be our best option. The Asgardians wouldn't have multiple access points to their fortress for security reasons. We may have to take our chances. Before we do anything, though, where did you find your little toy here?"

Jon led her down a narrow corridor to the large room with rune-covered walls. Jon ignored the room and focused on reaching his destination quickly. Kandi, on the other hand, stopped cold. She might have missed the runes, but the walls captured Sara's complete and undivided attention, forcing the shared body to stop.

Jon soon realized he was walking alone. He said, "Aren't you in a big hurry to find where I got the blaster thing?" Kandi's voice sounded far away, "I was, but Sara stopped me. Something about the runes here. With Halvar dead, the armory can wait for a bit."

Her voice shifted as Sara began reading, "This is quite fascinating; the runes are elven standard and document what happened to this Master stronghold after the gate collapse." She pointed at one wall section, "Here, the text indicates that Crystal was becoming scarce. Wars between the different gate Watchers around Gaia were commonplace."

"Over here," she moved over a little, "they document their attack on Skye. According to the record, there was sufficient plunder from that raid that they felt secure in their citadel. Safely hidden in the castle, they easily defeated everyone who came to steal their horde."

Sara continued poring over the surface, looking for the last section. "Ah, here we go. Twenty years after the collapse, the remaining Masters held a conference. Attendees included the Masters of Gomorrah Garrison at Sodom Gate, Olympus Gate, Ra Gate, and Asgard Gate. Experience had told them that help was not coming from Aeden. If they were going home, they would have to save themselves. With that goal in mind, they decided to pool their remaining resources and attempt to build a gate."

Sara continued, "Apparently, the Watcher commanders argued about the best location for the gate. The Asgardians felt they should be hosts because of their available crystal resources, with each other site also feeling their location was best. Finally, the group from Sodom presented the most convincing argument. Sodom Gate was the first established in the initial colonization effort. To establish a time lock, Origen used the Wellspring, his original gate, to form Sodom. The Watchers believed the tie to the Wellspring would provide the best chance for a link back to Aeden. Finally, in agreement, they opted to build their transmitter there."

Jon was finally listening. "Sodom is one of our earliest legends. There is no proof it ever existed. Do they say where this Sodom is?"

Sara looked back at him, "They don't need to. In our time-stream, Sodom still exists. I have the coordinates. If we can get out of here, I can get us there."

The pixie's body shuddered momentarily as Kandi resumed control and began talking to Sara and Jon, "Finally, some good news. Now," redirecting her attention to Jon, "where did you get your toy?"

Jon proceeded across the room to where the hidden door stood open from his earlier incursion, awaiting his return. Kandi couldn't believe her eyes. "This was the castle's armory, probably put in for the Watchers to respond quickly to an uprising of the giants. That would explain the portal to the plateau. They could immediately respond without leaving themselves open to a counterattack." She began trolling through the rows of weapons. "Impressive."

Jon continued with his line of questions, "So, am I to believe that all the stories of ancient gods are true? That Asgard and the Rainbow Bridge actually existed? Odin, Thor, Ra, and Zeus were real?" He followed Kandi through the rows of assembled weapons while he came to grips with all the legends of his youth being flesh and blood.

"I have no idea how your ancestors concluded the Watchers were gods. These were men and women – warriors. I guess that, over time, the stories of their crystal powers morphed them into deities. The Asgardians were unique. Most gates opened directly into the human cities surrounding them. The giants were far too warlike to make that safe, so the Watchers built a secondary gate in the castle to buffer against a giant attack." She stopped cold in front of a collection of devices.

"That was probably a good idea if they all were like him...." Jon's voice trailed off when he noticed Kandi's fixation on the wall before them. "What gives?"

Kandi smiled, "What gives could be our way out of here. Do you see these cubes? These are portable transfer devices. I used two of them to visit your father's place in Colorado."

Jon shrugged, "How do we know if they even work?"

"We don't until we try."

With Sara looking on from inside her mind, Kandi examined the device on all sides. From Jon's point of view, the contraption appeared to be a polished metal cube. He saw no flaws in the surface, indicating an access point. Kandi appeared increasingly frustrated in her attempts to open the device. "The ones we used had panels that opened," she volunteered. "This one has nothing of the sort. I can't get inside to set the coordinates and activate it."

Kandi, Sara's voice echoed in the pixie's subconscious; *this is the same model we used in Vermont. Because of the general fear of Gaian access to such things, the manufacturers built a failsafe that would lock the unit down if power levels reached a critical point. I believe that is what has happened here.*

Sara's comments made sense. "Great," was Kandi's reply. She looked at Jon and tossed him the cube, "Here, see what you can do with it. You managed to activate the blaster."

Jon caught the device in one hand and smiled, impressed with his catch. The now familiar blue aura almost immediately expanded from the stone and into the cube. Now, access points were visible across the cube's faces. Kandi and Sara were ecstatic. She grabbed the device from his grasp but then grew silent as the cube returned to its flawless surface.

It would seem that Jon's ring is required to power the device. Sara communicated. Kandi reluctantly agreed. "Here," handing the cube back to the human, "you hold it; Sara and I will handle the programming. OK?"

"Sounds like a plan." He took the cube from her hand, and once again, the blue aura surrounded the device, and the access points reemerged. Quickly, Sara entered the coordinates for Sodom gate and gave control back to Kandi. "We may only get one shot at this," looking at Jon, "Are you ready?"

"Ready as I'll ever be."

Just then, a loud cry rang out from below the parapet. Jon and Kandi were startled. They had assumed they were alone in the castle. Kandi ran to the edge and looked over the side. What she saw made her turn white. "Jon, we have a problem."

"What's that?"

"Halvar may have been a loner, but he wasn't alone here."

A gathering of giant forms huddled around the dead Helvar. Jon gasped just loud enough for one of the beings to look up and see him. A loud cry of rage rose as the group moved en masse toward the castle's base. Jon and Kandi could hear the giants' feet echoing on the stone steps below. Jon and Kandi knew they had only moments before the massive creatures would arrive - and attack.

Fortunately, in all the excitement, Jon had not released the cube. The runic figures still appeared on the surface, but there was no time. A giant entered the room on the run as Kandi reached forward and grabbed Jon by the arm, leading him over to the parapet. Without thinking or asking, she leaped from the ledge, taking Jon with her. As they fell toward the ice and rocks below, she pressed the glowing spot on the face of the cube. There was a flash of incandescent light.

Chapter 43 – Sodom Revisited

Traveling through a portal must still conform to most laws of physics. Even though Jon and Kandi had traveled thousands of miles across the planet's surface in the blink of an eye, they were still moving downward at several feet per second due to Kandi impulsively throwing them from the castle parapet.

Now, instead of snow and rocks, they hurtled downward toward sand and scrub brush. Fortunately, neither found any obstacles as they bounced along the ground, finally stopping at the bottom of the hill. However, Jon had to believe that snow would have been softer as he tumbled into some bushes blocking his path.

Affected by the impact and the nausea portal travel caused, Kandi and Jon stood gingerly and gazed at their new surroundings while brushing the sand from their clothing and checking for broken bones or cuts. The area was as desolate as the snow fields around the castle had been, with nothing around them but sand and scrub plants as far as they could see, which, from this vantage point, wasn't very far.

Of course, nothing was probably a good thing in their current situation. Suddenly appearing in the middle of a busy intersection in a major city in Norwegian winter gear would be much more conspicuous than landing in the middle of an arid desert landscape. The downside was that no one could help them either. To make matters worse, the sun was barely hanging above the western horizon with no shelter in sight.

After an eternity of awkward silence, broken only by the wind whistling across the sand, Jon spoke, "So…this is Sodom."

There was a slight quiver in Sara's voice when she answered, as though trying to convince herself, "I know the coordinates I set were correct. Whatever "this" is now, twenty-five millennia ago, this was the gate city of Sodom." Kandi's voice took over, almost nostalgic, "The last time I was here was just before my transfer to Babel. Then, the area around the city was a garden – beautiful beyond words – a paradise. What could have happened?"

Jon replied, "I would guess twenty-some thousand years happened. In that amount of time, a lot can change. Climates shifted, and the area dried up. Who knows, the gate collapse might even have initiated the process. At this point, we can't know for sure." Jon was throwing stones that littered the area around where they sat. "Don't suppose we could give this bugger another shot?" He tossed the crystal cube up and down.

Kandi was almost apologetic, "No. The Institute made portable transmitters for emergency use – one-time emergency use. Normally, I would've grabbed two, but time appeared of the essence."

"Yeah. I was there. By the way, thanks for the heads up before you threw us off the balcony," he said sarcastically. He tossed the object into the air one more time for good measure before heaving the device as far as he could. He laughed, "Hey, maybe some future archeologist will make history when he finds that."

Then, Jon got serious, "OK, so where do we go from here?" he asked earnestly, "We don't have any ID or even most of our funds. All we have are the serious winter clothes on our backs, the contents of my wallet, about three hundred in cash – Norwegian krone at that, and one of the pre-paid cards we've already started using. Do we even have a clue where we are?"

Sara replied, "No. I never downloaded the coordinate maps for this period. It wasn't considered vital for the mission, but we are in the desert. Surely, that narrows our search down a little."

Jon laughed, "I'm sorry, but it doesn't. Ear...Gaia is littered with desert landscapes. Every continent has several. Even if my scientific community is correct about the possible location of ancient Sodom, there are still thousands of square miles of real estate where we could be."

Kandi's military training came to the foreground, "Very well. We're lost, and our current position limits us from discovering anything more. Procedure indicates that we need to get to higher ground." She pointed toward the top of a nearby hill. "Perhaps we can see something from up there that will give us an idea of where we are in this timeline."

Jon didn't hold out much hope in her solution, but he didn't have a better idea, so he dutifully followed her lead. The hill was deceiving, much taller than they had first believed, and slugging through the sand was a lot tougher climbing than rolling down.

They weren't long into their climb before experiencing the problems of wearing Nordic clothing in a warm desert environment, and they began peeling off layers of clothing from the heat.

Truthfully, it wasn't that hot, considering the time of year. Jon guessed it to be around sixty-five degrees Fahrenheit. From digs with his father in similar climates, Jon knew the temperature would plummet overnight and insisted they hold on to some warmer clothing for then.

Kandi spoke up, "This is incredible. We have nothing on Aeden to compare to this."

Jon commented, "But surely, you experienced our deserts when they assigned you here, right?"

Kandi replied, "When our scientists created your ecosystem, they made it as close to Aeden as possible. We didn't have deserts, so you didn't have deserts. All of this developed since the gates collapsed."

Finally, after littering the landscape with assorted clothing items, they stood at the top of the hill. The view was depressing. All around them were more hills surrounded by identical swaths of desert. No living thing was in sight, so Kandi tried a different perspective. Quickly, she shed her clothing and allowed her wings to unfurl to their maximum size. She launched into the air, soaring like a giant bird of prey over the area.

Jon had forgotten entirely about his companion's aerial abilities. He watched in wonder as her naked form soared above him. After about ten minutes, she returned to the hilltop, breathless with the exertion, sweat shining on her forehead. "We are not as alone as we feared," she sputtered. Her news encouraged Jon, "What did you see? Anything that tells you where we are?" Kandi shook her head, "No. We are still lost, but I did discover a road in that direction," she pointed west, "and apparently, a small town in the same way. I suggest we go there."

Again, the absence of objects to measure against played havoc with the duo's perspective. What had seemed to Kandi a short distance from up above was, in fact, three to four miles on foot. Fortunately, a half moon lit the desert sands as if it were midday, and the temperature was cool enough to make the walk almost pleasant. The only thing that would have improved the situation was water, which was painfully absent from the surrounding environment.

"Can I ask you a question?" Jon asked innocuously.

"If you must," was the curt reply.

"Tell me about how humans got here, to Ear…Gaia."

"Are you certain that you want to know the details?"

"Yeah. I'm still hazy about the whole time travel thing."

"Very well. Aedenian scientists began looking at Gaia not long after Origen allowed us to do so – years before the Human Wars began. They were fascinated by the possibilities of using time dilation to watch a world evolve, multiple times if necessary, within their lifetimes." She continued as they headed up yet another hill. "They weren't disappointed.

When they first looked at your world, giant reptiles were the high point of local evolution.

The scientists continued jumping forward a millennium at a time until they arrived at a period when the planet was in complete disarray; some event had eradicated most life forms. They couldn't go back along the timeline. Origen forbade that, but evidence later indicated that a giant asteroid, an extinction-level event, must have impacted your planet."

"That sounds close to what our people think as well."

Kandi took a minute to catch her breath before continuing. "The scientists were overjoyed by the opportunities this new development presented. Without the native species in contention, they could recreate Aeden on Gaia using techniques that had been only hypothetical before. Never had they considered they would get to try such methods. Through careful seeding, the atmosphere, which had been heavy in carbon dioxide before, was now in a breathable balance, even if the nitrogen content was higher than we were used to having.

Using the portals, the researchers could transport to the planet and pursue their work. At that point, they brought in plants and animals and watched them spread across the planet in days while thousands of years of Gaian time passed. The scenario was a scientist's dream. They seemed more like children playing with toys than the men of learning, which they were. They were about to begin voluntary colonization when the wars began, and the council put their research on hold, redirecting them toward supporting the war effort."

"That had to be disappointing," Jon commented.

"Yes, but they also understood that if the humans won, they wouldn't be around to continue their work."

"I see." Jon was instantly uncomfortable by her comment.

"At the war's conclusion, most people wanted the remnants of humanity destroyed, a pursuit which Origen stopped. With no other option, the council instructed the scientists to establish a human sanctuary on Gaia instead of the elven/pixie colonies they had anticipated building. Although most humans had died during the war, a large contingent remained in confinement on the Eastern Continent.

"The science teams enthusiastically began renewing their experiments and analyzing life on Gaia. Even with the time constraints from the council, the gates gave them all the time they needed. In less than an Aedenian year, the world was ready to receive the prisoners."

Jon gasped at that revelation. "That's amazing! How would that be possible even with time travel?" he asked.

"Remember, not just time travel – time dilation as well. The researchers had multiple teams running projects simultaneously. Every minute of the Aedenian day, they put groups of AIs into motion at different points in Gaian history to work on tasks that they wouldn't finish for a thousand years but required only seconds in Aedenian space. The scientists would jump forward to check the AI's work, make adjustments, and then jump forward again until they reached completion. When they finished, Gaia became a flawed reflection of Aeden. Some problems science couldn't resolve. Your planet received far too much radiation from its sun to be a perfect match. Many Aedenian plant and animal life forms perished when we attempted to integrate them into your world.

Research indicated that solar radiation alone would significantly reduce human life spans, especially after the first generation. Of course, the Council wasn't concerned with that. All Origen required was that humans be allowed to live. All the Council cared about was that Origen was satisfied and that 'where' the humans lived wasn't 'here.'"

Jon gulped. He hadn't realized how close his race had come to elimination. "You said that the problems my world faces are not new. What did you mean by that?"

"After forming the colonies, we abandoned your people to find their way, only checking in on them occasionally to be sure they were not attempting to return. Your race, though short-lived, thrived on Gaia, and your population exploded. However, just as now, your people abused the environment and caused an imbalance in the hydro and magnetospheres. There was a resulting drop in the strength of the magnetic field. Remember, Jon, your magnetic field is what protects you from your sun's rays. Consequently, reducing the field strength would cause a corresponding spike in solar radiation, which, in turn, began shrinking the polar caps. That redistribution of water weight on the planet's surface by both causes resulted in your world tipping.

"We saw it coming, realized what was happening, and tried to correct the problem, but it progressed far faster than we believed possible. In the end, conditions left us with only one alternative - evacuation. Initially, we believed we had a lot more time, but ultimately, we could only manage to get a few thousand people off Gaia before the final moment. What remained of the Gaian population either perished in the "tip" or mutated in the bath of radiation that followed."

Jon was skeptical, "How could this happen? The planet spins at a thousand miles per hour. There is no way the world could tip."

Kandi nodded, "You are correct. The gyroscopic effect of Gaia's spin would keep the planet from falling over and staying there but would not keep Gaia from tipping wildly before rediscovering her equilibrium, something which would take thousands of years."

"What happened afterward?" Jon asked somberly.

"Humans were placed in the old holding prisons on the Eastern Continent until the scientists could re-evaluate the Gaian ecosystem. Origen was not pleased. He reminded the council of their pledge to him and that they were also responsible for the environment of Gaia. They were ready to reestablish the colony a few months later, translating to close to a million years of your time. By then, the magnetic field had recovered, the water returned to the ice caps and underground areas, and the planet's spin stabilized.

"There was a twist this time around. Incredibly, the initial colony had survivors. These 'old ones' had mutated into semi-human forms and would be in direct competition with the new colonists. Fortunately for all parties, most old ones moved to less hospitable parts of the planet to avoid the newcomers. If Fiona were correct, the resettlement would have occurred about 27,000 years ago in your time. I have no idea what has transpired here between then and now."

Kandi finished her monologue just as they reached the top of the last hill. Below them, the city's lights shone warmly, almost welcoming. Jon allowed his head to swivel to take in the complete view. All at once, he stopped, his eyes focused on something away from the city. Kandi allowed her eyes to follow his. There was a ridge silhouetted against the stars in the western sky. "I know this place," he said.

Kandi was incredulous, "What do you mean you know this place? We are in the middle of the desert."

Jon smiled, "See that ridge over there?" She nodded. "I remember that shape. I visited here with my father when I was a little boy. Its name is Tall el-Hammam. Inside that ridge are the ruins of a city destroyed by a meteor airburst about five thousand years ago. Many archeologists believe the event created our legend of Sodom. Unfortunately, for our purposes, the destruction of Tall el-Hammam would have been about fifteen thousand years too late."

Kandi nodded as she listened, but Sara spoke. "Over the centuries, there would be a strong likelihood that others would build on the same spot, especially if the area had maintained some of its garden-like appearances. This one site could be old Sodom, where the Watchers gathered after the collapse, and the site of a new city later."

Jon continued, "We may have a more pressing problem. If, as I believe, that is indeed Tall el-Hammam, we are in the country of Jordan in a volatile part of my world known as the Middle East. The lights below us would then be the village of ar-Rawda, where Father and I stayed while we were here. Kandi, war has plagued this area for millennia. The latest one ended not long ago, with Jordan on the losing side. Although they are now more friendly to Americans, they will likely not be forgiving to strangers without papers."

Trusting his memory from when he and his father visited, he set a course for a building that had been a hotel at that time. Jon didn't have a plan per se, but he knew they needed a place to lay up while they considered their options.

Chapter 44 – Strangers in Need

The hotel was still there. As they entered the foyer, Jon and Kandi got more than a few stares from the people milling about. Even after shedding much of their Norwegian gear, their attire still looked jarringly out of place here in the desert. Kandi became stressed, "Why are they looking at us like that? Do they recognize us from the news?" She was on high alert, and Jon tried his best to calm her, "Relax. Our clothing makes us an oddity here. After we get a room, we'll go out and get something more appropriate to wear. "

Jon cringed as he watched a considerable portion of his last debit card go away to secure a room. Late fall was peak season here, with moderate temperatures and occasional rain to settle the dust. This was tourist weather, and visitors from abroad packed the hotel. After all, al-Rawda was only a few miles from Jesus' purported baptism site, and pilgrims needed rooms. In truth, Jonathan realized they were lucky to find anything at all.

While at the desk, Jon was able to exchange his kroner for the Jordanian dinar and get directions to a clothing outlet nearby. He was so excited that he never noticed the looks the clerk gave him or the clerk's conversation with his manager after he and Kandi left him.

After returning to the hotel more appropriately attired, they settled in the restaurant for afternoon tea. Jon looked at his companion, "Kandi?" She sensed a serious tone to his voice and nodded her acknowledgment. He continued, "Is there anything more you can tell me about this ring?" Jon waved the blue stone casually in her direction.

"Not much," she said honestly. "I know that Origen gave each archangel one before assigning them to a gate on Gaia. They always wore theirs, which makes sense if they couldn't take it off, and the stone always glowed blue. I can't be certain, but Origen had to give them special instructions regarding the stone's use. Whatever those were, no one ever told. The rings were a closely guarded secret."

Jon paused. He knew he was on dangerous ground. "You never asked Iblees while you were together?"

Kandi's face paled, and her voice turned icy at the mention of the archangel's name. "No. The topic never came up, and I never asked."

Jon was instantly sorry for having brought the matter up. He knew well that former lovers were never a topic for polite conversation. Still, he could only imagine how a former lover who planted a demon in your skull like a time bomb would affect her. Iblees was a piece of work. There was no doubt about that.

Jon dropped his head and continued, "That was inconsiderate of me. Sorry." He steered the conversation back to his original question, "So, Origen, your crystal entity, created these rings for the archangels, and no one knows how they work? How is that possible?"

Kandi grew weary of the conversation, "Look, Jon, I know little more than you do. I didn't realize the rings pulled their power from the planet until Fiona shared that information with you back on Skye. Even the tale of the stone opening gates is more rumor than fact. You've managed to do more 'accidentally' with the ring than I knew was possible. Why is the ring so important now?"

Jon looked the pixie in the eyes, "Because," he said, gazing into the glowing blue orb, "I think this little beastie is trying to tell me something."

Kandi looked at him questioningly, tilting her head to one side, "You do know the ring can't talk, right?"

Jon laughed, "Not in words, maybe, but ever since we arrived in Jordan, I've felt the stone pulling; no, that's not right, directing me, leading me somewhere."

Kandi wasn't convinced, "If that's the case, where do you think the ring wants you to go?"

Jon pointed over his shoulder, "West."

Kandi replied, "Just west? That's pretty general information, Jon. There's a lot of things 'west' of here, including a lot of dried-up landscape?"

Jon's eyes held a dreamy, semi-conscious look as he shook his head, "I don't know. Crazy, right? I know it's ridiculous, but I can't shake the feeling that there is something to the West that we need to see."

Kandi laughed mockingly, "And you have no idea what it is?"

"No..." As Jon looked into the stone, a memory of his father's letter crept back into his consciousness. *Think of it as a good luck charm. I did. When I discovered the Jericho dig, I carried the box in my pocket, which turned out pretty well...* Jon jerked his body upright in the chair as he realized what they needed to do. "This will sound crazy, but I can only think of one place the ring can be leading me. During my father's last expedition, he claimed the ring was his good luck charm, leading him to his greatest discovery."

"And his great discovery is west of here?"

"Yeah, about thirty miles away."

Now, Kandi was getting interested, "What did he find?"

Jon laughed and shook his head, "Don't know. After the initial find, the whole expedition went dark. The authorities made Dad sign a non-disclosure agreement with a healthy penalty clause, including jail time if he broke it. Very odd for an archeological find. In return, the British Academy awarded him the Graham Clark Medal, one of the most prestigious awards in his field.

"All I know for certain comes from something I overheard one night at Christmas. Dad had fallen asleep in his chair. As I passed by, I realized he was talking in his sleep and was getting very agitated. I stopped to shake him awake but then decided to listen first. What he said didn't make much sense, but now, with everything that has happened, I'm not so sure...."

Now, Kandi was curious, "What did he say?"

"Four words that he repeated over and over. Winged man. Glass coffin."

Kandi stared at Jon in shock, "You're sure? Winged man? Glass coffin?"

"Yeah. I'm sure. Why, does that mean anything?"

"Maybe nothing, maybe everything. Jon, at the time of the archangel appointments, there were thirteen elves and one pixie, a 'winged man.' His name was Michael. I had the honor of serving under him during the last campaigns of the war and a brief stint on Gaia later. He was a brilliant strategist and one of the few generals, along with Iblees, that didn't favor eradicating the human population."

Now it was Jon's turn to be incredulous, "Really? You think my father discovered a twenty-five-thousand-year-old pixie? What about the glass coffin? How does that fit?"

Kandi continued, "According to Aedenian religious traditions, we are buried in a crystal coffin when we die, so our spirit can see where it is going. The type of crystal used is plentiful on Aeden and is clear as your glass."

Jon whistled, "So, correct me if I'm wrong, but you're saying that my father may have found the remains of one of your archangels?"

Kandi nodded, "I can't be certain without seeing him, but if true, this could be our next step in my getting home. Something in the tomb area might point to a gate site." She became more excited at the prospect, "Jonathan, there is no choice. We must go there immediately!" She jumped up out of her seat, excited at the prospect of finding an archangel so near.

Jon motioned her back down, "Not so fast, Kandi. Getting there is not going to be easy."

"What do you mean? Thirty miles? With provisions, we can easily walk thirty miles!"

"Kandi. The problem is where those thirty miles are. Humans live in a divided world. Our geopolitical areas are varied and not often in alignment with our neighbors. We are currently in Jordan, which, not so long ago, had an intense conflict with its neighbor, Israel – and lost. As a result of that war, Israel kept control of a large area of land that formerly belonged to Jordan, called the West Bank, which happens to be exactly where we need to go. With the proper passports and visas, we might be able to get there - in time. Without them, we might as well be on another planet. We can't get there from here."

Jon's words deflated Kandi's mood, but she remained unconvinced, "Surely there is a way. I am certain these countries of yours can't have perfectly sealed borders. Isn't there a way we can slip across unseen?"

Jon shook his head, "Not a chance. In this case, the border is the Jordan River, just west of town. Not certain what security is like on this side, but the Israelis put the "p" in paranoid, especially since they turned over nominal control of a lot of the area to the Palestinians." She looked at him quizzically as he continued, "It's a long story. Anyway, after the war ended, the Israeli side of the Jordan was so heavily mined with explosives that no one in their right mind would think about walking there. That was decades ago. Even now, only a small space around the Jordan is clear, and that was only because of the baptism site."

Something Jon said sparked a response, "That is the second time you have mentioned this site. What is it?"

"According to Biblical lore, this spot is where John the Baptist baptized Jesus."

"This Jesus? He is one of your gods?"

"One of our largest religious groups considers him God's son."

Kandi pondered momentarily, "Ah, so a very holy site indeed. I would very much like to visit this place."

Jon and Kandi were so engrossed in their conversation that they failed to notice as an older man passed by their table, stopped momentarily, and then returned. "Excuse me? Jonathan? Jonathan Martyr?"

Jon was shocked at being recognized, instantly afraid that the Feds had managed to track them here. He jerked his head up and locked eyes with a middle-aged man in khaki slacks and a worn Grateful Dead t-shirt, "I am. Who wants to know?"

The man apologized, "I'm sorry to intrude, but I wasn't positive it was you. My name is Dr. Emile Jacobs, a colleague of your father's. You and I spoke briefly at his funeral. You probably don't remember me. We also met once before when your father brought you here years ago to see my dig. You've grown a bit since then."

Jon mentally slapped himself as he recognized the man in front of him. Dr. Jacobs was the man in charge of the dig at Tall el-Hammam. Jon suddenly remembered the aging don, "I'm so sorry, Dr. Jacobs. I didn't recognize you without your three-piece suit!" The man before him in his fatigues and straw hat looked little like the gentleman in Boulder, and Jon had little memory of the man during Jon's earlier visit.

The professor shifted his attention and laughed, "No problem, my boy. There were many people there that day." He turned his attention toward Kandi, "and who is this lovely creature."

"This, sir, is my wife, Kandi." Kandi was visibly startled at the use of her real name.

"A pleasure to meet you, my dear." He kissed the back of Kandi's hand and smiled at Jon, "I don't remember seeing her at the funeral."

Jon covered, "She wasn't well and didn't make the trip from Boston."

The doctor nodded, "More's the pity." He turned his attention to Kandi, "You are exceptionally beautiful, my dear." Looking back at Jon, "You did well." Kandi smiled, despite the misogynistic nature of the comment.

Jon blushed a little as he returned the smile, "Thank you, sir. I think so, too."

The professor looked at his watch. "I'm afraid that I am late for an appointment. Would it be possible for the two of you to join me for dinner this evening?"

Jon smiled, "I think that would be wonderful."

"Shall we say seven?"

"Seven it is."

That evening, over coffee, the professor asked, "Now, curiosity is killing me. I've been trying to figure out what brings Stephen Martyr's son to my home away from home? Don't tell me you decided to follow in your father's footsteps after all?"

"Not exactly, sir. However, I must admit that ancient civilizations are becoming more and more intriguing to me. No, our meeting here is purely coincidental."

"Jonathan, being in this little piece of nowhere cannot be coincidental. If not work, what brings you here?"

Jon's demeanor shifted as he considered his response, "Honestly, we're in a bit of a fix, sir. Kandi is very religious." Kandi gave Jon a strange look, "She and I were on our way to Jerusalem for a gemologist conference and decided to stop at the baptism shrine on our way...Unfortunately, thieves spoiled our plans while on the way from the airport in Amman. They took our car and everything else we had - clothes, passports, and most of our money.

We decided to run for it while they were busy with our things. I didn't want to take a chance that they would kill us when they finished. They didn't follow us. I guess they figured the desert would finish us off. They left, and we felt lucky to escape with our lives."

The professor's face reddened with anger, "The devil, you say! Did you contact the police?"

Jon choked a little on his reply, "Sir, this is difficult to say, but the police were the people who robbed us. At least they were driving an official car. Contacting them is out of the question."

" Dear God!" The news shook the older man visibly, "Is there anything I can do?"

Jon continued his spiel, "We contacted the U.S. embassy in Amman and reported the incident without mentioning the nature of our assailants. They will expedite our reissued passports and visas to this address."

Dr. Jacobs nodded his understanding, "I see."

Jon sank the hook, "There is an additional problem. The thieves took almost everything, leaving us dangerously short on funds. My bank has a branch in Amman that should be able to expedite a new ATM card and wire us some money. We only need a little to carry us over for a few days." Jon was amazed at how easily the lies spewed out of his mouth.

The professor nodded understandingly, "Don't worry. I have no problem loaning you money to cover your room and essentials. My university does a lot of business here." He winked, "I can probably get you a better rate too."

Jon let out a long sigh of relief, "Thank you. That would help a great deal. You are a godsend."

After a bit more small talk, Dr. Jacobs excused himself and left them at the table alone. Kandi confronted Jon, "So, you contacted the embassy and the bank?"

"No, of course not," he confided.

"You lied to him?" she stated more than asked.

"An unfortunate but necessary fib," he answered.

"I am constantly amazed that your race has so many different words for lying. Must come from a raging desire to deceive all the time." She sounded a little angry, maybe even disappointed. She had begun to think that this human was different. "What will we do when our papers don't show up?"

Jon looked at her through tired eyes, "I don't know. I didn't know the man was here until he approached our table. I just wanted to give us a day or two to catch our breaths and make a plan."

The next morning found the professor still fuming about how the Jordanian authorities had treated them. "I'm furious about your situation and by His Majesty's police no less! I've got a good mind to call this general I know in the Jordanian military and let him get to the bottom of this!"

The suggestion shook Jon's core, and the lies started again, "Dr. Jacobs, Please don't. I don't know how far the corruption goes, and I don't want to raise flags until we are safely back in the U.S.A. I promise I will file a complete report with the state department when we return home."

Dr. Jacobs stroked his beard, "Very well. I still think we should strike now, but "he glanced at the two young people, "I see you're both frightened out of your wits. I guess that waiting a bit won't hurt. For the record, I think you are wrong, but it's your life, so I won't interfere."

He turned his attention to Kandi," Now, my dear, I assume your religious leanings mean you wanted to visit the baptismal site?" Kandi nodded her assent. "Very well. I am still waiting on the new interns for my dig, so I won't start working for a few days more. How about this old man shows the two of you around?"

Chapter 45 – Leaving Again

A short time later, Dr. Jacobs and his two guests loaded up in his dilapidated jeep and set off for the site where Jesus of Nazareth was baptized over two millennia earlier. Although the professor had no religious attachment to the area, he appreciated the archeological significance. He was excited to share his knowledge – especially with the son of Dr. Stephen Martyr and his delightful wife.

The drive to the Jordan River reminded Jon just how desolate this part of the world could be. He smiled as the professor regaled Kandi with stories of the other archeological ruins they passed and how they had survived the war when so many things had turned to dust in the melee. Finally, after trading their jeep for the compulsory shuttle bus at the visitor's center, they reached the site of Jesus' baptism.

At first, Jon looked back and forth, confused at what he didn't see. He asked, "Where is the river?"

Doctor Jacobs shook his head and tsked, "Jonathan, I'm surprised at you. The river isn't here anymore - hasn't been here for years, but it was two thousand years ago," he finished emphatically.

Jon did a mental face slap before responding, "Of course, I remember now. The river shifted to the west a bit, so how is there still water here?"

"Two words. Rainy season. This part of the country gets ninety percent of its annual rainfall at this time. When it rains, the river goes over its banks, filling the ravine. It dries up soon enough, though. This time next week, the site will be bone dry again."

Jon was still confused, "What about pilgrims? I understood they came here in droves begging for baptism in the Jordan."

"Yes, that is true, but they don't come here. The tourist site is about a half mile away from here on the current banks of the Jordan." The professor's face showed his displeasure with the government's attempts to make money from religious property, especially if the exploited property was not authentic.

"Doesn't that turn off the pilgrims?"

"No. The masses are clueless and will do anything to bathe in the Jordan, whether or not it is the genuine place where Jesus took the plunge. The rain raises the water level, but the river still doesn't flow so fast that the faithful can't fulfill their hearts' desires. The water quality is terrible, though. I'm afraid neither the Israeli nor Jordanian stewards of the river have done a good job keeping the waters – shall we say, pristine?"

Dr. Jacobs shrugged and continued, "Okay. May I gather from your comments that you want to see the tourist site?" Jon sheepishly nodded. The professor continued, "So much for history then; let's go to the bathtub, shall we?"

The minibus made two more stops before taking them to the river. When they arrived at al-Maghtas, two or three groups of pilgrims were queued up, ready to enter the water. Although the visitors weren't threatening anyone, armed soldiers observed them carefully.

Across the river, on the Israeli side, a similar tableau was taking place. The Israeli position was a national park and had been excluded from the current treaty with the Palestinian Authority, which maintained nominal control of the rest of the West Bank. He and Kandi stood quietly, taking in as much of the surrounding area as possible. Things didn't look too good.

Their silence continued as they returned to the hotel. The professor finally broke the spell, "OK, children. Who's going to tell me what's really going on here?"

Jon was stunned, "I'm sorry. What?"

The professor laughed, "I've had difficulty swallowing your story. Robbed by the police? En route to Jerusalem via Jordan? Really? I'm an old fool, but that was a lot to take on faith, and years in this job have left me sorely lacking in the faith department. Then, my friend, there is that interesting item you wear on your right hand." Jon checked to be sure he had the ring covered. "Don't bother, Jonathan. I saw the object plainly when you entered the car earlier today." He focused on the younger man, "I may be a fool, Jonathan, but I'm not an idiot. Please don't treat me as one."

Jon and Kandi realized lying further would only worsen things between them. Jon told him the Reader's Digest form of the story, cutting the tale down to the bare bones but not intentionally leaving any major items out.

The professor pulled the car over to the side of the road and turned off the engine before responding, "So, young lady, if I understand Jonathan correctly, you are an alien. You don't look like the stereotypical little green man to these old eyes." He smiled.

Kandi took the cue and didn't hesitate to pull her hair up for the older man to see her markedly pointed ears. Then, she turned as far around as she could in the tight space and pulled up her shirt in the back so he could see her compressed wings folded close to her body.

"Whoa! Okay, I'm convinced. I'm not sure what I'm seeing, but whatever it is, it doesn't look like it's from around here." He directed his attention to Jon, "And you're telling me that these NSA goons have chased you all over the world?"

Kandi spoke, causing the professor to turn toward her, "We assume they are NSA, but they could be from any part of the US intelligence community. They have been following us for over a month. They almost caught us a few times. We gave them the slip in Norway when we discovered an artifact that allowed us to transport directly here."

"Which brings up a good point. Why here?" Dr. Jacobs was deeply interested in her response.

Kandi continued, "We found information leading us to believe that the items we sought went to the former gate city of Sodom. We had the coordinates, so that was where we came."

That piqued the professor's interest: "You're telling me the legend is real? The biblical city of Sodom is around here?"

Jon nodded, "Quite possibly at the site you're digging, except what you are excavating is only the most recent city at that location, not Sodom. That iteration had the unfortunate luck of being destroyed much like the original city, only for them, destruction came via an aerial explosion, not a gate collapse. Sodom's remains are far below this one."

The professor's excitement was almost tangible, "Incredible. You've given me much to consider as I move forward…and downward in my excavations. So, what happens next with you two?"

Jon said, "As you implied, sir, the ring I wear isn't just for looks. The jewelry is an ancient artifact passed down in my family for hundreds of generations. The fact that the ring has survived to the present day is, in itself, a miracle. I inherited it when my father died."

The professor was confused, "I crossed paths with your father on several occasions, and I don't recall Stephen ever wearing such an item."

Jon smiled, "He didn't wear the thing. Instead, he kept it in a lead-lined case in his pocket. My grandfather had warned him never to put the ring on his hand. In his will, he gave me the same instructions."

The doctor returned Jon's smile, "I see you listen well." The professor laughed lightly. "So, what happens now?"

"The ring wants me to go west. I believe to the last place my father excavated….."

The professor interrupted, "The find in the hill behind St. George? Do you know what he found there?" referring to the monastery outside Jericho.

"That's the place. We don't know what's there, but from what little we have uncovered, we believe the find is alien, Aedenian, in origin and, right now, offers Kandi her best hope of going home."

Dr. Jacobs whistled lightly, "But that will not be easy. You must first get across a highly contested border with trigger-happy guards on both sides without passports or visas, right?" A light of recognition filled his eyes, "You weren't thinking about a river crossing, were you?"

"Actually, yes…"

"Don't be stupid. That would be suicidal. Don't you think people have tried doing this before? The Jordanians or the Israelis would catch or shoot you before reaching the halfway point. Both sides wouldn't hesitate to make your life hell for trying, especially with no papers."

Kandi addressed the older man, "Dr. Jacobs, what other choice do we have?"

The older man considered his response, "I have an idea. I'm sending a truck to Jerusalem tomorrow to deliver some materials and pick up supplies. Amman is closer, but the government severely limits what we can buy in the way of luxury items, and our American students expect American amenities, spoiled little brats. Israel has a much more relaxed view."

He looked squarely at his two passengers, "We'll hide you in the bottom of the crates and put the materials we're sending out on top of you. Of course, the border guards at the bridge will check them, but they've never looked past the top level of items before. We'll stop and let you out as we pass through Jericho."

Kandi was shocked, "So, you've done this before?"

The professor looked at her sheepishly, "Well...not exactly."

Jon wasn't as convinced, "Sir, What if they do look in the crates?"

"Well then, we're both caught, aren't we?" By now, the three of them were back at the hotel. "Now, children, get a good night's sleep. We'll pack you up before dawn and get on the way shortly after. Make sure you eat a substantial dinner tonight. Long ride." The professor waved goodbye as he started into the hotel.

Jon's voice made him turn around, "Sir, You know that I can't ask you to take this risk."

"Son, you aren't asking. I'm telling. You have just given this old man two gifts. One, I now know that Sodom is real and likely buried under my existing dig site. Two, I know that we are not alone in the universe, that another race is also present. Those two gifts are beyond price."

Jon wondered if he should tell him about how humans settled on Gaia but then realized that nothing good would come from that information, so he didn't. If everything went well, maybe he could tell him later.

Once Jon and Kandi were safely behind the door to their room, Jon told her what he was thinking. "Kandi, Sara, we can't follow the professor's plan."

Kandi answered candidly, "I agree. He appears a little too cavalier in his assessment of the situation."

Jon nodded, "Aside from putting him and his work at great risk, we would still have virtually no chance of success. When my father and I crossed over to Israel from Jordan, they didn't just use visual inspections; they used trained dogs and scanners. The prof may think he can fool them, but the odds of success are poor to none."

Kandi said, "But what other options do we have?"

"We go back to Plan A. We need to execute a river crossing, as we discussed earlier."

"But, Jon, as you pointed out this morning, that plan also has a minuscule chance of success."

"I know, but I don't see where we have another choice."

Kandi, for once, tried to be the voice of reason, "Why can't we wait a few days? Think our options through."

That was when Jonathan dropped the bomb, "Because I don't think we have a few days. I noticed a car following us to the baptism site and returning at the same time we did. They never got too close, but I'm sure that we were their target. They even stopped to eat at the same place. Kandi, I think we'll have company sooner rather than later."

Kandi grew quiet. *How had the human noticed a tail, and she hadn't? Her pride told her Jon must be mistaken, but if he wasn't...* "Okay, Jon. How do we improve our odds?"

The three conversed earnestly for over an hour before the plan began forming. Even then, Kandi couldn't believe what she was hearing.

Is he implying that we allow the guards to win? Kandi was adamantly against the idea. "Allowing capture is far too risky, especially if the authorities are already alerted to our presence."

Jon spoke calmly, "Look. The risk is there but manageable. If we eliminate the Jordanian threat on this side of the river, there is every reason to believe the Israelis will prefer to capture rather than kill. The facility on their side is a tourist spot, not designed for long-term imprisonment. They will have to transport out as soon as possible. That's where we make our escape."

"There are still too many ifs. We must find another way."

"I wish we could. I do. The point is that we can't complete your mission without reaching Jericho. With the authorities closing in on us, time is of the essence. Whether we cross the river or cross on the international bridge, I see no way to accomplish the goal that doesn't involve getting caught. On the bridge, security is crazy tight. There is a large contingent of soldiers on both sides ready for anything, but the number of security staff in the baptism park would be much less. In addition, the bridge team has high-ranking officers within the ranks. They would take us immediately to Jerusalem or Amman for debriefing, whereas at the water crossing, they would have to wait for orders from their superiors. I'm banking on that small window being all we – well, you need to get us out of there and on our way."

Jon took several more minutes to explain the rest of the plan he had to his friends. As much as the two hated to admit the possibility of failure, Kandi and Sara began to see the logic and agreed that as poor as their chances would be, their odds were better crossing the river on foot than taking a chance with the small army on the bridge.

"OK, so when do we go?" Kandi asked.

Jon looked at his watch and responded matter-of-factly, "Now. Waiting only increases the chances that the police will be banging on our door. Moonset is in about thirty minutes. We go then."

"And how do you propose that we get there? The baptism site is a long walk from here."

Jon dangled the keys to the jeep in front of Kandi, "I took the liberty of borrowing these when we got back. He can report it stolen in the morning."

Kandi was unconvinced, "Still, the security cameras in the site's parking lot will be tracking all traffic, I'm sure."

Jon pulled out a hand-drawn map he had made during their excursion that morning, "We won't be parking there," he pointed to a place on the page, "We'll leave the car here and walk the rest of the way."

She studied the map, "The terrain is very open. You are betting a lot on the moonset darkening things."

"That, and a forecast for rain tonight."

"What happens when we get inside the perimeter?"

"That's where your unique skill set comes into play."

U.S. Space Force, Cheyenne Mountain, Colorado

Captain Masters barely kept his emotions under control. The call from the commander just under an hour ago had been as unexpected as it was fortunate. The Interpol flag on Martyr and the girl had paid off – in Jordan, of all places. Interpol's report claimed that a hotel desk clerk had become suspicious of their outlandish clothing, enough so that he alerted his manager. A cursory glance at the Interpol most wanted list did the rest.

Masters couldn't believe their luck. The Interpol listing was a Hail Mary toss. No one, least of all him, expected it to bear fruit. The local police were ready to raid the hotel immediately, but the commander convinced them that their quarry had slipped through their fingers too many times. He wanted his team on site for the take-down. Neither he nor Masters wanted a repeat of the Boston fiasco.

That was why Masters and his team were back on the Force's SST cruising at Mach 3 for Jerusalem. He would have liked to have landed closer to their target, but Jordan was still a security risk, and the plane would stand out at Amman International. Masters shrugged his shoulders. In the long run, the extra time wouldn't matter. They would be in ar-Rawda long before Martyr shook the sleep from his eyes tomorrow morning. The captain could barely control his excitement.

A few hours later, as their Land Rover chewed up the road from Jerusalem to ar-Rawda, Masters received an update from Interpol. A thorough check of Jordanian Border Patrol records showed no record of the couple entering the country by car, boat, train, or plane. How they got to ar-Rawda was a mystery. *Yeah, a mystery,* thought Masters. *We barely got back from Norway when this call came through. How did they get to Jordan?*

Chapter 46 - Escape

As Jon expected, the car that had followed them earlier was still parked outside the hotel entrance. He and Kandi went out the service entrance at the back of the hotel, assuring that the night clerk didn't see them leave. The professor had parked the jeep just around the corner under a palm tree for its shade, which at night had the added benefit of effectively blocking them from any prying eyes. Jon started the car and exited the lot from the service alley with his lights off.

As they drove down Baptism Road, Jon was thankful for straight, flat roads. He had turned on the lights as they moved through the nearly deserted town, but now those lights were more of a liability than a help. By one a.m., the clouds hid the stars, and the rain fell heavily on the jeep's roof. A few minutes later, they were at the junction. From here, they would have to proceed on foot. Jon commented, "So far, so good. No other traffic on the road. Let's hope our luck continues."

They hadn't walked far when the blurred lights of the Russian Pilgrim Residence appeared on the horizon. That would be their next stop. The Residence took in pilgrims for the night to make money to support their mission, making it one of the few areas accessible by road. They had passed by the facility earlier that day while on their tour. One thing that appealed to them was the compound's decorative perimeter fence. Pretty, but not much for security. It would be easy to climb. Most importantly, the site's north edge abutted the baptism site, presenting a possible back door into the facility.

They waited outside the fence for an agonizingly slow hour, waiting for guards and patrols, which never materialized. The slightest sound would force them to stop and re-evaluate their position. *Peace is good.* Jon reminded himself as they worked their way over the wall and dropped onto the residence grounds.

Staying on the edge of the compound where the surrounding plant growth was tall enough to hide them in their shadows, the pair worked their way around to the back, where much to their surprise, they discovered a locked gate with a sign indicating no entry at this point. This was their access point to the baptismal area itself.

Kandi pulled Jon aside, "This is where you wait while I clear the way." She deftly scaled the gate, leaving Jon in the shadows.

"Remember the rule?" he whispered back.

"No one dies." She said begrudgingly.

With those words, she silently disappeared beyond the gate and was soon swallowed up by the darkness while Jon settled down to wait.

Kandi's aggressive shaking roused Jon from a fitful dream, "I wasn't asleep," he protested.

"Right, just resting your eyes then? Come on. Time to go." Kandi was taunting him.

Jon was still half awake and confused. Did Kandi crack a joke? Instead of commenting, he earnestly asked her, "I assume you got them all? All six of them?"

She gave him a mischievous grin, "There were eight."

"Eight?" Jon had carefully counted the guards earlier. He was certain there were only six. "Where were the other two?"

"There was a command center hidden behind the trees near the water. Some idiot lit a cigarette, which alerted me. I took those two out first, along with their communication lines. The other guards were patrolling in pairs. Easy targets."

"No one..."

"No one died, although they may hurt a bit when they wake up."

Jon breathed a sigh of relief. They didn't need to add any additional murders to the already long list of crimes attributed to their names. What they were doing was as illegal as hell.

"How long before their bosses discover the communication loss?" she asked earnestly.

"They probably check in regularly, say every half-hour. If there is no response, an alarm will go up. Still, the closest Jordanian outpost is about thirty minutes away, which should give us plenty of time."

"So, based on your estimates, we only have about ten minutes before the alarm goes out. Better get moving." Kandi was more focused than Jon had seen since the walk to the falls in Norway.

Only two minutes of those minutes had transpired when they stood on the shore of the Jordan, where crowds of believers had been joyously dousing themselves with water only a few hours before. The rains had stopped, and the cloud cover was beginning to break up, allowing a few stars to peek through. Jon smiled. It was swimming time.

The plan was simple. Swim to the boundary fence, flip over, and then use the river, swollen from the rain, to help float across the barrier into Israel. Of course, Israeli security would have tripwires and sensors for this scenario, but what fun is there in a sure thing?

Jon eased himself into the water and gingerly walked toward the invisible boundary. He knew he had passed into Israeli territory when bright lights from the West Bank illuminated the river in a glaringly white blast, and a voice in Hebrew blared from a loudspeaker. That was the cue. Standing chest-deep in the water, Jon jumped, waved his arms, and shouted at the top of his lungs, "American! American! Don't shoot!" Jon barely felt the slight breeze from wings flapping overhead.

Chapter 47 - Yardenit Baptismal Site, Israel

The impossibly young captain drummed his fingers on the table between himself and Jonathan. "Mr. Martyr. Let's go over your story again. You maintain that you are a helpless American citizen who was robbed of your money and passport, yes?"

"That is correct." Jon absentmindedly scratched at his nascent beard. He had left his razor with his other belongings in Eidfjord a few days before and the growth was beginning to itch.

"And rather than go through proper channels to reissue your papers, you crossed into Israel illegally and at great risk."

Jon kept spinning the story he had concocted earlier, "Well, the situation was a little more complicated than that. I wasn't certain what kind of reception I would receive in Amman. As I told you, the assailants were in an official Jordanian car."

The officer seemed bored with this interrogation, "Yes, yes. You were afraid the corrupt officials would silence you. Not a very believable tale, hmm? Still, your story must be true because why would you lie?"

"I am sorry, Mr. Martyr, if that is indeed your real name, I find the entire thing very hard to believe. Per standing orders, we tried contacting the Jordanian security team on the other side immediately after you arrived. There was no response. Apparently, someone cut their telephone lines. Only a few minutes ago, we received an irate call from the Jordanian military in Amman. They claimed a team of commandos attacked their guards and were, of course, blaming us for invading their sovereign space. They wondered why we would do such a thing, and coincidentally, so do I. Jordan is demanding answers, and Mr. Martyr, I'm going to give you one last chance to give them some. What happened on the other side of the river this morning?"

Jon tried to sound innocent, relying on the old axiom that the best offense is a good defense. "Come on, Captain. Could you take a look at me? I'm no warrior. Hell, I'm not athletic at all. Can you see me attacking anyone, let alone a group of trained military personnel?"

The captain sat silently. He had no idea what had happened on the other side of the river last night, but he was sure this person couldn't have done the damage his counterparts described without significant assistance. However, who's to say he didn't have associates who stayed behind while he crossed?

The captain again focused on Jon, "You are correct, Mr. Martyr. I find the idea inconceivable that you would be able to accomplish this – alone. So, that begs the next question: who else was working with you? Who was behind the operation? Why was it so important to get you to the West Bank today? Finally, was this supposed to be a coordinated attack, and another team was supposed to eliminate our side?" His steel blue eyes bore a hole into Jon's head, "I have sent your fingerprints and photograph to HQ in

Jerusalem. However, since this is now an international incident involving the United States...." His voice trailed off as the phone on the desk rang, begging him to answer.

"Captain Peretz here." He listened intently to the voice on the other end. "I see. Of course, we will do everything we can to assist." He hung up the phone. "Well, Mr. Martyr, it would appear that you are very much in demand. That was a call from my superiors in Jerusalem. Your fingerprints and description are on an Interpol warrant initiated by the United States government. They have a detachment at your hotel in ar-Rawda and were very disappointed when you weren't there. I am to hold you here until they arrive." The captain gave Jonathan a very focused look, "Now, I'd like to rephrase my earlier question. Where is the girl?"

Jon feigned ignorance, "Girl?"

"Don't try to play me again. The Americans claim that you were in the company of a young woman, a woman very adept at hand-to-hand combat with whom you shared a room in ar-Rawda. Do you remember her now?"

Jon made it up as he went along, "Oh, her! She was just a college student I hooked up with. No one important."

The captain shook his head in a disgusted manner, "Very well. Continue this charade if you insist. Your friends from the States will be here in a few hours. We'll see if they have any better luck getting information." He looked over at the guard by the door, "Sergeant. Take this man back to the holding cell."

Outside the compound, Kandi had been busy. She had noticed the armed guards taking Jon from what she assumed to be the cells to a central building, probably administration, and then returned after about two hours. Each of the facilities required a swipe card for access. Sara had been using her AI observational skills to see what little Kandi might have missed. Then, they compared notes.

"Sara. I have seen only ten security personnel on site; however, they all appear armed."

"I concur. Door security is minimal. I would have no trouble overriding it with computer access..."

Kandi finished Sara's statement, "...Which we don't have. Somehow, we need to get one of those cards."

"Kandi, I noticed a female security staffer going to one of the outlying buildings. She had loosened her uniform fasteners as if she were going off-duty. Perhaps that is her living quarters."

"Well done, Sara. Worth checking out."

Sara cautioned, "We can't assume that she will be alone. An outpost like this probably has communal living quarters like our Watcher teams. Plus, security will likely also involve a swipe card."

"Agreed, but I don't see where we have many options. The door may have card access, but I am willing to chance that it is not alarmed. We should be able to force the lock. Sara, we are simply running out of time. The sun will rise within the hour, and the odds of remaining undetected diminish rapidly."

The pixie stealthily reached the residential quarters, where she found the swipe card panel. Sara took over the body long enough to pry the panel cover off the door frame and then short out the electronics inside. The door opened without any accompanying alarms. Kandi regained control, "So far, so good."

They entered the darkened room, silently reassured that the occupant was sleeping. That feeling continued right until the occupant launched an attack of her own. The activity at the door panel had been anything but silent. The woman hadn't had time to retrieve her weapon or to alert her superiors, but as a well-trained member of the Israeli Defense Forces, she was a weapon herself.

As she careened off the wall, Kandi mentally kicked herself for letting her guard down. She had been stupid, making a mistake that would have resulted in a reprimand for even a new cadet. No matter. Her training kicked in, and she quickly countered the next strike. Still, the Israeli woman would not be the easy victory Kandi presumed her to be, and Kandi thanked fate for not having another person in the room to deal with as well.

After several minutes, Kandi finally struck the decisive blow, rendering the girl unconscious. As she gathered the soldier's key card and changed into her uniform, Kandi saluted her opponent. "You would have made a fine Watcher. I can pay you no higher compliment. Thank you for your effort."

Dawn was minutes away, the sky already beginning to glow brightly in the east when Kandi approached the structure where the Israelis were holding Jon. She held her breath as she placed the stolen card against the sensor, only daring to breathe again when the light on the panel turned green, and the door opened onto a single room with a twin bed against the far wall as its only furnishings. There on the bed sat Jonathan Martyr. However, the look on his face was not a look of relief. Instead, his face reflected a deep pain. "Kandi, why are you here?"

At the same time, the pixie felt a gun barrel pushing a hole in her side. "Good evening, Miss Mehra. So glad you could join us." Kandi stiffened, ready for a quick attack, "I wouldn't do anything rash. There are three other weapons trained on your back. You might disable me, but the others would surely kill you. We've learned from our earlier mistakes. We're not taking any chances this time." The man had hidden just inside the door and off to the side.

Chapter 48 - Yardenit Baptismal Site, Israel

Kandi didn't recognize the voice of her captor, but she did recognize the U.S. flag emblazoned on his shoulder. Jon hadn't imagined their tail the night before. The government had been following them in ar-Rowda. The other soldiers quickly manacled Kandi's hands and feet, making it nearly impossible to move, let alone escape. Then, they did the same with Jonathan before leaving them alone in the room.

Kandi started the conversation, "When did they get here?"

"Only a few minutes before you staged your entrance. The captain you just met had only started asking questions when the door opened."

Again, Kandi's training had fallen short. The scope of her rescue attempt had changed entirely in the few minutes she was in the Israeli sleeping quarters. "So, things are not looking good."

"That, my dear pixie, would be an understatement." At that point, the door reopened, and the captain and an armed escort entered the room. The captain placed a chair opposite the captives while the other man focused his weapon on the pixie's head. *Not taking any chances, indeed.* She thought.

Captain Masters lost little time in getting the interview started. "You have created quite the series of international incidents in your travels, not the least of which is the one you pulled off last night. Currently, the Jordanians, Israelis, and Palestinians are calling for jurisdiction. The U.S. State Department is having a hell of a time convincing them we have priority. If I had my way, we would already be over the Atlantic headed back to the good ol' USA instead of sitting here having our little chat. Now, where do I begin...."

An hour later, the captain had confirmed that Kandi was indeed the alien he had been chasing all over Europe and that Jon was, in fact, an accomplice to her activities more than an unwitting captive. Kandi was incensed at the way the American was treating her. It was one thing for her to expose her wings voluntarily and another with a rifle pressed against her temple. She felt violated.

Just as in Boston, the elusive ring refused to budge from Jon's finger, but the captain figured that was something the commander could resolve back in Colorado. He finished the interview with an observation, "I figure the suits will resolve all of the legal niceties soon, and we'll be on our way. We generally find that a liberal application of American tax dollars can fix anything. I wouldn't get too comfortable here." The captain turned to leave.

Kandi wondered aloud, "Why are you taking us back?"

"Pardon me?" The captain seemed distracted.

"Your men in New York, Vermont, and Boston seemed pretty focused on getting us out of the way, at least me anyway, not to mention what they did in England with the *Voyager Templar*. Why the change of heart?"

"Ms. Mehra. For whatever reason, my superior has changed his opinion of you and your abilities. He wants to see you in person before deciding on your future – a future I am sure will involve much scientific study." Kandi shuddered. She would have to find a way to guarantee that scenario wouldn't happen. The captain continued, "Mr. Martyr, on the other hand, has something my boss wants very badly."

"The ring?" Kandi said nonchalantly.

The captain smiled as he headed for the door, "Exactly. I don't know what the thing does, but the commander has one like it. I don't think he approves of another one wandering around the world. He'll figure out a way to get it off of you." The door clicked as it closed behind him, taking the armed guard along.

Jon said, "Any ideas on how we will get out of this one?"

"No. Keep your voice down. There is every possibility that the good captain and his friends are using audio surveillance. I suggest we speak in Aedenian while we are prisoners here."

Jon immediately shifted over to the other language, "Good idea. Hopefully, they don't have anyone versed in Urdu."

"We'll just have to take that chance. Sara and I have been communicating internally. Things don't look too good. These restraints are strong. I won't be able to get out of them unaided. How far is the dig site?"

Jon laughed, "With everything that's happening, you are still trying to get there?"

Kandi laughed as well. Jon approved. She didn't do it very often, but her face lit up when she did, making her seem less a soldier and more a girl. "That's part of my training. Have a goal. Accomplish the goal. Set another goal. Anything else would be admitting defeat."

Jon nodded, "If there is any way to complete this mission, I will be there for you. Right now, though, things are not going our way. For the record, the site should be about five miles from here."

Kandi seemed almost wistful, "So close, but still so far."

Captain Masters had barely exited the holding cell when he received a call from Captain Peretz asking him to report to his office at his earliest convenience. Assured that the politicians finally okayed prisoner transport, he headed right over.

"Hello again, Captain. May I assume you have some good news for me?"

Captain Peretz wasn't smiling, "Actually, Captain Masters, the situation is far from resolved. Jordan is screaming bloody murder at the attack on their compound, which they still claim we did. This accusation makes my superiors in Jerusalem very nervous and reluctant to release the two prisoners until they have a satisfactory response for Amman. Additionally, Jordanian border control has no record of our captives ever entering their country, which concerns them greatly. On a positive note, since the crossing occurred here, technically Israeli territory, the Palestinians have dropped any interest in the case."

This development was not the news that Masters had anticipated. "Look, captain; the United States should have jurisdiction here....."

"Stop right there, Captain Masters. I understand you have capital charges pending in the United States, but we have an international security issue. Wars have started for less. Your charges have been running for over a month; they will wait a little longer. It was all we could do to keep them from being sent back to Amman for interrogation. They want blood."

Masters nodded, "Of course, we are glad that didn't happen."

Peretz continued, "Our decision to keep them in Israel was encouraged by the question of the young lady's 'country' of origin."

"I don't understand."

"Did you think that I wouldn't monitor your interrogation? I saw her ears and what appeared to be wings under her clothing. I seriously doubt if she is a citizen of the USA. I also noted a distinct lack of surprise from you."

Masters could see that he wasn't going to get his way. "Can we at least accompany them to Jerusalem?" Masters figured he would have a little time to devise a backup plan.

"Are you implying we cannot perform such a menial task?" Peretz was tired, and his anger was beginning to show.

Masters backpedaled his response, "Not at all. It's just that my superiors are every bit as demanding as yours. If anything did happen to the prisoners, heads would roll."

Peretz nodded, "I can see your point. We are diverting an armored personnel carrier carrying a Palestinian prisoner to Jerusalem for interrogation. We suspect he instigated an attack on an Israeli command post last week. We will add our prisoners to the vehicle when it arrives. You and your men can follow in your jeep if you like. Once in Jerusalem, my superiors will decide on your future role."

Masters raised his hands in surrender, "I don't like it, but I'm a soldier and used to not getting my way. Please alert me when your vehicle arrives." Still angry at being treated in such a manner, Masters managed a short bow of acknowledgment before exiting the room and calling his commander.

"I know why you are calling, captain." The commander seemed uncharacteristically calm.

"Sir, I'm afraid there was nothing I could do."

"Nor could our people at State, captain. Our hands are effectively tied."

"Sir, they know about the girl." Silence came from the other end. "I disabled the obvious cameras, but they had others in the room."

"That is unfortunate. The Israelis will be reluctant to release such a specimen, as would we. We will have to let them have her...for now. Our people and theirs can negotiate her fate later. The important thing is that young Mr. Martyr's globetrotting stops, and he's returned here as soon as possible."

"Yes, sir."

Chapter 49 – Unlikely Help

Jonathan was surprised to find another prisoner in the transport; Kandi did not react. The other man was Arabic and barely looked up as the soldiers led them inside and chained them to the truck's walls. Only a few minutes later, they were on their way. Neither Kandi nor Jon had seen the American captain during the process. The Israelis had won the legal battle and were now the people in charge.

They were not long into the journey when an explosion lifted the truck and slammed it on its side, leaving the three prisoners hanging precariously at different angles and the inside guard unconscious. Another explosion followed the first. The truck only shook slightly in response to the shock wave. Some other vehicle must have been the target.

The prisoners didn't have very long to think about what had happened. The vehicle's back door suddenly flew open, revealing a trio of armed Arabic men peering through the opening. One slammed the butt of his rifle against the temple of the already unconscious guard, guaranteeing his silence, then turned toward Jon and Kandi's fellow passenger. "Akeem! You are unharmed!" he shouted toward the man. "Hurry, Asif, " Akeem responded, "get the keys from the guard's pocket and free me. They will send reinforcements soon. Why did you fire a second grenade?" Asif smiled, "The Israelis sent a second vehicle. Armed men jumped out. A second grenade seemed an appropriate response."

Once freed, Asif waved his pistol at Jon and Kandi, "What do you wish done with these two?"

Akeem replied, "They appear to be Americans, but the soldiers treat them as enemies. They picked them up at the Israeli baptismal site."

Asif nodded, "Want me to kill them?"

Akeem shook his head, "No. The enemy of my enemy may be my friend. If nothing else, we may be able to ransom them. Take them with us."

Jon hadn't understood any of the conversation between the two men, but the waving gun was hard not to understand. He had a distinct feeling that the two had just decided his and Kandi's fate, and he allowed himself to breathe for the first time since the attack. "Looks like we get to live."

Kandi replied, "You don't say that like it is a good thing."

"That's because I'm not sure yet."

Akeem stared intently at them, "Be aware that I speak excellent English. Even completed my schooling in England." He looked at Jon, "You are wise not to assume you are out of danger."

Kandi looked him in the eye, "So, why take us? What are we to you?"

Akeem laughed, "You are nothing to me, but you seem very important to the Israeli soldiers. They fear you, or they would not have chained you this way. I am curious as to why that would be. Besides, they also want you, which might make you valuable in trade. If not, and my curiosity is not satisfied, I can always kill you later."

Jon gulped at the man's statement, but Kandi was in full warrior mode and took the comment in stride. The new men had no idea who they were or what they could do. She smiled as she rubbed her hands, willing the circulation to resume. She nodded as she observed Jonathan doing the same. Their new captors did not attempt to restrain them again, for which they were thankful. They went along quietly as Asif waved them into the back of a dilapidated truck and were soon on their way to what she assumed to be the group's base of operations. Kandi didn't care one way or the other. Her hands and feet were free of shackles, and she would die before allowing anyone to constrain her again.

The two trucks wove in and out of the streets and alleys of old Jericho. There was little chance that anyone was following them, but Akeem would not underestimate his adversary again. After a half-hour, the two vehicles pulled into a garage for a truck repair facility, where the door quickly slammed down behind them.

The militia members treated Jon and Kandi respectfully, which Jon assumed was due to something Akeem had said when they arrived. They gave them food and water as well as a place to rest. It wasn't until the following day that Akeem summoned them into his presence. Jon whistled softly. The man before him bore little resemblance to the prisoner in the van. This person was a man used to having orders followed, a leader.

Akeem smiled as they approached, "Please. Sit, my friends. Make yourselves comfortable. We may be here for a while."

Jon and Kandi sat on the cushions arranged on the floor of the office area before Kandi asked, "What would you like to know?"

Akeem laughed nervously, "My apologies. Among my people, it is unusual for a woman to speak first. I forgot that in yours, it is quite normal. Let's start with why the Israelis had you in custody?"

Kandi again replied, "We crossed the Jordan illegally at the baptism site. The authorities were, shall we say, distressed that we did so."

A strange look crossed Akeem's face, "Interesting. Asif was just telling me about a raid on the Jordan side of the river. Rumor has it that Israeli commandos attacked and subdued ten Jordanian soldiers. I told Asif I had difficulty believing such a thing simply because none of the Jordanian soldiers died in the attack. Are you telling me you were responsible?"

Kandi looked a little sheepish, "My husband," looking at Jon, "insisted that no one die. Made the job a great deal more difficult." Jon thought, *Good girl. You remembered what I said about women traveling alone.*

Akeem continued, "Even so, taking on ten trained soldiers...."

Kandi interrupted, "There were eight."

Akeem stopped momentarily and began again, "...taking on eight trained soldiers would be no small task. You managed to create more trouble for our Israeli occupiers in one move than I have over the past year. Please pardon me if I ask you to prove your claim."

He stared at Kandi as he said this, somehow aware that she was the more dangerous of the two. Kandi smiled as she got to her feet, "I accept. Where do you....." Her words stopped short as a tall, bearded man with a knife ran toward her while two more, similarly armed, came from the sides. Asif held a knife to Jon's throat so he would not intervene. *No problem*, she thought; *Jon would only get in the way.*

The three men timed their assault, so they arrived simultaneously. Kandi didn't move until the last possible moment. When that moment was gone, the three men sprawled on the floor, their weapons impaled on their friends' arms and legs. Kandi turned toward Akeem and gave a pixie smile, "No one dies." Akeem laughed, "My curiosity as to your importance has been satisfied. Your demonstration tells me why your captors chained you to the wall of the transport van but not why you have not escaped from us. I am sure you could have done so at any time."

Jon answered this one, "You are correct in your assessment. We could have escaped at any time, but why should we? You have been kind to us, not even posting guards around our area. You have freely given the hospitality of your home. We have respected you in return."

Akeem seemed pleased at the man's response, "So tell me, young man. Why was it so important for you to get to the West Bank?"

Jon said bluntly, "We search for the winged man of the mountain."

The smile vanished from Akeem's face as he spoke, "This man's burial place is sacred to us. How do you know of him? Be careful how you answer. Asif has a rifle pointed at your head. You are fast, but I doubt you can outrun a bullet." Again, he looked at Kandi.

There was only one thing that Kandi could do to convince Akeem of who she was. She stood, turned her back to Akeem, and raised her shirt, exposing her retracted wings. "The man in the mountain was known to me as the Archangel Michael. I know him because he is one of my people. I am a Watcher assigned to take him home."

Chapter 50 – Surprise!

Akeem was dumbfounded. Not knowing what else to do, he fell to his knees. Soon, others in his group joined him, and their strange words filled the room. The men's response startled Kandi. She couldn't have known the religious significance of her actions, how claiming and demonstrating kinship with one of the ancient ones would also make her someone to be revered.

She turned toward Akeem and gently touched his shoulder, breaking the spell. "This must stop now. I am not a deity. I am flesh and blood as you are, as Michael was. Please, rise and let us speak as before."

After much convincing, Akeem reluctantly sat with them, "How may I be of service to one such as yourself."

"First of all, stop this nonsense! I am the same person who sat at table with you and spoke with you earlier. I am not worthy of your worship."

Akeem was unconvinced, "Yet, you are winged just as the one on the mountain."

Kandi asked, "That I can't argue, but this brings me to my first question. How do you know about the winged man?"

"My ancestors originated here long before the Jews came from the desert, and the old city's walls fell all those millennia ago. By word of mouth, our elders would charge each new generation with protecting the winged one's place of rest. We had always succeeded until recently when the blasphemy occurred."

Jon felt he knew the blasphemy of which Akeem spoke and his father's involvement in the process, so he attempted to sidestep the issue, "You refer to the scientists digging on the plateau?"

"I refer to the blatant disregard of our history and our beliefs. At first, we tried talking to them, to no avail. Then, we tried to convince them by raiding their camps and stealing their supplies, but they would not back down. After the infidels opened the burial chamber, we attempted to blow up the entrance they had created. During that raid, the Israeli guards at the excavation caught me, flagged me as a terrorist, and sent me to Jerusalem for interrogation. That you were also on that transport only confirms that God is at work here."

Kandi spoke earnestly, "Your actions also aided us. So, from what you just said, the site is guarded?"

Akeem answered, "I'm afraid I might be responsible for that. Since our raid, the occupation force has grown significantly. Currently, at least a hundred heavily armed soldiers are protecting the entry point. More are below, just outside the chamber itself. They stand guard, but they cannot enter. The religious powers secured the door against anyone getting curious. They keep the keys in a secure vault in the Vatican. This security would not keep out an invading army, but it suffices to hold back curious soldiers.

"Why, you ask? Once the scientists breached the chamber, the find's significance created much discord. Governments and religious leaders became involved. They still argue to this day. I thank God for that and pray he keeps them fighting for a long time."

"Yet, even against such odds, you continued trying to attack them?"

"We tried to blow up the entrance, close it off. Preserve the remains below until we can manage to extract the body."

Kandi reacted, "How could you extract the body if you blew up the entrance?"

Akeem smiled slyly, "The place they dug was not the original entrance. The ancient ones buried their dead in caves as people have done here for millennia since. The family of the one you call Michael was no different."

Kandi asked him, "Can I assume this cave still exists?"

"Indeed. The Christian infidels discovered the opening long ago but didn't understand its significance. They even built one of their monasteries around it almost fifteen hundred years ago. They claim it is one of the caves of the Jewish prophet Elijah. We saw no harm in their actions. Their presence preserved the access chamber from other prying eyes. Over the years, many monks have also been members of our order."

Jon finally spoke, "And, what order would that be?"

"We are the Knights of AnKi, the name given to God by our ancestors."

Kandi appeared shocked by the man's response, so Jon jumped in, "Can I assume this place is St. George's Monastery just west of Jericho?"

Akeem nodded, "You are correct."

Kandi asked, "Could you arrange a visit?"

Akeem nodded, "For one such as yourself, I will make the necessary arrangements."

Later that evening, after Kandi went to bed, Sara crept out of Kandi's subconscious to add her take on the day's events. After laying low for almost two days, she was ready to be heard, "Kandi? Why are you acting so strange around Akeem? Is it because their order carries an Aedenian name?"

"Yes. There have been many things about Gaia that have surprised me, but this, hearing the true name of God, shocks me to the core."

"Yet, he seems sincere."

"He is still human, Sara. What seems real now may not be true later. He will bear watching as we move forward. There may be a time when my wings are insufficient to dissuade him from other actions."

"What about Jon?"

"What about him?"

"He seemed bothered by Akeem as well. Might he have insight?"

"I suppose it is possible. I will ask Jon in the morning. Good night, Sara. Tomorrow should be an interesting day."

"Good night, Kandi."

Chapter 51 - Epiphany

Captain Masters walked through the ambush scene as he spoke with the commander back in Colorado. His arm was in a sling due to a fracture of the radius. It hurt like hell, but not nearly as much as the lashing he would receive over the phone.

"Status, Captain?" The commander was brusque.

"Three men dead, sir. Two others, including myself, suffered non-life-threatening injuries. I've taken the liberty of arranging transport back to the US for the deceased."

"Very good. What of our Israeli friends?"

"Four dead. The only survivor is the man from the back of the van. They airlifted him to a Jerusalem hospital with a traumatic head injury, currently in critical condition."

"Do you think this was a planned escape by Mehra and Martyr?"

"I don't believe so. All indications are that these were members of a local militant group. The Israelis were taking their leader to Jerusalem for interrogation, and the RPG fragments we found were of Iranian origin in keeping with other terrorist attacks."

"Why did they take our prisoners with them?"

"I have no idea. My first consideration was for ransom, but we have received no demands for money or prisoners. Of course, that could change today."

"Let's hope it does. I wanted those two back here yesterday. What are your plans from here?"

"Nothing right now. In my mind, I keep coming back to why. Why did they take the chance of attempting a river crossing? Any other border with Jordan would have been a cakewalk to sneak across compared to Israel. For that matter, why Jordan to begin with? Even with alien tech, going from Norway to the Jordanian desert seems odd. I can't help but think something nearby is drawing them, but I can't imagine what that would be. Do you have any suggestions, sir?"

"Unfortunately, no. I will check with my State and the CIA contacts to see if they can offer suggestions. For now, keep your eyes and ears open. Whatever the attraction is, it may not be overly apparent to others."

"Yes, sir."

After hanging up, Masters approached his Israeli counterpart as the man surveyed the scene. "Captain Peretz?" He waited patiently for the other person to respond. Masters knew what it was like to lose men under your command. The young Israeli had suffered the same loss as he, possibly for the first time.

"Yes, Captain." Peretz looked over the scene, still marked with police tape from the day before, "What a mess."

"Agreed. Are you still thinking that the perpetrators were locals?"

"Yes. The techniques they used are typical of the groups around here, plus their leader, Akeem, was in the van, although his presence was a closely guarded secret. We didn't send a convoy because we didn't want to draw attention to his presence. Command believed stopping at the baptismal site to pick your people up would add to the deception."

"Apparently not."

"Indeed."

"Captain Peretz, my command and I feel that Martyr and Mehra were heading somewhere when they crossed the river. Would you have any idea where that would be?"

"No. I can't help you. The West Bank is not a thriving tourist destination right now - far too much unrest. Many of the old sites are closed. Other than pilgrims from Jerusalem or Tel Aviv heading to the baptism site, our only major activity is the archeological dig west of the city."

Masters' ears perked up, "What's going on out there?"

Peretz shook his head, "No one knows, or at least no one is telling. The whole thing is a giant pain in my side. We have over fifty soldiers at the site, along with representatives of the PLO and the religious police of Saudi Arabia and Iran. Heck, even the Swiss Guard from the Vatican has a presence there."

"Wow. All those people, and no one's talking?"

"From what my people say, no one's seen what's there. The burial chamber, if that's what it is, has been sealed. Some guards, a few from each service, stay at the door below. The rest have set up camp around the entrance. Whatever's in there, the powers that be are taking no chances of a leak."

"And they've been doing this for years?"

"At least ten."

"Wow. That's something. Say, my arm is acting up. Think I'll check in with your medic if that's OK."

"Sure. I'll compare notes with you later. A royal screw-up like this will get a lot of attention. Pays to show a common front."

Masters had an Israeli corporal drive him back to the compound, but instead of heading straight to the medic, he used his sat phone to call back to the commander. "Sir. There is a mysterious dig just outside of Jericho. I remember reading in the background material that Dr. Stephen Martyr, Jonathan's deceased father, led a major dig near here. Could this be where he and the woman were going?"

"Interesting. I'll see what I can find out. In the meantime, I have a new assault team on its way to you. They should be there sometime tomorrow. Take them and go check out this site. Might prove useful."

"Will do, sir."

Back in Colorado, the commander wasted no time getting feelers into the intelligence community, but every inquiry came up empty. All the groups knew of the controversy surrounding the Jericho dig, but no one knew why it was so contentious. Any attempt to dig deeper came back with a warning to stop. Someone higher up the food chain was handling it.

The commander sat back in his chair and analyzed the situation. The landing in Jordan almost made sense. ar-Rawda was practically on top of the original Sodom gate. If the pixie was indeed gathering Aedenian materials, this would have seemed a logical place to go. Their use of a portable transmission device indicated they had found some ancient tech still working somewhere else, possibly in the Norwegian hotel. He made a note to have a crew investigate that site more thoroughly. Captain Masters did have a point, though. What did the two of them want in Jericho?

He pondered that question for almost two days when the answer struck him like lightning, suddenly illuminating everything in brilliant white light. How could he have been so stupid? Was it even possible? The location was right, but the odds of the tomb being untouched all these years seemed impossible. He chuckled. It was almost as unbelievable as an archangel's ring surviving all this time. He knew he had to get to Jericoh immediately. Not caring what his actions revealed, the commander disappeared in a flash of blue light.

Chapter 52 – The Way to Truth

Kandi and Jon met with Akeem around noon the next day. People came and went from the compound throughout the morning in a seemingly normal traffic flow like the events of two days ago had never occurred. Jon asked Akeem about the attack and if there were hints of any reprisals. Akeem laughed, "We hit and hide; never brag about our actions. To do so would demonstrate pride, which our faith proclaims as sinful."

He continued, "I have inquired at the monastery. My friends there tell me the site is closed to tourists at one in the afternoon. We will show up at six. He tells me that is when the monks are at prayer, followed by their evening meal. He will meet us at the side gate before joining the others. Since I know the location, I can lead you to the cave from there. I don't want to get your hopes up. I have been there many times and have not found any entrance to the burial chamber."

Kandi replied frankly, "I hope my brother's spirit will guide us when we arrive."

Akeem nodded his acceptance of her statement prayerfully.

Kandi and Jon had intentionally not told Akeem about Jon's subliminal guidance via the ring. They felt that knowledge would add more complexity to an already complex situation. Now that the moment of truth was at hand, the two fugitives discussed what might happen next. Kandi had to laugh to herself; she and the human worked efficiently together now. She would never have believed that possible.

As the two walked around the compound, Kandi began the conversation, "How are you doing? Do you still get the feeling from the stone?"

"Stronger than ever. My gut's telling me to damn the wait and go to the cave now. There is such a sense of urgency...I can't fully explain it. As to how I'm doing? I'm not certain that it matters anymore what either of us wants. Right now, the only mission is to reach the burial chamber."

Six o'clock seemed to take forever to arrive, but things happened very fast when the time came. Akeem, Jon, and Kandi were stuffed in the back of a van, hidden from view. The last thing they wanted was someone to identify one or all of them to the authorities. The mission would end before it ever began. They parked the van in the parking area across from the monastery. From here, they would have to walk.

Jon silently watched as the other three men grabbed weapons and ammunition, "Are you expecting trouble from a bunch of monks?"

Akeem wasn't laughing, "It's not the monks we worry about. If you manage to breach the burial chamber, there is an excellent chance we will face armed resistance from outside the fake door. If it is a perfect day, we will carry these out. If the day turns dark...well, I find it better to be prepared."

They arrived at the gate at precisely six, and true to his friend's word, a monk met them and allowed entrance to the compound before silently exiting. Akeem led them between the buildings to where the cave's outline peeked from behind the edge of a building. As they entered the relatively small space, Jon swore he heard voices. Alarmed, he started to alert the others when Akeem grabbed his arm and pressed his finger to his lips. Then he pointed upward to where the military guards were watching over the other entrance. Jonathan hadn't realized how close the guards were to the cave opening.

Once inside, Akeem and his friends turned on LED headlights to guide them to the back of the cave. That was where Kandi's heart stopped. In front of her was a small chapel with an altar on one side. Over the centuries, the monks had covered the walls with paintings of biblical themes. The place was beautiful. The one missing thing was a door, a crack, or a crevice they could enter. There was nothing here that might lead them to their goal. Was this all a big mistake?

Jon sensed what she was thinking. He stared into her eyes, shook his head, and pointed at his right hand. *We're Okay. My ring senses something here, something not visible, but what is it?* He walked around the chapel, becoming hyperaware of the stone on his hand, following its lead until it no longer led but stayed still.

Jon stood before a beautiful fresco, but that didn't matter. He wasn't interested in the art; he was concerned with the wall behind it. He took his hand and placed it in the center of the painting, causing the stone to erupt in blue flame. At first, nothing happened, but then the wall seemed to shake. Chunks of art-covered plaster fell away, slowly at first but with increased urgency as his hand remained steadfast. Akeem and his men looked on with fear and awe. They had seen the human as the woman's servant, but now they realized he was at least her equal. There would be hell to pay for the wall's destruction, but they would deal with that problem later.

When the last plaster fell away, Jon stood before a translucent material covering a hole leading outward from the chapel. Inscribed on the edge of the door was an inscription in Aedenian runes, for which Sara gladly gave the translation, "Here lies Michael, the greatest of the Archangels. Woe to the person who disturbs his rest." The words went on to describe the manner of his death and the names of those who survived him. Jon realized that one of the male names had to be one of his ancestors.

Jon placed his right hand firmly on the crystal wall. Again, the blue light flared, and the wall vanished. "I guess that means we're worthy? Right?" Akeem answered, "I pray, mighty one, that you are correct. Your worthiness is not in question. I worry about we who follow you."

The cave floor was smooth; only the accumulated dust of the ages lay on the stones. There was a downward slope to the path, which led for about fifty feet before they reached yet another seal blocking their way. Once again, Jon placed his hand and felt the energy surging within him. The seal melted away, revealing a sizable open space beyond.

The group gasped as the room's glories revealed themselves to their lamps.

Sara began interpreting the runes and drawings on the walls, "These describe the heroic acts of Michael Archangel. Here he is, herding his people to safety as Sodom's gate erupts into flame. For the rest of his life, Michael defended the humans around him. Over here is a depiction of him alongside his wife and children. Over here, they tell of attacks from outsiders where Michael defended them from harm."

Sara paused, "Kandi, you'll want to hear this. Here, they describe a great temple across the Jordan on the place where the gate collapsed." She looked at Jon, "That had to be the attempt by Yodin and his followers to recreate a gate!" Sara continued interpreting, "Michael aided the effort but did not follow them into the void beyond the temple. He returned to his family and lived out his life with them. The community wanted to give him a proper burial at his death, so they went to the temple's ruins and retrieved some of the holy stones. Some they used to create the casket for their hero; others went to make the floor....."

Jon had tuned out the pixie's voice. As he stared around the room, all he could think about was how his father must have felt, standing at this exact spot. He also knew how heartbroken his father would have been, unable to share his findings with the world. Jon then walked to an opening in the far wall. There, in a crystal coffin, was 'the winged man,' his ancestor. Jon laid his hand upon the crystal dome in a sign of silent respect. During the silence, he could hear people talking. They needed to hurry; company was coming.

A few seconds later, he realized the sounds were coming from the path back to the chapel, not from the newer door in front of him.

Chapter 53 – The Game's Afoot

Captain Masters was sitting down for his evening meal when the commander approached, "Good afternoon, Captain." Masters nearly spat out his food as he jerked himself to attention. "Commander? What are you doing here?"

The commander replied, "I might ask you the same thing. I ordered you to watch the dig site."

Masters stuttered, "I am...I just came from there to get something to eat and check on correspondence. I left two of the new team there with strict orders to call me if anything unexpected occurred. Sir? I spoke with you in Colorado Springs a few hours ago; how...."

The commander silenced him, "That, captain, is far above your pay grade. Suffice it to say I am here now. Shall we get up to the site?"

Masters left his dinner, sitting uneaten on the table as he leapt for the door. In less than a minute, his jeep was racing along the highway. The commander didn't say a word during the entire half-hour trip. Once on-site, he demanded to go down to the entry. There was some haggling with the Israeli commander, but eventually, the commander got his way. The entryway was just as Captain Masters had left it, with all the locks intact. Masters felt he needed to speak, "See, sir? Everything is fine. What is the big deal about this old stuff, anyway?"

The commander almost lashed out at his subordinate but caught himself before he did something he would have regretted. "Masters? Do any of these men know anything about what is behind this door?"

"No, sir."

"This matter is so high up the chain of command that I didn't know anything about it until you brought it to my attention, and I started asking the right people the right questions. This," he waved his hand at the door, "my dear captain, is a huge deal indeed. Tell me, is there anything below this place?"

Masters corralled an Israeli soldier, "Excuse me, soldier, is there anything below this dig site?"

The young woman was happy to assist, "Yes, sir. An old Greek Orthodox monastery exists in the cliff wall about fifty feet below us." She went on her way.

The commander was beside himself, "Captain. Gather your men. We're looking in the wrong place."

The commander was in agony. He dared not teleport with his men around, yet the time wasted in traditional transport was trying his patience. They had no rappelling equipment, so there was no easy way down from the ridge to the monastery. They had to take the roads; first, the recently created one from the dig site, and then the Wadi Alquat up to the parking lot. His anxiety only increased when they found an empty transport parked there, its engine cool. Time was indeed of the essence.

As quickly as they could run, they reached the monastery's locked gate. After beating it for a few minutes with no response from within, the commander ordered his men to break it down. He would deal with the fallout of their actions later.

By now, the monks had begun appearing from their sleeping quarters, surprised to find armed soldiers in their compound. The resulting confusion would have been comical had the situation been different. The soldiers used their headlights to brighten a landscape otherwise only lit by stars. With a general idea of where the cave must be, the commander ordered his men to push the monks aside. Soon after, they found themselves in the shrine's tiny chapel.

At first, the side cave didn't catch their attention. It was a sergeant who noticed that there was plaster on the floor of an otherwise spotless area. Once discovered, though, they plunged through the entryway. The commander smiled. He knew victory was within his grasp.

Chapter 54 – Where Angels Sleep

When Jon returned to the anteroom, he found Akeem and the others with weapons drawn. They had also heard the movements down the hallway and were preparing for battle. Sara had been reading the ancient runes on the wall, oblivious to everything else. Jon motioned to her to follow him to where Michael lay at rest. "Sara, time to let Kandi back. Things could get pretty messy shortly. "Very well, Jon," she said reluctantly. Her facial expression shifted in a way that was now normal for him. The pixie again controlled her body.

Kandi gasped when she saw the figure in the crystal sarcophagus, "He looks just like he did the last time I saw him." Somehow, after twenty-five thousand years, she expected something different, not the person she had once served beside. A noise in the other room refocused her attention. Was there anything here they could use? She asked Jon, "Is the ring giving you anything?" He shrugged, "It's giving me plenty, but I don't understand what it's saying. The strong sense of attraction is still there, but now it's all around me, not pointing in any one direction. I don't know what to do."

A short burst of automatic fire caused Jon's reflexes to throw himself to the floor. At the same time, he realized the time for decision-making was at hand. He had to find the answer soon, or all would be lost. There was another burst of gunfire, followed by a scream of pain. Jon was face down now, almost willing his body to merge with the floor. Kandi was standing over him, not ready to show fear to any enemy and ready to die before being captured.

While on the floor, Jon became aware that the substance below him was not stone. At first, he hadn't noticed the difference because of the dust that had settled upon it. Now that his body had wiped some of the dirt away, he could see that what was below it was opalescent – a crystal.

Jon was ready to shout at Kandi when a strong male voice echoed through the chamber, "So good to see you again, Kandi." Her body froze at the sound, "Iblees. Why am I not surprised to see you? After your little mind tricks with me earlier, I knew you had to be around still."

The archangel smiled like a predator, ready to finish off his quarry, "Had that little drone worked properly, we wouldn't be having this conversation, and your pet human would be long gone as well."

"So, what are your plans now?" Kandi forced herself to remain calm.

"The human will die." Jon's stomach churned at the man's words. "He has the last archangel ring. I can't afford for that to be wandering around the planet. Better that it joins the others in my vault."

"You killed the rest?"

"Some died in the gate collapses. The rest wandered the world, hoping for Aeden to mount a rescue - a rescue that never happened. They were easy to pick off."

"All except for Michael."

"Ah, yes. Michael. He went native, something I never anticipated. He showed up briefly when Yodin and his friends enlisted his help to build a gate at the old Sodom site, but then he disappeared again. We met again later, but then never heard another word until this," he waved his hand around the room, "was rediscovered. His human family must have loved him deeply to go through all the trouble of building a crystal casket."

Jon's voice suddenly rang out, "Kandi! Hit the floor now!"

For once, the pixie didn't hesitate to follow his lead. She hit the floor just as a blue light rose from within it. Too late, Iblees realized what was happening. He screamed in frustration as the room dissolved around Kandi and Jon, leaving them in darkness.

"Where are we?" Jon asked. The room was dark, and his hands found rock walls when he reached out. Only the nausea indicated that they had indeed teleported somewhere. Realizing he still wore his LED headlamp, He reached up, and suddenly, walls appeared on all sides.

"Unknown," replied Kandi. Her headlamp refused to turn on. Looking at it in Jon's beam, she saw a bullet hole in the side casing. "Well, that was close."

Jon's light caught a dark space on the other side of the room, which slowly became a passageway. They followed the upward path through the rock walls until they saw light streaming in from their right side. Trees and shrubs obstructed the opening. When Kandi saw them, she shouted, "I'm home!" She began clawing at the obstructions until they were free, standing on a cliff face overlooking a large valley. Jon was awestruck, "So this is Aeden. It's breathtaking."

Kandi looked sadly at her companion, "I spoke too soon. This is not Aeden."

"What do you mean? You said you were home, and I don't know any place on Earth that looks like this."

Kandi sighed, "The plant life appeared Aedenian, which first deceived me. The problem is that." She pointed up toward the sun. "Aeden has a red sun. This one is yellow."

Jon was confused, "So, where are we then?"

"I believe we are exactly where we were. The question isn't 'where,' I believe it is 'when.' I will know for certain after I take a look around." Kandi began removing her clothing, freeing her wings to fly. "This may take a few hours. I can only sustain flight in your atmosphere for a few minutes at a time before resting. If you get hungry, those large purple berries should suffice. I'll be back as soon as I can." With that, she took off.

The sun was setting, and Jon was getting worried when Kandi flew into view. She landed neatly upon the cliff face. Jon tried to appear angry, "About time you got back. Where have you been?" Then he took a closer look at her face. "Hey, are you alright? You look like you've seen a ghost or something."

Kandi sat on the rock, staring into the darkening sky. Finally, she replied, "I know when we are. Somehow, you have brought us twenty-five millennia into your past. Backward travel wasn't allowed; some even considered it impossible...except for your ring. Some rumors claimed archangels could travel backward in times of dire need. If you had doubts about your right to the ring, this should take care of them."

Jon stared at her with a dumb look, "25,000 years. What makes you so sure?"

"I served with the garrison at Gomorrah Station down on the coast. Sodom was within our protectorate, so I visited here many times."

"So, Sodom still exists? Do you have friends here? People who can help you get back to Aeden?" Jon found himself saddened that Kandi's mission might be coming to a close."

Kandi hung her head, "We're too late. "It appears that Sodom's gate suffered a cataclysmic explosion some years ago. Everything in front of the portal is gone, and what is left doesn't look sturdy. I located some tent towns around the city's perimeter, filled with refugees – human refugees. I saw no Watchers.

"I landed to get information, but when the people saw me, they screamed at me, more animal than even humans should be. They came at me with stones, makeshift spears, and knives. They cursed me as they hurled their weapons, some of which struck me." Kandi pointed at the injuries to her body, "Before I could gather my wits, the front group was upon me, attempting to hold me down until the others caught up. It was only through my augmented strength that I was able to escape. I returned as fast as possible."

After a minute, Jon found his voice, "Where do you suggest we go?"

Kandi replied, "We only have one option: go to Gomorrah. If the base survived, there will be a Watcher brigade there."

Early the following day, they set out for Gomorrah on foot, with Kandi occasionally taking flight to confirm their direction. At other times, Kandi took great care in covering her ears and wings. Any humans they encountered must not realize that she was a pixie. The humans of Sodom had made it clear that her kind wasn't welcome here anymore.

Chapter 55 – Once Upon a Time...

The trade guilds on Aeden had built Sodom as a center of commerce. Everything about the city spoke of wealth and glamor. The gate was large enough to accommodate the giant air carriers, bringing Gaia's wealth back to Aeden and handling the hordes of tourists coming the other way. The wealthy of Aeden flocked there. Sodom represented anonymity. What happened there stayed there. It would not follow them back to their real life on the home world. They could do all manner of unspeakable acts to the human occupants of the city, and no one cared. After all, humans were just animals.

The Institute built Gomorrah as a fortress, placing its back to the sea for added protection. They tasked the garrison there with the containment of all humans between the northern edge of Duat in the southern continent and the southern border of Babel to the northeast, an area that included Sodom. Because the supervised area was so big, the Institute assigned a large detachment of Watchers to the garrison, along with the necessary equipment and weapons they might require.

Like most military installations on Gaia, the builders put the base's gate away from the compound in a sea cave. That was probably why the garrison appeared intact as Jon and Kandi looked down from a nearby hillside. Air cars, which would have normally flitted back and forth, were few and far between. Here, as at Sodom, human refugee camps had sprung up around the complex. They were the only real change Kandi noticed. Aside from them, Kandi felt a strange sense of normalness that she had been lacking for a long time.

After monitoring the base for a while, Kandi said, "Okay. Here's what we'll do. You go down and check out the refugee camps. Your Aedenian is passable, and they are likelier to talk to a fellow human. See what you can discover."

"And you?" Jon replied.

"Same agenda, different people. I'll report to the local Watcher Commander, explain our situation, get supplies, and return, hopefully with some idea of how to proceed," Kandi said confidently.

Jon was reluctant to go separate ways, "And you think they're going to believe you? I mean, our story isn't exactly normal." Jon wasn't so sure.

Kandi smiled, "This is 25,000 years in your past; for me, it is not. I served at this base for nearly a year before transferring to Babel." She shuddered as visions of Babel and its resident archangel flashed through her mind, "I have a strong reputation within the Watcher community. The odds are good that I served with the current commander during the war or at least some of his senior staff. They'll believe me."

Jon shrugged. He didn't like separating but had to agree that Kandi wouldn't be welcome with the refugees, and his reception would be less than cordial in the Watcher stronghold. "Well, I guess we better get busy. Meet back here in a week?" Kandi nodded.

As she prepared to get up, Jon touched her lightly on the forehead. She looked at him peculiarly but then shrugged it off. Jon had no idea why he had done it. It had just seemed the right thing to do at the time. He waved goodbye and shuffled down the hill to the first human compound set aside from the others.

A tall, lanky man with a makeshift spear blocked his path as Jon approached the encampment's perimeter. Jon wished he had concentrated more on learning the variances in Aedenian as he smiled and tried his best to appear non-threatening, "Hi. I was wondering if I could join up with you guys. I am traveling alone."

The man just stood there, unmoving, giving no indication that he had heard Jon, let alone understood him. Jon tried again, "Hi. I was…"

"I am not stupid," the man spoke, "I heard you fine."

"So, can I come into your camp?" Jon moved toward the man's left in an attempt to outflank him.

The man moved effortlessly to block Jon, "Your speech is strange, as are your clothes. Why should we trust you?"

Jon delivered the speech he had been rehearsing just for this situation, "I am from Nasvilla, a village south of Babel. After the blast destroyed much of the city, we came south to see if Gomorrah had fared better. We hadn't come far before robbers attacked us; I am the only survivor." Fortunately,

Jon's confrontation with Helvar had left enough bruises and scabbed-over wounds to give credence to his story.

The man looked Jon over and was about to send him on his way when his eyes settled on Jon's ring. In a subdued voice, he asked, "How did you come by a Chosen's ring?"

"It's mine." Jon asserted. He hadn't planned for the ring to be so easily identified.

The man struck an attack pose, "You lie! Humans cannot have such a thing. It is forbidden."

Jon backed into a defensive position, "I do not lie. The ring has chosen me as its champion and cannot be removed from my hand without terrible effect. The fact that I wear it means there is no taboo." Jon hoped his words would keep the man from attempting to sever his hand to get the ring.

Deciding that a human with a Chosen's ring was good enough to allow Jon into the perimeter, the man motioned for Jon to follow him. "We will go to our council. I will kill you if you attempt to escape or harm anyone."

"Agreed." Jon gulped. He had no intention of harming anyone. As for escape, he had nowhere else to go.

Kandi's story was simple. She had been on a mission that terminated unexpectedly – literally the truth. She only had to tweak the locations and dates to fit the current situation. Ultimately, she had a plausible back story that should satisfy the base commander and stand up to routine scrutiny. Of course, she had to get into the compound first.

As Kandi walked through the refugee camps on the outskirts of the compound, she was more than a little uneasy. People stared, and conversations stopped as she walked by. Obviously, her attempts to disguise her appearance weren't fooling anyone. She only hoped to make the outer wall before the humans attacked, assuming base security would allow her entrance.

Walking up to the identification portal with a hundred human eyes boring into her back, she was shocked when the security AI greeted her, "Welcome, Master Watcher Mehra. We were not expecting you. Enter, and I will notify base command that you are here." Kandi was confused. She'd expected some confrontation for an unexpected entry. Was it really going to be that easy to get access? "Thank you. I look forward to meeting with the commander." The entry opened, and she passed through.

Kandi walked across the courtyard, observing other Watchers engrossed in hand-to-hand combat. She was surprised by the normalness of the scene and more than a little pleased that training continued even under the current emergency. Looking around the base, one never would have guessed a significant catastrophe had occurred. Across the quad, she saw a woman wearing a commander's uniform walking across the compound toward her with an enormous smile on her face.

"About time you showed up for some real work, Mehra," the commander stated. Kandi immediately recognized the voice. "Muhaimin? Is that you? You're base commander?" Muhaimin Avani had been the training officer at Gomorrah Station when Kandi was assigned there. The two had been good friends – practically inseparable. They had kept in touch after Kandi transferred to Babel Gate but lost contact with each other after Iblees had forced her move back to the Institute.

"It's me. Kandi." Commander Avani could see Kandi's question as her old friend looked at the emblems on her shoulders, "Call it a battlefield promotion. The commander and his two lieutenants were at Sodom investigating the gate shutdown when Sodom blew, taking most of the population. I was next in line, and since there's been no contact with the Director, the promotion stuck." The two women had been walking back toward Muhaimin's office as they talked, "Now, tell me how it is that you show up at my doorstep. Last I heard, you were a Master Watcher assigned to the Institute training staff. That was rather sudden, wasn't it? You had only been at Babel for a few months."

"Yes. There was an opportunity at the Institute, and I jumped at the chance." Kandi saw no need to go into detail about her liaison with Iblees or the subsequent events on Aeden, "We had an enviro-drone malfunction near Solapur. Since I helped install several of them, the Director asked me to do the assessment. I was fortunately away from the gate when it detonated."

Muhaimin nodded, "Huh. Honestly, I had forgotten Solapur had a gate for their mining ops. That's a fair distance by air car but walking it would be interminable. You, my friend, are lucky to be alive," she glanced disapprovingly at Kandi's attire, "and much in need of a bath and something resembling a uniform. You'll have to tell me where you got these rags. I don't recognize the fabric." She smiled again as she reached into her desk, pulling out a blaster, "Now...why don't you tell me what you've really been doing for the last thirty years."

Kandi let out a small gasp. Was that possible? Thirty years had gone by since she had left this station? She decided to tell the truth and hope for the best. "I didn't think you would believe the true story, Muhaimin, so I gave you the shortened version...." For the next hour, Kandi told her story with numerous interruptions by Commander Avani; the only variance from the truth was Jon. She left him out of the narrative. Trying to explain the human's involvement would be difficult. The gun didn't waver until the end.

Muhaimin sighed, "That's quite the tale, fantastic, yet I want to believe it. Welcome to Gomorrah Station, Master Watcher. However you came to get here; it's good to have you. We need all the hands we can get, and to have someone of your caliber drop in on us is a major boon. I'll notify the quartermaster that you are on your way. He'll arrange for housing as well as clothing."

Kandi stood and started to hug her friend. Reminding herself at the last minute that her friend was now her superior officer, she snapped to attention, saluted, and left the office headed for the quartermaster.

Kandi?

Yes, Sara.

Does this feel as weird to you as it does to me?

Weirder. Remember to only talk to me when we are alone, right?

Right. No need to raise any new concerns.

That, my friend, would be an understatement.

An hour later, freshly bathed and dressed in battle armor and tunic, Master Watcher Kandi Mehra set foot on the training ground. She smiled. Jon could wait. This would be the first decent workout she'd had in weeks.

Chapter 56 – The Chosen

The guard hustled Jon into a large tent at the center of the camp. The dimness of the structure's interior made it difficult to see; only with great difficulty could Jon surmise that multiple people were present. All talking stopped as he entered, and his guard told the assembly, "Elders of the Tribe of Ishen, this man was captured attempting to enter our domain."

The man at the circle's center, obviously the leader, asked, "So, why is he here? Weren't your instructions to turn back any intruders, to kill them if need be?"

The guard dropped his eyes as he continued, "Yes, Elder, and as I proceeded to do so, I saw what he wears on his hand - a Chosen's ring."

There was an audible gasp as the elders spoke among themselves. The leader rose and examined Jon before saying, "This is impossible, for he is human."

"Yes, Elder. He claims to have come by the ring honestly, and since he wears it without coming to harm, I assumed you would want to see him." He paused before continuing, "He also claims that any attempt to separate the ring from his body will destroy those who try."

"Very well, guard. Return to your post. Our enemies still plot against us, and I fear an attack is imminent."

The leader addressed Jon directly, "May I see your ring." Jon approached and presented his hand for the man's scrutiny. He carefully noted the facets of the stone along with the blue glow. He told the assembly, "I don't know how this man came by it, but the ring is genuine. As all of you know, I was blessed to serve the Archangel Gabri for many years. There is no question of this ring's authenticity." Turning back to Jon, "What are you called?"

"I am called Jonathan Martyr."

"Well, Jonathan Martyr. You possess one of the rarest items on the planet – both planets. There were only fourteen in existence. The mystic Origen gave all of them to pixies and elves – no humans allowed. How did you get one of them, and how does it accept you?"

Jon planned his words carefully, electing to tell the truth, "I come from a future time where I received the ring. I am a true descendant of the Archangel Michael. As to why the stone accepts me? I honestly don't know. I just know that it does."

"Jonathan Martyr. We are travelers. Our journey started south of here, near Duat, years ago. As he died, the Archangel Gabri told me of a place to the north where survivors, "he gestured at the people around him, "could find a place of refuge, guarded by another one of the fourteen. We follow his way. Are you the one we seek?" The elder looked at Jon expectantly.

Just then, from outside the tent, someone raised the alarm. The village was under attack. The tent evacuated quickly, each man grabbing a weapon as he left the chamber. Jon followed, not sure what he could do to help.

The attackers approached from the south, bearing knives, swords, and spears. They were a much larger group than the tribe Jon had joined, as if many other tribes had agreed to attack as one. The first assault nearly breached the perimeter. The community's women and youth quickly moved the dead and wounded out of the way, preparing for the second wave.

Jon realized that they wouldn't survive the next one. The aggressors were too many and too strong. The village would fall. In desperation, he spoke to his ring, "If indeed you were designed to protect, now would be a good time to prove it." He held the jewel over his head, willing it to strike, but nothing happened. No protective shield appeared, and no laser beams struck out. He didn't know what to do. *Maybe if I move closer to the action?*

Fearfully, Jon approached the defensive line. *Things do not look good for the home team,* he thought. He saw the torches of the opposing camp flash against metal blades as they prepared to strike. He could also see the fear in the eyes of the defenders. It was the look of men facing certain death who would never hold their loved ones again. When Jon turned around, he saw the women and children, each holding whatever they could grab to strike at the enemy. He was reminded of the story of Masada. Like that tale from Jewish history, there would be no prisoners here.

When the attack came, the defenders stood valiantly in its path. Now, calm in the face of death,

Jon raised his hand again. He didn't look upon the stone as a master but as a partner. He mentally asked it to protect the innocent. A blue shield erupted from his hand, creating a wall between the two forces. The attackers slammed against the light, which would not yield, stunning the ones who made contact with it.

Jon stood stalwart with his hand raised against the enemy. Try as they might, the would-be assassins kept trying to break through his barrier, and the stunned bodies continued to mount up around it. Finally, physically spent and severely reduced in numbers, the opposing force retreated. Jon's group had won. His arm fell to his side just before his exhausted body collapsed upon the rock.

Kandi's first full day of life at Gomorrah Base was eventful. Thirty years may have passed in her absence, but the Watchers continued their daily routine, albeit with a lack of enthusiasm. Commander Avani had announced that morning that Kandi would be the new training officer. Even though she skipped over several young officers, none seemed to mind being supplanted by a living legend in the Watcher community. From what Kandi had seen on the training ground yesterday, she would have plenty to do. The Watchers in the compound were complacent, and in the current environment, complacency could be fatal. She briefly considered her promise to Jon – to meet him at week's end. No problem; even with the new duties, she would have plenty of time to gather intel and return to the hilltop.

But the weekend came and went. Kandi was simply too busy to think about Jon and her promise. Truthfully, she was relishing her return to what she considered a normal life. She thrived on discipline and order. The Watcher community was exactly what she had been missing for the past few months.

Sara was finding her niche in the new scheme as well. At first, she had nagged Kandi incessantly about her responsibilities toward their human friend, but as Kandi became more comfortable, Sara found that she was also finding peace here. One thing bugged her: *Why weren't the Watchers helping the humans outside? Wasn't that their primary objective?*

Sara's mental questions crept into Kandi's consciousness, so she addressed her concerns during her next meeting with the base commander. "Commander Avani, may I ask a question?"

"Of course, providing you call me Muha," referring to Kandi's old nickname for her. "We were too good of friends back then for a little thing like a chain of command to get in the way. What's on your mind?"

Kandi smiled at the familiarity, then returned to a more serious mien, "Muha, I have stood on the battlements overlooking the area and find what is happening in the human communities unsettling. There has been fighting between the human tribes and even cases where groups are banding together against a single foe. I fear that if they do this against each other, they will soon conspire to attack us. There was even a rumor one of the tribes employed Aedenian technology. Why are we not doing something?"

The commander nodded, "Kandi, the truth is that we don't have the resources to do much. When Sodom Gate ceased operations, the merchants there panicked and demanded we protect them. The commander led a full brigade and took most of our armament to support their cause. They were all still there when the gate detonated. Now, we are alone. There are no reinforcements. The humans outnumber us ten to one. Even though the Watchers here are showing improvement thanks to your teaching, we are still far from being able to deal with a foe like this in hand-to-hand combat."

Kandi nodded her agreement, "I see. I didn't realize our armory was so depleted. Still, to wait until attacked is not viable either."

Muha smiled, "Agreed. Over the past year, we have reestablished voice communications with some of the battalions at other cities – Olympus, Duat, Asgard, and particularly Babel. Babel sustained heavy damage to their university, but their armory remains intact. Since most of the city's occupants are students and faculty, they are not experiencing our turmoil. Archangel Iblees has graciously offered to give us whatever we need to regain control. I would like for you to lead a team to retrieve them."

Kandi blanched at the mention of Iblees' name, something Muha did not ignore: "Is there a problem? Since you left here to be the Archangel's bodyguard, I figured you would be a logical choice." Muha's voice indicated that she had no idea Kandi had been more than a bodyguard.

Kandi's voice dropped in volume, "It's complicated. The Archangel and I did not end things well."

Muha continued, "Well, I need you to put your personal life behind you and deal with the situation. We need those weapons, or this garrison will fall. I am leading a delegation to Asgard to discuss building a new portal to Aeden. I can't be in two places at once, and as you pointed out, we are defenseless here without those weapons. You leave by airship in the morning."

Chapter 57 – Heroes and Demons

Jon awoke to a gentle swaying motion and a beautiful woman stroking his hair. *OK, it's not my usual dream, but I can live with it.* At that point, the cart hit a large rock, throwing things around the interior of what he could now see was an enclosed wagon. The woman smiled at him when she realized he was awake. "I was getting worried about you. You have been unconscious for a long time."

Jon was still a little fuzzy when he replied, "So...who are you, and where are we?"

The woman smiled happily, "I am Sheena, the chief elder's granddaughter. I was the first chosen to be your wife."

"My...what!" Jon sat up with a start, instantly regretting the move as dizziness and nausea hit him.

"Careful, my love. After you saved the village with your powers, the elders were beside themselves with gratitude. They wanted to give you something special. They chose me. We left Gomorrah the next morning, heading north. We have been traveling for two days."

Startled by the news he had a wife, Jon abruptly moved away from Sheena, "Have I done something to displease you, Jonathan Martyr?" She looked distraught, fearful, as if she had angered a god who would now smite her.

"No. I am not displeased or angry." Jon replied, trying to think fast.

Sheena continued, "I am glad to see you are better. We have been most concerned about your well-being." Sheena had begun rubbing fragrant oils into his skin. Jon grabbed her hands and looked her in the eye, "You are magnificent, and I greatly appreciate your care. It's just that I am already in a committed relationship. I'm not available to marry anyone."

Sheena was shocked, "How is that possible? You traveled alone, and no one came looking for you. Your clothing was torn and worn. No wife would allow that to happen."

At this point in the conversation, Jon realized he was naked except for a piece of cloth wrapped around his lower body like a diaper. "Sheena, where are my clothes."

"They were not considered worthy of such a wondrous man as yourself. We burned them. The women of the tribe are making you proper clothing, one suitable for a man of your stature." Sheena returned to the original subject, "Can you tell me about your wife?"

"First of all, what happened to the items in my pockets."

"I don't know what pockets are, but we found these in your side bags." Sheena presented a small leather sack containing Jon's wallet, watch, comb, and coins. Jon breathed a sigh of relief. If he ever returned to his time, the money in that wallet could spell the difference between life and death. Sheena obstinately continued in her questioning, "I am still waiting on an answer. Tell me about this mysterious wife of yours."

Jon smiled at the mention of Kandi and proceeded to fabricate a story of their life together, "She is an amazing person, a partner more than a wife. She is beautiful beyond words, but more than beauty, she is smart and wise. She is my equal in most ways and, in some, my superior."

Sheena gasped at that revelation. "That is not possible. Men and women are never considered equal."

Jon continued, "We hadn't known each other long before we realized we were destined to be life partners." The words startled Jon even as he said them. In the distant future, Fiona had asked him if he loved Kandi. He realized now that he did. Barba had been fantastic, but Jon realized his love belonged to the pixie and no one else, even if she didn't return his affections. He closed his eyes and wished to see how Kandi was doing and was startled when a vision came immediately to mind. She was in an open area wearing the black body armor she had worn when he first met her. She was facing off against other pixies and elves. She was happy. Jon didn't know how, but he knew this was the truth. He relaxed.

"So, where is she this wonder among women?" Sheena's question brought Jon back to his reality.

"Kandi and I had different jobs to do back at Gomorrah. We were to meet on a hillside," Jon did the math, "tomorrow. If what you tell me is true, I probably won't make that meeting."

"You shouldn't worry. You made quite an impression on the other tribes. There will be many to tell your wife where you went if she comes looking for you. After your demonstration, the others welcomed our leaving, and because of their fear, we are certain they will not be following." Sheena looked adoringly at Jon, hoping he would change his mind, taking her in place of his lost love. Being the wife of such a powerful man would give her much standing, even more so if she became the mother of his children.

Jon didn't take the bait. Something more pressing spoke to him, not so much words as a feeling. "Sheena. I must speak with the elders when we camp for the night. There is much for us to discuss."

Kandi and her small team arrived at Babel Garrison around mid-morning only to find the base in complete disarray. On the way, they had passed over the remains of Babel University and its Gate. The destruction was beyond belief. Whereas some of Sodom remained unscathed, Babel was a total loss. Its gate had been within the university's walls – nothing remained.

Ironically, Iblees had given the Gomorran commander the impression that Babel was in pretty good shape. That impression did not translate to the scene in front of Kandi now. The garrison was intact, but chaos reigned within its walls. With some difficulty, Kandi found the quartermaster, who had no idea why she had come to him. Apparently, Iblees had not told anyone about their visit, nor the weapons Babel was to provide Gomorrah.

Okay. The easy way didn't work. I guess I will have to talk to the Archangel himself; not my idea of a good time.

Kandi found Iblees in an office overlooking the compound. "Enter," was the only reply to her knock.

"Master Watcher Kandi Mehra, reporting from Gomorrah Base." She kept the conversation as formal as possible.

The man behind the desk looked up with a start, surprised to see his old lover here - and alive. "Master Watcher Mehra, I am delighted to see you well."

Kandi's voice ran cold, "I believe we can dispense with the niceties, don't you? I'm here to pick up the weapons you promised to Commander Avani."

"Of course, if you will just go to the quartermaster...."

Kandi interrupted, "Would that be the same quartermaster who knows nothing about weapons leaving the base?"

"Ah, an oversight, I am sure," Iblees sent a message to the quartermaster and arranged for the transfer, something the quartermaster seemed quite against. "There. You will have no further trouble."

Kandi contacted her team and told them to try again before turning her attention back to the elf behind the desk, "I see you still have your winning ways."

"Kandi. You know you were always my favorite."

"Until you traded me in on a younger model. Whatever happened to her? Did she die in the blast, or did you kill her like you tried to kill me?" Kandi had felt Iblees pressing against her mind, trying to find the mind drone he had left inside her. The skills Fiona had taught her allowed her to block him. "Don't bother. The mind drone's not there anymore."

"I see. I also sense some fairy magic keeping me out. I wonder how you managed that?"

"Just an old friend helping me out."

"I see. Was your fairy friend the one who also put the protection drone in there?"

The comment shook Kandi, "Protection drone? The only drone I am acquainted with was the one you sent to kill me. Is there anything else, Archangel?"

"No, that is all."

Kandi snapped to attention, saluted, and returned to her ship.

Archangel Iblees sat for a moment behind his desk; *I don't know why the other drone failed or how she got a fairy to help her. No matter. I can't plant a new one in her, so I must find another way. Kandi Mehra must die.*

The rest of the weapons transfer completed, Kandi and her team prepared to leave, only to be surprised by Iblees making an appearance to see them off. Kandi was immediately on her guard, but he did not attempt to approach her personally. Instead, he chatted with the rest of the team. *He is a charming bastard.* As he was leaving, he gently touched her lieutenant's forehead. The motion was negligible but still caused Kandi to cringe. *Did something just happen?* She put it behind her, boarded the craft, and set off for Gomorrah. Her lieutenant seemed fine, so she put the casual contact aside and continued her preparations for departure.

Chapter 58 – Meeting Your Heroes

After Jon's conversation with the elders, the caravan changed direction, away from the familiarity of the coastal regions and more inland toward unknown territories. Jon still wasn't sure why he knew this was right; he just knew. Somehow, he knew positively that there would be someone at the end of this journey who could help the tribe in their quest for peace and prosperity in a world currently with precious little of either.

On the third day, they reached a valley with a small river running through its middle. There was ample space for crops and homes. No other humans were around. The elders looked at Jon expectantly. He nodded his assent. This place was where he envisioned in his dreams. He left the group to set up their encampment and went deeper into the valley. He needed something – no, someone to help him make sense of what was happening, and the vision had indicated he would find it here. He hadn't gone far before he got his answer.

"Why have you come?" The voice made Jon jump.

"We come seeking peace and an opportunity to prosper," Jon replied.

"No. I believe that is the reason the others came. Why are you here?" The voice was insistent.

"Something, a feeling, led me here. I know that doesn't make sense, but it is the truth. May I turn around?"

"Granted."

Jon turned. He had no idea what he expected, but what he saw was something infinitely more. The being in front of him was his height. He had Kandi's pointed ears, facial features, and wings - enormous wings fully unfurled. They were magnificent. His eyes dropped further to the being's hand to see a ring not unlike his own, glowing a brilliant blue. The creature in front of him continued, "Yes, we both wear the mark of the Chosen which, as a human, you shouldn't be able to bear, and more importantly, why does your ring sing to mine like no other before it?"

Jon glanced at his hand and saw his ring glowing as brilliantly as the one on the stranger's hand. "I don't know. I sensed something or someone here who could help the tribe, so I followed that feeling." He continued, "We mean no offense. We can continue if we hinder you."

The man-pixie paused before replying, "There is no need to move onward. I can sense the truth in what you say. Others have wandered here and are under my protection. Your tribe may stay and join the others, although I sense the people you are with are not your tribe. You still have not told me how you, a human, wear that ring and live."

Jon began telling his story, the complete truth, not changing anything from what occurred. When he finished, the archangel before him contemplated Jon's words before replying," I believe I have an explanation for our rings' strange behaviors. They are acting this way because they are the same ring. I can't understand how I could be the ancestor of your distant past. I have no mate, human or elf, and no intention of finding one. What is your name, human?"

"I'm called Jon, sir."

"Well, Jon, I am known as Michael."

Holy crap, Jon thought, *I thought he looked familiar.* Jon flashed back to the cave under the monastery and the man encased in crystal. The one in the crypt was much older but was no doubt the same person as the one who stood in front of him now.

Michael continued, "Are you all right, Jon? You look pale."

"I'm sorry. You are quite a shock. I've heard stories about you since I was a child. To see you in person is unsettling, to say the least."

Michael laughed, "Well, I hope the stories were at least good ones. Shall we go meet your friends?"

The meeting with the tribe went well. The people had seen archangels before, so Michael didn't present that great a shock. The elders were relieved that their search was ending and that they could begin setting up a permanent site. Over the following weeks, Michael instructed Jon about his ring, its powers, and Jon's responsibilities to it. Something told Jon that this was why the ring had thrown him back here in the past. It was tired of him mucking around. When he and Michael concluded their talks and lessons, Jon felt like his life was complete.

Jon hadn't forgotten about Kandi. He still dreamt of her and what she was doing every night.

Dream wasn't the right word. The visions he was experiencing were far more lifelike than any dream. He found himself pining for her and was jealous of how easily she had fallen back into her old life as a Watcher. Apparently, Jon had no place in her life anymore. After all they had been through, he'd hoped she would miss him at least a little.

Several weeks later, once Michael had completed Jon's lessons, Jon found himself adrift with no plan or idea of where to go or what to do. He did what he normally did when melancholy struck. He went to the small pond not far from the village. Here he could think. Staring into the water, he almost didn't recognize the face staring back at him. Weeks with the tribe had allowed his hair to grow out and his beard to grow. He didn't particularly care for the look, but the others in the tribe approved. Who was he to contradict them?

Ironically, as Kandi grew farther away from him, Sheena, who had been throwing herself at him at every opportunity, also began distancing herself. In a similar manner, the rest of the tribe began to relax in his presence. Although still treated with honor and respect, he was no longer the "hero of the hour." He now found himself alone more and more often.

One day, after dinner, Sheena approached him with eyes down, seemingly in fear. Behind her, he saw Michael sitting around the fire with the elders, glancing in his direction. Jon looked at the girl before him, "What can I do for you, Sheena?"

"I don't know how to begin, Jonathan Martyr. You have been so open to us and faithful to your wife;

I felt I needed to be as much to you." Her voice trailed off to a whisper.

"What is it, Sheena? I won't be angry." Jon felt that he was talking to a small child.

"I have met someone, Jonathan Martyr - someone who wants me, and I want him. I let him believe I was unattached, but he became suspicious when I kept us from being seen publicly. Finally, I told him the situation, and now he tells me I must make things right. He and I cannot continue seeing each other unless you publicly renounce me before the elders."

Jon stood, took her hand, and said, "Sheena. I have never stated a claim on you. That was something the Council did without my approval. I hadn't realized there was a bond to break for you to have a normal life. Of course, I will do anything to guarantee your happiness."

Together, they walked to the council fire, where Jon formally renounced any claim to Sheena as his wife. He spoke of Kandi and confirmed that he and Sheena had never consummated their marriage. The elders around the fire relaxed like a great conflict had been avoided. Michael jumped up and ran over to Jon and Sheena. He took Sheena into his arms and, looking over her shoulder, thanked Jon for what he had done.

Jon had a lot of conflicting emotions at that point. Michael and Sheena? Really? Jon remembered the nights he had almost given in to Sheena's pleadings. He shuddered at what disasters such a pairing could have created in the timeline. After all, it appeared that she would be his VERY great-grandmother.

Chapter 59 – Unfinished Business

After takeoff, the aircar AI took over, making all the necessary calculations and adjusting for weather conditions much more efficiently than the crew. They were just along for the ride. About halfway through the trip, Watcher Kling, serving as loadmaster, checked on their cargo to guarantee nothing had shifted during their ascent, which was standard operating procedure.

Not long after, their perfectly normal flight was shattered by an alarm, indicating a problem in the cargo bay. The aircar had just reached apogee and began its long descent to Gomorrah Station. Kandi commed back to Watcher Kling, "Everything okay back there?"

Kling's response was swift, "No, Master Watcher. Some of the cargo shifted. I'm going to need a little help."

"Be right there."

As Kandi passed the loading platform, someone blindsided her with a body block into the bulkhead, temporarily stunning her. She looked up just in time to see Watcher Kling pointing a blaster at her head. Kandi reacted with a quick body shift, which allowed the door to absorb most of the blast. The two Watchers fought briefly over the weapon before Kandi managed to kick it under some of the crates. She then turned and faced her adversary.

"Mari. Explain yourself."

Kling had assumed a fighting stance. Kandi knew the girl well. They had sparred in training and knew there was no way Kling could beat her in a one-on-one fight. Kandi noticed something strange about her opponent. Kling's eyes were dilated to the point where the irises were practically non-existent in the black field of her pupils. Her movements were jerky, not as precise as Kandi had observed in training. It was like she was fighting herself as well as Kandi,

"Mari. We're comrades. I don't understand what's going on here?"

Mari's voice was hardly a whisper, "Please forgive me, Kandi. This is not my doing. My body is not my own." She shook her head and began speaking in a halting manner. "I'm sorry. I must do this. The master commands …." The young Watcher's words drifted away as she threw herself into Kandi's open arms, almost hugging her in a haphazard embrace. With Kandi distracted, Kling pressed her palm against the emergency cargo release, setting off more alarms as the crew was notified of the impending emergency depressurization. Kling looked Kandi in the eye as her expression and voice changed, "You must die, Kandi. This time, there will be no escape." Before Kandi could react, the outside door opened, and Kling and Kandi flew through the opening and into the stratosphere, the explosive decompression pushing them clear of the aircar's jets.

Kandi was immediately gasping for air. The airship had just started its descent from 80,000 feet, and there wasn't enough oxygen to draw a breath or to spread her wings. Kling fell alongside her, drifting only a few feet away, lifeless. Kandi realized what had happened. Kling was the one Iblees had touched before liftoff. He must have planted a drone in her. *I have been a fool!* That thought was her last before lapsing into unconsciousness. Sara wasn't so lucky. She was not bound by the need for oxygen. She screamed inside Kandi's mind, lost in fear for many seconds before succumbing.

Although he now considered his pursuit of Kandi a lost cause, Jon had to know for sure. He announced to the tribe that he was leaving them and returning to Gomorrah to find his "wife." There was really no reason for him to stay. They had Michael as a guardian now. He and the other tribes in the valley had welcomed the newcomers unconditionally. Several inter-tribal relationships had begun, and weddings were on the horizon. With their security all but guaranteed, Jon could leave in good conscience.

Before setting out, Jon stopped to say goodbye to Michael and Sheena. The three of them had become good friends over the last weeks, and Jon would miss them terribly. He waved to Sheena as he entered the clearing surrounding their hut, but then collapsed as a blinding light stabbed a dagger into his brain. He fell to the ground unconscious.

Jon awoke to see Michael and Sheena looking down on him, worry written on their faces. Jon tried to sit up but failed, his head telling him he wasn't ready for that quite yet. Michael spoke, "Brother

Jonathan, we saw you grab your head and collapse. What happened to you?"

Jon's voice was strained, "I wish I knew. One second, I was coming to say goodbye, and the next, there was a stabbing pain and then nothing."

Michael thought carefully, "Was there anything else?"

"Yes. Now that I think about it, there was an intense feeling of dread and sorrow, like something terrible had happened."

"Jonathan. You once told me of the visions you had of your wife. Do you still have them?"

"All the time. That's the reason I have to go back to Gomorrah. I have to get them to stop so I can move onward."

Michael asked earnestly, "Was there any time when you were together that you touched her forehead?"

Jon thought that a strange question, but as he thought back, he remembered touching Kandi's forehead before they left on their separate ways. He remembered thinking it odd at the time but later disregarded it. He relayed the circumstances to Michael.

"Jon, can you see her now?"

Jon attempted to create a vision of Kandi as he had done hundreds of times before, but this time nothing came. "No. Nothing."

Michael sat beside the bed. "Jon, I believe you planted a protection drone in your wife's mind."

Jon was horrified. "No, I wouldn't have done that."

"I don't think you meant to. I believe you only wanted to wish her safety, and the ring complied by issuing the drone."

"So, what does it mean that I can't see her now?"

"I'm sorry, my friend. It means she has died."

His words threw Jon into a panic. *Kandi dead? No. Impossible.* He thought back over all their adventures together. She had been the strong one, the one to overcome obstacles. She couldn't be dead, yet deep in his heart, Michael's words rang true. "Is there nothing I can do?"

Michael said, "Maybe. Before the gate collapse, it would have been forbidden, but now.... Reach back to where your mind lost contact with her. Protection drones are always active and transmit their findings even when not requested. You should be able to see what happened to her. I need you to describe it to me."

Jon did as Michael asked, "I see her on the bridge of an airship. There's an alarm. She goes back to the cargo area. She's attacked! Her assailant grabs her and presses a panel. Oh God! The door opens, and she is blown out. She can't breathe." Jon opened his eyes, "Then the vision goes dark."

Michael shook him, "Jonathan, stay with me. Go back to the point in time where she fell. You see her, correct?"

"Yes"

"If you see her, you can grab her."

"I don't understand."

"We did this the other day with the grapes in the forest, remember?"

"Yes, but that was in the present."

"You have an archangel's power. The same thing will work in the past. See her in your mind and reach for her. Do it now."

Jon focused on Kandi; he saw her falling, the thin air blowing her hair back, her eyes closed, and frost forming on her cheeks. "Michael, this isn't grapes."

"I am here with you, brother. Focus."

Jon felt the archangel's hands on his shoulders, the energy of his aura filling him even as he willed Kandi to come to him, and the next thing he knew, she was there in his arms. He gently laid her on the ground and began CPR, begging the pixie to breathe. After a minute, she coughed and sputtered, then started breathing independently. Michael picked her up and took her to his hut, where Sheena promised to look after her. Michael then steered Jon outside.

"Brother Jonathan?"

"Yes?"

"Would you like to tell me how you happen to be married to a pixie?"

"Well..."

"And not just any pixie. I know this one personally. Kandi Mehra is the most vocal pixie in all of Aeden. Her opinion of humans was well known, mainly that they should all be dead."

"Well..."

"I can barely accept that you know one another. That you are traveling together is a stretch of the imagination, but I can't conceive a universe where the two of you are life-partners."

"Michael...I can explain. Please don't tell Sheena." Jonathan went on to explain everything, including his feelings for Kandi, feelings that he had never shared with her.

Michael pondered, "Your earlier deception is safe with me. My wife does not need to know, but what happens when Kandi wakes? She will demand answers. You must know that we violated the most basic law of time travel. We intentionally changed the past. There is no telling what effect this will have on Kandi."

"We'll cross that bridge when we come to it. For now, Kandi is alive and safe. That's all that matters."

Chapter 60 – All Good Things...

A few days later, Jonathan found it necessary to cross that bridge. Kandi had awakened, wondering where she was and what had happened to her. She was confused with memories of a fall from a great height...a nothingness that enveloped her. What had happened? Where was her ship? Were the crew okay?

Sheena didn't have the answers to most of Kandi's questions but was more than happy to explain the ones she could. Before long, Kandi was hearing all about how Kandi's husband was so worried about her and how wonderful it was that she was here with him. She told her how Jon had saved the tribe and how proud she must be. Then Sheena said how forward-thinking Kandi was, being a member of the Watchers and married to a human. In typical Sheena style, a full ten minutes passed before Kandi could get a word in edgewise.

"Stop!" Kandi was on sensory overload, "What do you mean...my husband?"

"Jonathan Martyr, your husband. After he saved the tribe, the elders gave me to him for a wife, but he wouldn't even look at me that way, so devoted he was to you. I am surprised you're a pixie, but then Michael and I have a similar situation, and we...."

Sheena looked like she was going to launch into another lengthy monologue.

"Sheena. Please stop!" Sheena stopped, and Kandi continued. "I am not married, not now or ever. Jon and I are…traveling companions, nothing more. Where is he, anyway. It would seem that we need to talk."

Over the next hour, a lengthy argument ensued as Jon attempted to explain his "marriage" to Kandi. He carefully avoided any acknowledgment of his true feelings for her. Now was not the time.

When the discussion changed to how Jon had saved her, she was fascinated that Jon's command of the ring had come so far, but how had he known she was in trouble, and how did he find her? The conversation circled back to the presence of the protection drone.

Kandi was incensed. What gave him the right to invade her that way? The sting of Ibless' incursion was so recent in her memory that it only worsened matters. Michael jumped in and assured her Jon had no idea what he was doing. He also quickly added that without the implant, Kandi's death would have been permanent. She shuddered. As it was, she remembered clearly what it had felt like to die.

Kandi's ordeal had left her weak. Days turned into weeks and then months. She spent much of that time in conference with Michael. Even considering the years since the gates detonated, he had changed so much from the battle-hardened veteran she had known during the last campaigns of the war. Most confusing was his marriage to Sheena, a human. Kandi had difficulty seeing the pairing, but Michael appeared happy and content with his life. He could imagine no better companion than Sheena as wife and mother to his children.

When Kandi had regained her strength, she and Michael set out for Gomorrah. She had rebuilt relationships there and needed to let the garrison know she was alive. Visions of her "death" still haunted her. She couldn't explain what Jon had done to her, so she certainly wouldn't try to do so to her comrades. Thinking of Jon reminded her that it was his love for her that allowed him to yank her through space-time and save her life. She glanced over toward the human. She still wasn't sure how she felt about him. She no longer hated him, but love...that was a step too far.

When Muha got over the shock of Kandi being alive and in the company of an archangel, she filled them in on happenings in the compound. Work had commenced on a new gate at Sodom. Muha's efforts at forming an alliance with Asgard and Olympus resulted in the construction being here. Michael agreed to help but insisted that Kandi remain in his camp until the completion of the project.

After months of work, the day came when the gate was completed. The Watchers were attempting a transit in five days - there was no time or excess crystal for a test. Kandi delivered the news with excitement. Jon was not as pleased.

The following day, Jon happened upon Kandi while she was sitting quietly alone. "Can I bother you?"

Kandi glanced toward him, "Certainly."

Jon sat beside her, "Michael announced he was staying with Sheena. So, I was wondering what your plans were?"

Kandi resumed her downward stare, "Sara and I have been debating that. The stories we heard from Fiona told of the attempt but never indicated whether the Watchers succeeded. Jon, if they make the connection, I finally have a way home. My quest was always supposed to end this way - find a way back and fix things if possible. The attempt might be dangerous, but it's a risk I must take. Besides, your own timeline is in great danger as well. This might be the way to save them too."

Jon's soul felt very heavy, "This is what we have been pushing toward, to get you home, fix the problem, and return to help us, but...."

"But, what?" Their hands touched, and neither of them pulled away.

Jon wanted to say, "What about me," but instead said, "You could die. We do know what happened. We're pretty certain that they didn't fix the problem. After all, no one came to Vermont to reset the timeline. No one came to help."

Kandi was quiet, "Jon. We've been over this before. That's not how time works. You proved that when you grabbed me out of the air before I died."

Jon took her hand in his, an act he wouldn't have considered a few months ago, "I'm afraid that, even if you make the trip, things on Aeden will be too broken. Something will happen to prevent your interference."

Kandi stared at him long and hard, "Please understand. I still have to try."

Jon gulped, "When do you leave?"

"Tonight." Kandi paused before continuing. "You'll be fine here, you know? The tribe has adopted you, and every eligible girl practically swoons when you walk by, especially now that they know I have no claim to you. Michael sees you more as a brother than a descendant. This will be a good life for you. Besides, if all goes well, I'll be back before you know it."

Jon's reply caught her off-guard, "I can't stay here. You have a mission, and so do I. I'm not able to bridge to Aeden, but Michael has taught me how to move through the time stream. By joining the power of the two rings, I should be able to return to my present. I may be unable to stop what is happening there, but I can try to help those affected the most."

Kandi appeared shocked, "So, you will be going too?"

Jon nodded.

Kandi nodded, saddened by the prospect and unable to explain why, "So, this is goodbye then?"

"Look, Kandi. I won't stay here without you. The place will be too empty. I wouldn't be able to bear it." He stood and faced his friend, "Safe journey. I hope you succeed, and we meet again." They hugged the embrace of soldiers before battle.

"You too."

Jon wandered away to gather his things, leaving Kandi blinded by her tears. She had been able to reconcile her leaving with Jon being safe here with Michael and the tribe, but the knowledge that he was returning to a world aimed at destruction made her doubt her decision. In the end, though, logic dictated that she needed to try her way. It might be the only way to save both worlds. Kandi stood, spread her wings, and flew off toward Sodom. She prayed that they would succeed. She would miss Jon and hoped she would see the human again.

Jon found Michael working in the field beside his hut. Jon found it strangely normal that one of the most powerful beings in the world was happy planting crops and taking care of his very pregnant wife. Jon told him of his and Kandi's decisions and that Jon was ready to go if Michael would help him.

Michael understood that with Kandi gone, Jon had no real reason to stay, and he respected the human's decision to aid the people in his time during their need. Still, he had grown fond of his descendant and proud of the legacy that had produced the one known as Jonathan Martyr. "You are certain, Brother Jonathan? Without the joined stones, you will not be able to return."

"I'm going to miss you guys too, but without Kandi, this life has nothing for me anymore. At least in my own time, I might be able to make a difference."

Michael nodded and put his right hand over Jon's. The two rings that were really one glowed with a blinding intensity. The two archangels, pixie and human, joined their thoughts as they sought the way back to Jon's present. A moment later, there was a flash of light when the portal opened. When it closed, only Michael remained.

End of Book 1

An excerpt from *A Clash of Tomorrows Book Two: Aeden*

Jonathan's Journey

Trapped. Stuck in a web of intersecting lines, his body detonated into atoms only to be reassembled and then exploded again. Jonathan tried to think. He and Michael had been standing in the field when they opened the portal...but it hadn't looked like the other doorways Jon had used in the past. This one was more of a rip in the fabric of reality, a tear that desperately wanted to heal itself but instead found this meager human thrust into its maw.

Jon was convinced that something had gone terribly wrong as the web transformed into a translucent, semi-solid membrane that held him immobile much like an insect trapped in tree sap. He kept reminding himself not to panic. After all, he was coming from thousands of years in the past. He ceased struggling and waited for his prison to send him on his way.

After an eternity, his trap immersed him in a turbulent liquid. At first, Jon was intrigued about this new manifestation of space-time. That was before he took a breath and immediately regretted it.

The water wasn't an illusion; it was real. Jon had made it to the other side of the transit, but where was he? He was unable to determine which direction was up, totally disoriented by the turbulent liquid that surrounded him.

Purely by chance, his feet grazed the muck lining the bottom. Positioning his feet against the gooey surface and fighting the urge to expel the liquid from his burning lungs, he shoved himself upward with all his might, erupting above the surface, coughing and sputtering.

Jon had barely managed to clear his lungs a bit, when a tower of water came out of nowhere, crashing down on him, crushing him under the frothing surf. Water again flooded into his nose and mouth, and not just any water. This stuff was nasty. He gagged from its foulness. It wasn't just the taste, either. The smell that accompanied it was equally awful. He did learn one thing. The water was salty. He must be in the sea and with the bottom so close below him, he had to be near a shore.

Jon was confused by his circumstances. He had never ported anywhere other than an open field, mountainside, or sand-covered desert – all landing points devoid of any physical impairments, like walls – and water. He had assumed that there was something in the port process that determined the suitability of the receiving environment. He now realized that he was incorrect in that assumption.

Jonathan turned just as another wave towered above him. Diving into the breakwater as it arrived, he was able to avoid most of the bad effects. He relaxed a little and noted that the ten-foot surges of water appeared to arrive at regular intervals. He was surprised to find that what he had initially thought was daylight was actually hundreds of rocks protruding from the water, each of them glowing with an intense white light. By their glare, he glimpsed the shoreline about a hundred yards away. At least now he knew where he needed to go.

A large, nearby stone, whose monolithic stance was easily eight feet out of the water and three feet wide, looked as good a place as any to seek temporary shelter. During the next break in the waves, Jon made a lunge for it and took shelter in its shadow. Then, he took time to better able to assess his situation.

Obviously, Jon was in the water. The salinity and the pounding surf indicated he was near the shore of an ocean or sea. Surrounding him were hundreds of stones similar to his shelter. They were of various sizes, some barely sticking up above the water and others easily twice the size of his current resting place. The aura emanating from the stones was so intense that staring at one would temporarily blind him. Occasionally, electrical flares arced between them, adding to the surrealness of the experience.

Jonathan turned his vision to the night sky where clouds blocked any view of the moon or stars. These were not normal clouds. They seemed to be alive with their own luminescence - a dark reddish glow seemingly from within. The overall effect was not unlike an artist's rendition of a hellscape.

Now calmer, Jon focused and put himself into the rhythm of the waves; he began maneuvering his way between stones during the lulls. Traveling wasn't easy. When he got to where his feet touched the bottom, the muck sucked at his feet. Jon would have sworn the shoreline was moving ever farther away.

On the third such shift, he felt something like a mild electric shock on his leg. His body jerked in response, almost causing him to slip. A short time later, he received another shock. This time the source lingered a little longer against his calf.

Jon could feel his leg going numb, and he knew it wasn't from the cold water. He knew he had been poisoned when the numbing sensation began moving farther up his body every second. His situation was now dire. He needed to get to shore now or not at all. Throwing caution to the wind, he began moving away from this new threat as fast as the sucking mud on the sea floor would allow. A wave caught him off guard halfway between two stones, slamming him under the water as it collapsed. In the glow of the stones, he managed to catch a glimpse of the thing that had touched him.

The monster appeared to be a huge eel-like creature roughly two feet in diameter and ten feet in length. It had long, ropy tentacles that stretched toward Jon like they were searching for their next meal, which, he realized, they were. However, it wasn't the pseudo arms that had Jon's undivided attention. Rather it was the tooth-encrusted mouth gaping open behind them, one that would have given H.P Lovecraft nightmares.

There was no question of the beast's target. It came straight for Jon, assured that this hapless fool would soon succumb to the poison it had given him. In its mind, the man would offer little or no resistance. Jon longed to prove him wrong.

Even though his body was getting more and more sluggish, Jon raised his right hand and willed the ring to respond. At first, nothing happened. The ring's power wasn't infinite, and most of Jon's and Michael's energies had gone into the transfer from the far past to here. He knew that the ring desperately needed to be recharged but hoped he would be able to call up enough energy for this.

A second later, he sensed a mild force field emanating from the stone, slapping the creature in the face. There wasn't enough strength to kill or even cause harm, but it did get the monster's attention and offered sufficient deterrent to make the beast rethink its next meal. It quickly turned and swam outward, looking for more manageable prey.

Jonathan now had to deal with his own injured body. He forced his nearly paralyzed limbs to move once more. Wave after wave struck, attempting to pull him back into their embrace. Still, he pushed himself onward. Finally, just as his body succumbed to its fate, he found himself thrown onto a narrow beach with a makeshift sea wall positioned just behind it. A final wave's thrust pushed Jon onto the sand where he lost consciousness. He never saw the hooded figure walking his way.

About the Author

After retiring from a career in information systems, Bruce M. Baker taught English Literature and Writing to middle school students, primarily Hispanic, first and second generation, immigrants. He is the coauthor of 2022 Oklahoma Book Award finalist and 2023 Next Generation Indie Book Award finalist, *The Chance: The true story of one girl's journey to freedom* and *Faith Through Trial: A true story of hope and survival.*

A Clash of Tomorrows is Mr. Baker's first work of fiction. He lives with his wife Deborah in Oklahoma City.

Made in the USA
Coppell, TX
19 May 2024

32507890R00285